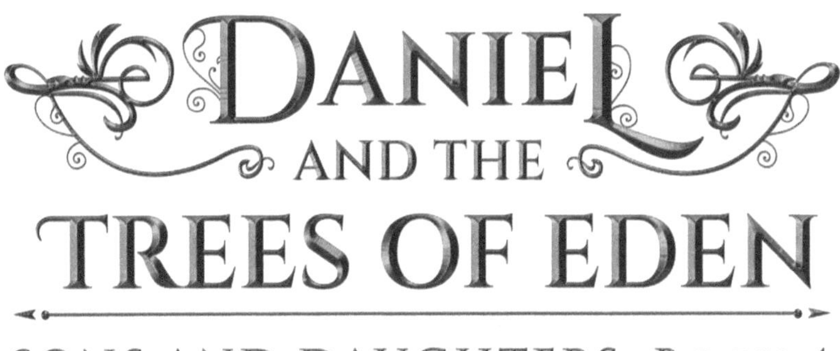

DANIEL AND THE TREES OF EDEN

SONS AND DAUGHTERS · BOOK 4

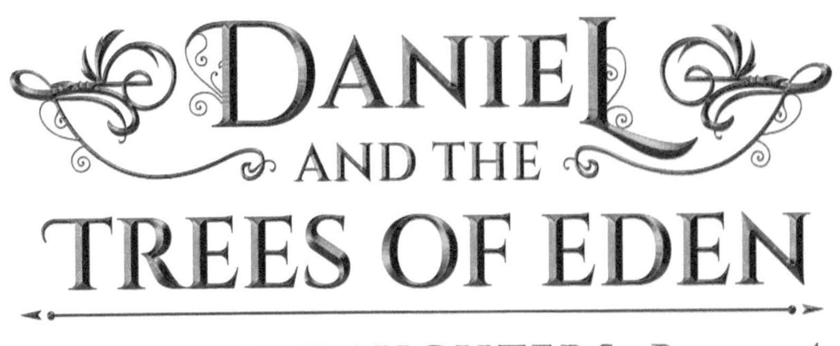

Daniel AND THE TREES OF EDEN

SONS AND DAUGHTERS · BOOK 4

NATHAN LUMBATIS

For other books by Nathan Lumbatis, including Books One, Two, and Three in the *Sons and Daughters* series, visit:

nathanlumbatis.com.

Daniel and the Trees of Eden:
Sons and Daughters Book 4
Published by Dove Christian Publishers
P.O. Box 611
Bladensburg, MD 20710-0611
www.dovechristianpublishers.com

Cover Design by Donika Mishineva

This is a work of fiction. Names, characters, places, and incidents either are the product of the author's imagination or are used fictitiously. Any resemblance to actual persons, living or dead, events, or locales is entirely coincidental.

ISBN: 978-1-957497-35-8

Printed in the United States of America

For Ariel,
whose creative and brilliant writing
is an inspiration.

1

Substitutes and Roadkill

Daniel wove through a group of football players huddled around the door of his math classroom and made a beeline toward an open desk at the back. Garland decked the walls, heavily burdened with gaudy red bulbs and other Christmas ornaments. Someone had scrawled, "Math is evil. It's Christmas Break. Let us leave!" across the dry-erase board. Most of the class stood around talking about their plans for Christmas break once school let out. Daniel didn't join the conversations. He unslung his green backpack and tossed it on the ground, then slid into his seat and pivoted toward the door. Other students trickled through, mostly in twos or threes, while finishing conversations from the hallway. Four cheerleaders slipped in. One smiled at Daniel and gave a small wave. He politely smiled back, but his attention was elsewhere.

Ben walked by the doorway and paused. "She's coming," he mouthed before disappearing into a group of other students heading in the same direction.

"Here we go," Daniel muttered. Every Friday since their last quest, it was the same thing. One of his teachers was mysteriously absent due to a sudden sickness, family emergency, or an inexplicable urge to travel somewhere far away. In their place—

"Good afternoon, class." A woman with a pixie haircut the color of dishwater, long red fingernails, and eyes concealed behind dark glasses stalked into the classroom, her voice a raspy wheeze. She wore a disheveled pantsuit that was so threadbare it could have been fished out of a dumpster behind a thrift store. It smelled like it, too. "I'm Miss … uh … Miss …" The Creep glanced around the classroom, clearly at a loss for a fake name.

"Garbles Matlock?" Daniel offered, tossing out the most ridiculous name he could invent on the spot.

"Yesss," the woman hissed, peering at Daniel over the rims of her glasses. "Garbles Matlock. But you can call me Ms. Garbles, because that's a suitable name." She studied Daniel while muttering. "Let's see: brown hair streaked with white, brown eyes, tall, slightly muscular frame, defiant and cheeky. He's the one." She eagerly clicked her fingernails together.

The other students exchanged confused stares. Daniel didn't know why. He figured they would be used to this by now. Last week, it was Mr. Mange, a squat, middle-aged man who smelled like manure. The week before, it was a Ms. Bloodmash. Daniel could never quite place what she smelled like, but it somehow made him think of a meat processing plant. There had been a Ms. Gore, a Ms. Wratch, and even a Mr. Murder. Every class had ended the same. Ben had similar experiences, and this one would undoubtedly be no different.

"Take out your history books," Ms. Garbles barked. "Turn to page—"

"This is a math class, Ms. Flarbles Baggeldy-Goop," Daniel said. "See, it talks about math on the board behind you. Also, it's the last day before Christmas Break, and we only have thirty minutes before the bell. We get out early today, so you don't actually have to teach us anything."

"My name is Ms. Barbles Fladbock," the Creep snarled. "And I've had just about enough from you! Out into the hallway. Now!"

One of the cheerleaders leaned over. "Daniel, why do all the substitutes hate you so much?"

Daniel shrugged. "It's a long story." He hurried into the hallway. The door slammed behind him, and before he could turn, he felt the

Creep's hands on his shoulders.

"Master will reward me for capturing you," she said, practically salivating. "Power. Slaves. Wealth."

Daniel ducked and spun away from her hands. "Look, you must be new at this. All the other Creeps have taken me around the corner and into the stairwell. There're no cameras there, and since class has started, no one will see you attack me." He nodded back toward the classroom, where students were leaning out of their seats to watch.

The Creep lifted her sunglasses and perched them atop her head, revealing black and depthless eyes. She chuckled, and her teeth began to elongate. "Well, then ... into the stairwell we go."

Daniel casually slid his arm through hers and guided her along the hallway.

The Creep looked confused by his lack of fear. "The Master has wonderful things planned for you," she wheezed, her voice strained like wind through a cracked door.

"Let me guess," Daniel replied. "Remove the Image of the Three? Join him or face torture? Death? Yada, yada, yada?" He pushed the door to the stairwell open and ushered the Creep in. Two people already stood on the landing: a tall, gray-haired man with a scraggly beard leering down at a younger teen with blue eyes and white-streaked black hair. "Oh, look! Ben's here too with *his* Creep of a teacher. Hi, Ben!"

"Hey, Daniel!" Ben waved happily. He gestured toward the man who was towering over him. "This is Mr. Horibal. He came up with that name himself, by the way. He's my 'substitute teacher' for English today. See, Mr. Horibal? I told you if you waited long enough, Daniel would come, too. Two for the price of one. You can't beat that."

Mr. Horibal gripped Ben loosely around his neck and fixed Daniel with a menacing but thoroughly bewildered look.

"Hi, Mr. Horibal!" Daniel waved cheerily. "This is Ms. Marbles. You two know each other?"

Ben slipped away from Mr. Horibal and inched behind Daniel.

The door to the stairwell finally clicked shut.

"Get them!" Ms. Garbles hissed.

The Creeps lunged for the boys. Instead, they found the wavy blade of the Sun Sword as it completed its sweeping arc through their bodies, leaving a bright trail of orange and yellow fire in the air. Great clouds of black spirit billowed out of their mouths, and both collapsed to the landing, unharmed and purified. He counted to ten. With a pop, the predictable blinding light filled the stairwell, signaling that the man and woman, now free from the Enemy's power, were taken into the Father's service.

Ben yawned. "Are Creeps getting easier to defeat, or is it just me?"

"When you've faced the Serpent," Daniel replied, "everything seems easy."

"I suppose." Ben opened the door to the stairwell, lazily side-stepping as a different female Creep lunged through and fell to the ground in a crouch.

She grinned. "Two Vessels! Master will—"The Creep's gaze ran up the sword from its intricately woven metal hilt hovering just beyond Daniel's right hand to the end of its tip-less blade. She nervously glanced around the stairwell. "I see you've been busy. Perhaps I should come back another time."

With a sigh, Daniel flicked the Sun Sword through her startled face and released the weapon. It transformed into fire, spiraled around his arm, and flew back into his chest.

The Creep disappeared as Ben walked through the doorway, waving over his shoulder. "See you at the car line."

Daniel grunted and plodded back to his classroom, his mind racing with thoughts of their next quest. The waiting had been agonizing. Sure, he was eager to see the Spirit of the Age sealed into the Serpent, but the interim had also meant long separations from Gabriela. Two months ago, she disappeared into the Mist to help her people in Aguas Calientes, which meant two months with zero contact. To make matters worse, he knew she put her life on the line every day.

Hardly an hour passed by that Daniel didn't receive a notification on his phone about military conflicts all over the world, including

Peru. The reports centered mainly on the Middle East, though. It was worst there: wars embroiled country after country, each falling to mysterious groups of militants. With every triumph, the new governments all but subordinated themselves to Ealim Wahid, the Enemy's sham international peace organization. Its figureheads, the nefarious twins Amira and Abida, seemed to haunt every news program, YouTube ad, and talk radio show. Their message of international peace through the unification of nations under their banner never wavered.

Daniel gritted his teeth at the thought. Peace? Yeah, right, if by peace, they meant covertly removing the Three's Image from huge groups of people and strong-arming policymakers to limit the rights of anyone opposed to their mission. Predictably, the Father's children were targeted through unjust detentions, persecutions, disappearances, and expulsion from their countries. Even the U.S. felt Ealim Wahid's influence to pledge money and troops for their mission—troops which frequently returned to the U.S. with dogmatic loyalty to the organization.

At the time of their first quest, Peru had all but fallen to the Enemy. Now, after the country signed on with Ealim Wahid, it was a veritable bastion of darkness. This is what Gabriela had gone to fight, all while battling demons and Creeps. Not that she was defenseless.

Daniel slid back into his seat. Ignoring the questions from his classmates about their missing substitute, he laid his head on his arms and shut his eyes.

No. Gabriela was definitely *not* defenseless. Before their quest to the Serpent's Abyss to save Raylin and find the Abyssal Staff, the Three had gifted her with superhuman strength and the power to travel through a different dimension called the Mist. She was smart, athletic, beautiful, and powerful. Daniel moaned. And she was far away. According to Granny, their next quest would begin by helping Gabriela free her people, which was supposed to be soon. He prayed that "soon" didn't mean another several months. The Three didn't always have the same timeframe as he did.

Father, can you please keep Gabriela safe? While I'm at it, could the quest start before long? I mean, Creeps for substitutes? The Enemy is getting desperate.

Daniel waited, hoping to hear some sort of confirmation from the Three. Instead, the bell rang, and the classroom erupted into loud cheers and a rush toward the door. Daniel sat at his desk until everyone cleared out before scooping up his backpack and drifting into the hallway.

The sooner the quest started, the sooner it would be over, which meant the sooner he and Gabriela could finally be a normal boyfriend and girlfriend. The memory of her kiss was so strong, he felt it on his lips. At least she had left him with that. Not that it did much good beyond making him insanely over-analyze it for a few days. Was it simply a "goodbye" kiss? An "I love you and can't wait to be back" kiss? A "You're sweet, but I'm sorry I can't date you" kiss? What had his breath smelled like? Did he look stupid when she was that close to his face?

Daniel ran his hands through his hair like a madman. What did it matter? She made it abundantly clear she couldn't focus on a relationship while her people (and the entire world, for that matter) were in danger.

Daniel made a beeline toward the front of the school.

Ben slipped out of his classroom as Daniel passed by. His blue eyes glinted with mischief. "I know that look: longing eyes, insane hair, desperate, startled glances over your shoulder at the sound of every girl's voice. Pining away for a certain Peruvian bombshell?"

Daniel groaned. "It's bad today."

"I can tell. Of course, I'm not one to talk. The last time we were at Granny's, Raylin barely breathed in my direction. I'm still depressed."

Daniel threw his arm over Ben's shoulder. "Nah, man. She laughed when you tripped over Janice sleeping on the floor and crashed into the ironing board. That's got to count for something."

Ben rubbed his forehead, gingerly feeling the goose egg still visible just above his left eyebrow. "It counts for a headache."

The cold sunlight of December in Oregon streamed through gathering clouds heavy with snow. A thin blanket of old ice already lay on the town, spotted with patches of mud and road grease waiting expectantly for the pure white of a new dusting.

Ben pointed at the line of cars. "Mom ahoy. Plus a Janice."

Daniel didn't need Ben to point them out. Above their Suburban, a glowing woman floated, a little more than a shell of light. Three interlocking circles shone on her forehead, and a glistening gown of ethereal blue draped her frail frame. Her lips moved in song. The sound didn't reach them on the school steps, but Daniel knew what it said.

> *The Mighty Three, my protection be,*
> *Encircling me, you are around …*

The memory of the rest of the song played through his mind. It was the prayer of encircling protection that Janice's spirit sang when she fell asleep while interceding for someone. The words were beautiful, but Daniel knew they were also powerful. When Shakti had first attacked him and Ben on their second quest, the prayer resulted in a fiery barrier strong enough to shield them from the Bolt of Pestilence. Thankfully, Seren and Raylin had discovered normal people couldn't see Janice or her barrier. It happened one evening when Gator, Barf, and Barth, their enormous and bombastic neighbors, came to deliver the Christmas popcorn Janice had ordered. She was asleep on the couch, but her spirit hovered around the yard, singing away. Barf stomped right through her and was none the wiser. Since then, her presence on car rides home had been extremely useful.

Ben opened the backdoor to the SUV and threw his backpack in before sliding over to make room for Daniel, who jumped in behind him.

"Good afternoon, boys!" Leah, Daniel's biological mother, waved from the passenger seat. Her blond hair was plaited into a thin braid over one shoulder, and her warm, brown eyes were a perfect match for Daniel's.

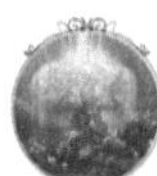

"Mom!" Daniel exclaimed, launching forward to embrace her over the console. "When did you get in town?"

"Your mother thought I should come in to surprise you guys. I'll be staying through Christmas!"

Daniel's adoptive mother, Mariah Jones, turned around and smiled, one dark eyebrow raised over icy-blue eyes. "It's one of your Christmas presents, Daniel. And I think I deserve a greeting, too, young man."

"Oh, you know I'm happy to see you," Daniel chuckled, leaning over to give her a quick peck on the cheek. "Thanks. I was just so surprised to see my *other* mom. Wait, if she's up front, where's Janice?" Daniel asked, looking around the SUV.

"Floorboards of the third row," Mrs. Jones explained as she drove forward in the car line. "Poor thing tumbled down there after she fell asleep on the drive."

Daniel sat back and buckled, then joined Ben to crane his neck around. He caught sight of frizzy-red hair and darned socks poking out from opposite ends of a blanket on the floor. "Oh, well, she looks comfortable. No use disturbing her."

Mrs. Jones pulled out of the school car line and onto the road. "Yes, now keep your voice down. We absolutely don't want her to wake up." She tucked graying-black hair behind both ears, gripped the wheel, and stared straight ahead, her jaw set in grim determination. "Some nasty characters were stalking along the road up ahead. The last thing we want is for Janice to wake up and lose our barrier."

Ben rolled his eyes and searched the wooded plots stretching along the road. "Don't demons want a Christmas break, too? Good grief. What is it this time, a Grinch demon?"

"Raccoon and armadillo demons," Mrs. Jones replied. Her words were short and clipped as she focused on driving. "At least, that's what I think they were. Didn't get a good look at them, but they seemed nasty. Skulking about the shadows in the trees as we drove by."

Leah pointed ahead to where the forest grew thicker and crowded the road. "That's where they were. Are you sure we'll be okay?" she asked nervously.

"Perfectly fine," Mrs. Jones reassured her. "Janice's barrier will plow right over them if needed."

Leah went a little pale but nodded resolutely. She was still a novice with the type of spiritual warfare Daniel and Ben were used to. The Three had allowed her to watch the battle in the Serpent's Abyss, but it was clear she found it unsettling. Daniel couldn't blame her.

Mrs. Jones, on the other hand, had taken right to it after their last quest. She was terrified at first, of course, but her anger at seeing her sons attacked through the Orb of Seeing quickly overcame any anxiety. She launched into full battle mode after Granny gave her and their dad orders on spiritual defenses.

Daniel turned his mind back to the monster awaiting them and prepared to summon the Sun Sword. He knew it might not be needed, though. Janice's barrier could handle most ordinary demons. The attacks had begun immediately following their quest to the Serpent's Abyss. Demons possessing all manner of things started assaulting them to and from school. But, because the area was not under the Enemy's power, they weren't allowed to show themselves to normal people, much less attack them outright, unless there was an Orb of Concealment cast. Since Janice began riding with them, though, they could blaze through pretty much any Concealment or demonic attack without worrying about a battle.

Right on cue, a giant raccoon with tire marks along its back, bear-like claws and fangs, and wisps of demonic spirit trailing out of its ears, bounded out of the woods.

"Looks like roadkill," Ben commented. "Man, demons will take over anything."

The raccoon demon jumped onto the lane behind them, launched itself on top of the SUV, and slammed into Janice's fiery barrier.

My life, my home, encircling me,
Oh, Sacred Three,
The Mighty Three …

Janice's spirit sang on above the car, unflinching and seemingly unperturbed by the giant demon hissing and spitting just feet from her.

"Ah! Give me the Vessels that I might eat them!" it shrieked, its claws burning away as it dug them into the barrier, doing its best to hang on for the ride.

Daniel opened the sunroof. "No," he replied, deadpan.

Mrs. Jones took a sharp turn, and the raccoon demon was flung into the woods.

"Take a hike, you overgrown rat carcass," Janice muttered in her sleep.

Ben smiled back at her.

"Incoming," Leah whispered, her voice shaky and her eyes wide. "I think that one's an armadillo. Or was, once."

Daniel and Ben leaned over to gape out the window as a pile of bones, discombobulated armor plates, and a scaly tail came running out of the woods and jumped onto the road directly in front of them. It charged with surprising speed, even though its head was where one of its hind legs should've been. Its sorry state certainly took some of the intimidation out of its threats, especially since it couldn't get a full sentence out without stepping on its own mouth.

"I'm going to dest—argh!—roy you Vessels. The Mast—ack!—er will give me a place of hon—orf!—or when I capture you. You bel—erg!—ong to me! Muhahah—aaakkk!"

Mrs. Jones plowed right over the demon. It was unclear whether the barrier or the SUV did more damage, but the remaining mass of seething roadkill stayed plastered to the road, a matching pair of flaming tire marks added to its battle scars.

"Loser," Janice chuckled through her sleep. "Now, I need to go see a woman about a cardigan."

Leah sighed. "Is this what it's like every day after school?"

"After school. Before school." Daniel shrugged. "Grocery shopping. Every time we order a pizza."

"That much?" Leah asked, wringing her hands.

Ben waved her concern away. "That was all before Mom and her friends prayed up a barrier around the neighborhood. Some Creep disguised himself as a pizza delivery man. Of course, he couldn't

approach the house, but when Mom went out to get it from the car, he was foaming at the mouth. He threw the pizza on the ground and climbed out the window to get at her."

"That's awful!" Leah exclaimed.

"I know!" Daniel replied. "The pizza was completely ruined! Probably poisoned, in any case." He sighed. "The barrier around the house stopped him, of course. Mom was fine." His stomach rumbled. "Man, I'm hungry. Could go for some pizza right now."

Leah shook her head and cast anxious eyes over everyone in the car. "You've been attacked even at home! Can't you get a moment's rest?"

Mrs. Jones turned on her blinker and pulled into their neighborhood. The Sweetbay Bottom sign looked a little worse for wear: claw marks all but obliterated some of the letters, and half the sign was charred. "Don't you worry about us," she said, her tone reassuring. "I got all my prayer partners from church to pray for protection around our neighborhood. I told them there were some illegal things happening and some 'unsavory characters' loitering around, putting our kids at risk. Didn't mention all the demons and Serpent stuff, but they got right to work. It's not that hard to convince women with children to start a prayer chain. Within a week, there was a barrier around the neighborhood. Creeps and demons can't get past the entrance. They don't stand a chance against my prayer circle."

A black-eyed woman on a bicycle rode out from behind the sign and pedaled furiously toward their Suburban.

Mrs. Jones rolled down the window. "Not a chance!" she repeated, her fist in the air.

The Creep crossed an invisible line, and a flaming barrier roared to life. She froze mid-stride, hissed and spat, and then vanished.

"Goodness!" Leah's eyes bugged out. "She was just burned up! That poor woman! What does everyone think about this? I mean, how do you explain it to the rest of the neighborhood when they see people going up in flames?"

Daniel put a reassuring hand on her shoulder. "The Creeps aren't killed, just purified. The Father takes them somewhere to help them."

Ben reached around behind his seat to rouse Janice. "The neighborhood barrier is just like Janice's. Normal people can't see it, and the Creeps and demons aren't allowed to attempt anything if normal people are around anyway. It's the Three's rule, and they have to follow it."

"Janice, wake up," he said tenderly. "We're safe in the neighborhood now."

Janice sat bolt upright. Her frizzy red hair and magnified eyes, fluttering behind thick glasses, barely cleared the back of Daniel's seat. "Home already? Gracious me. How'd I get on the floor?"

"Tumbled down at a stop sign, dear," Mariah called back. "Want me to drop you off at Granny's?"

"If you could." Janice yawned, then hoisted herself back into the seat. "I've got a few things to get done before you all come over this evening." She tossed the blanket off to busy herself pulling on boots and straightening out her disheveled knit-cardigan and ankle-length plaid dress.

Snowflakes drifted down and slid off the windshield. Within moments, a steady flurry began dusting the pine forest on either side of the road. Granny's, a solitary, white wooden house on the outskirts of the neighborhood, peered out from its happy prison of large trees and English ivy. Seren and Raylin sat on the front porch swing, covered in blankets.

As Mrs. Jones pulled into the driveway, Daniel slid the car seat forward to let Janice out. The girls waved eagerly as they caught sight of her.

Ben waved back, desperately trying to be seen over Janice's poofy hair as she fumbled out of the vehicle.

"They're waving at Janice, Ben. Don't look so desperate," Daniel whispered.

"Mind your own business," he snapped back.

"You poor dears!" Janice chortled when she caught sight of the

sisters. "It's so cold, and you're out here waiting on me. Right where I left you. Come on inside and let's get things straightened up before everyone arrives. I've got some knitting to finish, too. Not sure why I need to, but it suddenly seems important."

Mrs. Jones cracked her window. "We'll be up with takeout once Alan gets home from work. Five-thirty sound okay?"

"Just right."

"Close the door, Ben," Mrs. Jones said over her shoulder. "Raylin's already inside. She's not coming back out, and we have to get home."

"Mom!" Ben shouted, slamming the door shut and folding his arms in a pout. "Don't be ridiculous. I was just … enjoying the snow."

Leah and Mrs. Jones exchanged knowing glances.

"Of course, my son. The snow. You really think I haven't noticed all those longing glances and awkward attempts at conversation? You're about as obvious as Daniel." She backed out of the driveway and onto the street.

"Hey, I'm not trying to hide anything," Daniel replied. "I own my crush. Besides, she likes me, too. We kissed, so it's official."

"Here we go again," Ben snorted. "The Kiss. Like it was amazing or something. It caught you so off guard you almost wet yourself, Daniel."

"I did not! I was cool about it."

Ben rolled his eyes and watched the passing trees. "Well, there goes the evening. Hope you all like talking about Daniel's romance with Gabriela because that's all he'll blather on about tonight. It'd take an act of God to get him off that subject."

2

An Act of God

"**A**ll I'm saying," Daniel said very matter-of-factly as he and Ben climbed the stairs to their room, "is that I didn't make a total fool of myself when Gabriela left through the Mist. There, now we can stop the conversation."

Ben followed close behind. He rubbed his temples and groaned. "Sure, with you having the last word. Typical. Look, I don't care. Can we please stop talking about this?"

Mrs. Jones stood with one foot on the staircase. "Be ready to go once your father gets home," she called after them. "Don't take too long up there either, Daniel. Come down and talk with your wonderful mother about the past couple weeks."

Daniel heard his biological mother reply with some grateful comment before he walked into his room to change. He froze.

A scroll, glowing with a soft golden light and sealed with an eight-pointed star, floated in the center of the room.

"Ben." Daniel nodded toward it.

Ben gasped. "What do you suppose that is? Is it safe?" He walked around it with an appraising eye. "From the Enemy? Oh, eight-pointed star. That's got to be from the Three."

Daniel reached up and took hold of the scroll. The star dissipated, and the scroll slowly unfurled. "I don't think the Three need to send letters. They can just talk into our minds OH MY GOSH IT'S FROM GABRIELA!" He quickly scanned the letter.

Dear friends,

It's finally time for you to join me in Peru! Get your stuff ready and go to Pedestal Hill this evening at 5:00.

See you soon!

P.S. Inti said hi before he left for battle.

P.P.S Pack for Babylon, too. Once we're done here, you won't return home before transport.

P.P.P.S Give this note to your parents when you're finished with it.

Daniel passed the scroll off to Ben and immediately grabbed his backpack to dump out the contents. Once certain everything related to school was out, he hastily stuffed it with supplies and clothes. His mind raced. He was going to see Gabriela tonight! Would they get a chance to talk? Would she want to kiss him again?

"What's with the circle at the bottom?" Ben asked, looking at the front and the back of the scroll, then holding it up to the light.

Daniel shrugged. He hadn't really stopped to even notice it. Not with his reunion with Gabriela so close! He checked himself. They weren't meeting up for some date; she had been battling evil in her hometown, trying to free her people from the spiritual oppression of the Enemy. Romance was almost certainly the last thing on her mind. *Breathe, Daniel. Relax,* he told himself. *Focus on the task at hand.*

Father, help me to chill out, please. Help me concentrate on the quest. His mind slowed, and he felt a sense of calm.

"What does one wear to Babylon?" Ben asked, oblivious to Daniel's inner struggle. Or, more likely, totally apathetic. He grabbed his own bag and began packing. "It's probably hot."

"Desert," Daniel said. "Oven during the day. Chilly at night. I'm going to wear jeans and a long-sleeved button-down over a T-shirt.

And the stuff Janice knitted for us, of course." His own words gave him pause. In his smitten stupor, what clothes had he even packed? He emptied his backpack of all the random clothes and supplies to restart more mindfully. "Don't forget your knives," he said to Ben.

"Duh. First thing I packed." Ben pulled his golden daggers halfway out of his bag and went back to rummaging through his drawers.

A Celestial Arrow struck a fir tree outside their window, encasing it in a temporary shell of blue light.

"Hey," Daniel said. "Arrow." He jabbed a thumb toward the tree.

Ben barely looked up. "Seren and Raylin probably got a scroll, too. You know, it'd be so much easier if Janice would just buy them phones. That poor tree. Want us to come to Granny's? Shoot the tree. Got a message from the Three? Shoot the tree. Want to know if we have any more donuts left over from breakfast? Shoot the tree. I swear, Seren is just messing with us half the time. Likes the power, no doubt."

"Please. You gawk at it all day, hoping it gets lit up. The second you see an arrow, you're out the door like a racehorse."

"Maybe," Ben allowed. "But I still think Seren is abusing her power. Ooh! Do you think we all have the power to write spirit messages now? Maybe I can send Raylin—I mean Raylin *and* Seren scrolls like that."

"Nice save. But that's a good question. I could actually communicate with Gabriela if we're separated again."

"Oh, holy Three," Ben intoned, folding his hands and falling on his knees beside his bed. "Will you give me the power to send spirit messages?"

Daniel paused from packing. "Anything?"

"Nope. Guess it's just one of Gabriela's special powers. She's so cool."

Daniel sighed and read back over the scroll. "Yeah. She is." He carefully placed it on the top of his dresser and then paused at the mirror hanging on the wall over it. Daniel brushed his bushy, brown

hair to the side. He sniffed his underarms and crinkled up his nose. "Ew. I smell bad."

Ben smirked. "Shocker. Would you quit fussing in the mirror? Your hair looks stupid and always will. Let's just hurry and get ready so we can go meet the girls."

"I'm getting a shower first. You might want to freshen up, too. You really want to start off the quest looking like a doofus and smelling like you just got out of P.E.? Because you do."

"I don't look like a doofus!" Ben ran to the mirror as Daniel disappeared into their bathroom. "Do I?"

Thirty minutes later, Daniel and Ben walked down the stairs together. Both wore jeans with long-sleeved camo shirts and brown T-shirts underneath, all concealed beneath Janice's prayer-infused, knitted, stealth-black ponchos and beanies. Their backpacks bulged with supplies, with just enough room left for food and water. Daniel held the rolled-up scroll in his hand, ready to present it to Mrs. Jones when the litany of questions began. The best way to handle breaking the news to their mothers was to let the message speak for itself.

Leah was the first to notice the boys. She looked up from a magazine she was reading at the table and tilted her head to the side as she regarded their clothes. "New fashion statement?"

Mrs. Jones walked into the kitchen holding a basket of laundry and promptly dropped it on the floor when she caught sight of the ponchos. Her face went pale, and a hand strayed to her forehead. "Does this mean what I think it means?"

Daniel held out the glowing scroll. Mrs. Jones snatched it from his hands and unfurled it so both she and Leah could read the message.

Keys rattled in the door to the garage before it swung open, and Mr. Jones's light brown hair and lanky frame appeared around the corner. "I'm home," he sang from the hallway, dropping his briefcase and plodding into the kitchen. "I got off early today so we could ..." His voice trailed off as he surveyed the scene. "Something happen?"

Mrs. Jones held out the scroll.

He took it from her hands, his dark blue eyes quickly scanning

the note. When he finished, it pulsed brighter, and an Orb of Seeing popped out of the circle at the bottom.

"Oh my!" Leah gasped. "What's that?"

The Orb hovered in the air in front of Mrs. Jones. She took it in her hands and frowned. "That's how the Three expect us to keep up with what's happening while the kids are on their quest," she said, her voice saturated with self-pity. "Keep vigilant and pray; that's all we can do."

The Orb floated to Leah, who cupped her hands around it.

Mr. Jones patted his wife on the shoulder. "It allows us to see through the eyes of whoever is in need on the quest. Sometimes Ben, sometimes Daniel. Last quest, it flashed over to Raylin's viewpoint quite a lot, but I think it was through Seren's eyes half the time."

Ben approached his parents and gave them a hug. "Sorry, guys. I have a feeling this will mean we might miss Christmas."

"But your last quests," Leah began, letting the Orb float back into the air as she crossed the distance to Daniel, "didn't they only last a few days? There's still a week before Christmas."

Ben shrugged and passed the question off to Daniel.

"It might take longer this time," Daniel explained. He stood between the Joneses and Leah, not sure who to hug first. "We have more to do this go around. We're off to Peru this evening. I don't know how long that will take. Then it's straight to Babylon to do whatever it is we have to do to seal the Spirit of the Age. We don't really know much about how big of a battle that'll be." He held up his hands helplessly.

Leah pulled him into a tight hug, her grip surprisingly strong for someone with such a small frame. "I guess we don't have much choice in the matter?" She pulled away and squeezed his shoulders before pushing him toward the Joneses.

Mr. Jones shook his head. "No. We don't. That doesn't mean we can't help them, though." He nodded at the Orb of Seeing, now floating around the smoke alarm. "Our prayers helped to literally shield them from the Enemy on the last quest. You remember. They'll do the same on this one."

"How can you act so calm?" Mrs. Jones snapped, pulling away to grab a dining chair from the table. She stood on it to retrieve the Orb. "You talk about it like it was a little rain we protected them from. There was a seven-headed dragon and a horde of monsters, Alan. Christmas is ruined!"

Mr. Jones seemed to know when he was defeated and fell into an apologetic silence.

Leah studied the Orb. "All we'll do is pray?" She looked confused and let her gaze drift out the window to the falling snow.

Daniel was about to explain more about prayer when Ben nudged him.

"Don't you think we should go?" Ben held up his watch.

Daniel felt a stab of urgency. It was already 3:30, and they still had to meet up with Seren and Raylin, field whatever goodbyes Janice would throw at them, and hike up to Pedestal Hill before 5:00. "Yeah. Sorry, everyone, but we need to hurry." He pulled away from his parents and inched toward the door.

"Oh, now, hold your horses," Mrs. Jones's voice rose in alarm. "Let me make sure you kids packed everything you need." She grabbed their backpacks and hastily rummaged through them while muttering to herself. "Ok. Looks like everything's in order." She grabbed her coat from where it was hanging beside the garage door and tossed Mr. Jones his. "Although I can't understand why you both can be so thorough when packing for death-defying quests, but you can't pick up all the socks from your bedroom floor."

Leah, still lost in thought and quiet, pulled her overcoat on and waited beside Daniel for the Joneses to be ready. "I … I'm proud of you, Daniel," she whispered. "I still feel like a stranger in your life, but I love you, and I'm proud of all you've accomplished." She reached out and took his hand, studying it as if it were something precious. "It's funny, isn't it? You spend so long looking for someone, and suddenly, they're in your life. Then they're gone. Just like that."

Daniel felt a warm sensation spread through his body. "I love you, too. In all fairness, my life is awfully strange. Anyone would feel

like a stranger. Even I do sometimes. But, um, we've made it through three other quests. I'm sure we'll survive this one. Just pray for us."

Leah looked up into Daniel's eyes. "I'll pray every second of every day." She gave his hand one final squeeze and stepped back as Mr. and Mrs. Jones filed through the door.

"We'll all be praying furiously," Mr. Jones said. "Come on, boys. Grab your bags and let's go before your mother tries to stall."

"I heard that, Alan," Mrs. Jones annoyed voice drifted back inside.

Daniel and Ben snickered to each other and quickly followed.

* * *

Seren and Raylin waited on the front porch, poised like soldiers with their weapons summoned—Seren with the white starlight limbs of the Celestial Bow held by her side, and Raylin leaning casually on the obsidian black Abyssal Staff. Like the boys, both girls wore dark colors: jeans and earth-toned shirts. Raylin opted for a dull green long-sleeve, while Seren sported a muddy brown. These were mostly concealed beneath the same black ponchos and stocking caps Janice had knitted for the boys. Raylin's straight, snow-white hair was pulled into a tight braid that snuck out of the bottom of the cap to hang halfway down her back. She leveled her green eyes at the boys and gave a curt wave. Seren's hair was similarly braided, although hers draped over her right shoulder, her white-streaked blond standing out in stark contrast to the pitch black of her poncho.

Janice could be heard flitting around inside, crashing into furniture or clanging in the kitchen. She stuck her frizzy red head out the door. "You girls positive you packed enough food? Clothes? Underwear? I can whip up a few more pair if you need them."

"You've made us plenty of underwear, Janice," Raylin said gently. "More than we could possibly wear in a year, actually."

Janice stepped onto the porch and put her hands on her hips. "How many times do I have to tell you girls? Call me 'Mom'. I know that's a touchy subject, and I can never replace your real mother, but I can't bear being called by my name by you two dear little ducklings."

She launched herself at both girls and pulled them into a wild, yarn-filled hug. Her eyes brimmed with tears, each magnified through her glasses before falling onto their stocking caps and absorbing into the dark fibers.

Daniel half-expected Raylin and Seren to pull away in annoyance, but surprisingly, both seemed to enjoy the affection. They muttered something inaudible.

"Oh! There it is," Janice exclaimed. "Music to my ears." She ushered the girls off the porch and down to the group. "I assume another one of those Orbs came with your note, too?" She reached into the oversized pockets of her cardigan and pulled out a glowing scroll identical to Daniel and Ben's.

Mrs. Jones held up their Orb and frowned at it. "Yes, we got ours. Now we can stare through it at all the horrible things happening to our children. You got one, too?"

Janice rummaged through her pockets. "My gracious. What did I do with that thing? Is that it?" She pulled out a ball of yarn. "Hardly. Oh, for goodness' sake. Orb!" she called in her nasal voice. "Orb, are you there?" She whistled loudly, and surprisingly, the Orb drifted out of the open door and down the steps to Janice. "Let's keep you in my pockets where I won't lose you." She dropped it in along with the yarn ball and spun around to engage the other adults with a slew of questions.

Ben stepped closer to the girls. "Why do you both have your weapons summoned?" He asked, directing the question at Raylin.

She shrugged. "Didn't know when we would need them. We wanted to be ready. The Creeps attacked before the first quest even began."

Seren gestured toward Ben with the Celestial Bow, its radiant limbs glinting in the depths of her blue eyes. "I attacked you in your front yard before the second quest."

Daniel nodded sagely. "Abida and his goons *did* show up right before we left for Ireland. I guess we should be ready." He summoned the Sun Sword. If Abida visited again, they'd be in real trouble. He

broke through Granny's barrier like it was child's play, and the power of the Sun Sword wasn't enough to permanently purify him.

Would Daniel have that power even if the Sun Sword was whole? He held up the sword, floating just beyond his fingertips. They were beginning their last quest, and still, the Three had not given him any clue about the whereabouts of the missing shard, no matter how many times he had asked them. They needed the sword to be complete if they were going to all have the Father's superpowered Blessing like Daniel had at Intipuncu. Otherwise, they'd be going into the biggest battle of their lives with only a fraction of the power needed. The Three were cutting it close.

Ben snorted. "I feel kind of left out. Look at you all, brandishing your weapons just because you can."

Ben's comment brought Daniel back to the present conversation.

"You could summon the Triune Shield," Raylin said, her voice, slightly deeper than Seren's alto, was tinged with mischief.

Ben seemed relieved by her attention. "Oh, sure, I'll just hang out as the Triune Shield. It's perfect for conversation." He whipped out his golden feather daggers and encased them in the blue light of the Triune Shield. "I guess I'll have to settle with this."

Daniel held the Sun Sword up next to one of Ben's daggers. "That's cute, Ben. They're so little!"

"Shut up."

"So, Raylin," Daniel said, looking up from the blades, "how does it feel to be starting your first quest?"

Raylin's eyebrows narrowed. "This isn't my first quest."

"I mean your first quest fighting for the Three instead of against them." Daniel held his breath. All their interactions had been like this since returning. He couldn't say anything without getting under Raylin's skin, accidentally insinuating something negative about her, using the wrong words, or bringing up a sensitive topic.

Raylin paused for a moment as though uncertain of Daniel's meaning. She looked away. "I'm not sure what I feel. Hopeful, I guess. Looking forward to kicking some Enemy butt."

Daniel breathed a sigh of relief. Awkward conversation averted. He didn't see why Raylin had to be so touchy on the subject of her betrayal and possession. It *was* her choice to betray them in Peru in the first place, and Granny had warned her about the Voidblade's spirits possessing her if she kept using it. Why should he have to tiptoe around her decisions?

Ben sidled up closer to Raylin and took advantage of the silence. "I know what you mean. I'm looking forward to fighting, too. Gets the blood pumping, you know?"

Seren rolled her eyes, but Raylin smirked.

"I guess so," Raylin replied. She gripped the Abyssal Staff with both hands and activated the eye. Iridescent green swirls eddied in the staff's obsidian black. The half-foot-wide circular head separated into fragments, expanded, and orbited in a perfect ring. Triangles of yellow light flickered into being within and orbited in the opposite direction. A pitch-black point appeared at the center of the orbits. "But that'll mean dealing with the Enemy—the Serpent—again. Face to face." She shuddered. "I hope I can handle that."

Ben let his daggers fall to his side. "You'll do great. Besides, we'll all be together."

A smile played at the corner of Raylin's mouth. "Thanks."

"I mean, I think we will. Daniel? How does sealing the Spirit of the Age thing work, exactly? You're supposed to be our leader. Know something?"

Daniel waved the Sun Sword back and forth, trying to ignore Ben's desperate flirtation. "I know as much as you do. The Three haven't been exactly specific on how we're supposed to do this. Or what the Spirit of the Age is, you know? I mean, is it Supai, Shiva, and Arawn all together or something? Or maybe all his incarnations combined into one?"

Ben hugged himself. "Don't even put that out there! Ugly Town, here we come."

"Surely we'll get some instructions," Daniel continued, moving from Ben to the girls. "I mean, I hope we'll get instructions. But you both have some inside information, right?"

Raylin released the Abyssal Staff so that its form returned to its resting state. "Even when I was on the inside, I didn't know anything about sealing away the Spirit of the Age. I can't imagine the Enemy likes talking about it."

Seren walked over to Ben and patted him on the head. "Don't make such a fuss. First of all, the Serpent *is* all the Enemy's incarnations combined into one. They're an extension of him. Duh. You've already faced him, so go change your pants."

"Hey!" Ben objected. "I didn't—my pants are just fine, thank you." He glanced at Raylin.

"Second of all, ditto with Raylin. But I think it's safe to say that sealing the Spirit of the Age has something to do with Amira and Abida. From what I understand, the Enemy has always had one or two people he worked directly through at the culmination of each age."

Daniel let the Sun Sword float straight up in the air. The interwoven braids of golden metal comprising the handle hovered just beyond his fingertips as though he were performing a magical balancing trick. "What'll happen to the Generals when we seal old Nasty Snake?"

Ben shook his head. "They'll be totally ticked, that's for sure. Maybe they can return to a normal life or something."

"Just imagine Wanu"—Daniel laughed—"with her weird shark teeth and insane personality going grocery shopping. Who'd want to be friends with that possessed freak? Or Vinaash? That crazy, pestilence wielding ..."

Ben glanced meaningfully at Raylin and Seren, who regarded Daniel with chilly expressions. He walked his fingers over the razor edges of his daggers.

A prickly feeling crawled up Daniel's spine, and he quickly shut his mouth.

Raylin shook her head. "I used to be that messed up too, Daniel. You're friends with me. I think."

Seren rolled her eyes. "Four arms and blue skin, and I'm standing here because of the Three. Real smooth, Slick."

"Right. Sorry, I didn't mean it that way. I just meant … Don't be so sensitive, okay? I mean, you know that Wanu is different from you guys, so yeah."

Ben gave Daniel a thumbs up. "Nice save."

Daniel groaned and edged closer to Ben. "Why can't I ever say the right thing to them these days?" he muttered.

"I don't know, but I wish you'd get a grip and quit making things weird," Ben whispered back, putting his arm over Daniel's shoulder and turning him away from the girls.

"Listen, I wasn't the one that let myself be possessed by the Enemy like the demon-sisters over there. I'm trying my best to avoid stepping on their toes, but it seems like I can't say anything without offending them."

Seren stepped in front of Daniel. "The demon-sisters have very good hearing. You two done with your powwow?"

Daniel craned his neck around to find Raylin waving at him. He cradled his forehead in the palm of his hand. "Yes."

"Kids?" Mr. Jones walked over from the huddle of adults. "We better go. Forty minutes until your departure time."

The other adults ambled toward them. Janice chattered on about the ponchos she had knitted for the companions, but Mrs. Jones plodded by in agitated silence, crunching her way through the now thickly falling snow. She parted some low-hanging branches and struck out on the wooded path that led up to Pedestal Hill.

Seren and Raylin fell in step behind the adults while Daniel and Ben took up the rear.

Daniel found his gaze frequently drifting to Raylin's back. He exhaled, his breath becoming visible in the freezing air and momentarily obscuring her form. He shook his head. If that wasn't appropriate, he didn't know what was. She was impossible to read and always confusing. All he had to do was blink, and she'd be insulted. If he wanted the quest to go smoothly, he'd have to watch what he said to Raylin. The last thing any of them needed was to be distracted by conflict or misunderstandings.

They had just crossed into the thicker part of the woods when a twig snapped in the underbrush behind them.

Daniel and Raylin spun around. A sparrow darted out of the powdered bushes and flew past. Their eyes met, and after a moment of awkwardness, they rejoined the others, who hadn't seemed to notice.

After hiking a hundred yards up the path, they passed the gully where Daniel used to practice swordplay. As usual, fallen trees and boulders crowded the ever-widening ravine.

A thud, followed by a low, muffled growl, came from down the path behind them.

That caught everyone's attention.

"I think we've got Creeps on our tail," Daniel whispered. He remained fixed on the bushes for a moment, thinking. He hoped it was Creeps. Demons would be a problem. He and the other Vessels could transport away, but that would leave the adults to deal with them. "I'm going to use a Sunstorm."

The other Vessels nodded in unison. Raylin activated the Abyssal Staff and stood at the ready. Seren raised the Celestial Bow and drew back while a white arrow of brilliant starlight glittered into being on an invisible string. Ben began to glow, ready to summon the Triune Shield in an instant.

With one last glance behind them, Daniel mentally prepared himself for the Sunstorm and flung the arc of fire.

3

A Hair-ifying Purification

The group stood motionless, staring at the path after the muted thunder of the Sunstorm dissipated. No dark spirits tore through the air. No guttural screams of anger echoed over the hillside. No terrifying demons broke out of the bushes.

Everyone relaxed except for Leah. She looked still and small, frozen in fear. The whites of her eyes were a perfect match for the snow caught on her jacket and muffler.

"An animal, maybe?" Mr. Jones asked.

"Could be a black bear," Janice suggested. "I've seen a few poking around in the woods from time to time. Mind you, I kept my distance. Mostly saw them through the window of the house, but once when I was—"

Mrs. Jones stepped in front of Janice. "Should we keep moving?" she whispered.

Daniel nodded. "I think so."

The group quickened their pace almost to a jog and reached the top of Pedestal Hill within five minutes. Daniel and Ben helped the mothers down the incline to the ledge outside the cave while Seren and Raylin helped Janice slide down it carefully, one on either side of her. Mr. Jones brought up the rear.

The curtain of ivy overhanging the entrance to the cave, now covered in ice, clinked like chimes as the companions filed through. The inky darkness of the cave gave way to the brilliant light of the Celestial Bow and Sun Sword.

The Vessels quickly scanned their surroundings, weapons at the ready. It was empty, save for the familiar form of the pedestal standing like a sentinel in front of the back wall.

Seren released the Celestial Bow and made a beeline toward it. "Question: whose hand will the pedestal be keyed to? All our quests for the weapons are over."

Daniel scratched his head and shrugged. "We could all try, I guess."

Raylin joined Seren in studying the handprint engraved into the stone plinth. "It'll probably be Daniel's hand. We are going back to Machu Picchu, after all. Don't see why it should change."

Ben nodded. "That makes sense."

Leah followed Janice, who hovered behind Seren and Raylin. "What are we talking about?" she asked, eyeing the pedestal over Janice's shoulder.

Mrs. Jones pointed at the handprint. "It transports them to different places all over the world where the kids can risk their lives fighting demons and the Enemy." She frowned at the pedestal as though it were a disobedient child.

Mr. Jones gave her a nudge. "I know that look. You can't destroy it. Granny will just show up in a fireball and transport them away. Or Gabriela could open the Mist, and then they'd have to walk there."

Her scowl deepened until, seemingly satisfied she had demonstrated enough displeasure, she turned to the Vessels. "We'll be watching you kids every waking moment."

"And praying like mad," Janice interrupted, poking her head out from behind Seren's shoulder.

"Don't take any unnecessary risks." Mrs. Jones raised an eyebrow. "Understand?"

"Yes, we know," Daniel and Ben mumbled in unison.

Mr. Jones produced the Orb of Seeing from his coat pocket. "No fighting with each other, either. When Seren ran off from you all last time, it about gave your mother a heart attack."

Janice flitted toward him with raised hands. "I quite agree. If I see you all arguing, I'll … Well, I don't know what I'll do. I can't imagine being angry with any of you, but I'm sure I would be. Please don't make me get—"

"Why are we still following them, Dear?" a gravelly, all-too-familiar voice whined from the ledge outside. "They tried to blow us up. I have half a mind to call the police."

"Be quiet!" Gator snapped, her voice low and commanding. "They might hear us. What if they're right inside this cave?"

Daniel locked eyes with Ben.

Seren and Raylin exchanged sideways glances.

Everyone else watched the cave opening with bated breath, except for Mrs. Jones, who looked so annoyed, Daniel was surprised she didn't march out onto the ledge and launch into a lecture. Daniel hoped she would resist the urge. Their only hope of not being discovered was to release their weapons and pray the darkness of the cave dissuaded the Gurges from venturing in.

Daniel released the Sun Sword. Raylin and Ben quickly followed suit. Darkness enveloped the cave.

"I didn't know this was here," Barth grunted. "Dear, let's leave. Maybe Ms. Julie gave those horrible weapons to them so they could kill us. Wouldn't surprise me. You can thank our lucky stars we had just fallen into that gully. Or maybe they're aliens! Gator, I bet they're aliens! That would explain how horrible Daniel is. Lying to the judge and getting you taken away. Destroying our life. Constantly meddling. And now he's trying to blast us to bits with his evil space technology!"

"Hush!" Gator replied. "I'm going in." The iced ivy rustled as Gator cautiously parted it.

Daniel stole a glance at his watch—4:58. His heart sank. They didn't have time for this.

Father? he asked, trying to quiet his anxiety and listen. *I've got two seconds, so I'm just going to do what I think I need to. Stop me if I shouldn't.*

The failing evening light of the gray sky filtered into the cave. Daniel gave himself one second extra, but no divine messages slipped into his mind.

He walked toward the entrance just as Gator forced her way in. Barth followed directly, clinging to Gator's right shoulder. Both wore heavy jackets, work boots with mismatched woolen socks pulled up and over their pants, and stocking caps. Barth's flaming red chest hair bristled out from the jacket interior as if he carried around his own cheery fireplace.

Daniel summoned the Sun Sword, throwing back the darkness of the cave with the sudden, blinding flare.

Gator and Barth blinked in shocked surprise.

"Aliens!" Barth screamed.

Gator threw her right arm up to shield her eyes. "What the heck?"

"Merry Christmas, Gurges. Sorry about this, but I think you'll thank me. Eventually." Daniel swung the sword in a blazing arc through their chests, and both promptly collapsed facedown in the cave.

Mrs. Jones and Leah cried out in shock.

Mr. Jones ran to Daniel's side and grabbed his sword arm. "Daniel! What have you done?" He stared down at the Gurges in horror. "They're not monsters, son! Why did you kill them?"

"They're not dead," Seren stated matter-of-factly. She knelt beside the Gurges, grabbed their arms, and attempted to pull them completely into the cave. "Whoa! That's a two-person job for sure," she laughed, dropping Gator's arms and grabbing Barth. She easily dragged him into the interior. Raylin joined her in towing Gator over toward her father.

"Not dead? That's good," Janice prattled. "Always liked the Gurges. Silly people. Fun from a distance. Sell good popcorn. That man has hair like an orangutan. Though I suppose I'm one to talk. Mine's so frizzy."

Leah paced back and forth with one hand on her forehead and the other on her stomach, all the while staring at the motionless figures on the floor. "Okay, if they're not dead, what happened to them when they got cut with your sword?"

Daniel released the Sun Sword and joined his mother. "It purifies them just like the Creeps. Only, they don't have any demon spirits." He took her hands in his and patted them.

Ben snorted. "As far as *you* know, anyway." He turned to Leah. "If they're anything like the last normal people Daniel struck with the Sun Sword, they'll wake up in a little bit and ask about the Three. They're fine, don't worry. Honestly, it'll help things if the Gurges had a little God in their lives."

Raylin cleared her throat. "Don't we need to leave? It's 5:02."

Daniel spun around. "Yes. We do." He jogged to the pedestal. "Can you guys take care of them for us?"

The adults all mumbled their consent, eyeing the Gurges with significantly less care now that they knew they weren't dead.

"Just be careful," Mrs. Jones ordered. "And know that we'll be miserable, worried, and praying feverishly until you return."

Leah nodded in agreement. "I'm not really sure what you're in for, but please don't take any unnecessary risks."

Janice flew toward Raylin and Seren and wrapped them in a tornado of cardigans and hugs before flitting to the other adults.

Mr. Jones gave the boys a serious look and tipped his head toward them with a somber expression. "Love you, boys. Be safe."

Daniel held his hand over the pedestal. "Everyone ready?"

"No," Raylin muttered. "Just get it over with."

Ben and Seren grunted in agreement.

Daniel blew out a slow breath and touched the handprint. His hand stuck fast to the pedestal, and the circle of fire spun out around them, filling the cave with blinding brilliance. He and the others floated into the air. Predictably, the fire's whirlpool motion locked in place, and the cave itself launched into a spin. Everything suddenly blurred: his parents, Janice, the Gurges' prone bodies, and the woman's figure in the cave doorway.

Daniel couldn't clear his vision. Was that Granny? The cave swirled into a tunnel of fire, yanking him and the others through.

"Here we go," Ben shouted, his voice muted and distant. "I hate this part with a passion. It's like we're stuffed in a blender and sucked through a straw."

Daniel could feel Ben and the girls being towed behind him through the portal.

"Quit being such a baby," Seren snickered. "You've been through worse."

"Yeah, *Seren*, I have. Thanks to you. It doesn't make this any better, though."

"On the bright side," Raylin joined in, "you haven't thrown up yet."

"Give me a minute."

Daniel was still troubled by the figure in the cave. "Did anyone else see a woman before we transported?"

"It was Granny," Ben said, groaned, and then continued. "I saw her blue nightgown and broom."

"I didn't see anyone," Raylin added. "Where was she?"

Daniel directed his voice toward Raylin's. "I saw her outlined against the ivy curtain."

"Granny was probably sent to give our parents some special instructions," Seren offered.

Daniel considered this, but there was little time to ponder the issue more. The raging vortex of fire stilled, and he found himself standing back in front of the pedestal. Three flashes of light burst into his field of vision to his sides, and the others dropped out of the air and collapsed to the ground. Tongues of orange fire burned over their heads.

"I think we got the Gift of Tongues in transit," Ben said, pointing above Daniel's head. He shifted his legs beneath him and stiffly stood.

Daniel looked up and saw the same flickering fire hovering above him. "Must need it soon."

He took in their surroundings. That wasn't the only difference. When they first transported to Peru on the quest for the Sun Sword,

the cavern had been pitch-black until his foot crossed the line of residual fire left over from the vortex. Daniel pulled his hand back from the pedestal, which rose from an octagonal platform in the center of the chamber. Now, the stadium-sized stone cathedral was already lit with bright, cheery torches, all reflected in the gargantuan, sun-shaped mirror fixed to the ceiling. House-sized pentagonal stone slabs formed the floor, stretching toward smooth walls hewn into the seamless, living rock beneath Machu Picchu. To his front, two sets of double doors flanked a six-story-high staircase that climbed to the compartment where he'd found the first shard of the Sun Sword. Where the doors met, a golden inlay in the shape of the wavy-bladed sword stretched from top to bottom, and similarly fashioned letters arched along their top. The Gift of Tongues allowed Daniel to read the once indecipherable words. "Blessed are the pure in heart," the left door read. Over the other was the phrase, "For they shall see God."

As before, soft, ceaseless music, like wind blowing through unseen pipes, filled the vast space. Somewhere, it found its way through the rocks and carved stone to periodically tease massive chimes. Their knell gave the chamber the ambience of a magical temple, calling its hearers to worship.

Ben stood up, gingerly rubbing his backside. He nodded toward the doors on the right. "Didn't the Devourer blast those off their hinges the last time we were here?"

"Well, yeah," Daniel replied. "But that was before Supai totally destroyed the whole passageway. I seem to remember him tearing through that wall right before we transported back home." He spun around to scan the room again, looking for the one thing he was most curious about. "I wonder where Gabriela is."

Raylin joined them, eyes flitting around. She breathed rhythmically as if trying to calm herself. "Maybe Granny fixed everything. Or Inti."

Daniel shrugged as he walked off the platform.

Seren was the first to follow. She pointed to the top of the staircase. "What's up there?"

"The chamber of the Sun Sword. Man, this brings back memories, doesn't it?" Daniel tossed the question back to Ben and Raylin. "I wonder where Gabriela is," he repeated.

Raylin blanched. "Yeah, just not so good memories. And I have no idea where she is."

Ben listened nervously. "Oh, come on. Surely, the memories aren't all bad. You did help us get all the shards. Without you, we couldn't have escaped from Wayna Picchu. It all worked out in the end, right?"

"Maybe. I guess." Raylin pulled her poncho tighter. "I mean, I know you're right. It's just hard to feel that right now."

Seren continued her study of the staircase. "Is there also a school up there? I hear a bunch of kids."

Daniel furrowed his brow and focused on the noise. He had been so immersed in memories that he hadn't noticed the low chatter of young voices.

Right on cue, several heads popped over the lip of the topmost stair and broke into laughter. "They're here! The Vessels are here!"

A bustling mass of children and teenagers walked out on the landing at the top of the staircase and began waving. They nimbly bound down the steep steps, chattering in excitement.

Daniel instinctively summoned the Sun Sword even as Seren and Raylin summoned their Weapons of Power.

Ben waved at them to put the weapons away. "They're just normal kids. Don't scare them. Look at their eyes."

The bustling crowd of nearly twenty quickly surrounded the Vessels, and Daniel could immediately see Ben was right. None had the telltale signs of a Creep, and all seemed like normal children. Most of them wore old clothes sporting patched holes and dirty stains. All were too thin, but their faces beamed with joy.

"It's the Weapons of Power!" one little girl squeaked in excitement. "Are you going to save my mommy?" She approached Raylin and raised her arms to be picked up.

Raylin shot a confused look at Seren before releasing the Abyssal Staff and lifting the child into an uncertain hug.

"Your hair is so pretty," the girl said, touching the wisps of stark white that escaped Raylin's stocking cap. She pulled the cap off, and Raylin's ponytail cascaded down her back. "It's beautiful! How did you get it so white? Mine's just plain brown."

Raylin blinked in surprise at the question. "I … it … mine used to be dark." She looked around the room. "Well, Supai turned it white."

The girl looked sad and gingerly touched Raylin's face. "I'm sorry. He's mean, but I love your hair, and you're nice." She planted a kiss on Raylin's cheek and tightened her grip, wrapping herself around Raylin in a full-body hug. A smile broke through Raylin's look of surprise.

"What about my parents? Will you save them, too?" a preschool boy shouted, jumping up and down to be noticed from behind a group of taller kids.

A chorus of similar questions erupted from the crowd.

Before anyone could answer or ask for clarification, one of the teenagers stepped forward and held up his hands to shush the younger children. He was half a foot taller than Daniel and sported the same olive skin as the rest of his group. His chin-length hair was light brown and perfectly framed a face that could've been on the cover of some teen heartthrob magazine. Instead of ponchos or tattered clothes, he wore cargo pants and a dark blue jacket over a red T-shirt. Once things had calmed, he turned toward the Vessels. "Gabriela said you'd be coming. Are you here to save us?"

Daniel wasn't sure how he felt about another guy hanging around Gabriela the whole time she'd been gone, especially one who looked like him.

Seren tore off her hat and quickly fixed her hair. She shuffled forward. "Y-y-yeah. I guess we are. I'm Seren. This is Raylin and Ben. And you are?"

"Cristiano." He winked at Seren.

Daniel stepped in. "I'm Daniel. Thanks for remembering me, Seren." He turned toward Cristiano. "We honestly didn't know you all would be here. Gabriela didn't mention anything about *any* of you in her letters to me."

"Letters?" Ben asked. "We only got one, and it was basically a group message."

"Shut up, Ben. I take it you're from a nearby village?"

"Most everyone here is from Aguas Calientes or Santa Teresa," Cristiano answered. "I moved here from Cuzco several years ago, right before everything fell apart. Before my family was taken." He swallowed hard and fell silent.

"But then Ms. Gabriela came through the Mist!" the girl in Raylin's arms exclaimed. "She beat up all those bad people. She's so strong! She should be back now, though. I wonder where she is?"

"Where did she go?" Daniel had to keep himself from rushing toward her, but he couldn't keep the eagerness from his voice. "When did she say she'd be back? Was she okay when she left?"

"You're scary. She was supposed to come home the same time you arrived."

"Maybe she ran into more of the shadow people," someone else offered from the crowd.

Daniel remembered that when he and Gabriela had met for the first time, she referred to the Creeps as shadows—normal men and women twisted into shells of their true selves so that they didn't even recognize their own family. He immediately thought of the shadow sins he'd seen come out of all the Vessels' hearts, including his own. No doubt, there were some still lurking there. If it hadn't been for the Three, the Enemy could've easily filled them with evil as well.

"Gabriela calls them Creeps." It was Cristiano again. "She's been capturing them and taking them into the Mist."

"Yeah, unfortunately, we know all about the Creeps," Seren said. "We can handle them, though. At the risk of sounding like my neurotic friend over there," she tilted her head toward Daniel, who twisted his face into a look of bitterness, "where did Gabriela say she was going?"

"There're hardly any trains that bring food to Aguas Calientes anymore, so she went to Cuzco to get some supplies. But our real problem is that all the Creeps and demons know we're hiding here. They've surrounded Machu Picchu."

Raylin set the little girl down and approached them. "I thought Cuzco was protected by the Three. Why didn't she just take you all there?"

"I'm not sure. Gabriela taught us about the Three, and she did mention something about a Cuzcoan Seal. The Father's children were fleeing, and it's weakening." He shrugged. "That's all I know. Does that even make sense?"

"Yes," Ben replied. "That's the same problem we're having with the Babylonian Seal."

"Babylonian?"

Seren waved the question away. "That's not important right now. Why didn't Gabriela just keep you all in the Mist? Surely, you'd be better protected from attacks."

A deafening boom shook the mountain. The children whimpered and crowded closer to the Vessels. The other teenagers tried unsuccessfully to quiet them down.

"Exhibit A," Daniel said. "Do you know what kind of demon is attacking you?"

Cristiano's face paled. "Who knows? They're all terrifyingly weird combinations of dead animals." He pulled the children closest to him into a hug. "Gabriela insists this is where we're supposed to be; though, I'm not sure how long we'll be safe here."

"They shouldn't be able to get this close to Machu Picchu," Raylin's little girl whined. "What about the barrier?"

A little boy latched his arms around Cristiano's right leg. "The demons must have broken through. Are they going to get me?"

"Everybody pray for protection," Cristiano ordered. "Maybe the Three will strengthen the barrier." He knelt on the ground amid the children and led them in a prayer.

Boom!

The sound of scraping claws, leathery wings rasping stone, and wheezing voices filled the staircase behind the gilded doors.

Terrified, childlike prayers filled the cavernous cathedral.

Daniel summoned the Sun Sword and spun around to the other

Vessels. "I think we should get everyone to the top chamber. It'll be easier to fight without worrying about the children."

Raylin fixed determined eyes on the shaking doors. Her hands glowed with a hunter-green light as she folded them together and then drew them apart. The obsidian Abyssal Staff appeared within her grasp. She expertly whirled it around to build up momentum. "Daniel and I go on the offensive." She looked at Seren. "You support from behind."

"Agreed," Seren replied. The lights of the Celestial Bow shot down from her forehead and expanded into the brilliant limbs and arrow of starlight. "Ben, maybe you should surround the kids while they climb the—"

A familiar rush of wind silenced her as Gabriela strode out of the parting Mist. She paused in front of the staircase, hauling a wooden wagon laden with fruits, bread, cheese, and bottles of water. Three globes of light hovered around her like fireflies, illuminating her way. Her straight, brown hair, disheveled and tangled, escaped her stocking cap to fall around her shoulders. Her knit parka, once totally black, now bore stains of mud and grime.

Daniel rushed to help, but before he reached her, Gabriela yanked the rest of the wagon through the portal and pushed the whole thing sideways so that it skidded to a halt several yards away. "Oh, right. Super strength. Guess you didn't need me."

She looked at Daniel and blinked in surprise. Her chocolate eyes were red-rimmed and offset by dark circles of exhaustion. Despite her display of power, it was obvious she was tired and emotionally spent. She burst into tears and yanked Daniel into a hug. "I'm so glad you've come! I've needed help, and then the Three finally said to send for you, and now you're here! You can free our parents." The refugees caught her eye. "Is something wrong?"

Boom!

Both doors shook violently on their hinges.

"Oh. I see we have company."

4

A Demonic Playdate

Gabriela wiped her eyes as she looked away from the doors and turned toward the other Vessels. "Raylin. Seren. Ben." She said their names as if she didn't believe they were there and then breathed a sigh of relief. "Thank you all for coming."

Daniel gently touched her arm. "You take the kids into the Mist, and we'll fight off the demons.

She shook her head. "No. They don't need to be in there without us. I'll explain later. Besides, you'll need me out here. Just prioritize defeating the demons and rescuing the Creeps that come through the door. Then we can all go through the Mist together."

Their time for questions ran out. Another blow from the outside shattered the door to the right.

The children cried out in fear as twenty Creeps streamed into the room. The possessed men and women wore an assortment of military fatigues and ragged civilian clothes, and all sported the typical tan complexions and brown hair of the region. They leered at the kids with jet-black eyes, eagerly clicking ragged fingernails and licking their yellow fangs. Two figures bounded through behind them. A hulking, slavering bear demon with horned ridges down its back landed to the left, shattering the stone with claws like plows. Mottled black and brown fur bristled out from its rotting, leathery hide. To the right, a lithe jaguar demon eagerly bounced back and forth. Steaming saliva oozed from its mouth, melting the stone wherever it fell. Its once spotted, golden coat now glowed an unhealthy iridescent green, and fangs stuck out in every direction except straight. The Creeps and the demons parted on either side of the door.

"Imagine running into you people here," a familiar voice said from the darkness of the stairwell. The accent was unmistakably northern European. Tyr stepped out of the shadows and kicked one of the shattered doors out of his way. It flew across the room and slammed into the wall, spraying the air with shards of stone. His blond hair, brushed neatly to the side, had grown several inches longer than his previous military cut. He wore a sleeveless, blood-red tunic with matching pants. His muscles bulged as he hoisted the Hammer of War off his shoulder and whacked the other fallen door out of his way, sending it spinning through the air and straight into the opposite wall. He scanned the room and frowned. "Huh. I sense all five of you, but I can't see you." His eyes raked over Daniel and Gabriela but couldn't seem to focus on them. "Must be the two lovebirds, standing so close. But where are the others? What magic is this?"

"It is as we said," the jaguar demon complained. "The girl from Aguas Calientes can hide from us in plain sight. That is why we cannot stop her."

"No excuses," Tyr snapped, still scanning the ruins with a hint of humor in his eyes. "Can't you feel their weapons? They make it easy to locate the children even if you can't see them. Even the local girl emits the Three's power."

The Creeps sniffed the air, confused.

The demons glowered around the room, weaving their heads from side to side as though struggling to catch a glimpse of the companions out of the corners of their eyes.

"It is not as easy for us," the bear demon grumbled.

Daniel glanced at everyone and shrugged.

Seren reached up and touched Janice's poncho.

"I sense the Celestial Bow right there," Tyr said to the demons,

pointing in Seren's general location. "Be careful of binding arrows from that direction. And let's see, the Sun Sword and Abyssal staff are over there." He vaguely gestured toward Daniel and Raylin. "And your problem girl is in the mix with them. No need to worry about the shield boy." He turned around and went to lean against the broken door frame. "I got you in, now do your part."

"And how do you expect us to do that?" the bear growled. "What if they hide and purify or bind us as we run right by them?"

"Why fear purification? Master granted you extra power to repossess your bodies. At least a few times, anyway. As far as their hiding goes, that's easy," Tyr smirked. "Target the children. The Vessels won't have a choice but to intervene. Just don't make me clean up your mess. I have a date with Amira after this, and she doesn't like it when I get dirty."

Daniel's heart sank. Facing off with some Creeps and demons didn't bother him that much. But Tyr was a different story. As a human vessel of the Enemy's spirit, he had at least triple the power of most demons. Worse, he couldn't be purified because of his link with the Enemy.

Father, please help us. He glanced back at the group of cowering children and teens. Only Cristiano wasn't crying, but he still had a look of horror as the demons leered at the group with hungry eyes. *This could get bad quick. Give us the strength we need.*

Focus on those who can be saved. The Father's calming presence seeped into Daniel's mind. Once, he was confused about the Three's roles in prayer; he now knew the Father spoke to them with the Son's voice and that it was the Spirit's power that settled upon him to bring peace and empowerment. With all three attending to their fight, Daniel felt any sense of uncertainty dissipate. *Purify the men and women under the Enemy's control and leave this place.*

Daniel scanned the other Vessels and saw them similarly relax with certainty and calm. "We all know what to do?" he called over his shoulder.

Tyr gestured curtly with his hand, and the jaguar demon and

Creeps advanced straight toward the children. The bear demon hung back, however, still warily scanning the room.

"On it," Ben replied, dashing into the middle of the children to summon the Triune Shield. His radiant blue borders expanded just as the jaguar demon reached them, freezing its rending claws a foot away from the nearest child and rebounding the demon onto its back.

The children screamed and cowered close to the center, where Cristiano huddled the younger ones together.

Seren followed up by releasing a volley of Celestial Arrows toward the demon. Seeing their approach, it rolled to its feet and bounced out of the way as the arrows spread their binding blue light over the flagstones where it had lain.

"It is only a matter of time, little children!" the jaguar demon purred. "Come out of that silly shield. I'm hungry!" It jumped around the room, avoiding Seren's arrows until it was on the opposite side of the shield from her. It slashed wildly at Ben's borders.

Seeing that the children were no longer easy targets, the bear demon finally decided to join the fight and bore down on Gabriela. "Even if I cannot see you, I can still smell you, you little worm. You took my slaves. Where are they? Give them back! Worthless scum! Worthless! Worthless! Worthless!"

Gabriela grunted. "Not too bright, are you? Here, Daniel. This one's for you. Catch!" She kicked the demon under its jaw as it lunged toward her. Its head flew back against its back with a bone-snapping crunch as its body hurtled toward Daniel.

In one fluid motion, Seren let three arrows fly at the bear. The blue casing quickly spread over it mid-air. Once it covered its body, a circlet of fire appeared around its head.

At the same moment, five Creeps stalked Daniel's general area, unsure of his exact location, while the other fifteen cautiously surrounded Raylin.

Daniel flung a Sunstorm at the demon, blasting it higher into the air and purifying it at the same time. Its angry spirit exploded out of the desiccated corpse of a small, black bear. However, the

attack instantly gave away his location to the Creeps, who promptly charged him. With the Sun Sword raised, Daniel focused its power as quickly as possible and stabbed the ground, sending the purifying wave of the Fire Strike through the Creeps before they could change directions. The controlling spirits exorcised from the Creeps snaked into the air and then divided. Half streamed into the raging spirit of the bear demon, which stormed around the giant mirror at the top of the ceiling. The other portion flew toward the jaguar demon, which promptly inhaled the spirits with a snarl.

Its rage exponentially grew, and it doubled down on its attempt to get to the children.

"Ben! Are you holding up?" Daniel shouted.

The Triune Shield's radiant blue momentarily glowed brighter. "I'm good. He's actually not that strong," Ben replied. "Kind of pathetic, really."

Seren dashed around the shield to get a clear shot.

Gabriela followed close on her heels, leaping over her to follow up with a heavy blow.

The jaguar demon shrieked in anger and flipped over the arrows as it spun in the air toward Raylin. She barely had enough time to switch her attention from the Creeps attacking her to catch the blow of its jagged claws with the center of the Abyssal Staff. The force knocked her back against the pedestal platform, but before the demon or the Creeps could pin her down, she nimbly spun around and leaped up the steps. "I think you're just stronger now, Ben. These guys are no joke. A little help here, please!"

The Triune Shield blushed a slightly rosy color, then returned to its normal blue.

Daniel shook his head and joined Seren and Gabriela in their dash toward Raylin.

Sensing Daniel and Seren's approach, the jaguar demon left Raylin and rushed them. It flung its mouth wide open and spat a huge blob of saliva in their direction.

Daniel and Seren dove to the side while Gabriela nimbly jumped

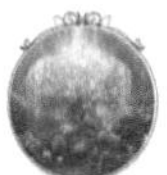

over it. Her trajectory carried her over the sizzling crater in the stone straight toward the demon, which she flattened with an earth-shattering punch.

The spotted bag of bones skittered around the floor before reforming into a very disorganized jaguar corpse. The neck, now collapsed, nearly absorbed the entire head. One front leg stuck out from the top of the back, while the other had somehow changed places with the tail. The remaining legs dangled uselessly below as the demon skittered away from Gabriela with a shriek.

"Need some help?" Tyr yawned from the doorway, lazily swinging the Hammer of War from one hand to the other.

The bear demon's spirit flew like black lightning toward him. "No! Please! Let us have revenge on the girl."

Tyr shrugged. "Fine. You get five minutes."

Daniel overheard this exchange, and his heart sank. Five minutes to wrap things up and escape with all the Creeps before Tyr got serious.

"Bear, you fat idiot!" the jaguar demon screamed. "Quit floating around whining. Join your strength with mine."

The spirit growled at the insults but winged through the air toward the jaguar, scooping up its own carcass as it passed it on the floor.

At the same moment, the remaining fifteen Creeps charged Raylin and Seren. Seren bound three, and Raylin swept the legs out from under two more before six dove over their defenses and knocked them to the ground.

"Raylin!" Daniel shouted, running past her to join Gabriela in rushing the demons. "Seal him before they combine!"

"You may have noticed I'm busy at the moment!" she yelled back. "A little help, please!"

"They're just Creeps!" Daniel replied, alternately flinging Sunstorms at the bear and jaguar demons. Both wove around the blasts and collided in an explosive storm of vile spirits and carcasses. "Can't you handle it yourself?"

The Creeps had now pinned down Raylin and Seren's arms and weapons.

"Newsflash!" Raylin shouted. "It's hard to fight the Creeps when we don't really want to hurt anyone. Not to mention, there's a lot of them!"

The demons flew around to the opposite side of the Triune Shield so that it was between them and Daniel while they continued their unholy amalgamation.

Gabriela leaped straight over the shield. "I'll handle them. Help the girls!"

"Fine!" Daniel spun around and dashed toward the Creeps. Out of the corner of his eye, he noticed Tyr watching the fight with a haughty sneer and had to resist the urge to fling a Sunstorm at his face just for kicks. He slid up to the Creeps. Two released the girls and charged him.

"It's about time!" Seren snapped, kicking at the Creeps holding her arms now that one of her legs was free.

"I was busy, too," Daniel replied. He stabbed the ground and sent the purifying power of the Fire Strike through all the Creeps before they had a chance to escape its reach.

The spirits controlling them screamed through the air toward the two demons while the men and women collapsed to the ground, unconscious.

Raylin jumped to her feet and activated the Abyssal Staff. Its circular head unlocked, and the pieces began orbiting triangles of light circulating in the opposite direction. A point of swirling darkness appeared in their center, and the fleeing spirits froze directly above the Triune Shield before they could rejoin their demons. With a slurping shriek, the dark mass was drawn through the eye of the staff. Once finished, Raylin spun around and cocked her head at Daniel. "You ran straight past us to get at the demons." She poked him in the chest. "A quick Fire Strike would've been simple."

Daniel threw his hands up. "Raylin, we were in the middle of a battle. It's not always easy to make every right move. Besides, you did the same thing to Ben when we were first here for the Sun Sword, remember? It's not a big deal."

She leveled a challenging stare directly at Daniel. "Yeah, I do remember. I did that when I was the Enemy's slave *before* the Three saved me."

"Look, can we talk about this later?"

A loud thud shook the room. Daniel and the others looked up to see Gabriela, fist still extended from her Herculean punch, and the demon plastered against the cavern wall. The jaguar and bear had combined into a horrendous chimera with eight legs, each armed with razor-sharp claws, bones projecting from its back like porcupine quills, and two fang-filled heads joined on one body. It slid to the floor with a growl and readied itself to pounce.

"Sure, Daniel. Later."

Behind them, all the exorcised Creeps disappeared in a flash.

Tyr pushed himself up from the wall. "Time's up. Now it's my turn."

The demon hissed. "Fine. But the children are mine. And the girl from Aguas Calientes." It waved a jagged claw in Gabriela's general direction. "She took all my slaves, and I want her to pay!"

Tyr shrugged. "That can be arranged."

Gabriela quietly shifted behind Daniel. "We need to retreat," she whispered. "Fighting Tyr would be pointless and dangerous, and all the Creeps have been rescued. Let's go."

"The Mist?" Daniel asked.

Gabriela gave a curt nod and dashed toward the cowering children, still safely enveloped within the Triune Shield.

Seren drew back on the Celestial Bow as Gabriela passed by. "How much time do you need to get the kids out of here?"

"Seconds. Just stall them and follow. Quickly now!" She raised her hands and drew them apart. The air at the base of the Triune Shield grew gray as the curtains of the Mist opened beneath it.

"We're going down?" Ben asked in surprise. "I feel like an elevator."

"Oh, I don't think so!" Tyr laughed, still leaning against the doorway. He pushed himself up and jumped into the air, the Hammer of War raised high overhead, and smashed the Transportation Pedestal

and platform. A fissure opened at his feet and extended toward the Vessels.

The flagstones beneath Daniel and Seren crumbled, and both tumbled into the crack. Raylin deftly jumped backward quickly enough to evade the attack.

Daniel slid to a stop between two upended slabs as Tyr leaped over him toward the Triune Shield. He instinctively flung a Sunstorm, catching Tyr in the leg, and then grabbed the lip of the stone and yanked himself out of the fissure.

Tyr spun in an uncontrolled descent to the ground, crashing at Gabriela's feet even as the Enemy's spirit billowed out around him. She jumped back toward the Mist while the chimera demon, hot on Tyr's tracks, charged the foggy portal in one last attempt to get the children. She cocked a fist back, ready to give the demon the uppercut of its life, when Seren, already freed from the mess of shrapnel and broken stone, sent a volley of Celestial Arrows into its hide.

It froze in its tracks directly over Gabriela, rending claws extended but bound in midair.

Daniel raced under the demon, the Sun Sword raised above his head to exorcize it even as he grabbed Gabriela and pulled her away.

Its spirit, untethered from both carcasses, joined Tyr's spirit to rage in a maelstrom.

Seren and Raylin dashed to Daniel and Gabriela's side as they ran toward the Mist. Ben and the children were now completely inside and gone.

Raylin spun around even as Seren and Gabriela jumped down into the fog and activated the Abyssal Staff. The chimera demon's spirit whirled through the eye of the staff with a howling curse. Tyr's spirit, however, remained connected to his body.

He leisurely pushed himself up off the ground and flexed all his muscles. The Enemy's spirit crashed back inside him, and he relaxed. "The Three's feeble power is useless," he sighed. "Even if I wanted to be free, it wouldn't do any good."

A curious look came over Raylin's face, and she lowered her staff.

"If you wanted to be free, they would save you. I should know."

Tyr scoffed in response, then flung the Hammer of War at Daniel and Raylin.

At that moment, Gabriela's hands reappeared from the Mist, grabbed their ankles, and yanked them down, shutting the portal and drawing them into the world of cloud and starlight.

5

A Creepy Family Reunion

Daniel felt his body relax as he gently floated out of a cloud and dropped to the ground within the peaceful, twilight world of the Mist. Trees towered overhead but grew far enough apart to allow gentle starlight through their tangled bower. Curtains of fog clung to shimmering branches and sometimes floated on the breeze to temporarily obscure the more distant scenes of forest and meadow. Thick grass carpeted the ground, itself wet and glinting with the clinging dew drops. Far away, snatches of singing echoed through the forest. It was a different song than Daniel remembered: less lilting and peaceful and more like a battle hymn.

The others stood quietly by, flanked by the refugees from Machu Picchu. The children beheld the Mist in silent awe, wide-eyed and open-mouthed at the beautiful landscape.

Ben, back in his human form, nudged Gabriela and pointed to his ear. "I hear singing again. Are the Children of Llyr and the Sons of Don going to swing by?"

Gabriela shook her head. "No, they're on the front lines in Babylon. But their songs still fill the Mist. We'll see them soon, but first, we have our own battle to fight."

"That wasn't it?" Seren asked, nodding upward.

Gabriela shook her head. "That was to save the last of the Creeps from Aguas Calientes. The real battle is already happening right now. Inti fights the Prince of Peru in the spiritual realm, and I'm supposed to bring you all to him once we're done here."

"What are we supposed to do here?" Raylin asked.

"I'm about to show you," Gabriela replied, moving closer to where the children still huddled around the older teens.

Cristiano stepped forward. "Where are we?"

"A safe place in the Mist," Gabriela replied. She clapped until all the children looked directly at her. "Listen, I want everyone to walk between me and the Vessels. If you wander off, you might get lost. Understood?"

The refugees glanced back and forth, clearly confused. From the oldest to the youngest, fear reflected in their eyes.

"We understand," Cristiano replied. "Right, everyone? We're going to do exactly as Ms. Gabriela says."

The younger kids answered in chorus like a class to their teacher.

"Good," Gabriela said. "Now, everyone hold hands and follow me." She strode through the trees, expertly leading the group through the pathless landscape.

There didn't seem to be any actual trail or markers Daniel could discern, just varying kinds of ancient trees swaying their soaring branches in the breeze. The ambient light of the Mist reflected off every surface, creating a kaleidoscope of dancing shadows in the ghostly drizzle. After a short time, however, a flickering yellow-orange light warmed the gloam of the woods.

Gabriela held up her hand for the procession to halt, and she spun around. "This is where I've been bringing the Creeps I captured over the past months. Kids," she turned around, "your parents are here, but they're still possessed." She gestured for Daniel and Raylin to join her at the front of the line. "They need to be purified before you can go to them. Until then, you *must* stay back and guard your hearts against anything they say. Understand?"

The older children nodded, but the younger kids simply stared at Gabriela, clearly too overwhelmed to process her commands.

"I'll be sure to keep them back," Cristiano said, holding the hands of the youngest children among them. He tried to look calm, but his chest heaved with quick, almost panicked breaths.

Seren ambled up next to him. "I'll help you tend to them." She placed a calming hand on a little boy who shivered with fear. "Don't worry," she added, placing the other on Cristiano's shoulder. "Daniel and Raylin know what they're doing. Your parents will be fine."

"Do you need me?" Ben asked as Gabriela waved everyone forward. He jogged to the front of the line.

Gabriela pulled aside a branch and pointed. "No. The Creeps are detained. Granny made sure of that."

In a wide clearing, Granny's fiery barrier burned in a circle big enough to comfortably contain at least a hundred Creeps. They slavered and growled at the approaching group, flexing their claws and baring sharp fangs. Some ran back and forth like angry, caged animals, crushing leftover fruit and old bread that Gabriela had no doubt supplied during their incarceration.

"Hello, little children! Come closer," a female Creep tempted. "Let us see your lovely faces."

A male Creep sauntered up to the barrier. He wore a torn parka, and mud matted his dark, disheveled hair. "Once we break out, we'll take you to our master," he hissed. "He'll have such fun with you! He's a powerful bear demon, you know, and he's always hungry."

One of the little girls nearest to the front gasped. "Papa?" she whimpered, breaking away from the group.

As she passed Ben, he reached out and pulled her back. "No further. Just wait, and he'll be your dad again." He turned to the Creep. "Dude, your master just got purified and sealed into the eyeball of that freak seven-headed Serpent. Sorry, not sorry."

The possessed man took a step back, vibrating with rage.

Tears rolled down the girl's cheeks even as other children found their parents in the group and called for them. The Creeps jeered and grimaced, no recognition of their own children showing in their faces.

"This is why I couldn't let them in the Mist," Gabriela explained, taking Daniel's hand into her own.

Daniel felt goosebumps go up his arm. He leaned closer.

"It wasn't safe to have them in the same place as the Creeps. Not to mention, it was too risky that they would wander off. And Inti had placed a barrier around Machu Picchu anyway. It kept the demons at bay until Tyr showed up. But the Three's timing is always perfect, right?"

"There you are, Gabriela." Two Creeps, a man and a woman, broke away from the group and edged right up to the barrier. It was the woman who spoke. Her long, chestnut hair fell in stringy cords around a face twisted in cruelty. Her eyes seemed familiar. "Have you come to visit with us again? We do so look forward to our time together. Did you miss your own dear parents? Let me reassure you of our affection. We'll figure a way out of this prison, and when we do," she stifled a wicked chuckle behind dirty claws, "you'll be executed by your own loving father."

The man—only slightly shorter than Daniel, balding, with brown hair and a broad face—clapped his hands eagerly. "Master promised me I'd be the one to do it. Won't that be special? Father and daughter."

Daniel now understood the horror and abuse the children would've faced if Gabriela had allowed them into the Mist without her. It would've been torture.

"How often have you come to talk with them?" he whispered to Gabriela.

"Every day," she hoarsely replied.

"I'll take care of it." Daniel raised the Sun Sword. "Raylin, you ready?"

Raylin gripped the Abyssal Staff in both hands, the dark green swirls eddying faster as though eager to get to work. "Ready."

Daniel approached the barrier and raised the sword, channeling all his energy into the blade. The Creeps stepped back, snarling at the blazing weapon with rabid fear. The barrier, somehow responding to the power of the Sun Sword, began to shrink, pulling all the Creeps closer to the purifying power. Daniel stabbed the ground at the base of Granny's seal and noted with satisfaction as the shockwaves of the Fire Strike purified them all at once.

A tornado of demonic spirit whirled into a raging storm above Daniel and Raylin. "Disgusting, mortal Vessels!" it screamed in the double voices of the jaguar and bear demons. "Once Master takes over, all flesh will be destroyed, and only we spirits will remain!" The demons paused in silence, and Daniel imagined they were looking around for something. "Where is the rest of my spirit? I cannot sense it."

"Have you met Raylin?" Daniel asked, gesturing behind him.

"Hi," she said, tossing a casual wave in their direction. "If it's the rest of your spirit you want, I'll send you to it." She activated the staff.

The demons shrieked as the eye sucked their essence through its tiny portal. Moments later, the peace of the Mist returned like a gentle rain.

Daniel ran to Gabriela and grabbed her arm. "Quickly. Go see your mom and dad before they disappear!"

She patted his hand and calmly walked toward the man and woman who had only moments before relished the prospect of her torment and death. "It's okay. They won't disappear."

Daniel followed closely behind and was soon surrounded by the children swarming to find their parents.

Gabriela's parents were all eyes and mouths as they gawked at their surroundings.

"Where are we?" her mother asked. Recognition lit up her face when Gabriela stepped into view. "Gabriela. Is that you? My little darling! You're so big. How are you so tall?" She stroked the side of her head, and a shadow of fear clouded her face. "I remember … I remember being taken."

"The demons," her father whispered. "How long has it been?"

Gabriela knelt between them and pulled them into a hug. "Many years, now. But now you are free."

All three broke into tears and simply held one another. All around them, shouts of recognition and joy broke the quiet tranquility of the Mist. Out of the corner of his eye, Daniel saw Cristiano run toward a woman kneeling in the grass, her face buried in her hands as she sobbed.

Seren and Ben joined Raylin as Daniel himself stepped back to be abreast with them.

Ben raised his hand. "Question: why aren't the Creeps—former Creeps—disappearing?"

Seren shrugged. "No idea. I expected them to vanish same as you."

"Likewise," Daniel replied. "I'm sure Gabriela knows," he whispered. "But I don't want to bother her at the moment."

Raylin leaned on the Abyssal Staff and gestured casually to the left. "Maybe that lady knows."

A tall, glowing figure, draped in azure robes that mirrored a clear scene of the night sky, stepped out from behind an ancient pine. A crown of stars languidly orbited her head, and her eyes sparkled like moonlight on a rippling sea. She had to bend her head to pass below the branches, which were nearly fifteen feet above the ground. A long, bronze dagger hung naked at her hip, its blade sticking through a delicate chain of silver. Black, wavy hair, intermingled with galactic lights, cascaded down her back to sweep the ground behind her. With each step, stars shook loose to float happily into the air around her. She raised her hand in greeting.

"I *do* know, in fact," she said, her voice airy. "Earthborn formerly enslaved to the Enemy and his legion of spirits walk in vision while the Spirit instructs them. Now, they will gather here."

"Oh, is that right?" Daniel nodded. "Was that supposed to clear things up?" he whispered to Ben out of the side of his mouth.

"I'm sure Gabriela will rescue us with a more human explanation," Ben said smugly, folding his arms. "See, right on cue."

At the sound of the woman's voice, Gabriela had taken her parents by the hand and led them over. "Coyllur!" she exclaimed, her face beaming.

Coyllur bent down and pulled Gabriela into a hug. "Greetings, sister. I am overjoyed that your parents are released."

"Thank you! And the others?"

"I have them here." Coyllur stood and spread her left arm so that the gauzy robe hung like a curtain. With her right hand, she drew

her dagger and cut a long, luminous slit from top to bottom. The movement sent a fresh nebula of starry clusters drifting into the air. "Come out, children."

"Okay. Guess I was wrong," Ben muttered. "Man, how could Gabriela let us down like this?"

Daniel elbowed him in the ribs and shushed him.

Moments later, men and women walked out of the brilliant opening and into the twilight of the Mist. Many wore the telltale garb of the Indian Creeps: baggy pants and loose-fitting shirts or red and gold dresses. Others sported the dowdy robes of the druid Creeps purified in the British Isles. A few wore army fatigues or regular civilian clothes. They intermingled with the former Creeps from Aguas Calientes and Cuzco until a group, about a couple hundred strong, stood milling quietly.

Daniel recognized familiar faces. In fact, the more he studied them, he was pretty sure he'd seen most, if not all, of them before. The last group to step through bore shocking resemblances to his substitute teachers over the past several months.

Ben tapped him on the back. "Hey! It's Ms. Garbles and Mr. Horibal! Ah, I've been wondering how they were."

He waved happily as they shuffled out from under Coyllur's shadow. "Hey guys! Nice to see you again!"

They cast uncertain smiles back. Mr. Horibal gave a half-hearted wave in reply but kept glancing over his shoulder as if uncertain Ben was talking to him or someone behind him.

The cut in Coyllur's robe sealed itself back up after the last of the former Creeps walked through.

"These are all the Creeps I've purified," Daniel said, walking closer to Gabriela and her parents. "Ever since our first quest."

"Yes," Gabriela replied. "They've spent their time asleep on the Father's Mountain learning through visions about the way of salvation, and now they'll gather here."

Ben folded his arms and winked at Daniel. "Ah, see? She always comes through for us. Crazy, overly spiritual explanation? Gabriela's your woman."

Seren cast Ben a sideways glance as she turned to Gabriela. "Why are they coming here?"

"And who's Coyllur?" Raylin added quietly. "I mean, obviously a Firstborn, but is she going to help us with the quest?"

Gabriela cleared her throat and passed the question to Coyllur. "Will you be helping us in Babylon?" She nodded toward the murmuring crowd of former Creeps. "And what's next for them?"

"Before this quest is over, and the Spirit of the Age sealed," Coyllur lowered her arm and glided around the group, "a great revival will break out—the New Awakening." She beamed affectionately at the purified men and women like a mother to her children. "These, having been taught by the Spirit, will spearhead that movement. Each will return to their homes to tell of the Father's love and the Three's redemption." She completed her rotation around the silent crowd and returned to the Vessels. "It was my job to attend to their needs during their teaching, and I will do so until that time."

Raylin released the Abyssal Staff and hooked her arm into Seren's. "I guess that means you won't be helping us fight."

Coyllur shook her head.

"In the last quest," Seren said a little apologetically, "most of the Firstborn were busy fighting and didn't have time to help us. It was ugly until the Spirit showed up."

Coyllur's luminous gaze swept over Seren to settle on Raylin. "Do you fear failure on your first quest as a child of the Father?"

Raylin blushed, and her eyes found the ground.

"Be comforted, sister. You will have the help you need. Even I do not know what is in store for you. The future is only known to the Three. But certainly now, after all, you do not fear death." Coyllur knelt before Raylin and lifted her chin so their eyes met. Three white stars drifted toward Raylin and illuminated her face.

Raylin's breath caught in her throat at the gesture as if suddenly exposed and vulnerable. She held Coyllur's gaze and swallowed hard. "Not afraid of death, just of being separated from those I love."

Coyllur's eyes flitted to Seren, Gabriela, Ben, and finally Daniel. "I see," she said quietly, her voice filled with compassion. "You have

many connections. Many you love. Yes, separation by death is a sorrow, indeed. The Champion overcame death, though, so that you and those you love might have a way into eternal relationship with the Three and each other."

She stood, releasing Raylin and drifting into the crowd of former Creeps, touching faces and patting heads. "Come, lie down and rest. Tomorrow, there will be much to learn." She gestured to the Vessels. "You, too. Rest now. You are called to Inti's side in the morning. With him, you will face Kon and hopefully restore the Peruvian Seal."

Daniel's eyes immediately flew to Gabriela. Her face shone pale even in the twilight of the Mist. "Is this something we should worry about?"

Gabriela shuffled her rumpled poncho around and tucked stray hair back under the beanie. "Probably not. With Inti at our side, I'm sure we've nothing to worry about. It's more about what's on the line."

Seren gently pulled away from Raylin and joined in. "That sounds important. What do you mean 'on the line'?"

"If Kon is sealed, then revival can start in Peru." Gabriela put her hands over her heart. "My parents can finally return home. *I* can finally go home. All my people could live normal lives again. But if he's not sealed, Peru will continue playing host to demons. Even if we help Inti defeat him, but he's not sealed, he can keep enslaving humans and prevent the revival Coyllur mentioned."

Ben sagely nodded. "I see. So, he's that powerful of a demon? I mean, we've battled the Enemy face-to-face. Could he be worse?"

"Let me guess," Raylin said. "He's a Prince?"

"The Prince of Peru," Gabriela replied. When Ben looked confused, she added, "The strongest Firstborn govern each country. He may not be as bad at the Enemy himself, but he's extremely powerful. He was the main instrument the Enemy used to take over Peru in the first place."

"I see," Daniel joined in, reaching a nervous hand over to take Gabriela's. Thankfully, she didn't pull away. "So, if he was the conduit for Peru's fall, his sealing will open the path for Peru's revival."

Gabriela squeezed Daniel's hand harder. "Exactly. With Inti's help and the Three's power, I'm sure we can manage it. Then, it'll be straight to Babylon after that."

Ben groaned and plopped both hands on top of his head. "Please tell me we won't be facing the Enemy immediately. I don't think I could handle two major battles in a day."

"Definitely not!" Coyllur laughed, suddenly behind Ben.

Ben jumped forward, tripped, and stumbled to his knees. He craned his neck around. "Where did you—? Are you trying to shock me to death?"

Coyllur cast a look of motherly compassion down at Ben. "My apologies. No, you will not head into battle with the Serpent right away. There is a task you must accomplish in Babylon first. One that will purify you all and make you ready for the battle."

Raylin extended her hand to Ben.

He hastily grabbed it, and she hoisted him to his feet. "Thanks," he said, breathless, looking expectantly at Raylin as if hoping she had something more to do or say.

Raylin narrowed her brow in confusion and glanced around before opting to pat Ben on the shoulder. She then eased closer to Coyllur. "Any more details about this task?"

Ben awkwardly reached out as if to pat her back, decided against it, and fell to brushing away the dirt from his knees. "We'll probably just get some mysterious gobbledygook for an explanation," he muttered.

"Inti will give you directions tomorrow," Coyllur said. "Clear instructions," she added, winking at Ben. "For now, rest." With that, she glided back to comfort the former Creeps, still milling about in confusion or catching up with their children.

Daniel turned to face the other Vessels. "I guess we'll have to be content with that. Hopefully, this purification thing isn't that big of a deal."

"Yeah, right," Ben snorted. "Because that's how things *always* go on quests. Smoothly."

"Way to be optimistic," Raylin said flatly.

Gabriela slid her hands upwards to Daniel's arm, and all his attention was immediately on her.

"I want to introduce you to my parents," she whispered. "Come on."

Daniel followed like a puppy, all thoughts of the quest now a million miles away.

6

The Prince of Peru

Instead of the calm, soothing music of the Mist, a mariachi band played in a clearing. Gabriela led Daniel by the hand toward her parents. Raylin, Seren, and Ben milled about, each engaged in various activities. The trumpeter gave Daniel an enthusiastic thumbs up.

"My name's Daniel, and I'm Gabriela's boyfriend!" Daniel bawled. "I chase after demons and fight monsters and stuff, and I'm going to marry your—AHH!" He tripped over his foot and face-planted into a pile of Coyllur's stars, which all somehow had her eyes.

They turned disapproving glares onto Daniel before indignantly floating to Raylin, who leaned against a nearby tree. She pulled them into a hug. "I know, I know," she soothed. "He's a jerk. Ben, do you want to talk about feelings?" She skipped over to Ben, who was in the form of a small Triune Shield on the opposite side of the clearing.

"No thanks," Ben replied. "Seren and I are playing checkers. We simply haven't the time."

Seren nodded condescendingly, barely looking up from the gameboard.

"Fiddlesticks," Raylin pouted. "Oh well, at least I have my little buddies to talk to." She squeezed the beaming stars in a vigorous hug. "Come on! Let's go snuggle."

"Yay!" the stars all squealed.

Tyr danced out of the woods in ballet shoes and waved amid various leaps and pirouettes. "Hey guys, whatcha doing?"

"It's our best friend, Tyr," Seren, Ben, and Raylin sang in unison. "Come play with us!"

"He's so handsome," Gabriela swooned.

"Now that's the kind of boyfriend you should have," her mother muttered.

Her father vigorously nodded. "And just look at those dance moves."

Daniel jumped to his feet, screaming and tearing at his hair. "What sort of nightmare is this?" Lucidity finally set in, and he dropped his hands. He was dreaming. The content itself didn't come as a surprise, though. The scenes continued to unfold before him, but he was aware enough to see them for the crazy caricature of his actual interaction with Gabriela's parents. He recalled their conversation had *not* gone smoothly.

Her father, Sandro, was less than thrilled with the idea of his little girl suddenly grown-up and in a relationship with a foreigner he had never met. He had given Daniel a long, cold, appraising look before introducing himself. Saying little else by way of conversation, he mostly ignored Daniel and focused on catching up with Gabriela.

Alessa, her mother, didn't even give Daniel a greeting. When Gabriela announced him as her boyfriend, the joy of reuniting with her daughter quickly faded, and she wouldn't meet Daniel's eyes. She gave a disturbed look to her husband before directing a barrage of questions to Gabriela.

Gabriela had noticed their cold interaction, of course, but brushed it off. "They've just been freed from the Enemy and discovered they lost years of my life. Give them some time." She then gave Daniel's arm a squeeze and walked off with her parents to sit at the base of a glistening beech tree.

Daniel shook off the memory and looked around. The bizarre images of his nightmare faded away, and he found himself floating high above Peru. To his right, a maelstrom of storm and fire raged

over the mountains. The earth rotated beneath him, abruptly bringing him to the edge of the tempest. In the sky high above the mountains, Inti battled a demon wreathed in storms.

Inti was colossal, dwarfing even the peaks below him. Instead of the light and airy robe he often wore, bronze armor, intricately fashioned of woven cords, fit tight around his body. It burned red hot, presumably from the white flames dancing around him, obeying the movements of his hands. On his head, he wore a golden helmet with a half-disc of metallic sunrays arched over the crown from ear to ear.

A circle surrounded by heavenly script appeared over the demon, spinning as it rained down columns of fire and light.

Other than a gargantuan, humanoid body, Daniel couldn't see the demon's features amid the hurricane of clouds churning about him. He flung a network of raging lightning at the sudden onslaught of holy power, pushing it back up and eventually breaking the circle.

Inti snapped his head toward Daniel. "It is time, Daniel!" he shouted, his voice strained with exhaustion. "When you wake, tell Coyllur to send you all at once. My battle with Kon must end so I can join the war in Babylon. Hurry!"

Daniel flew downward toward the earth, but an invisible force gripped his body and froze him in place. The clouds around Kon's body parted, revealing a muscular chest, bare but for a heavy medallion of black metal hanging from a green-beaded string. A grinning feline mask, decorated with strange symbols and indecipherable letters, hid his face. In his hand, he carried a staff, and skulls rattled around his waist. He wore a stark white kilt, which contrasted with his dark gray skin.

Kon pointed his staff at Daniel. "Stay a moment, young Vessel," he commanded, and Daniel felt himself pulled toward him. "I have a gift for you." He grabbed the medallion from around his neck and threw it like a frisbee toward Daniel.

Inti flung fire at the disc, but Kon's clouds expanded to form an intercepting barrier, ricocheting the flames. "Do not listen to him," Inti ordered, unscathed by the white-hot inferno rebounded toward him. "Guard your mind! Do not put it on!"

The warning came too late. Inti's voice faded into the distance, and the scene dimmed as the necklace slipped over Daniel's head and around his neck, shrinking as it did to fit his body. The force holding Daniel in place relinquished its hold, and he felt his momentum resume as he hurtled toward the fading earth below.

Daniel sat bolt upright. Sheets of fog drifted silently on the breezes of the late twilit world of the Mist. Ben, Raylin, and Seren slept beneath trees to his right. Gabriela, embraced even in slumber by her parents, lay to his left. The other men and women rested in the clearing where Granny's barrier once held them prisoner. Coyllur was nowhere to be seen.

The medallion.

Daniel was suddenly aware of its weight around his neck. He cautiously reached up to touch it, remembering Inti's desperate warning, and gingerly lifted the disc to slip it off. The moment it reached eye level, something stirred in its depths. At first, it was nothing more than a blurred movement of colors, as if he were watching TV through muddy water. The images soon cleared, however, and Daniel realized he had a panoramic view of a large chamber backlit by an eerily familiar light. He was staring into the Abyss. The myriad of alcoves, some empty and some still housing the hideous avatars of the Enemy, spanned from the floor to the ceiling, covering every space in the immense walls. And on the floor, the seven-headed Serpent—red, titanic, horned, writhing, and seething with rage. The point of view tracked along the Serpent's body, giving Daniel an unnecessary survey of his titanic coils. It paused on the two unbound heads. The Serpent's eyes glared through the picture straight at Daniel.

A cold, uneasy feeling crept up Daniel's back. If the Enemy could see into the Mist, did that mean he could send demons to find them? Or worse, his Leaders and Generals? Daniel closed his eyes and tried to tear the medallion off his neck. It wouldn't budge, and he felt an invisible force binding the beads to his body. The image shifted to the Serpent's coils, which parted to reveal the Leaders and Generals standing amid a five-pointed, glowing star. Daniel recalled them using it to transport to and from the Abyss during the last quest.

"Our plan progresses perfectly," Amira reported, kneeling before her master.

Abida followed suit. "No matter the power given to the Vessels, they can't withstand this. Their greatest weakness belongs to us now."

"Make sure they suffer," the Serpent commanded. "I want the Vessels broken and shattered when I attempt to remove the Three's Image. Even if it cannot be broken, I want them to feel cast away, destitute, abandoned, alone."

The scene swung away, and the Enemy's following words were faint and muffled. Daniel jumped to his feet, his eyes glued to the scene. He strained to hear more details to clue him in on the Enemy's plans. If he could hear just a little more, they might be able to prepare.

Something rustled in the grass behind him. It barely registered until Raylin dashed into view and swung the Abyssal Staff hard against the medallion. The force of the blow yanked Daniel forward onto his face, but not before he saw the medallion rocket through the air. Coyllur appeared in a haze of starlight on the opposite side of the clearing and caught it. She squeezed the medallion. It creaked and whined as it lost its shape.

"Where did you get this?" Coyllur asked, letting the balled-up metal hang limp from its chain.

It vibrated angrily.

Dumbfounded, Daniel pushed himself up, rubbed his nose, and stared around.

Raylin gazed down at him with furrowed brows, then extended a hand to help him up.

He batted her hand away and jumped to his feet. "Why did you interfere? I could see into the Abyss," he shouted, a sudden wave of anger fueled by fear surging through his body. "The Enemy was talking about some secret plan to weaken us. If I could've heard more—"

"Daniel, calm down." She stepped toward him and grabbed his arm. "Stop screaming, or you'll wake everyone up."

"I don't care!"

"Okay! Okay. Fine. Just calm down. What did you see?"

"The Serpent. He's meeting with the Leaders and Generals. They have some plan to defeat us. But you smacked the medallion off me, and now we've lost our chance to get a leg up on them!"

Raylin raised her hands apologetically. "Look, it felt evil. Like it was possessed," she replied, her voice insistent but hushed. "I thought you were in trouble. But," she spun around to Coyllur, "is Daniel right? What he saw—was that really happening, or was it just some trick?"

Coyllur looked up at the sky even as a cluster of stars floated out of her hair and surrounded the medallion with a stellar cage. "That I do not know. This is Kon's, but how did you come by it, Daniel?"

Daniel ran toward her and tried to scan its inky depths. Nothing was there beyond the dull black of the metal surrounded by a fog of demonic spirit.

"Daniel?" Coyllur repeated.

He sighed, exasperated and anxious. "I dreamed about Inti and Kon fighting. Inti needs our help and wants us to come as soon as possible. When I was waking up, Kon sent his medallion to me. I tried to take it off, but it wouldn't budge."

Coyllur shook her head and placed a calming hand on the top of Daniel's head. "Like all demons, Kon delights in deception and despair. Did he show you truth or lies that you might despair? I do not know."

Her attempts to calm Daniel only served to agitate his frustration even more.

"I am certain, however, that despair was his goal," she continued, "and therefore, you must not allow those images or his voice into your heart. Purify the medallion," she looked hard at Daniel, "which is what you should have done in the beginning." She nodded at Raylin. "Be ready. Kon is immensely powerful, and his necklace likely holds a generous amount of his spirit."

Daniel reluctantly summoned the Sun Sword even as he fell into prayer. *Father, what did I see? Was that real? How can we be ready for what the Enemy has planned?*

Why did you wait to ask for my help? The Father's voice calmed him, but the reprimand was clear. *You are in battle, and the Enemy*

seeks any means to corrupt your heart with darkness. Be on your guard.

I … I know. But what I saw in the medallion was so overwhelming, I couldn't … Daniel shook his head and sighed. He knew better than to offer excuses to the Father. *I'm sorry. But what about the Enemy's plans? Will we be okay?*

Remember what you learned in the past, Daniel. I am with you always. I am trustworthy and loving, and what I allow or forbid is for your good. So, have faith in me now. If it were good for you to know every scheme of the Enemy's, I would reveal it to you and the other Vessels. For now, follow Coyllur's advice. Purify the medallion.

By this time, Seren, Ben, and Gabriela were standing next to Raylin, looking on with questioning glances to one another but not daring to interrupt.

Coyllur stepped back, her stars still holding the necklace in place, and gestured for Daniel to hurry.

He raised the Sun Sword and slashed the crumbled disc. A storm of lightning, wind, and dark spirit tore into the air, bending the trees around them in a horrific gale.

"Did you see my Master?" Kon's spirit roared, laughing maniacally despite his imminent sealing. "I hope it brings you comfort. The Master will shatter your hope and your power, and he will certainly kill you all!"

Screams of alarm went up from the crowd of former Creeps as Kon's deafening voice startled them all awake.

Raylin activated the Abyssal Staff.

"Losing a little of my spirit is nothing to me," Kon jeered. "Take it, and welcome. I have more than enough power to defeat Inti and all four of you together. Come to our battlefield; witness my strength, and despair!" Kon laughed.

The raging spirit lowered to hover over the medallion. Kon's masked face materialized, followed by his claws, which he sank into the metal. "You know, I think I would like to stay for a moment. Would you enjoy knowing more of the Master's plan? It is guaranteed to succeed and will certainly bring torment to you and those you love."

Raylin gripped the staff harder and strained with all her might, but the core of the spirit remained, locked in a tug-of-war between her sealing power and Kon's stamina. "He's not budging!" she shouted, her voice clipped with effort.

Daniel flung a Sunstorm at his claws. In the second before it landed, Kon released his grip and was sucked toward the eye of the Abyssal Staff, avoiding the purifying explosion. At the last moment, however, he dug his talons into the ground, and the struggle began all over again as he inched himself back toward the necklace.

"Enough!" Coyllur commanded. She stepped in front of Kon's spirit and raised her arms. Three stars, each the size of a house and in a perfect line, instantly materialized in the air above her. The air vibrated with power and heat, and a beam of star fire blasted Kon directly in his masked face.

The attack drove his spirit, screaming and spitting with rage, toward the staff. Raylin braced herself hard, her feet spread apart and both hands white-knuckled around the obsidian black shaft of the Abyssal Staff. In the second that followed, Kon disappeared through the point of sealing, and silence filled the Mist.

Once satisfied he was gone, Coyllur waved her arms, and the stars ceased their attack, shrank, and drifted into her hair.

Raylin, shaking, released the Abyssal Staff and fell back into Seren's waiting arms.

Daniel released the Sun Sword and went to join them. Murmurs from the crowd of men and women, punctuated by the alarmed questions of their children, filled the air. It was a perfect echo of the apprehension stampeding around his mind. The images from the Abyss were so real that he couldn't shake the weight of dread that pressed down on his heart. The Enemy had some horrible trap planned for them. Could he have discovered their greatest weakness? Whatever that was. Vessels had died in the past; that he knew. What would it mean for the world if they failed? Would they have to wait for other Vessels to be chosen and trained while the Enemy grew in power? How many more would suffer? What would it mean for him and Gabriela? For all their families?

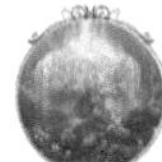

"What was all that about?" Ben asked, pulling away from Raylin and Seren.

Gabriela silently approached behind him.

Daniel felt like Kon was on vacation in his mind, wreaking havoc with his raging storms and cruel suggestions of torment and death.

Peace, Daniel. You and all you love are safe in my hands. Is my Spirit not always with you?

Daniel sighed, feeling the Father's peace knocking at the door of his heart. For some reason, he couldn't quite let it in yet. He glanced at Raylin. If only she hadn't interrupted the vision when she did, he might have had some closure—some definitive answer. He felt a nagging resentment well up inside him.

Coyllur placed heavy hands on his shoulders, startling him. She turned him around and cupped his face. "The Three know all your needs. Right now, the most important thing is not to know the Enemy's plans but to allow the Father's peace into your heart. So, the Enemy has a new plan to defeat you. So what? How is it different from all his other schemes? There is no difference. The Three foresaw and overcame those and will do the same with this one."

Ben held up his hands. "Wait a minute. What about the Enemy's plan? Did he invent some horrible new way to kill us?" Frantic anxiety tinged his voice.

Daniel explained what he had seen. Predictably, Ben spouted all the same questions that ran through his mind. Daniel didn't have the patience to go through it all again and tuned out Coyllur's responses.

Gabriela stepped in front of him. "Daniel, it's not like you to be so angry—not anymore. Why are you so scared of the Enemy's plans? Coyllur's right; this is just one more evil strategy the Three will overcome. Whatever you saw and whatever you're feeling now, let it all go."

Daniel slowed his breathing. There was something about Gabriela's voice that made him more willing to open the door to the Father's peace. He paused and closed his eyes, allowing it to trickle into his whole being. "Thanks. I needed that."

Someone approached through the trees. "Are we safe here?" Cristiano asked, his voice trembling. The noise from the crowd of refugees sounded as if they were close to panic. "Should I prepare everyone to leave?"

"You are safe," Coyllur replied, striding toward him. "Reassure your people that the Three are protecting them. Daniel and the others are about to leave. You all will not witness any further fighting tonight. Go. Rest."

Cristiano nodded and turned but paused with his hand on a low-hanging branch. "Will I … *we* get to see you all again?" His eyes scanned the Vessels but paused on Seren.

Raylin grinned and nudged her forward.

"Stop it," Seren hissed, awkwardly pretending she hadn't noticed.

"Once the quest is over," Coyllur said, "the Vessels are free to *see* whoever they choose. Now, however, they have a date with Kon and Inti."

Seren discreetly nodded back at Cristiano.

He grinned and hurried back through the trees to a chorus of terrified questions.

Coyllur faced the Vessels. "Ready yourselves. You leave straight away."

Everyone left to gather their things.

Gabriela gave her parents one last hug and a few words of reassurance before regrouping with the others.

Daniel returned to the tree he had slept under and scooped up his backpack. Despite Kon's obviously malicious intent, Coyllur's warnings, and his prayers, Daniel still wished he had seen more. Images from the vision played over and over in his mind like a video stuck on a loop.

Father, are we safe? Can you please at least tell me if there is something planned that we won't be able to overcome?

You are safe in my hands. You and your future.

Daniel waited for more but felt a sense of finality in the pronouncement. That was all the reassurance he was getting at present.

He interlaced his fingers behind his neck and tried to clear his mind. He certainly didn't want to struggle through the same lessons he'd already learned in the previous quests: trust, prayer, and faith during times of weakness. Certainly, this quest would have enough spiritual lessons to keep him occupied without redoing the old ones. If he had learned anything, it was that whatever the Three allowed, it was for all their good, and the Three would save them from the Enemy even if they waited until the last minute to do so.

Even if they were allowed to die.

Still, the Three would save them. But Daniel knew he wasn't scared the Three would abandon them. He was nervous that after all their trials, waiting, and suffering, the Three might allow them to be defeated. Sure, they'd go to Heaven. That was awesome and all, but Daniel wanted to build a life with Gabriela. To one day get married, have kids, and have a real *life*. Still, if only Raylin had butted out a moment longer. If only Daniel could've heard more of the plan. If only.

Daniel grabbed his hair in frustration as though he could simply yank out the images and leave them in the Mist.

He joined the others at Coyllur's side as she reached into the folds of her dress and pulled out an Orb of Passage. Daniel gritted his teeth.

Wonderful. A perfect end to a perfect night.

7

Kon Is a Jerk

Ben moaned. "Here we go."

"You will join Inti in the spirit realm over Peru," Coyllur explained. "The battle reaches a crescendo, and your coming will turn the tide. Do all he tells you without question. Now go!"

She threw the Orb of Passage at their feet, and fire exploded around them. Daniel felt himself unmade within the flames and violently yanked through the air. As usual, traveling by Orb gave one the sense of hurtling through space in all directions at once. At first, he could tell they were streaking through the sky of the Mist. But, at some point, they passed through a wall of water to rocket straight up into an expanse of open, clear air. Their momentum slowed, and they materialized far above the range of mountains Daniel saw in his dream. A dark blue expanse, gloriously illuminated by bands of the Milky Way and all the planets of the solar system, stretched out above them like a canopy. Below, a glowing boundary line zigzagged through mountains, jungles, cities, and fields, circumventing a long, narrow swath of land. And dead in its center, a luminescent circle turned within a triangle of faint yellow light. Within the center of the triangle, letters of heavenly script spelled out something that, at first, was indecipherable. The letters blurred and shifted until Daniel could read them.

"Belonging to the Three," it read.

As if barely plugged into a light socket, the symbol and words flickered on and off.

"The Peruvian Seal!" Gabriela exclaimed, her voice panicked. "It's almost gone!"

On the horizon, a storm of fire and lightning shook the air.

Seren pointed. "I'm betting that's where we'll find the battle."

No sooner had the words left her mouth than some power yanked them swiftly through the air directly toward it. Within seconds, they found themselves on the outskirts of Inti and Kon's violent clash, dwarfed by the titanic Firstborn locked in mortal combat. Neither touched the earth but trod on the air as though it were solid.

The Firstborn appeared just as they had in Daniel's dream. Kon, wearing his demonic feline mask frozen in a hideous, toothy grin and bedecked with a belt of human skulls, surrounded himself with waves of violent storms. He pointed his staff at Inti, and four balls of angry electricity appeared in the air around him.

Inti, radiant in glowing bronze armor and wreathed with flames, folded his hands and closed his eyes. At the last moment, a half second before the bolts struck, he and Kon switched places.

It was so sudden that Kon's own attack hammered him to his knees before he could defend himself.

"Fighting by deception, Inti?" Kon howled. He leaned forward onto his hands, smoke rising from his charred body. "How unlike a servant of the Three. Maybe you should come over to Master's side."

The switch seemed to take all Inti's remaining power, and he stumbled backward, catching himself from falling only at the last moment.

Daniel and the others floated to the edge of the battle, hovering motionless. He glanced at everyone's faces, silent and pale in the gray, stormy light. Though Kon's malevolence was nothing compared to the Serpent's, it was clear no one wanted him to take notice of their presence. He hoped the power of Janice's clothes would conceal them until they were under Inti's protection.

"I do not deceive," Inti gasped, straightening himself back into

a fighting position. "You reap what you sow, Kon. The Three have heard my prayers and the prayers of his children in Peru. They will take it back now."

Kon pushed himself to his feet and spat. "How? You think your pathetic Vessels will come to your rescue. The Vessel of the Sun Sword is likely dead—driven mad and strangled by my medallion. I will overcome you and—"

"They are here now!" Inti pointed at the Vessels. All at once, the four of them flew to his side; Daniel and Raylin hovered in front of his shoulders, Seren his chest, and Ben his forehead. Gabriela, as if knowing all along what her role in this battle would be, fell to her knees and began interceding for them. Inti raised his finger and pointed toward the heavens. "And *He* is here."

The Spirit, unmistakable but in a form Daniel had never seen, descended as a condor to fly directly above Inti's head. Power wafted off the Spirit's wings like waves, washing over Inti and rejuvenating him.

One by one, his calming presence visibly filtered into the others, Ben first and then Raylin and Seren. For some reason he couldn't explain, Daniel felt agitated. The Spirit's eyes bore into his back and searched his innermost being. Daniel could sense it, but his presence didn't bring the peace he remembered.

Kon took a step back and dropped his staff by his side. His eyes narrowed as he searched the air around Inti. "Vessels? I sense their power," he muttered, "but they are hidden from me." He seemingly gave up pinpointing their location and looked up at the Spirit. "The balance of Peru is in my favor. My servants have enslaved too many of the people for you to rightfully take it back." His eyes danced between the Spirit and Inti with a nervous energy. "You have to follow the rules the Father put in place at the dividing of nations! You are cheating."

"Silence," the Spirit commanded. "The Vessels freed all the slaves around Machu Picchu and many from Cuzco. The balance was restored in our favor. Peru is under Inti's governance once again."

Inti whipped his head around to look down at the Peruvian Seal. Unlike before, its light burned bright and steadfast. The faintest smile played at the corner of his mouth as he fixed Kon with a victorious expression.

Kon snarled, lifting both arms. "Master!" he screamed. "I offer you my essence. Inhabit me. Strengthen me. Take back my land!"

Serpents, familiar in their similarity to the Enemy but smaller, erupted out of the air around Kon and sank their fangs into his arms and legs. He clenched his teeth but made no sound as a sickening green pallor spread over his body. His eyes burned red, and the pupils elongated into slits. "Ah. I sense you much better now," he crooned, fixing each Vessel with his baleful glare. He paused on Daniel. "I will kill you first. Did you enjoy the vision of the Abyss? Or maybe you did not see the end."

Daniel felt a weight around his neck as though the medallion were still there. He reached up to rub his skin where the beads had hung as visions of the Serpent crashed like a wave over his mind, replaying quickly. Along with them, the frustration he had felt toward Raylin burst to the forefront of his thoughts. Why had she interrupted? Did she not want him to know what the Enemy had planned? She was always getting in the way—the quest for the Sun Sword, their time in India, the debacle with the Abyss—in each quest, she either dogged their steps, frustrated them, attacked them, or deceived them.

"Daniel!" Inti's voice shook him into the present. "Come back."

Daniel looked around. He was halfway between Inti and Kon, floating subconsciously toward their enemy.

Kon sneered with smug self-satisfaction as Daniel returned to Inti's shoulder.

"What was that all about?" Seren demanded.

Raylin pointed to her neck. "Something with the medallion again?"

Daniel shook his head, still too clouded by the images and the onslaught of anger to clearly explain what had happened. "It's nothing."

"You sure?" Ben persisted, his brow knit in concern. "It looked like you were under some spell."

"I'm fine," Daniel snapped. "Can we focus on the fight now?"

"Hey, don't get snippy with me. We were just worried for you."

"Do not listen to the Enemy's lies, Daniel," Inti interjected, his voice quick and commanding. "Deception, isolation, and despair are his tools. You know this. Do not be so easily tricked. Now, all of you, be anointed with the Spirit and fight with me!"

Everyone shut their eyes and prayed. Daniel, chagrined by Inti's reprimand, felt like that was the last thing he wanted to do, but he tried.

Um, please help us. Help me to … to …

The Spirit's voice trickled into his distracted mind. *Why are you far from me?*

Daniel craned his neck to see the Spirit, slowly flapping his expansive wings directly above and behind Inti.

I'm not. I've just got a lot to think about.

Let it go and trust me.

I am! I mean, I'm trying. Daniel still felt a slight pressure on his neck. Was it his imagination, or could he feel the medallion there?

Kon attacked. Lightning bolts, wide as rivers and blood-red, rained down all around them.

Ben expanded into the Triune Shield—huge, now that he was anointed with the Spirit—and surrounded Inti. The bolts struck against his barriers and were thrown back, rebounding in random directions. One even ricocheted directly at Kon, catching him full in his mask. The ghoulish feline mask fell to the ground, split in two and charred. His actual appearance wasn't much better; he had a human-like face, gray-green and pock-marked with scars, singed eyebrows, numerous missing teeth, and a nose so hooked it played about his mouth. His yellow, beady eyes had slit pupils reminiscent of a crocodile's rather than a cat's.

Now free from the concern of Kon's attack and energized by the Spirit, Inti calmly raised both arms in front of him, one above

and one below, so that both palms faced each other. Two discs of fire, each comprised of ornate and intricate interlocking circles and heavenly script, appeared above and below Kon. "Seren. Bind him."

Seren summoned the Celestial Bow. Its radiant white limbs of starlight, now much longer than her body, branched out from her extended hand. She drew back on the invisible string, and a luminous arrow appeared. She released it as soon as she had completed a full draw. The arrow tore through the air faster than Kon could react to flee Inti's trap and struck him between the eyes.

Kon grunted and flailed about in shock until the binding casing froze him in his place and the circlet of fire appeared on his forehead.

Inti brought his palms together, and a column of raging yellow fire filled the space between the discs. "Daniel, ready yourself to approach him, but be prepared. He will attempt to deceive you. Do not listen to his words. Strike with the Sun Sword, and do not hesitate."

Daniel floated away from Inti and summoned the sword. It was its usual size. He turned it from side to side, looking for any evidence that something was wrong. The others' Weapons of Power had grown with the Spirit's presence. Why hadn't his? He cast a glance back at the Spirit.

Why are you far from me? The Spirit's azure eyes remained fixed on Daniel. *Turn over your fear and anger.*

Daniel turned back around and blew out a small breath. He tried to center his mind. *Okay. I give you my fear. I don't feel it, but I choose to trust that everything is okay. I choose to trust you.*

You, your friends, your family, your future—they are all in my hands.

Daniel felt a sense of calm, barely perceptible, as the Spirit's power gently rested upon him like a blanket. The Sun Sword grew longer and brighter as he reached Kon, who still lay frozen in Seren's binding. The tongues of fire licking the edges of the blade burned a white-hot, distorting the air around it.

Kon struggled against his binding to turn his head, fixing Daniel with an unblinking, reptilian stare. "I can smell your fear. Your uncertainty." He sniffed the air. "Your anger." Kon's eyes flitted to Raylin.

Daniel followed his line of sight to where she hovered at Inti's shoulder. With a quick gesture from Inti, Raylin summoned the Abyssal Staff. It hovered, long as a light pole, in front of her. Its eye activated automatically as if hungry for the rest of Kon's spirit.

"Ah. I see," Kon sniggered. "Your look explains it all. The traitor interfered with my vision. She interferes with everything, does she not?"

As though physically entering his body, Daniel felt Kon's words inching closer to his mind and stirring up emotions in his heart.

Do not heed his lies. The Spirit's power washed over Daniel again, pushing Kon's influence back.

Daniel gritted his teeth and didn't answer Kon. The pressure of the demon's presence warred with the Spirit's within him, battering his body like a nauseating wave of chaos. He raised the Sun Sword above his head.

"It was her fault the sword lost its tip, no?" Kon continued. "And I heard it was for her that your friend over there died." He raised his eyebrows toward the Triune Shield.

"Ben?" Daniel asked. "Well, he had to die to get the Triune Shield." Even as he said it, however, Daniel didn't feel the logic of his words. He knew they were true, but he felt that Kon had scored a point somehow. It was because of Raylin that Ben had died, throwing himself in front of the Bolt of Pestilence. No matter if it was Seren throwing the bolt and Ben had been resurrected.

"She dogged your steps through the British Isles. Hounding you. Interfering. Attacking. All while you and your *true* friends tried to help her. How many times did Gabriela risk her own life during the quest to save Raylin?"

The Sun Sword fell to Daniel's side, and he gaped at Kon. His true friends? He pictured Ben, Seren, and Gabriela encircling him, and outside their group, Raylin, sneering and annoying.

He lies. The Spirit's voice eased to the forefront of his mind. *Deceiving and distorting for his own gain.*

The Spirit's power once more pushed Kon's back, but for some

reason, Daniel didn't want it to. He reached out in his mind and pulled back the feeling of resentment toward Raylin. It felt familiar, like an old, worn shirt that fit just right.

"Daniel," Raylin shouted, her voice shrill in his ears. "Hurry and purify him. He's tricking you."

Daniel snapped his head around and glared. "I know what I'm doing, Raylin. I don't need any help from you!" The Sun Sword shrank to its normal size as Daniel swung it through Kon.

Seren's binding broke, and half of Kon's spirit erupted into the air, wailing and howling like a hurricane. The other half shot down toward the mountains, streaking as a lightning bolt straight toward a peak Daniel knew all too well. Wayna Picchu: the entrance to Supai's realm. Raylin activated the Abyssal Staff's power and began sealing away the portion of the demon's spirit left storming in front of them. Within moments, it was gone, and a deafening silence filled the sky.

Daniel floated back to Inti and the Spirit, embarrassed and confused. The moment Kon fled, the clattering arguments ceased in his mind. He couldn't quite remember why Kon's points seemed as weighty as they had.

"Hey, I got half of him," he offered, trying to laugh. "The Sun Sword *is* still missing its tip. Maybe that's why I couldn't get it all." Even Daniel didn't believe this, but he pressed his point. Looking up at the Spirit, he said, "When will we find out where the tip is? Don't we need it to receive the full power of the Father's Blessing?"

Silence.

Gabriela floated nearer to them, her eyes looking everywhere other than at Daniel.

"Half of Kon is too much," Inti replied, disappointment evident in his tone. "And the missing piece of the Sun Sword would not account for Kon's escape. Not with the Spirit empowering you."

The Spirit, still flapping his wings slowly in the air above Inti, held Daniel's gaze and addressed him alone. *You have grieved me, Daniel. To you, the Sun Sword's tip is lost. To us, it is exactly where it needs to be. You will find it when the time is right. My power is sufficient for you*

until that time. My power was sufficient for your battle with Kon. Why were you far from me?

I don't know, Daniel replied. *It was so confusing.*

Seek the answer to that, and all will be made clear. Look within yourself.

Ashamed, Daniel dropped his eyes to the ground below, not daring to look at the others for fear they would read everything in his face. He wasn't sure what had happened with Kon, and the Spirit's command to "Look within" wasn't exactly helpful. Especially when everything "within" was so mixed up. He shut his eyes and tried to focus.

The Spirit now broadcasted his voice to everyone, and Daniel put the conversation behind him.

Kon nurses his wounded spirit in the underworld and will seek to regain his old power over Peru. Now, instead of a time of rest for my people here, a new persecution will break out.

Gabriela gasped. "Certainly, it won't be as bad as before! Will my people be enslaved again?"

No. Not until long after your time. Do not fear, daughter. Your family and all those who are mine will have peace. But in the age to come—the last age—Kon will rise to power once again and much sooner than his successor would have. Inti will once again face him.

Inti heard the pronouncement and lowered his head, glowering resolutely down at Wayna Picchu.

Tears welled up in Gabriela's eyes, but she blinked them away and cast Daniel a sideways glance. Seren and Raylin floated down to her, each on one side, and placed comforting hands on her back.

Seren looked up at the Spirit. "The next age could be hundreds of years from now, right?" she offered hopefully.

Its advent will occur at the sealing of the Spirit of the Age. And with its coming, the end will be as a flood.

"What does that mean?" Ben asked. He released the Triune Shield and joined them at Inti's feet.

Inti broke away from Wayna Picchu and fixed his glinting eyes on

the Vessels. "It means that the next age, once it starts, will be short. Until now, each age has been thousands of years long. Not so, the last. It may endure only a century. Two at the most. Only the Three know the exact times."

Everyone turned to look at Daniel.

He squirmed. "What? I … I don't know what went wrong, okay? Something happened with the Sun Sword, and Kon was in my head. I was trying. I promise. Besides, the Spirit did say Kon wouldn't rise again until after Gabriela's lifetime. So even though the next age will start soon, we won't have to deal with him again."

"No, but my people will," Gabriela replied. "Maybe my children. Maybe my grandchildren. To think they will have to endure the same horror that me and my parents did is awful."

A torrent of emotions churned through Daniel. Frustration, anger, sadness, confusion, shame, embarrassment—they were all there. He released the Sun Sword and floated closer to the others.

Ben nudged his arm. "What was Kon saying? How did he make the Sun Sword shrink like that?"

Daniel felt a pervasive sense of relief. Until now, he feared the others had been able to hear some, or all, of what Kon had said. Apparently not. He thought back on Kon's litany of accusations against Raylin and thought it best to avoid bringing those up. "I really don't want to talk about it. It was overwhelming, like when the Enemy gets in your head with one of his spells. Look, I'm sorry. But you all are acting like this was all my fault. It's not like I wanted Kon to escape."

Inti, and above him, the Spirit, fixed him with looks that Daniel could feel penetrating his mind. He blushed.

"Okay, what's next?" he asked, hoping to change the topic.

You will go to Babylon and find the Gates of Eden.

Raylin and Seren looked like the pronouncement made sense. Gabriela, too. She silently nodded her head as though the plan was all coming together in her mind.

"I feel like I've been left out of a secret," Ben said to Daniel.

"I know what you mean," Daniel replied.

Ben cleared his throat. "Gates of Eden? Care to explain? Because we're in the dark."

She let her hands run down her staff as she spoke. "Well, when I served the Enemy, breaking back into Eden was always on his mind. He wants to destroy it."

Seren joined in. "It's the only place on Earth where he has absolutely zero power. He can't stand that. To him, it's like a nagging splinter in the bottom of his foot, always working its way deeper."

"Isn't it guarded by a really powerful Firstborn?" Raylin asked. "Someone who keeps the Enemy at bay?"

"Uriel, the Cherub," Inti answered. "He keeps the gates locked from any who would enter by force."

Raylin nodded. "The Enemy was nuts about getting in. He constantly ranted and raved about destroying the Tree of Life and turning the garden into an ash heap."

"I remember that, too." Seren broke away from Gabriela and looked up at the Spirit. "Why would he care about that?"

As you both said, it is abhorrent to him that he can no longer enter Eden—that some place exists in the world where he has no power. But there is more. He considers it an abomination for Earthborn to live eternally. That is a gift only the Firstborn should have, he believes. He considers destroying the Tree of Life a way to shut the Earthborn out of Heaven.

The Spirit and Inti exchanged exasperated glances.

"As if he could," Inti said, shaking his head.

The Spirit continued. *Before you can seal the Enemy, you must be purified. The battle against Kon showed how necessary that is. Uriel will let you into Eden and, from there, direct you to the Tree of Purity. But guard yourself against temptation, and do not try to take of the Tree of Life on your own. Its fruit is forbidden unless given by our hand.*

Daniel furrowed his brows. "But if the Enemy can't get into Eden, how could we even be tempted to take the fruit of the tree? I remember the story of Adam and Eve. It was the Serpent that tricked them."

"Do you forget, Daniel?" Inti asked, tapping his chest. "The Serpent is not the only enemy. The flesh, riddled with your own sins, holds iniquity enough to tempt you. You will bring your own evil into Eden, and it is *that* you should guard yourself against."

Daniel lowered his eyes. "Surely that goes for all of us, though. Not just me."

Yes. All of you. The Spirit flew higher into the air, and suddenly, the veil between them and the Father's Mountain drew back. A sigh of wind, warm and spiced with the smells of every good living thing, washed down around them. Brilliant light spilled from the top of the peak like rain, bathing the forests, fields, rivers, and waterfalls in an effervescent sheen. Everyone beheld the mountain with longing, including Inti. *I take my leave. But remember, I am with you always. Go now and finish the quest.*

The Father's Mountain was cloaked once again, and the Spirit with it. Inti shifted in his molten armor and waved his hand.

Before Daniel had time to realize what was happening, they were streaking through the air down toward Machu Picchu. In that split second, he caught a glimpse of the sun setting behind the mountains. That meant that, even though the time battling over Peru had seemed to last only a short time, nearly a full day had elapsed on Earth. His observations were quickly drawn back to their trajectory as the side of Machu Picchu fast approached. He braced himself for the landing, but instead of crashing into the side of the ruins, they passed through the mountainside and found themselves back at the Transportation Pedestal. Inti, now in the same form as he had kept in Coricancha—tall, robed in white, wearing a red, sun-shaped jewel inset into a golden diadem, light-blue eyes, white hair—gestured toward the plinth, still shattered and cracked from Tyr's attack.

The broken stones of the pedestal snapped back in place while the crack in the floor eased together with a quiet groan. Within seconds, the entire room had returned to normal.

Seren, still breathless from their descent, steadied herself on the side of the dais. "An Orb of Passage, flying with Inti through the air,

and the Transportation Pedestal all within a day? This is too much fun." Her deadpan comment stirred up a series of groans from the group.

"Do we have to?" Ben gasped. "Can't we just walk through the Mist or something?"

Gabriela, still somber and avoiding Daniel's eyes, unslung her backpack and pulled out a piece of bread. "Babylon is on the other side of the world," she explained between bites. "It would still take us several days to walk there."

"It would be impossible had you a hundred years," Inti said as everyone gathered around the dais. "The way to Babylon is shut through the Mist. You will not be able to use it once there. Remember, the Babylonian Seal is broken, and you will be in the heart of the Enemy's territory. The pedestal is on the outskirts of the ancient city of Eridu, which you know by its modern name: Tell Abu Shahrain."

"That's unlucky," Raylin said, blowing out a long, slow breath. She inched closer to Seren, who studied the ground while rubbing her temples. "We can't even hide in the Mist or anything?"

Inti shook his head. "And once you leave the transportation site, the Enemy will know you are in his land. You must make haste to the Gates of Eden."

Ben raised his hand. "As usual, I have a load of questions. First, Raylin and Seren, I get the feeling Babylon is going to be awful. Am I correct? Second, isn't Tell Abu Shahrain where Ealim Wahid is? You know, where the Enemy's Leaders and their gang hang out? And probably the Enemy himself in whatever stupidly monstrous form he's taking in Babylon? Do we honestly have to transport there of all places? Three, Eridu? Some explanation, please." He put his hands on his hips and raised his eyebrows.

Daniel jumped in with a raised hand. "Four, don't we get some more instructions on what to do? It can't be as easy as going from point A to point B, right? Let me guess, Eden is far away from our transportation site, and we'll be chased by demons the whole way." He casually moved closer to Gabriela, but she still avoided his eyes.

Inti folded his hands. "The pedestal," he began, fixing each of them with a serious look, "is within the House of Enki: E-Abzu. Raylin, Seren, no doubt over the years, you overheard the Enemy searching for this place."

"Yes," both girls responded in unison, but it was Raylin who continued. "Enki is a Firstborn, and the Enemy knew he guarded the Transportation Pedestal that was somewhere in the borders of ancient Babylon. He figured if he could destroy it, regaining his foothold in the land would be easier."

"But he could never find it," Seren continued. "That's how it was when I served him, anyway." She looked to Inti for reassurance.

He tipped his head and continued. "Once the Babylonian Seal was broken, Enki left E-Abzu and took his place in the heavens to fight the Enemy. His power still conceals its location, however. As he is not there to instruct you, you must listen closely."

Inti slowly passed his steady gaze over each person. Once everyone had made some gesture that they were listening, he continued. "E-Abzu is a place of water. Long ago, by your reckoning, it was located on the edge of a swamp. Now, it is an oasis beneath the desert. Water from the ancient rivers, Pishon and Gihon, still flows underground there, mingling with the waters of Enki's house. Dip all the Weapons of Power into those waters. Do not leave E-Abzu until you do. From there, follow the Euphrates River until it joins the Tigris. Where both rivers mix at the edge of the Persian Gulf, bathe your weapons once more. These are the four rivers that flowed out of Eden when the Three created it. With your weapons baptized, the portal to Eden will be triggered to open when you approach its threshold."

Gabriela lightly touched the Pedestal but then quickly pulled back. The handprint flared brightly and pivoted on its fingertips around the dais's surface, leaving three other indented prints in its tracks.

Inti placed his heavy hands on Daniel and Ben's shoulders. "The pedestal is now keyed to all four Vessels. Gabriela, you must be touching one of them to transport alongside."

Daniel nudged her and tried to take her hand. She gave him a weak smile and pulled away.

"Not now. I'm still too shook up." She lifted her head. "Are the Gates of Eden at the edge of the Persian Gulf, then?"

"They lie fathoms beneath its surface," Inti replied. "The Sun Sword will guide you."

Raylin took off her beanie and straightened out her hair. "We'll need a boat."

"Maybe we could pick one up on the river somewhere," Seren suggested.

"Let's just ask old Soupy for one," Ben muttered. "Sounds like we'll be practically transporting into his garage."

"All will be provided for," Inti reassured them. He pointed at the pedestal. "But your mission, as usual, is dangerous. Do not take off the clothes Janice made for you. They will shield you from enemy eyes. It is time."

Daniel looked over at Gabriela. She ambled closer to him and lightly touched his shoulder. "Everyone ready?"

"Nope," Ben muttered.

Seren shook her head. "Quit being such a baby."

Raylin nodded. "Let's do this."

All four stuck their hands to the pedestal.

"Babylon," Ben burped as the room began to swirl, and they were yanked into the vortex, "here we come."

8

A Desert of Monsters

Daniel could tell they had transported somewhere underground. Nowhere else could possibly be so dark. He pulled his hand away from the pedestal. The air smelled as if there was water nearby, but that was to be expected. He listened intently and thought he caught the gentle lapping of small waves somewhere around them, but it was hard to be certain over the mesmerizing thrum that permeated the air and even the stone he stood on.

"Everyone here?" Seren's low, authoritative voice asked from somewhere in front of him.

A retching sound came from Daniel's left. "Present," Ben groaned. "Maybe I should take some Dramamine before I transport places. Or invest in one of those bracelets with the pressure point thing to help people with motion sickness. This can't go on."

"Little late for that now," Raylin replied. "You probably should've thought about that before you were on your last quest."

"True," Ben muttered. "True. Where are you? I can't see."

"That's my hand you're touching," Raylin replied. "We're all in the same position we were before leaving Machu Picchu, obviously."

"Right. Right," Ben replied, the brightness in his voice giving away his evident happiness.

"You're still touching my hand."

"Oh. Sorry."

The room suddenly lit up as one of Gabriela's light globes floated into the air.

"Gabriela," Daniel said, blinking in the sudden brightness. "Have I ever told you how glad I am of all your powers?"

"Couple times," she replied, then gestured toward the globe hovering two feet behind them. It floated backward, revealing dark waters just beyond their platform. Its glow did little for Raylin and Seren's side, however. "I think this requires more light." She held her hands together and then lifted her arms, drawing her palms apart. Ten more globes materialized in the air between them, floating around the pedestal to illuminate the chamber in soft, white radiance.

They were standing on a circular shelf of stone, which extended out about two feet from the base of the pedestal. If anyone had attempted to take more than a step away, they would've fallen straight into the water.

The pool was placid and clear. With a flick of Gabriela's wrist, three globes plopped into the water, sinking below the surface until they landed on the bottom twenty feet below. A shoal of pale fish swarmed them as they sank, sending flickering shadows flitting about the rocky pool floor.

"So, this is E-Abzu. Looks like we're in for a swim," Daniel said. "Maybe we should go ahead and dip our weapons in. Better now than when we're being harassed by fish."

Seren peered over the edge of the stone lip at the orbs still glowing below. More fish had joined the fray. Apparently, this was the most exciting thing that had happened to them in a long time. "True," she muttered, summoning the Celestial Bow.

Daniel and Raylin did the same, and the white light illuminating the cavern was awash with vibrant greens, yellows, and oranges. As they held their weapons under the frigid water, more fish appeared and happily gamboled about their glows.

Ben frowned at them. "I'm not so sure swimming across this place sounds like a good idea. I just know I'm going to get a fish in my pants or something."

Raylin craned her neck around. "What about the Triune Shield? Don't you need to dip it in?"

Everyone else cast inquisitive expressions at Ben.

Ben squirmed, looking back and forth between their eyes like he was trapped. "Obviously, but it's a little different for me! I'd have to actually get in the water myself and then summon the Triune Shield. And, you know, there're fish in there."

"We're in a hurry, Ben," Gabriela reminded him. "No choice."

Daniel pulled the Sun Sword out of the water, studied the blade for a moment, and then released it. "I guess that's long enough." He jerked his head toward the pool. "Come on, dude. Get it over with."

Ben reluctantly turned and dipped his hand in the water. "Yikes! That's cold! I know, maybe this'll work."

The others released their weapons and shuffled around Ben as he pulled out one of his golden daggers and cast the Triune Shield around it. Without the other Weapons of Power distracting and dividing them, the horde of fish gathered around the blue light. Even a few of those swarming Gabriela's globes quickly made their way up to this new curiosity. The water boiled with their excitement.

Ben drew back uneasily. "That's probably got it, don't you think? I mean, no need to overdo it."

Daniel exchanged glances with the girls. They all nodded their heads silently. Seren made a shoving motion with her hand and gave Daniel a thumbs-up.

With a grin, Daniel silently shifted around behind Ben, placed his foot on his back, and pushed. "Sorry, Ben."

"For what—what are you doing? Ahhh!"

After Ben violently sank beneath the fish ball, the Triune Shield expanded outward, its upper arc barely clearing the surface of the water before the entire shield disappeared beneath the water and sank to the bottom.

"Huh," Raylin said, leaning intently over the lip of the shelf. "The shield doesn't float."

"Looks that way," Seren observed a little nervously.

"Can he breathe?" Daniel asked.

Gabriela chewed the bottom of her lip and leaned a little farther over the stone edge. "If he couldn't, surely he'd release the shield and swim back up, right?"

The light of the Triune Shield flickered out.

"I think," Daniel said, nervously tapping his fingers on the stone, "we're about to find out."

Gabriela waved her hands in the air, and all the underwater orbs converged onto Ben's frantically swimming form.

Within seconds, he burst through the surface of the water, teeth chattering and sputtering for air. "No!" he thrashed violently in the water. "That is not your home, little fish. Get out of there. It's not your home!" he shrieked.

Ben finally made the lip of the platform where Gabriela and Daniel hoisted him onto its narrow shelf. He scrambled to his feet, squirming, and reached his hands down the back of his pants to pull out a flat, blue and black striped fish. It wriggled wildly in Ben's hands before slipping out to plop back into the water.

"Those are *my* pants! Mine!" Ben shouted, pointing at his rear and still shaking from shock and cold.

Daniel prepared himself for an onslaught.

"You," Ben said through gritted teeth, turning carefully on his heel so that he didn't fall back into the writhing water. He placed an iron grip on the pedestal to keep himself anchored there and dripped all over the surface of the dais. His eyes were dark with anger. "You pushed me."

"Now hold on a second, Ben," Daniel said, holding up his hands and shifting back a few inches. "I know it seems like—"

"Silence! You shoved me into an icy cold nightmare of fish, Daniel. It was fish hell, and I got an up close and personal look. All of me. Do you understand? All. Of. Me."

Daniel shuddered. "I … I understand."

"Now, my backpack and all my extra clothes are wet, too!"

"To be fair," Seren intervened, "we all told him to do it. We just

couldn't risk the shield on your daggers not being what Inti meant when he said to dip our weapons into the water."

"That's right," Daniel rejoined. "It was all our ideas."

Ben growled through gritted teeth, "I almost lost my dagger, by the way. Barely had time to slide it back in my belt before I had to summon the shield. And then I sank like a stone to the bottom." He flung water off his hands into Daniel's face. "It's even colder down there!"

"Could you breathe under the water?" Raylin asked.

Ben's tone softened. "Come to think of it. Yeah, sort of. I mean, I don't think I was technically breathing air since there wasn't any down there, but I was okay." He wrung out the bottom of his shirt, doing his best to fling the excess water onto Daniel's face again. "Now that you mention it, it was almost like I just pulled oxygen out of the water. I guess I could've stayed down there forever, or at least until I couldn't maintain the Triune Shield anymore." He jerked his head back to Daniel. "Not that that should give you any ideas!"

Daniel wiped the remaining water out of his eyes and held up his hands defensively. "I literally have zero ideas in my head right now."

"Good." Ben poked him in the chest. "Keep it that way."

"If you're done," Gabriela said, "I think we should think about getting out of here. Only, I'm not sure which way to go." She folded her arms under her parka and scanned the cavern. "Daniel?"

"Yes?" Daniel eagerly replied.

"She wants you to summon the Sun Sword for directions," Seren explained, exchanging a weary glance with Raylin. "Not get all doe-eyed and desperate," she finished under her breath.

"I heard that," Daniel hissed in her direction, then addressed Gabriela with a brighter tone. "One second."

Daniel reached back to hold on to the pedestal and summoned the sword. It floated in the air in front of him, pulling strongly off toward his right.

"I guess that's our bearings. I'll leave it summoned while we swim so we don't get lost."

"Swim?" Ben burst out, his voice an octave higher. "Who's swimming?"

"We are," Raylin replied.

Seren felt the water with her hands and then hastily rubbed her arms. "Brr! Okay. This is going to be tough."

"Give me all your backpacks," Daniel said. "I can hold them above the water while the Sun Sword pulls me to the other side."

"Oh, right," Ben replied. "What a stupendous notion. Because it would be bad to get our things wet, huh? This way, we can all change into dry clothes when we get to the other side. Right. Right. Oh wait, except for me!"

Seren slipped off her bag and plopped it at Daniel's feet. "Yikes. Sounds like someone's going to milk this for all it's worth."

"You better believe it," Ben said, tossing his backpack into Daniel's chest.

Gabriela gently set hers at Daniel's feet and then sent all her orbs underwater behind the dais. "Hopefully, most of the fish will stay around them while we go by the Sun Sword's light."

"Great idea," Raylin replied. "I'm not sure Ben could handle another incident."

Ben blushed and shuffled anxiously to the edge of the water, muttering something unintelligible under his breath.

With grunts and groans and significant shivering, everyone slipped into the water. The pull of the Sun Sword was luckily strong enough to keep Daniel afloat while he glided through the pool, holding everyone's backpacks by their grab handles above water. To everyone's relief, no other fish friends decided to visit. After swimming about a hundred yards, they found solid ground in the form of a gradual underwater ramp that led up to a high stone wall. They were about knee-deep now, and there were no signs of stairs or a doorway.

The Sun Sword pointed directly at the stone.

Daniel passed out everyone's backpacks and fell to studying the boulder. "We're clearly supposed to get through here. I could try blasting it, but—"

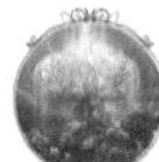

"That could cause a cave-in," Raylin interrupted. "I wouldn't do that."

"As I was about to say," Daniel replied, "it could cause a cave-in. Believe me, I don't want another broken leg or worse."

Seren was ignoring the conversation and cautiously shuffling her feet around underwater.

Daniel waved the Sun Sword back and forth for light, studying the surface of the stone. "Maybe we could look for a keyhole or something."

"Found them," Seren said. "There're four, actually, all underwater at the base of the stone. They're shaped just like the keyholes at the door to the Serpent's Abyss. Only, there's one now for the Abyssal Staff."

"I see the sisters are both anticipating me," Daniel grumbled under his breath.

Gabriela raised her eyebrows at his comment and waded closer to the wall face, feeling under the water with her feet as well. "This one feels like a bowl. The Triune Shield goes here, obviously. Next is the Abyssal Staff. Just a simple circle for you to slip the shaft in, Raylin."

"Well, well, well. Isn't that something," Ben said bitterly. "Looks like I would've had to summon the shield in the water without being kicked in and sinking to the bottom after all. Glad I had that experience." He frowned at Seren and Daniel but conspicuously left Raylin and Gabriela out of the reprimand. "Of course, I don't blame you girls," he continued, nodding to both while finding his position. "No matter what Seren said, I'm sure you had no part in pushing me in."

Raylin looked up after she had found her keyhole. "Oh, uh, it's all a blur, really." She summoned the Abyssal Staff and carefully pushed the shaft down below the surface of the water.

Gabriela shared a chuckle with Raylin before moving on. "Next one is the Sun Sword."

Seren had already found her position. She summoned the Celestial Bow and laid it down sideways in the water.

Daniel trudged toward Gabriela and, after she had stepped back, lowered the Sun Sword down into the clear water to see. At the base

of the stone was a slit the same size as his blade. He slid the sword in until he heard a click.

Last of all, Ben summoned the Triune Shield. As soon as the borders had expanded, the stone face shuddered and, with a loud grinding noise, slid beneath the surface of the pool.

The water rushed in, swirling around the sides of the threshold and splashing against the ramp, which continued its climb past the submerged stone door. Everyone released their weapons and plodded up the walkway. Gabriela recalled her lights, dispatching them ahead to station themselves along the ramp. As the last person passed by, the stone doorway rose from the water, sending one last wave greedily surging around their ankles.

Seren shivered. "The air feels so cold and dry up here."

"And dusty," Raylin coughed. "It brings back unpleasant memories."

"Too many to count," Seren replied, her voice small and haunted in the shifting darkness.

Daniel led the way past Gabriela's sentinel lights. "If you both have been here before, does that mean you can quickly get us to the Euphrates?"

Seren shrugged. "Babylon is modern-day Iraq, so it's pretty big. Tell Abu Shahrain was in the process of being built when I served the Enemy. I visited with him every now and then, but I was usually kept somewhere else. And I never saw Abida and Amira or the other Generals. I guess he wanted to keep them a secret. From how fast he replaced me with Vinaash—"

"Which was like, immediately," Ben interjected with a snort.

Seren frowned. "Thank you for emphasizing how unimportant I was. As I was saying, from how fast he replaced me, he never intended on keeping me a General very long. I was probably an experiment. So, sorry. I don't know much about the surrounding area."

Raylin swiveled her backpack around to her stomach to fish out some water. "Same. I only ever passed through on missions, and those were rarely to the same place in Babylon. Never stayed." She

took several swigs. "But, unless you're right at the rivers, everything is brown, dry, and lifeless. It's hard to get your bearings in the desert."

"Have you ever been on the Euphrates?" Daniel asked hopefully.

"A couple times, but not enough to know my way there from wherever we are."

The ramp stopped at a dead end, blocked by a boulder set in the wall. Daniel pushed against it with his shoulder and then, meeting only resistance, decided to scan the base. "I guess we'll have to risk the light of the Sun Sword for guidance once we're out of here, then. I'm guessing it's going to be risky." He pointed to the ground. "I don't see any keyholes for our weapons."

The others spread out around him, searching the area.

"I don't see anything either," Gabriela said. She put a hand on the boulder and gave a gentle shove. The whole thing shifted, sending a shower of sand down on Daniel's hair.

He fell into a fit of coughing and hurried backward as more fell to the ground from the ceiling. "A little warning, please."

Ben reached up and dusted off Daniel's head. "Your hair's a nice reddish color now. So pretty."

"Thanks. I'll keep that in mind the next time I go to the salon to get my roots done."

Gabriela studied the ceiling and gestured for everyone to move back. "I'm going to try to move the boulder without everything collapsing. If it does, stay back," she said to Daniel. "I can handle some rocks. The last thing we want is an injury."

"Roger," Daniel replied with a salute. "I do solemnly swear to remember that you have superhuman strength and do not need rescuing."

Gabriela laughed. "Glad to hear it."

Daniel relaxed. That was the first time she'd smiled at him since the debacle with Kon. Maybe she had forgiven him, and things could return to normal.

After making sure everyone was at a safe distance, Gabriela reached both arms around the boulder and casually lifted it. More

sand sprinkled down on her, but she ignored it and took a few steps back until the boulder was free of its resting place. Evening sunlight flooded in as she set the boulder to the side of the ramp.

Everyone cautiously approached the opening and peered into the vast desert stretching out before them. To the north and south, the land was a blight of dull red sand, devoid of any vegetation and dotted with broken rocks.

In the distance, a network of roads, lined with periodic lamp posts, stretched across the desert. A weary sun, reddish-orange in the dusty haze, languidly sat to their left. In the same direction and nearly out of sight, a portion of a metallic gray compound snuck around the rocks. It was evidently part of a larger building.

Grey and green tanks, each sporting a fifteen-foot gun from their turrets, patrolled the roads. Creeps, perched atop the lumbering war machines, growled or barked greetings as they passed one another. Hummers zoomed back and forth like worker bees, weaving around the trudging tanks on the highway, themselves no doubt piloted by black-eyed Creeps.

Dinosaur-like dragons, sixty feet tall and heavily armed with shining scales, stalked over the desert. Their long, needle-sharp claws dug into the sand and tossed up a dusty plume with each step. One long, straight horn grew between their eyes. Two more coiled upward above flopping ears, which hung limp like folded hand fans around the dragons' jaws. Their heads, triangular and grinning, swung side to side as the beasts patrolled the area with unblinking eyes. Tails as thick as pine trees jutted out behind them, whipping back and forth to provide balance and occasionally pounding the earth to leave slender craters in their wake.

Golden-crowned demons flew above the scene, each sporting four wings, mouths overflowing with ragged teeth, grasping talons dangling from hawkish feet, and one sand-brown serpent coiling around their torso. The snakes helped them scour the desert for any sign of threat, their heads bobbing between the demons' legs to peer down at the barren wasteland with vigilant interest. The demons'

iridescent red skin glistened in the setting sun, which barely hung on to the hazy horizon in the west.

Some other species of flying demons, smaller and covered in brightly colored feathers of green and yellow, darted through the air above the golden-crowned monsters. They sported only two wings, and their heads were bony and shaped like some bizarre combination of a lion and a bull, while their bodies were horse-like. Short, black tail feathers fanned out from their rumps, matching the black of their front and back legs. Their forepaws were almost human except for the jagged nails, while the hind legs appeared to belong to some sizeable bird of prey.

Toward the gently sloping horizon, just visible as it arced around their field of vision, an intricate pattern glowered on the sand in burning red script and interwoven lines. There was no doubt in Daniel's mind that it completely encircled the area, and he had a hunch they were at its very core.

"It looks like a seal. Only, I'd bet Ben's daggers it's not the Three's," Daniel muttered, scratching his chin. Once the Enemy had broken the Babylonian Seal, he likely placed his own mark on the land.

Ben elbowed him in the ribs. "Bet with your own stuff, but you're probably right."

The others studied it in solemn silence.

Wisps of eerie, gray haze seeped out of the desert along the glowing lines, floating up into the air. As they all marked their ascent, the sky changed before their eyes. Like a kaleidoscopic supernova, a scene of spiritual battle unraveled above them.

The expanse of the evening sky was a clash of spiritual beings. At first glance, the scene played out in extreme slow motion. Once Daniel focused on the details, however, it was as if someone pressed the play button on a movie, and the battle lapsed into real-time. Like a panoramic view of a war projected onto a screen, the actual battle between the Three and their Firstborn and the Serpent and his demons unfolded.

The Father's Mountain rose like a spire over the setting sun. The

brilliant light at the top rippled with power that cascaded down the peak in waves. Lines of resplendent Firstborn standing at the roots of the mountain gratefully received the overflow of luminescent energy. On the frontmost slope, the Son stood on a rocky outcrop above his armies below. He was arrayed in a gleaming robe of the purest white with a myriad of colors reflected and refracted in the air around it. A dazzling golden sash, rippling and undulating like a river, flowed from his right shoulder down to his hip. A halo of fire, wood, water, electricity, rocks, and visible wind whirled behind him like a symbol of authority, showing that all creation was at his disposal. His fiery white hair flowed around his head like a candle flame, standing in stark contrast to his dark, tan skin. Encapsulated within his face, Daniel found pure love intermingled with pure indignation and marveled that such seeming opposites could be so perfectly embodied in one being.

The Spirit, in the form of crackling blue fire shaped like a triangle within a circle, surrounded the Son's halo. Above them, in the beaming glory, Daniel felt the presence of the Father, shrouded from the world as though the very sight of him would unmake the universe.

The myriad of Firstborn crowding around the mountain fought directly with the demons, keeping the hordes of monstrous ranks at the borders of Babylon. However, one Firstborn towered like a giant above the others, his size rivaling the Serpent himself. Dark hair, outlined and permeated with an incandescent glow, fell thickly around broad shoulders. His eyes were torches boring into the Enemy. He wore armor of green and gold metal woven together in flexible plates. On his breastplate was an emblazoned insignia of three interlocking circles of emerald, each with a yellow flame in the center, and a halo of white fire rotated above and behind his body. In his right hand, he gripped a sword of black—not the ruinous pitch of the Voidblade, but a depthless, shining onyx. A shield of gold he held in his left hand.

"It's Michael," Gabriela whispered. "The Prince of the Holy City."

Daniel gawked in awe. "He looks like one tough dude. What's the Enemy going to do against *him*?"

Opposite them, the Serpent—titanic, red, and undulating all seven heads—coiled directly above E-Abzu. He was a mountain of ridges and horns and teeth as large as redwood trees. Five heads had eyes sealed shut, with tar-black human shapes stuck on his forehead between them. The other two heads snaked back and forth, constantly scanning the battlefield with venomous glee. The wisps of power seeping out of the land floated around him like a miasma of evil power. He mocked the holy armies with rumbling laughs and sent pulses of dark spirit into his minions on the front lines.

The force of darkness, a chaotic throng of every conceivable demonic conglomeration Daniel had encountered on their quests, seethed forward with renewed bravado. It was a mass of claws, wings, leering eyes, jeering, teeth-filled mouths, numerous animals possessed and distorted, and swelling storms of demonic spirit. More than anything, the army resembled a black sea of pollution, tossing to and fro with frenetic energy before crashing upon the bright shore of the Firstborn. The Serpent raised all seven heads and spat rivers of green fire toward the Father's Mountain.

The Son stood motionless as the hellish assault neared his front lines and dissipated harmlessly against a barrier, which materialized at the fire's approach.

Michael straightened and held out his sword. "You have no authority here," he proclaimed. His voice was thunder heralding a storm. He cleaved the air in front of him with his onyx sword, flinging an arc of black power toward the Serpent.

The Serpent's heads drew together and summoned a shield of their own—a spinning, red pentagram encircled by gray script. The arc of fire crashed into it, halted momentarily, and then cracked through the shield before slamming into the Enemy. He roared, convulsing and jolting as if Michael's power electrocuted him. Then, recovering and gathering himself, the dragon heads curled all seven lips. "Your power is miniscule!" he jeered triumphantly. "Even after all these millennia, I am still your senior. I will always remain above you! Babylon is mine. The earth is mine and all that is in it. Mine

to blight. Mine to destroy. Mine to free from the Three's hideous material life. All will be flame and spirit and rock again, and the Earthborn will have no soul for you to save! They will return to the dirt and grime of their creation."

"Your power dwindles," Michael replied matter-of-factly, unharried by the Enemy's words. "You have wrapped yourself and your followers in hell. You have gained nothing."

"But it is *MY* hell. Mine!" The Serpent roared in his seven-fold voice. "Mine and no other's!"

Daniel let his eyes fall back to the desert. As soon as he did, the battle resumed its glacial pace. It gradually dawned on him that the sky was dim and the sun had already fallen below the horizon. Everyone else, still absorbed in the scene unfolding above them, hadn't seemed to notice. "Guys? I think time sped up. Either that or I'm losing my mind."

One by one, each person pulled themselves away from the heavenly fight and took in Daniel's meaning.

"It's like we were pulled into a different stream of time," Daniel continued. "We must've been watching it for at least an hour."

Ben furtively glanced at the sky and took a step back into the shadows of the cave. "The Three must be on a different clock. If an hour went by that quickly, you could easily lose an entire day without realizing it!"

Raylin rubbed the back of her neck. "Memo to self, don't get sucked into the battle if I'm in a hurry."

Seren allowed herself one more hasty look. "I'm not sure where the Serpent is getting his bravado from. Seems like Michael handed his tail to him."

"Maybe he was Michael's superior once," Gabriela replied, "but I think he's lost power with each successive age and sealing."

"That's so like him," Ben said. "Delusional."

Seren leaned out of the opening and scanned the desert, then pulled herself back in. "When we were in the Abyss, didn't the Serpent mention something about erasing all life from the universe?"

"I think so," Raylin responded. "I seem to remember the twins and the Generals being surprised by that. I wonder if they really understand what he's doing?"

Ben joined Seren at the opening and craned his neck around to see more of the spiritual forces above and behind them. "I doubt it. Then again, they're all so twisted, maybe they want the same thing."

"Well," Seren continued, "I was just wondering if that's why the Enemy chose Babylon. I mean, it's already a barren wasteland, except for right at the river."

Gabriela shrugged. "I don't think it was always like this. In the beginning, this was a lush place. Remember, the Garden of Eden is near here. I think in the calamities that followed the Fall of the Earthborn, the land changed."

Seren opened her mouth to respond when a dragon's foot crashed down in front of her. They all remained frozen as the beast trudged past, thankfully unaware of the newly opened hole in the rock.

Gabriela touched Seren's shoulder guided her backward into the shadow of the ruins. Once out of the way, she gripped the boulder and silently put it back in its place to once again block the opening. "I think I'll shut this for now until we figure out what we're doing."

"That was too close," Raylin whispered. She gripped Seren's hand.

Daniel leaned his back against the boulder and slid down to its base. "Man, this is just like India. Wherever the towns are around here, I'm sure the people are freaking out with all this weird stuff walking around and playing out in the sky."

"You're assuming there is anyone left who is normal," Gabriela said, shifting the boulder a bit to ensure it was snug in its place, "which I doubt. This isn't the backwoods of some small Indian town like Khireshwar or the jungle hills around Aguas Calientes. Even in Cuzco, the Enemy still hides and disguises his servants. But here, it's a free-for-all. This is his territory now. Although"—she took off her knitted cap and tucked it under her arm so she could put her hair back up in a tighter ponytail—"it's possible any normal people in the city can't see *everything*. I mean, like the battle in the sky and all

the demons. Who knows? Maybe part of it is shielded from them or something."

Seren plopped down on the barren rock. "I think it would be best to wait until nightfall to leave."

"Agreed," Ben said, unzipping his backpack to rummage through the contents. "I'm going to see if I have any dry clothes to change into"—he pursed his lips and scowled pointedly at each person—"and then I'm going to take a nap. I'm exhausted, and I have a hunch we'll be dodging dragons and demons all night."

Everyone agreed that a nap sounded like a good idea, and once they had changed into dry clothes, the cave quietly echoed with their shallow, rhythmic breathing.

9

Dreams, Dragons, and Demons

Given the last dream with Kon and his obnoxious medallion, Daniel couldn't help but feel a little nervous about drifting into sleep, especially now that they were in the heart of the Enemy's territory. But, between the dark cool of the cave and the occasional watery noise from the pool, sleep came quickly.

He was pleasantly surprised to find a forest spreading out around him instead of a glut of demons and deserts.

A bright light shimmered through boughs of redwood, sequoia, and aspen, and moss and ferns thickly carpeted the ground. A sapphire blue sky stretched overhead, but the stars, moon, and sun all shone with equal brightness. To the east, another bright light illuminated the sky, but Daniel couldn't see its source. Somehow, despite its blazing fierceness, it didn't mute the celestial bodies. The sound of running water and people laughing drew his attention, and he ambled through the forest toward it. Everything around him felt safe and good.

Before long, he found himself looking over a shallow mountain creek. Amid the smooth rocks half-submerged in the gently flowing water, jumping fish, and a family of otters, a man and woman lazily waded in the shallows. Both wore robes of pure white that dragged in the water behind them, drifting around their legs in the current. He couldn't quite see their faces but found a host of other things to capture his interest anyway. A herd of elk knelt beside the water. Those closest to the creek lazily craned their necks over the bank for a drink without getting up. Nearby, bears sat in the current, happily splashing in the cool pools.

A mountain lion stalked a buck and pounced. The deer bellowed in delight, rather than pain, and rolled with the lion in the dust, each one jockeying for supremacy but neither harming the other. A few moments of uncertainty passed until the buck gained the upper hand by plopping down on top of the lion. The tawny cat, now on its back, accepted its position and reached up to lick the victor affectionately. After bugling in victory, the elk returned the friendliness with a kiss of his own. They reshuffled and then knelt side by side.

Daniel peered farther into the woods, his eyes drawn by the movements of other animals and people ambling through the shade: horses, birds, the biggest butterflies he had ever seen, maybe a giraffe or two, a colossal, plodding shape that could've been an elephant, a pack of wolves intermingled with a family of foxes, a skittering mob of raccoons, and dozens more creatures too concealed to identify. The myriad of animals intermingled at the bases of towering tree boles or rested in beds of fern, and most were attended by a man, woman, or child. But his curiosity pulled him back to the couple now sunbathing on one of the rocks in the middle of the water. They were still too far away for Daniel to clearly see their faces. The woman seemed more familiar than the man, but there was something about both that Daniel felt drawn to.

"Daniel," a soft voice behind him said.

Like an anchor pulling him into the waking world, Daniel felt himself drawn backward out of the forest. The scene faded, and he found himself once more in the cave.

"Daniel," Gabriela said again. "We need to get moving."

He sat up and rubbed his eyes in the glow of Gabriela's lights. Everyone else was already awake. Ben grumbled something under his breath while wringing water out of his socks. Seren shuffled her poncho around to make sure she could get her hands free. She practiced summoning the Celestial Bow several times before she

was satisfied the bulky clothing wouldn't hinder her movements. Raylin spun the Abyssal Staff, shifting it from hand to hand while it whirled expertly around her body. Gabriela, backpack on and hair tucked in her stocking cap, leaned against the boulder, waiting for everyone to be ready.

Daniel rummaged through his bag for a drink before joining her. "I had a dream," he said.

"Me too," she replied. "I was on the Father's Mountain while the battle with the Enemy carried on below me."

"I was in a forest with tons of animals and people. There was a man and a woman. They looked so familiar …" Daniel stared blankly into the darkness.

"Did you figure out who they were?"

Daniel shook his head.

Raylin approached. "The Spirit came to me in my dream. Told me not to fear our enemies and then something about being merciful. He kissed my forehead and left."

"He must've walked out of your dream and into mine," Seren laughed. "He said he had just seen you and that I didn't need to worry about your safety. Just to trust him."

"I had a dream, too," Ben joined in, his teeth clenched. "I was the Triune Shield floating at the bottom of a river. All of you were there inside me, enjoying the fish and the crocodiles swimming through the water while I floated you downstream until a monster ate us. It was muddy and gross and dreadful. Gee, I wonder where I got the inspiration for that dream from. So glad you all had lovely spiritual visions. Bunch of no good, dirty, rotten—"

"Okay!" Gabriela sang, turning to the boulder. "We all slept about three hours, so it should be good and dark now, if that even matters."

Daniel shrugged. "Didn't Inti say the Enemy would be aware of us the second we set foot out of here?"

"Yes, but that doesn't mean all the demons and Creeps will. And I don't think the Enemy will know our exact location, just that we're in Babylon. Janice's clothes on top of the darkness will hopefully give us enough cover to make it to the Euphrates."

"All right." Daniel turned to make sure everyone was prepared. "Are we a go?"

Seren and Ben stood at the ready. Raylin released the Abyssal Staff and grabbed her backpack.

"Good. No Weapons of Power unless we absolutely can't help it. We don't want to draw any unnecessary attention. Not to mention, if we exorcise something, and any part of its spirit gets back to the Enemy, he *will* be able to pinpoint where we were."

"True," Gabriela said, quietly pulling the boulder out of its resting place and setting it down to their left. The cold desert air rushed into the cave. "If there's a problem, let me and Ben handle it."

"Me?" Ben asked, his voice cracking in surprise. "Oh, right. My daggers. Of course. Yeah, I'll do what I can."

"If needed," Raylin added. "I can fight with my staff. Its summoning isn't that bright, and the staff itself doesn't glow like the other Weapons of Power."

Seren sucked in through her teeth. "I guess. That makes me nervous, though."

"I may be your little sister, but I'm not a little kid, Seren."

"I know, I know. I just don't want any monsters targeting you."

Gabriela patted them both on the shoulders. "We're all in this together. If a demon targets Raylin," she made a fist and popped her knuckles, "they'll get the rest of us."

"Just don't be reckless," Daniel added. "Only summon the staff if absolutely necessary."

"Got it," Raylin said with a curt nod.

A crescent moon glimmered through the heavenly battle scene to cast a ghostly sheen on the desert. A cacophony of noises punctuated the dark wasteland, but the only things they could see clearly were the well-lit road with its seemingly constant convoy of military vehicles and the spirit battle unfolding above them.

Daniel paused. "All of you stand in front of me to shield the light. I'm going to summon the Sun Sword for directions."

Once everyone was in position, Daniel summoned the sword

and braced his arms against the mouth of the cave while it floated in the air. After a moment of wavering, it pointed slightly northeast with a strong tug directly to their right. Daniel picked a large white star in the same direction as his bearing.

"We'll use the night sky to keep our direction straight," Daniel whispered, releasing the sword. "Let's go. Quietly now."

They all crept out of the cave.

A soft, yellow glow faintly illuminated their immediate area. In every direction, the unmistakable growl and bellow of dragons echoed over the rocky flat of the desert as they called back and forth to one another. A few of the beasts, dull gray and black in the night, lumbered nearby. Nothing in their behavior indicated they were aware of the companions flitting out of the cave and crouching next to neighboring boulders. The whites of everyone's eyes shone in the dimness, each alert and tense as a bowstring.

Once they moved out of the shadow of the rocky mound housing E-Abzu, the boulders disappeared, and there was no cover. Daniel kept fixed on the star, making sure that every few moments, he reoriented himself to its direction.

A few minutes passed, and E-Abzu was now several hundred yards behind them. Raylin scanned behind them. "So that's what's making the yellow light," she whispered.

Everyone turned. In the distance, behind E-Abzu, sat an imposing, triangular building of metal beams and glass faintly lit with points of lights outlined against the night sky. It was very much like a pyramid, only instead of straight, steep angles from top to bottom, Daniel could just make out distinct levels, each slightly smaller than the one preceding it, as the building stepped up into the sky. The top-most level was flat rather than culminating to a point. A portion of the structure trailed off toward the right in what looked like a series of long, squat warehouses. This was the part of the building Daniel had noticed when they peered out of E-Abzu earlier.

"I think I've seen something like that before," he said, scratching his head.

"In your history class, probably," Raylin said. "It's a ziggurat—a step pyramid. The Enemy loves those, though I'm not really sure why. He's opted for the more modern-looking skyscraper model than the old-fashioned bricks and stones. Didn't he make humans build one not long after they fell into sin? I don't remember the details of the story."

Seren joined in. "Something about languages and people groups being divided and placed under the dominion of certain Firstborn. Anyway, there's an older ziggurat not far from here that I used to visit on official 'Enemy' business."

"Oh?" Ben said with a cocked eyebrow and a low, thickly smug voice. "Official Enemy business, you say? How delightful it must've been to accompany Lord Soupy upon his errands."

Seren smirked. "Indeed. If you count drawing up plans for destroying mankind's hope in the Three as delightful."

Daniel tugged at his chin as he studied the building. "I'm pretty sure that's the headquarters for Ealim Wahid. At least, it looks like what I've seen on TV."

"I think you're right," Ben said, his voice small.

Gabriela whispered, "Enki must be super powerful to conceal E-Abzu from the Enemy. We were basically transported into their basement!"

Raylin pointed at the top of the pyramid. "Guys, something's happening."

A flash lit up the roof of the structure, and a bright fire flared up into a column of flames, throwing back the darkness and casting the building's shadow across the desert.

Roars and bellows shook the desert air, followed by the hurried thunder of the dragons galloping around them in the dark. Excited shrieks filled the sky, and stars, which still shone through the scenes of heavenly battle, periodically blinked out as shapes flew back and forth overhead. The hummers and tanks patrolling the road leading to Ealim Wahid groaned to a halt as if listening. Then, like horses darting out of their pens at a race, they zoomed off the road at full speed, each taking a different direction into the desert.

"And they're off!" Ben said. "The jig is up. Plan?"

Daniel broke into a run. "We keep following our bearings as quietly and quickly as we can!"

Everyone fell into step behind him. They steadily jogged along, hastily picking their way around small rocks dotting the desert's surface. A thundering gallop approached from behind, and everyone skidded to a halt.

Ben whipped out his daggers, but Daniel put his fingers to his lips and crouched down, motioning for the others to do the same. "Make sure Janice's poncho and cap are covering as much of you as possible. Maybe we can avoid notice."

Seconds after they had huddled together, one of the dragons ran up on their trail, sniffing the ground as it swung its head from side to side. A large, dark shape fluttered in the air above the beast, hissing and growling. Its orange eyes, big as headlights, glowed in the night air.

Daniel felt everyone tense, ready to spring into action if the demons got closer.

The smell was awful, like a dead animal left in the sun for days. A cloud of biting flies followed the monstrous duo and now buzzed around the companions.

"Find them. Kill them. Eat them," the demon flying in the air hissed. Its searching eyes scoured the desert while it obsessively repeated itself.

The flies made their way into every nook and cranny they could find within the folds of the ponchos, their sharp bites drawing an irresistible stinging itch that had to be scratched.

"I smell blood!" the flying demon shrieked gleefully. "But where? Where are they?"

The dragon now stomped ten feet from where the companions crouched, sniffing the air and snorting its rotten breath all over them.

Ben retched silently and held his hands tightly over his mouth.

"So close," hissed the demon overhead, now lowering its circle of flight around them. "But where? Where? Where?"

Daniel noticed a faint hunter-green light coming from within the folds of Raylin's poncho. She was readying herself to summon the Abyssal Staff. He reached over and gave her wrist a strong squeeze, drawing a sharp look of irritation from her. He shook his head and pushed her wrist down into the sand to hopefully shield any light from their assailants.

"I sense their power!" the flying demon wheezed with glee. "Close. Very close!"

The dragon bared its teeth as it took one uncertain step closer. Its toothy jaws were now only a few feet from Gabriela.

Father, please get us out of this situation! Daniel's mind screamed. Sweat beaded up on his brow and fell down his cheeks. Being discovered this early in their quest would be disastrous. They were already surrounded by enemy minions in the heart of Babylon. It would almost certainly lead to some, if not all, of them being captured. *Help!*

Glancing up at the heavenly scene, Daniel thought he noticed the Son's eyes on them. And did he imagine a wink? A moment later, loud bellows and shrieks in the direction of E-Abzu brought the dragon and the flying demon spinning around. With lightning reflexes, both tore away into the darkness toward the clamor, and the companions found themselves unexpectedly alone.

"I don't know what's happening, but let's go before we get pinned down again," Daniel suggested.

In answer, the rest jumped to their feet and raced toward the white star acting as their guide. The desert breeze, cold and gentle, soon helped to settle Daniel's nerves, but there was one thing still bothering him.

"Raylin," he whispered, falling back to be abreast with her and Seren.

"What's with you slamming my hand into the dirt?" Raylin shot back at him before he could say what was on his mind. "That hurt."

"What? I was … No, listen. I didn't mean to hurt you. I was trying to keep us from being noticed. You didn't need to summon—"

"We were already noticed," Raylin snapped. "In case you didn't realize it, we were pinned down and seconds from being attacked. I kept my hands under the poncho and got ready to summon the Abyssal Staff just in case."

"I know!" Daniel said a little louder than he intended.

Ben smacked his arm. "Shh!"

"I know that, too!" Daniel hissed. "Look, in moments like that, the best thing to do is pray for help. They started to sense our power. Didn't you hear the demon?"

"I'm aware, Daniel, and I was praying. I was also preparing to defend us. Next time you feel the need to give me direction, please don't shove any part of my body into the dirt."

"E-Abzu has been discovered!" a flying demon screeched as it streaked through the air directly above them. Two dragons followed close behind it, galloping at full speed with their tongues lolling out of their heads and fire leaking out of their maws like flames from a chimney.

A blob of dragon spit landed on Ben's face as the dragons thundered past on both sides.

"What is happening?" Ben whined, flailing his arms in the air to ward off any future attacks. He fumbled with the bottom of his poncho to wipe the sticky saliva out of his eyes. "Could we talk about group problems some other time and not when we're being assaulted by dragon snot?"

"Fine." Daniel rolled his eyes. "It's not like I meant to hurt her wrist or anything. Just trying to keep us alive."

"Same as me," Raylin replied. "Trying to protect us."

Seren and Gabriela both sighed in frustration but thankfully didn't join in the argument. The last thing Daniel needed was to have two more girls frustrated with him.

The group fell silent and continued their race. After half an hour of jogging, a new sight emerged from the horizon ahead: a line of dim lights outlining a structure of some kind. The features of the building were muddled by the darkness.

They raced on, following their guiding star straight toward the structure. Ten minutes later, a faint crunching, tapping noise began to register in Daniel's ears. It was fast, as if a dozen feet raced across the desert somewhere behind them and to their left. He studied the darkness, but nothing seemed out of the ordinary. Still running, he turned his head further around and noticed a myriad of dark shapes zipping through the air toward them, their silhouettes black and tiny against the flaming beacon upon the ziggurat. The scene was punctuated here and there by the waving dinosaur necks of the dragons, small as pencils, growing closer as they thundered toward the group. The enemy was on their trail.

"Daniel," Seren warned. "Stop."

The rest of the group slowed down while Daniel, still eyeing the horde's approach from behind, quickly passed them.

"What? Why? The demons are on our—"

Daniel could only figure he had crashed into a chain link fence by the sound and feel of it. He crumpled to the ground on his side, gingerly feeling the diamond-shaped pattern newly etched onto his face. "Ow," he moaned, raising his head to study the barrier. Some of the lights he had assumed to be on the structure still looming in the distance actually belonged to the fence, with one perched on each pole. The group gathered around him as he picked himself up. "A little more warning next time would be appreciated. I was distracted by them." He waved back toward the ziggurat and the approaching demons.

Raylin spun around to hastily scan their surroundings. "They must have our scent. No use standing around here and letting them catch up. Where to? Climb over the fence and make for the building?"

Daniel did his own survey. Beyond the barrier, the structure looked like a long line of storage units. Something like shipping containers, placed in stacks of two or three, cast impenetrable shadows throughout the yard within the fence. Hiding in there would, at best, do nothing more than delay their being caught.

Gabriela paced back and forth, studying the fence as if it held

some secret. "I don't think so," she finally said, drawing up in front of Raylin. "We're supposed to make it to the Euphrates. Maybe we go around and then keep following the star until we hit water."

More of the fast tapping, now to their right. And along with it, a husky, multi-layered wheezing as though a crowd of asthmatics played hide-and-seek in the desert.

"I don't like the sound of that," Ben muttered, pulling his poncho tighter around him.

"Me neither. Gabriela's plan sounds good," Seren agreed. "Mad dash to the Euphrates?"

"Seems about right," Daniel said, breaking into a sprint.

Keeping the compound to their right, they followed the fence as it wound its way around the buildings until they could get back on track.

"I smell water," Gabriela said, sniffing the air. "And it doesn't smell good."

"Blech!" Ben agreed. "Like sewage. Please tell me that's not the Euphrates."

Gabriela drew up next to him. "I doubt it. I don't hear any water flowing or see any trees."

Ben, now parallel with Daniel, glared at him. "So help me, if you or anyone tries to push me into *this* water, they're going with me. What do trees have to do with anything?"

"The Euphrates," Raylin explained, "is the only area around here where trees really grow. Since we're not seeing any, it must be something different. Maybe a drainage ditch or canal."

"Or a toilet," Daniel added. He was about to say something more when the tap-dancing asthmatics showed up again, this time behind them. "Whatever that is, it's definitely tailing us," he whispered. "Toilet or no, I imagine all water around here runs to the river."

Ben growled. "I *so* bet we have to travel by sewage in Babylon. That'd just be perfect, wouldn't it? And even so, it'd probably be better than all the other ways we've blasted around the world during other quests. Typical."

"To the toilet, then," Raylin joined in.

They followed their noses until the rocky ground gently sloped downward to a pale sliver of liquid moonlight running off straight toward their star. As if standing guard, scrubby shrubs flanked the banks of a narrow canal. Down at the water's edge, cloistered by a thicket draped with cloth, the warm glow of a dying campfire lit up a man's figure. He crouched over the coals for warmth and drew his rags closer about his frail frame.

Everyone skidded to a halt and silently studied the man. Excited cries haunted the desert from the direction of the fenced compound, and the ground rumbled with the distant approach of the dragons.

Ben nervously rocked back and forth from one foot to another. "Do we approach this guy or jump in the ditch or keep running or what? Someone please make a decision and quick."

Daniel shrugged. "Without the Sun Sword guiding us, who's to say?"

"Just use it," Gabriela said. "Our enemies already know where we are, and we need to decide fast."

A sharp crunching of sand, as if someone rhythmically stabbed the ground as they stalked nearby in the darkness, brought them all spinning around.

"I'll tell you," Raylin whispered, peering into the darkness, "whatever that is gives me a worse feeling than the dragons. It reminds me of the Nightstalker."

Ben shivered. "Oh, he was the worst! Daniel, do the thing."

"Shield me from behind," Daniel commanded and summoned the Sun Sword once everyone had formed a wall to shield the light as much as possible. The sword hovered in place until it pointed directly at the stranger, who went from huddling over his fire to jumping up in alarm at the flare of the Sun Sword.

Without another word, the companions dashed toward him.

"We're friends," Seren hastily reassured, holding up her hands in a show of peace. "We've been sent by the Three to fight the Serpent, and we're trailed by demons. Can you help us?"

"Shh!" Ben hissed, tugging wildly at her poncho. "Should you be blabbing all that before we figure anything out about this guy?"

"There's no time, Ben," Daniel said, releasing the Sun Sword to hopefully reassure the man they weren't a threat.

The man strode toward them with a marked limp as they approached his camp. He leaned on a crooked stick for support. A scraggly white beard splaying out from leathery, sun-worn skin was a perfect match for the roughly cut hair framing his dark eyes. "I know who you are. You just startled me, is all." His voice shook with age. "My name is Issar, and I've been sent to help you. Take my boat and go. Now." He pointed a crooked and wrinkled finger down at the canal.

Daniel gave a cautious glance down to the water where a long rowboat floated, moored to a scraggly bush. A tarp draped lazily over the gunwale, with one corner sunk below the murky water.

The group hesitated, which seemed to agitate Issar.

Raylin narrowed her eyes. "How do you know—"

"The Father sent me a dream that you'd find me, need my help, and that demons would be chasing you. Please, take the boat and go," he pleaded.

"Okay, okay. We understand," Gabriela replied, her voice a mix of hurry and caution. "What about you, though? Are you supposed to come with us?"

Issar returned her question with an eerie gaze. "My family is all gone. Wife, children, grandchildren. They're all gone. All because we follow God. The persecution has been terrible, and few of us are left in this land. Most of my friends have been captured and taken to the tower"—he gave a shuddering glance back toward Ealim Wahid's ziggurat, whose blazing searchlight still dogged the horizon—"or have fled." His voice grew quieter until little more than a whisper. "But my family are all gone to the Three in Heaven. I wait here only to fulfill this one last duty, and then I'll be taken home with them."

Seren and Raylin reached out and held one another's hand. Issar's tale of loneliness and death clearly drew up unpleasant memories

of either their time in the Enemy's service persecuting others, their own experiences losing family, or most likely both.

Gabriela listened, nodding resolutely as though she had accepted his declaration of impending doom.

Daniel marked their responses, still uncertain of how he felt or what they were supposed to do. *Father, should we save this man? Surely, you mean for us to take him with us.*

He waited. His only response was Issar's ragged and desperate breathing.

"That's awful," Ben muttered. "Come with us. We'll protect you, and you can—"

The sand erupted behind them, showering them in a cloud of dust and pebbles. A huge figure emerged from the cracked ground and stalked into the dim firelight.

Daniel, Raylin, and Seren all summoned their Weapons of Power; Ben's body gave off a ghostly blue glow.

The added light brought their assailant into focus. It appeared to be a ten-legged insect halfway between a spider and a scorpion. Two pairs of oversized fangs—two on the top and two on the bottom of its mouth—quivered in the air, attached to its head with bristled, bulbous appendages. It stretched them open as if showing off. They were more horrifying than Daniel had originally thought. Instead of spider fangs, they were shiny, black, razor-jagged pincers. The sickly-yellow body was heavily bristled and segmented like a scorpion's, though it thankfully lacked the stinging tail. And, where a scorpion's abdomen might have been flatter, its was rounded like a spider's. Two beady eyes glinted in the light of the weapons, but beneath them, directly between the fangs, a human-like face leered.

"Camel spider demons." Issar shuddered. He took a halting step back. "Flee. You must flee!"

"It's just one," Daniel said, raising the blazing sword and preparing a Sunstorm. "It's okay. We'll protect you."

He felt Gabriela's strong hand come down on his shoulder.

"Look," she whispered, pointing beyond it in the darkness.

Daniel peered into the desert beyond the demon. A dozen sets of eyes reflected the light of the Sun Sword at him. They crept forward, their myriad feet tapping the desert sand with every cautious, crunching step toward their prey. Each gave off the asthmatic wheeze he'd been hearing since running into the fence. They hissed and sputtered as if needing a puff from a giant inhaler.

Gabriela pulled him back. "If you all fight here, we'll be surrounded in seconds. Not to mention, the dragons and flying demons will soon arrive. You all run. I'll distract them and meet you where the canal ends. Go! And take Issar with you!"

Gabriela yanked Daniel backward and then leapt onto the nearest demon, punching it into the ground with such force that a crater formed. The demon's human face gasped in surprise, its eyes bulging as Gabriela deftly snatched it up by the leg and used its body to pummel the other demons now hungrily joining the fray.

Against every fiber of his being, Daniel spun around and motioned for the others to follow him to the boat. Ben reached out to grab Issar, but the old man shook off his grip and ran into the battle with surprising speed.

"Flee," Issar repeated matter-of-factly, whacking the nearest demon with his stick as he darted by.

Gabriela had torn through the mass of leggy monsters, pounding and tossing one, kicking another, breaking off fangs here, and hurling them at a demon there. Most zeroed in on her as the prime threat, and any who edged toward Daniel and the others found themselves hastily squashed.

Issar wound his way through the limping and wheezing demons, slipping from view into the very middle of the horde as he worked his way toward her.

"Issar!" Daniel and Ben shouted in unison, but it was too late. The only way of catching him would be to join in the fight, and the air was already alive with the excited cries of the flying demons, wheeling like furies toward the skirmish. If Daniel and the others didn't flee now, they'd be spotted and encircled.

Take the boat and go.

All four Vessels snapped to attention, and Daniel knew the message hadn't been for him alone.

Flee to the Euphrates and await Gabriela there.

Daniel pivoted to follow Raylin and Seren, with Ben close on their heels. At the very least, the Three's order reassured him that Gabriela would be fine. *But, Father, what about Issar?*

He is my child. I will care for him.

They slid down the bank, and the others piled into the boat. Daniel shoved it out into the canal and jumped in, getting tangled in the tarp as he did.

"Throw that into the canal and grab a paddle!" Daniel said, shoving the tarp off him and feeling around the bottom of the boat. "Where are they?"

"I don't feel any," Raylin replied, balancing in the rocking boat, now drifting toward the opposite bank. She held the tarp in her hands and studied it.

"What should we use?" Seren asked, throwing her hands in the air. "Wait. Raylin, summon the Abyssal Staff. If we stay near the bank where it's shallow, you could push us along."

Ben snapped his fingers. "Like those guys in the boats in Venice. A granola!"

"Gondoliers," Raylin corrected.

"Just what I said."

"That's a good idea," Daniel said to Seren. "Raylin, summon ... would you get rid of that dumb tarp and summon the staff already? We're in a hurry."

The water rippled with the rumble of the approaching dragons.

Raylin returned Daniel's comment with a sigh. "I've got a better idea. The Sun Sword pulls you when you summon it for direction. Use it to pull the boat."

"We'd be spotted the second it appeared!"

"Not if we're covered by the tarp. We could coast along quieter and faster than if I was pushing us through the water."

Daniel felt a twinge of irritation. "I guess," he muttered.

"She's right," Ben added. "Everyone, grab the tarp."

A scream split the air behind them, and everyone tensed. The darkness writhed with hulking shapes and darting figures, but nothing was clear. The thundering of the dragons was now almost upon them, and Daniel thought he could make out flapping wings amid the melee with the camel spider demons. Daniel put a foot on the edge of the boat and leaned forward, debating within himself whether to return to help or flee.

Seren caught him before he could make a move. "She'll be fine. We need to get out of here and now. If they get any closer, they'll pick up on the Sun Sword's power. Raylin, Ben, the tarp. Daniel, the Sun Sword!"

Daniel reluctantly sat down at the bottom of the boat, feet braced against the bow. Once the tarp had covered the gunwale, he summoned the Sun Sword, careful it didn't pierce the prow. The boat coasted away from the bank and was soon skimming down the middle of the canal at a steady pace.

"Issar's hut just got destroyed," Raylin whispered.

Daniel craned his neck around and saw her peeking out from beneath the tarp.

"Torn apart by those flying demons and then blasted on fire by one of the dragons. Seems we were seconds from getting caught."

Daniel gritted his teeth. "Well, *sorry*, I was worried about Gabriela and Issar. I can't just shut off my feelings." He wasn't sure if Raylin even heard him, but he didn't care. He was more worried about what was happening behind them. He lapsed into a stream-of-consciousness prayer.

Fervent as he was, though, he couldn't help but feel his prayers were bouncing off the tarp and right back into his own head. It was almost like the Three weren't listening or maybe weren't receiving his prayers. But that was nothing new. There'd been plenty of times in past quests that he felt they weren't listening, even though they always were.

"Any sign of pursuit?" Seren asked, her face aglow with the orange light of the Sun Sword.

Raylin shifted her angle. "Not that I can see. Sky looks clear—you know, other than the battle in the heavens. I don't see anything pursuing us on land."

Ben leaned back and sighed in relief. "Gabriela must be drawing them away. How can she fight all of them at once?"

"She doesn't have to," Daniel replied with more certainty than he felt. "She just needs to lead them on a wild goose chase. Hopefully, Janice's clothes do the trick, and she can disappear when the time is right."

The group fell into an uneasy silence for the next hour, the only noise being the smooth wake of their boat rippling against the banks of the narrow canal. After a while, Daniel noticed the absence of other noises. There were no birds, frogs, or insects, which he figured would be abundant on the tangled banks of the canal, if nowhere else. It was as if all of nature had either left the area or was in hiding.

The sound of rushing water soon reached them, and before long, the Sun Sword angled to the right, guiding the boat in a tight arc toward the nearest bank and into the low-hanging boughs of a tree. Once they had stopped altogether, the sword turned up on its end.

Daniel released the sword and joined everyone else to peek out from beneath the tarp. They had reached a river, fast-flowing and broad enough to be the Euphrates. A tangle of buildings, illuminated by unorganized clusters of lights and streetlamps, spanned the far shoreline about fifty yards away. The flat rooflines were broken by silhouettes of the occasional tall palm tree. The features of the nearby bank were blocked by the brush concealing them, but Daniel noticed the absence of lights and wondered if it was farmland or maybe an uninhabited flood zone.

Ben shuffled around next to Daniel, and the tight quarters of the boat were gently filled with the blue glow of the Triune Shield around Ben's daggers. "What now?" he asked, trying to stretch his legs. "Can we get out and walk around a bit? I'm starting to cramp."

"Fancy being spotted by a demon?" Seren asked. She let the tarp close and slid down, her back against the gunwale.

"No, but we can't stay in here forever. Besides, I need to … you know."

"Ah. I see. Well, I suppose if that's the case, then go ahead." Daniel snorted. "Yeah, we wouldn't want the Orbs of Seeing all locking in on you."

In any case, he could use a break as well. They just needed to be careful that they weren't discovered and forced to leave the area before Gabriela could locate them.

"Oh yeah, that was hilarious," Ben retorted, deadpan. "Gabriela fixed the Orbs, remember?"

"Okay," Raylin whispered, clearly confused. "I'm not sure I want to know more about this. Is this something I need to know?"

Seren sighed. "They're just being boys. It was nothing. The Orb of Seeing his parents had on the last quest was too sensitive and let them see through the eyes of whoever was in 'need.' And Ben *needed* to pee. But the Orbs don't do that anymore."

"Gotcha. Well, we *need* to be careful," Raylin urged, still keeping vigil from beneath the tarp and ignoring the conversation. "If something or someone spots us, we'd have to move, and that'd be a problem for Gabriela to meet back up with us."

"I agree," Daniel hastily added. "I was just going to say that, actually."

"Lady's first?" Ben said, squirming.

"Sure," Seren replied, giving the area one more scan before sticking her head out from beneath the tarp.

She and Raylin tossed their legs over the side of the boat and carefully navigated the muddy banks of the Euphrates before disappearing into the gloom.

After everyone had taken their turn, they slid back beneath the tarp to wait. Minutes passed into an hour and beyond. All the while, the river lapped against the banks like a monotonous lullaby, leading Daniel into a sleepy stupor. He could tell by their breathing that the

others had already succumbed, so he needed to stay awake to keep guard. The last thing he remembered was a cool breeze finding its way through the opening beneath the tarp.

10

A Scenic River Cruise

Somehow, Daniel knew he wasn't far from the mountain stream he had visited in his last dream, even though he was surrounded by a boundless forest and there was no sight of the stream anywhere. He felt he was in a Holy Place; the very air around him vibrated with the Three's power. Here, the trees were all hardwoods: towering ash, sprawling oaks and beech, massive magnolias surrounded by ancient hornbeams and poplar. A myriad of other species grew there, too, though Daniel had no name for them. Their trunks soared into the canopy like pillars in some great hall, and each bore a word in a strange script engraved upon its base.

Daniel waited for the meaning to become clear, but no understanding came. It was as though the trees themselves wanted to keep it secret. There was a strong feeling of being watched, and he intuitively knew the forest was very alive and very alert. A dim, golden light softly illuminated the wood. Birds rustled in the branches, occasionally calling out to one another in haunting voices. Strange insects, glowing and leggy, with wings like dragonflies and long, segmented bodies, floated on the breeze, happily dancing about the trunks. In the distance, just visible between the foliage, a small knoll rose to half the height of the trees. It was overshadowed by their boughs, which were so thick throughout the wood that Daniel couldn't glimpse the sky.

A cry of happiness joined the birdsong. There was a flash of movement on the knoll, and Daniel felt himself drawn toward it. His barefoot steps fell silent in the soft moss that carpeted the forest like a green, feathery sponge. He rounded the last giant tree. At the apex of the hill, a group of people laughed and cried as they hugged one another under the green canopy, breaking away for only brief moments to exchange some comments before embracing once again. The group, originally only three or four people, grew with each moment as more crested the hill from the opposite side.

The man looked familiar, and there was something in his voice Daniel recognized. He couldn't place his name, though. The others, a mixture of men and women, children and adults, Daniel certainly didn't know.

A stick cracked toward Daniel's left, and giggling whispers, mixed with the gentle clapping of leaves, floated on the breeze. He whirled around, glimpsing a man and woman peeking from behind one of the enormous trees. It was the same couple from his earlier dream of the creek. Before he could even think to say something, they laughed and fled, waving, into the shadows, their soft footsteps somehow loudly reverberating through the woods.

Footsteps. A hand on his shoulder. A voice.

"Daniel."

The vision faded, each tree melting into the leafy gloaming—a watercolor of greens and browns, laughter, and warm light—until the scene dimmed into darkness.

"Daniel, wake up."

He touched the hand on his shoulder. "Gabriela?"

He pulled himself into a seated position. The others still slept. She leaned over the gunwale, gently shaking him awake.

"I'm back." Her voice was sad and quiet.

"Is everything okay?"

Their conversation roused Ben with a start. He sat bolt upright, which rocked the boat, disturbing Raylin and Seren.

"Gabriela's found us," Daniel whispered.

"What happened?" Seren asked, groggily staring around. "Where's Issar?"

Gabriela shook her head. "The demons got him almost as soon as he ran into the fight. He was no match for them."

"That's awful," Ben muttered. "We did hear a scream, but we hoped for the best."

"I don't get it," Daniel said, shaking his head. "The Father said he'd take care of Issar. I know I heard him say that."

Everyone sat in silence. Daniel pictured the old man recounting the loss of his family, his story a testament to the hopelessness he felt in the material world and his longing for what was to come. Issar was basically a stranger, but he'd given his life to help them.

Daniel's dream trickled back into his consciousness. The man, a stranger but somehow familiar, reunited with his family in bliss—it was Issar. The full realization set in. Yes, Issar had died, but now he was given new life away from the strife and horror wreaked by the Enemy and his servants. The Father had taken care of him, just not in the way Daniel had prayed for. He shared the details of the dream. Gabriela didn't seem surprised, while the others, like Daniel had, took the revelation with an evident mixture of acceptance and grief. But, for him at least, those feelings were fleeting, pushed out by the imminence of their own danger.

Overhead, the spiritual armies remained locked in combat, their movements set to some cosmically slow pace.

Ben interrupted the silence. "What did you do after we left?"

Gabriela stretched her arms over her head and yawned. "I pounded some demons into the ground and kicked them around. Once I got all their attention on me, I double-backed to the fenced buildings we saw earlier, let them chase me for a while, and then lost them. These clothes came in handy. I followed our same path back to the canal so I wouldn't lay down a new trail for them to follow." She shrugged. "It won't be long before they figure it out, though. We should get moving."

"You must be exhausted," Seren said. "Hop in. We'll make room for you. Ben, move closer to Daniel."

Daniel smacked Ben's legs before he had a chance to obey. "Ben can scoot back. There's enough room for Gabriela right here." He patted the bottom of the boat behind him.

Ben slapped Daniel's hand. "Hey man, didn't Barth ever teach you to keep your hands to …" He cast a hasty glance at Raylin and slid backward until he pressed up against her knees. "Yeah, Gabriela, you must be exhausted. Take my seat."

"Boys," Seren sighed, holding her head in her hands.

Raylin shrugged at Seren, pulling her knees closer to her chest.

Gabriela climbed in and leaned against the side of the boat. "I'm just glad to sit anywhere." She searched the shadows of the boat. "Hand me a paddle or something. I'm not too tired to help."

"There's no need," Daniel explained. "The Sun Sword pulls us quicker than we can paddle."

"Won't the bright light make us a target?"

"Tarp," Seren replied, sliding it forward for each person to grab.

Before covering himself, Daniel stood and hooked a leg over the railing to shove them off the bank and farther into the current. Once he was sure they were far enough away from the branches to avoid being snagged, he pulled the tarp over himself.

"Fantastic," Gabriela sighed, "because I may not be too tired to help, but I'd sure love a nap."

Daniel summoned the Sun Sword and braced himself against the front of the boat as it pulled them forward.

Before long, the boat was filled with the rhythmic breathing of four sleepers. Daniel was glad for his earlier naps; otherwise, he'd have drifted off to sleep as well. As it was, the strain of maintaining the Sun Sword was just enough to keep him alert.

Daniel's reflections, like the boat, drifted over the next hour down a winding path. The two dreams from that evening played out in his mind. Issar's reunion with his family made sense, but who were the man and the woman he saw in both? Why did they keep showing up? On the other quests, he'd always had dreams and visions for a specific reason, and those reasons were usually self-evident. The

vision of Kon and Inti fighting was obviously to prepare him and the other Vessels for the battle. The dream of Coricancha had been to give him direction. The shared dream he and Ben had of the Father's Mountain was intended for comfort and guidance. But these were different. He was simply a spectator.

Father, am I supposed to be figuring something out? Will these dreams help us somehow?

Daniel paused, hoping a reply would be quick in coming. He let his mind go quiet, listening to the gentle swish of water on the bow of the boat as they pushed through the current. Then, just when he was about to lapse back into prayer, an answer trickled into his mind.

Store these scenes in your heart. Let go of your resentment. Forgive, that you might defeat the Enemy.

Resentment? What resentment?

The Sun Sword pulsed, and where the tip would have connected to the rest of the blade, a line of electricity crackled along its edge. He didn't understand.

Does the missing tip have something to do with my dreams? I'm confused.

The answers will come in time. Search your heart and let go of your resentment. Obey this, and more will be revealed when the time is right.

The words faded softly away, leaving Daniel even more perplexed. How were all these things connected? Did he resent someone in his dream? What did forgiving have to do with fighting the Enemy? In India, he and Ben had been angry with each other, but it certainly didn't prevent him from battling. His heart felt heavy with uncertainty.

Daniel craned his neck around. Everyone else was asleep, slumped over in various uncomfortable and cramped positions. The flickering glow of the Sun Sword cast dancing shadows on their faces. He wondered if the Three were sending them dreams as well.

The boat hit something in the water and jolted up and down, startling the others awake.

"What was that?" Ben hissed, breathless, as he fumbled for his knives. "We hit a deer or something?"

Daniel maintained the Sun Sword, allowing it to continue pulling the boat as he inspected the bottom for leaks. Everything looked okay. He shook his head. "Don't know. Could've been a log in the water."

Seren cleared her throat. "Do you think we should get to the bank and—"

The boat hit something again. This time, the jolt was so rough that the little craft stopped its forward momentum and listed dangerously to the left. Water spilled over the gunwale for a terrifying second before they righted, bobbing back and forth, and continued their trajectory downriver.

Everyone breathed a collective sigh of relief.

Raylin shifted to her knees, her palms glowing with the green light of the Abyssal Staff. "I don't think that was a log."

"Could've been a rock," Daniel offered. "Or maybe we're just really shallow and drifted into a sandbar."

Something splashed and swished in the water off their port side, noisily swimming alongside them before falling silent.

"Definitely not a sandbar," Seren whispered, peering from beneath the tarp. "Something moved in the water and just dove beneath us. Suggestions?"

Gabriela leaned forward. "The Sun Sword isn't changing directions, so we clearly need to continue downstream. Maybe we could paddle toward the bank with our hands and follow the river where it's shallower and safer."

Ben shook his head. "You want us to stick our hands into the water where some animal—or, let's be realistic, murderous demon—is probably waiting to attack us?"

"We might not have a choice," Daniel replied. "At least we wouldn't be sitting ducks trying to fight in the middle of a river."

Something tapped the bottom of the boat, rapping it directly beneath Daniel. The craft was lifted out of the water briefly and then plopped back down with a splash. Everyone braced their backs and feet against the boat, their eyes wide and alert.

"I don't like this!" Ben hissed. "How do we fight in water?"

Daniel picked his fingernails as his mind raced to come up with an answer. "If we're knocked out of the boat, everyone swim toward the left bank. There seemed to be more buildings on that side when we looked earlier. Easier for us to hide."

"Do we summon our weapons?" Raylin asked.

"Only if necessary. Ben, you bring up the rear. If something's after us, you can summon the Triune Shield and block its attacks."

"Or envelop us if there's no hope of out-swimming this thing," Gabriela said. "I'll take the lead. Everyone can grab onto me. I'm assuming I'll be the fastest swimmer."

Daniel and the others lurched forward as the boat suddenly stopped in its tracks.

"That's probably a safe bet," Ben said, his voice a husky whisper. "And yeah, I'd love to purposefully take up the rear while we're fleeing. This'll be so fun."

"Children," a wet, guttural voice gurgled outside the boat. "I sense your power. I hear your voices. I smell your fear." Loud, gargling laughter vibrated the air. "It is delicious to me." A tentacle, dark in the shadows at the back of the boat, slid beneath the tarp and pulled it into the murky water. "I do not want to share you with other demons. Let us agree that I, alone, will destroy and consume you. No screaming or fighting, yes?"

A dozen slithering tentacles snaked their way up the sides of the boat and into the light of the Sun Sword. Each sported a single, bony claw on the end, with barbs sticking out at random along the shaft. They sank into the rickety wood of the gunwale and tightened. The boat's joints creaked dangerously. Another searching appendage found Ben and slithered delicately around his shoulders as if tasting his clothes. With surprising dexterity, it hooked one of the stitches and yanked the poncho and stocking cap off Ben.

"Give those back!" Ben shouted, fumbling with his daggers. But it was too late; the tentacle was already beyond his reach.

"Ah. This is what shields you from my eyes. Disgusting. A garment drenched in prayers to conceal and protect. It tastes like they were

muttered by"—the voice mumbled and mused to itself—"a frail and lonely woman." The garments were pulled swiftly under the black water with barely a noise.

Raylin stood, her glowing palms together. In one fluid motion, she drew them apart, summoning the Abyssal Staff. "I don't plan on waiting for this thing to attack."

"Wait, Raylin!" Seren said, shifting to her knees and summoning the Celestial Bow. "Let me bind him before he retreats underwater!"

But it was too late; Raylin had already launched into a series of deft, lightning-fast jabs with the head of the staff, jabbing the tentacles where each gripped the boat.

"Impertinent girl!" the demon gurgled, releasing the boat and pulling its arms back into the frothing water.

The river went eerily silent, and the boat resumed its path down the river, pulled by the Sun Sword's power.

"Raylin," Daniel said, irritation tingeing his voice, "Seren had a point. Now we don't know where this thing is going to attack us from."

"Sorry," Raylin said, still standing in the back of the boat. "It was about to tear the boat apart."

"Ben, summon the shield," Daniel ordered. "We can't hide our power now anyway. We might as well protect the boat and keep floating as long as we can."

Ben nodded, his body glowing blue.

"That will not do," the watery voice said from beneath the boat.

The river erupted around them. The little craft launched into the air, jettisoning everyone into the water before they could land an attack. Dozens more tentacles wrapped around the boat, ripping into the wood and tearing it to pieces.

Daniel maintained the Sun Sword even as he plunged beneath the foaming black of the Euphrates. The light of the sword illuminated the water and the demon directly below him. Its long, sleek body sported shark-like fins, a crocodile tail, a mess of tentacles surrounding the likely location of its mouth, and a circle of glinting eyes crowning what looked like some fish's head. Daniel didn't know if it would

work underwater, but he attempted a Sunstorm. The demon, looking in every direction at once, zeroed in on Daniel swinging the blazing Sun Sword sluggishly through the water. With a powerful flick of its tail, the creature slid through the murk, easily evading the lethargic arc of fire. The Sunstorm spun, end over end, until it exploded into the river bottom twenty feet below.

The white light of Celestial Arrows, all encircled with brilliant rings, streamed through the water at half their normal speed. The demon laughed, once more slipping through the water with lightning dexterity to easily dodge them.

Daniel scanned the water above him and swam toward the luminous limbs of the Celestial Bow. He broke the surface and gasped for air. Everyone was scattered in the middle of the river, flailing to get their bearings in the darkness. Raylin and Seren struggled to swim while maintaining their weapons. Ben still glowed but hadn't summoned the Triune Shield, no doubt waiting for the group to make for the bank so he could take up his position at the rear.

"Swim for the shore!" Gabriela shouted. "It's useless fighting this thing in the water!"

"Thing?" the demon bubbled from beneath the water. It surfaced amidst the group with a rush of water that pushed Daniel and Raylin toward the left bank and the others toward the right. "I am the god Enbilulu!" the demon roared. "Ancient. Powerful. Worshiped and feared by you insignificant humans throughout millennia. You are nothing!"

Raylin swung the Abyssal Staff with all her might, but without footing, it glanced harmlessly off the demon's hide.

"You see?" the demon gloated. "Your power is nothing. You are nothing." Three tentacles quickly wrapped around her, pinning the staff and her arms around her body.

Now that most of the creature's body was above the water, Daniel flung a Sunstorm with its usual speed. Before the demon could drag her underwater, the arc severed the tentacles with a pop.

Enbilulu roared as wisps of dark spirit disappeared into the

darkness, fleeing too quickly for Raylin to capture with the Abyssal Staff. The Enemy would undoubtedly know their exact location in a matter of minutes, but Daniel didn't care about that now. Getting to the bank without drowning was his top priority. He reached out and grabbed Raylin's arm, yanking her toward him.

"Thanks!" she coughed.

"Swim!" he shouted. "I'll cover you!"

There was a commotion and bright flashes of light from the opposite side of the demon's body.

"Fleeing so soon?" Enbilulu bubbled, its crown of eyes glinting at Daniel and Raylin. "You will not leave my … domain … alive."

The demon grunted out its last words with effort as the blue encasing of Seren's Celestial Arrows crept over its body from the other side.

"How … dare … you!" Enbilulu gasped, straining against the binding. "I … will—GAH!"

A heavy thud reverberated through the water, and Enbilulu violently lurched to the side. Gabriela had no doubt followed Seren's attacks with a bone-shattering blow, leaving a perfect opening.

Daniel raised the Sun Sword for a Fire Strike, then plunged it into the water. The purifying power radiated across the surface toward the demon.

"I will never succumb to your power!" Enbilulu roared. Its lower half not yet covered with the Celestial binding, the demon gave a powerful flick of its tail. It rushed forward in the water and disappeared below the surface before the power of the Sun Sword could reach it.

"Now's our chance!" Ben shouted. "Everybody, get to the bank!"

Seren, Gabriela, and Ben swam toward Daniel and Raylin, but before they could go more than a few yards, the river reverberated with a sound like breaking glass, and a myriad of blue lights flared beneath the water.

"Oh, no!" Seren gasped. "I think he's broken my binding!"

The river seethed into a roiling maelstrom of tentacles and fins as Enbilulu breached the surface, separating Daniel and Raylin from the group again.

Daniel flung Sunstorms as quickly as he could, but the demon protected his main body by intercepting them with a tentacle, sacrificing one after the other.

"I have hundreds to spare, but you—you will perish in the depths of my kingdom!" it gurgled furiously.

The sky back toward the desert crackled with green lightning, and a noise like a flock of flying demons reached the river. Daniel glanced up long enough to see a poisonous-looking cloud streaming toward the battle. His heart sank. They were already helpless in the water. Once Vinaash showed up with her Pestilence, it would be game over.

"We've got Vinaash coming in hot!" he shouted.

"You are *my* prey," Enbilulu growled. "I will not allow that human upstart to have you."

"Vinaash! Enbi-woo-woo! Dragons! Camel spiders!" Ben yelled from the other side of the demon. "This is so stupid. Look, just come rescue me when you get a chance, okay?"

Seren's confused voice called out over the chaos. "Ben! What are you doing?"

In a split second, the Triune Shield expanded around Enbilulu, and the demon's body began sinking under the frothing water.

"What have you done?" it shrieked. "Release me! Release me this moment! Ahh! This feels so pure and holy. I feel sick!"

"If you throw up inside of me," Ben's voice thundered ominously. "I swear. I don't know what I'll do, but it'll be unpleasant."

Only the top of the Triune Shield remained above the surface. "Apparently, I'll be at the bottom of the river for a while. I'll try to figure out something. Just come and rescue me once Vinaash is gone."

"How are we going to do that?" Daniel demanded. "If you release Enbilulu, he'll attack you. You'll have to stay down there with him!"

"I know!" Ben's voice was desperate. "But what choice do we have?"

A Bolt of Pestilence zinged through the air not half a mile from the river, turning a building to ash seemingly at random.

"Just get out of here and hide. I'll keep Mr. Enbidoodoo under control so you all can get to the bank."

"Enbidoodoo?" Enbilulu raged. "How dare—"

And then they were gone under the murky gloom of the Euphrates. Within seconds, the blue glow of the Triune Shield faded in the depths, and the only noise was the rumble of Vinaash's approach.

"Daniel, Raylin!" Gabriela shouted; she and Seren had already washed to the opposite bank by Enbilulu's thrashing. "There's no time for us to make it over there. We'll hide on this side. You guys get to your bank and disappear into the city. Meet up downriver. There's bound to be a bridge. Hurry!"

She and Seren were already trudging through the mud and quickly disappeared into the brush.

An arc of Pestilence struck a lone palm tree on their bank. Against the heavenly battle scene in the sky, Daniel saw its silhouette crumble to ash. There was no time to waver. One bolt into the water would no doubt radiate out to everything in the river, including him and Raylin.

"Let's go!" Raylin hissed, releasing the Abyssal Staff and swimming through the water.

Daniel allowed the Sun Sword to return to his chest and followed, swimming with all his might toward the shore. Perfect. Gabriela and Seren were on their own. His only ally was Raylin. If Daniel's communication blunders during this quest were any indication, she wasn't exactly the best person he could've been partnered with for a battle. And Ben was stuck imprisoning Enbidoodoo at the bottom of the Euphrates.

Father, I don't suppose you could send the Spirit to help us?

Daniel pulled himself out of the water and followed Raylin up the muddy bank and into a narrow alleyway between two buildings. He glanced up at the heavenly battle. The war continued to unfold— glacially slow and silent.

11

Psychopaths, a Wolf, and Quills—Oh My!

Vinaash flew over the rows of houses and buildings, her vomit cloud crackling with angry Pestilence. "Come out, little Vessels!" Her jeering echoed within the city. "You've faced me before; certainly, you're not afraid."

Daniel and Raylin lay flat beneath an abandoned military hummer, hoping Vinaash would eventually move on and they could begin their search for a bridge to cross the wide Euphrates.

"I sense you," Vinaash muttered, irritation evident even through her thick Indian accent. "But it is as Tyr said. Your clothing shields your presence, if only a little. Interesting."

Daniel could only catch glimpses of her from their hiding place, but he could tell her appearance hadn't changed much since their last encounter in the Serpent's Abyss: long, dark hair, green lightning gracefully arcing over her shoulders and head, a red, ankle-length sari dress, its edges embroidered with some intricate, metallic design.

An arc of Pestilence zinged through the air and nailed the front of a brick building. The building turned ashen white and crumbled inward, revealing a darkened interior strewn with rubble.

"Must I destroy everything before you come out and play?" she continued in a sing-song voice before passing over a row of structures to Daniel's left and moving toward the heart of the city. "Do not come all the way to Babylon to hide like cowards." Her mocking voice trailed off into the distance.

Raylin tapped him on the arm and whispered, "You think it's safe to move on?"

Daniel shrugged. "Maybe." He surveyed the buildings and homes lining the street as best he could from ground level. The city, even abandoned as it seemed, appeared chaotic. A few streetlights cast weak glows onto the pavement below, but most flickered, if they worked at all. The details he could catch showed a mishmash of architecture—square, flat-roofed businesses mixed among homes and apartments, most of mud-brown stone or brick adorned with random graffiti and busted windows. Stray heaps of litter dotted the roadside. The streets appeared abandoned, but in the Enemy's territory, who knew who or what hunted from the darkened doorways?

Daniel turned to Raylin, "This street seems to follow the river. We'll stay on it and use the buildings for cover. Hopefully, it won't be long before we—"

Raylin covered his mouth and put her finger on her lips. She pointed behind Daniel and shook her head.

Across the street, Tyr had just emerged from an alleyway. Behind him, a gargantuan wolf demon plodded along, voraciously sniffing the air. Its back towered over Tyr's six-foot-something frame by at least a meter, and it sported the usual yellow fangs and rasping claws that most beastly demons did. Its eyes were a baleful, luminous orange, which strongly contrasted with its ghostly white fur. Around its neck, a mane of bristling, black quills rattled every time the wind blew or the wolf turned its head. The barbs continued in a thin line down its back and then resumed in full force around its tail.

"I hunger," it growled in a low voice. Its accent held the same Northern European inflections as Tyr's. "You had better be right about the Vessels, or you will be my dinner. So hungry. So. Hungry. I will eat them. Crunch them. Where are they? I hunger. I will eat them. Or I will eat you. Eat."

Tyr rolled his eyes and swung his club in front of the monster.

"I'd like to see you try. Also, shut up. That's an order. I know you're hungry; you don't have to keep saying it over and over again."

"But I hunger!"

"Fenrir!" Tyr spun his club around and smashed a hole in the side of the building next to the demon.

Fenrir bared its teeth, its quills bristling out like a bottlebrush.

"I told you to be silent. You've done nothing but slaver and complain since we left the tower. Do you imagine the children will come running at the sound of your whining? Besides, Master wants them alive and UN-eaten. Get yourself under control, or I'll do it for you."

Rather than back down, Fenrir moved closer to Tyr with a low, rumbling growl. "No human gives me orders"—it breathed heavily, its breath blowing Tyr's hair back—"except Abida and Amira. You are not spirit like me, and you never will be. You are flesh. Earthborn!" the demon spat. "You will perish once Master's plan comes to fruition, but we will endure for eternity."

Tyr gave a disgusted sigh and turned his back on the demon as though to show his contempt and utter lack of fear. "That's what we're all counting on," he muttered. "Oblivion is true freedom. I have no wish to live for an eternity, not with the likes of you, anyway. Now, search the other side of the street. I'll look inside the buildings." He turned and rested a muscular arm on top of Fenrir's snout. "And remember, the children have clothes that make it difficult for us to see them. You'll have to use your nose if you want to avoid getting purified."

Fenrir let out a low growl of warning, but Tyr simply patted the demon's nose and walked toward a building on the opposite side of the street. "I'm so sick of you all," it complained.

Daniel snapped his head back around to Raylin. Instead of finding her alarmed, however, she seemed distracted. "Raylin," he whispered and tilted his head toward the approaching demon. "We've got company."

Raylin finally focused on him. "I know," she whispered. "Sorry. I assume escaping isn't an option."

Fenrir was now in the middle of the street and heading behind them. Tyr was nowhere in sight.

"No, it's not. Summon the staff," Daniel said and rolled out from beneath the hummer. The Sun Sword flamed out into the air at his fingertips. He flung two Sunstorms almost before Fenrir realized it was under attack.

With lightning reflexes, the demon leaped over the arcs of fire, which exploded into a nearby business with muted thunder. It landed with a howl and tore toward them.

Daniel summoned a Fire Strike, but the demon easily jumped over the purifying waves of power and sailed directly over Daniel.

"Fool!" it snarled, bearing down on him with rending claws. "I may not be able to see you clearly, but your attacks give away your location."

It had all happened so quickly Daniel knew he wouldn't have time to pull the Sun Sword out of the ground and prepare a Sunstorm. He yanked the blade free and tried to dive out of the way, but it was too late.

The demon's jaws snapped down.

Two of its teeth shattered as it closed on the Abyssal Staff. Raylin stood over Daniel, her weapon brandished above to catch the jaws on its indomitable obsidian shaft.

She spun the staff around and swept at Fenrir's legs and then followed with a swift uppercut with the head of the staff.

The demon unsuccessfully attempted to dodge both, and Raylin forced it back long enough for Daniel to scramble to his feet and fling another Sunstorm.

Fenrir dashed to the right, narrowly escaping the purifying arc that singed off its left whiskers. It crouched, growling, eyes flames of hellish orange. Gingerly, it licked its broken fangs and searched the ground until it found the shattered pieces at Raylin's feet.

"Daniel," Raylin said, keeping her eyes locked on the wolf. "Purify these fangs for me, would you?"

"Certainly," Daniel replied, dragging the Sun Sword over both.

Each popped like a balloon, turning into vapors of dark spirit.

"Let's take care of those, shall we?" Raylin said, unlocking the top of the Abyssal Staff and sealing them away before they could return to Fenrir.

The demon snarled, and its quills raised up like hackles. With a quick shake of its barbed main, a dozen quills shot through the air.

Raylin spun the Abyssal Staff, catching three on the shaft of the staff and dodging the rest.

Daniel swatted a few out of the air, but they were coming so fast that one grazed his left shoulder, drawing a red line of blood. Intense, searing pain like fire shot through his arm.

"Ow!" he screamed as the left side of his body began to convulse and cramp. Gasping with the agony, he instinctively held the Sun Sword up to the cut. A high-pitched noise like metal rubbing on metal whined from his arm. Daniel felt something wriggling out of the wound. With a faint clink, a black splinter, apparently fractured from the main quill, fell to the ground. The burning sensation vanished, but the wound still throbbed.

"You okay?" Raylin asked, her eyes glued to the demon.

"Fine. Now, anyway. Don't let those things get you. They feel like you're being jabbed with red-hot irons."

"Cool," she replied. "Yeah, no thanks."

Fenrir growled with pleasure. "Did you enjoy that? So weak and fragile. One little splinter can nearly bring you to your knees. What would a dozen feel like to you? That would be pleasant to see … or hear, in this case."

In the distance, Vinaash's Pestilence thundered through the city.

"We need to finish Mr. Wolf and quick," Daniel said, drawing abreast of Raylin.

"Yeah, not to mention Tyr is still somewhere close. I wonder why he hasn't joined the battle. Not that I'm complaining, mind you."

"I, too, wonder where he is," Fenrir rumbled. "Worthless human."

"Hey!" Daniel replied, charging the Sun Sword for an attack. "Private conversation here. Mind your own business."

Fenrir raised its head and gave an ear-splitting howl. Nearby windows and streetlamps shattered at the noise. Daniel and Raylin quickly covered their ears until it died down, echoing out over the city like a siren.

"That should get everyone's attention," Fenrir said with a devious smile. "We will see how you fare against a host of demons. And, the Generals, I suppose, will come, too."

Daniel flung a Sunstorm, then hastily charged the sword.

With cat-like reflexes, the wolf leaped over the first arc straight at Daniel.

Daniel jumped backward and plunged the Sun Sword into the ground.

Fenrir cracked the asphalt as it landed five feet in front of Daniel, the purifying waves of the Fire Strike buffeting it repeatedly and forcing him back. As with many of the more powerful demons Daniel had faced, the attack alone wasn't enough to totally purify it. Stray wisps of demonic spirit snaked into the air from Fenrir's fur as though each hair was a separate entity needing to be purified.

Raylin sped to the demon's side, striking his foreleg with a powerful sweep of the Abyssal Staff, followed by a blinding series of quick thrusts into its ribs and a crushing wallop onto the top of its back. She dashed backward as the demon spun around and snapped its jaws where she had stood.

With a pained whimper, Fenrir whipped its tail toward them. A scattershot of venomous quills peppered the air.

Daniel had thankfully already flung a Sunstorm, which purified the barbs aimed at him.

At least twenty targeted Raylin. She spun the Abyssal Staff in front of her, but a few got through. Most stuck into the car at her back, but two sank into her leg.

She gritted her teeth and crouched low, brandishing the staff in front of her even as she grabbed the ends of the quills and yanked them out of her thigh. Breathing heavily, she tossed the barbs at Daniel's feet. "Sword," she wheezed, her voice low and shaky.

"Right! Sure." Daniel, surprised by her ability to still stand, quickly obeyed, drawing the Sun Sword over the quills.

Fenrir looked confused. "I may not be able to see you, but I felt my quills sink into your thigh. Are you enjoying the pain? Excruciating, is it not?" it asked with a voice mixed with theatrical cruelty and genuine bewilderment.

Raylin returned its malicious, searching gaze with a withering expression. "That's nothing. Try carrying around the Voidblade for a couple years of your life, and then talk to me about pain." She sealed away the wisps of evil spirits fleeing through the air back toward Fenrir.

"This ends now." Fenrir galloped toward her.

She cracked it in the mouth with the head of her staff and then jumped backward. Her wounded leg gave out, and she stumbled to the ground even as Fenrir bore down on her.

Daniel darted between them and let a Sunstorm fly directly into Fenrir's open maw.

The arc landed, instantly exploding in a purifying blast of power. The demon yelped and backpedaled so fast it tripped and sat on its haunches, looking more like a startled puppy than a fearsome monster. It licked its mouth as its fangs vaporized into dark spirits.

From where she crouched on the ground, Raylin extended the Abyssal Staff and sucked in the tendrils.

Daniel sighed. "Do I have to purify every individual part of you before you disappear? Come on, man! That was a direct hit!"

Fenrir jumped to its paws, raking grooves in the asphalt with its claws. "I am moo powaful dan you can imathin!" it said, toothlessly fumbling over its words. Fenrir went cross-eyed as it looked down at its muzzle, attempting in vain to view its now fangless mouth.

Daniel took advantage of Fenrir's distraction and flung another Sunstorm into its chest. Spinning around, he pulled Raylin to her feet so they could flee while the demon was occupied. "We need to get out of here. This is going nowhere."

"I know. And now I'm wounded," Raylin grumbled in disgust.

Daniel looked down at her bleeding thigh. "Yeah. It doesn't look good." He held the Sun Sword up to the wounds to make sure no splinters were left. Nothing came out. "Look, next time, just dodge an attack like that. It'd be impossible to deflect all of them with your staff."

"I know. You don't have to tell me that." She hobbled next to him, using the staff and his shoulder for support. "But it all happened so fast, I didn't have much of an option to jump."

Daniel frantically searched the area and made for an open doorway, releasing the Sun Sword as they fled. He whispered, "Put away the staff so he doesn't notice us."

Raylin released her weapon and leaned heavily on Daniel's shoulder to compensate.

He ducked into the building just as the cloud from the Sunstorm cleared. Fenrir howled behind them, and they risked a backward glance only to see a brand-new set of jagged fangs burst out of the demon's gums.

"Ah. That feels much better!" Fenrir laughed and then scanned the street for them. "Where did you morsels disappear to?"

Crackling thunder vibrated the air, and Fenrir's hair stood on end.

Daniel shot Raylin a desperate glance before rushing further into the building. Hopefully, there would be somewhere to hide, or at least a backdoor into an alleyway where they could zigzag between buildings.

Vinaash's sing-song voice rang out over the streets, permeating the broken windows and ajar doors. "Having trouble with the little rats?" she asked Fenrir from somewhere in the air above him.

Fenrir's reply was lost amid Daniel and Raylin's labored breathing. The building's interior was a bedlam of broken furniture, stray papers, and empty bookshelves. Before its owners abandoned it or were captured and enslaved, it was probably some sort of business. Raylin and Daniel turned a corner into a hallway and leaned against the wall.

"Can you keep going?" Daniel asked.

"I'll be fine," Raylin replied. "The pain is getting better. I just

need…" Her eyes fell on torn strips of cloth, maybe from old curtains or clothes, strewn over the floor. "Actually, I just need that exactly." She snatched up a long strip and deftly wrapped it around her thigh before tightly tying it off. "Much better," she said, putting more pressure on her leg and even risking a jump into the air. "Yeah. That'll do."

Daniel peered around the corner of the hallway and out the door. Vinaash and Fenrir were out of sight, but he still caught snatches of their conversation. The street was aglow with the puke-green light of Vinaash's Pestilence. "Good, because we need to get out of here and fast. Let's hope there's a back door or, at least, a window. Follow me."

Daniel continued down the hallway until it led straight into a small office. A desk piled high with emptied drawers and loose paper rested against the left wall. About seven feet above the ground was a half-moon glass window, about two-and-a-half feet high and three wide.

"You think it opens?" Raylin asked.

Daniel jumped onto the desk to look. "No. But we could break it," he said with a shrug.

"I give the orders!" Vinaash shouted, her voice carrying down the hallway. "Search the buildings. I'll search the streets."

Fenrir roared. "I am a god! You are—"

Whatever it was about to say was snipped short by a thunderclap and a yelp.

"I'll break it," Raylin said. "Or we'll be trapped in here between an angry demon and a psychopath. The staff won't be as noticeable if someone's watching from another window."

She summoned the Abyssal Staff and used it to vault onto the desk next to Daniel. "Elbow room, please."

Daniel shuffled to the side and shielded his face while Raylin swung the staff into the window. It shattered outwards, leaving jagged pieces sticking up and down like teeth. She cleared these away with a sweep of the shaft.

"Careful," she said, cautiously climbing onto the sill, palms splayed out as she wormed her way into position to swing her legs up. Once

perched on top, she carefully brushed a few stray shards of glass out onto the street below, then jumped down after them.

Daniel jumped up after her and got both legs up. He shifted position to drop down and cut his thumb on a sliver of glass. "Dang it," he said just as a loud crash shook the room and showered the desk with the debris.

Fenrir stood in the shattered doorway, forcing the rest of its body through. "Where are you, little morsels?" it barked, swinging its head around and sniffing the air. "I smell you. Oh, I smell blood. Right. There!" It lunged toward the window.

Daniel was in no position to summon the Sun Sword and opted to throw himself out the window just as Fenrir's snapping jaws crashed through the frame after him.

"Get back here!" the demon howled, splattering Daniel and Raylin with saliva. "I hunger!" It got both legs through and, with a massive heave, shook and cracked the wall of the building.

Daniel summoned the Sun Sword, but Raylin grabbed him by the shoulder.

"Put it away!" she hissed, pulling him after her. "Remember, Vinaash is hovering around somewhere. She'll know right where we are if you start firing off Sunstorms. Just run!"

Daniel pointed back at Fenrir, still struggling to break through the wall. "But it was trapped. I could've at least stabbed it a few times. That wouldn't have attracted more attention than it bringing down the building."

The alleyway was piled high with trash bags and crates and led in the same direction as the street on the other side of the building. Daniel let the Sun Sword hover in front of him as they ran. Mercifully, it pointed in the direction they were already heading.

Two dumpsters on their right disintegrated with a thunderclap, and the air around them turned acrid. Daniel and Raylin darted toward the building on their right and pressed themselves flat against the wall. Daniel released the Sun Sword.

"Alley rats!" Vinaash called from the air above them. "Where did

you go?" She floated over the alleyway until she was directly above their intended path. The buildings here were close together, and she seemed to dislike flying down into such cramped quarters during a fight. "What sorcery was used on your clothes?" She swatted a fly away and put her hands on her hips. "That sword of yours makes an easy target, though. Pull it back out, and let's have some fun."

Fenrir howled, and a loud cracking noise reverberated through the alleyway.

"Keep running," Daniel whispered. "I'll distract Vinaash and give us some cover."

"Wait," Raylin said. "I have an idea."

Daniel whipped out the Sun Sword and flung a Sunstorm at Vinaash. "There's no time. Just run!"

The wheeling halo behind her shifted to shield her from the attack, but the blast still exploded into a fiery cloud, obscuring her vision long enough for Daniel to dart beneath her and continue down the narrow path.

Once under her, Daniel fired two more to keep her vision obscured while they ran. He glanced behind him and saw that Raylin wasn't following. With the Abyssal Staff in hand, she charged one of the walls and scampered up the side. Once she had reached as far as she could, she leaped to the other wall and then back and forth until she cleared the top of the buildings. The Abyssal Staff held high, she sailed through the air above the remnants of Daniel's last Sunstorm.

The air cleared for a moment to find Vinaash facing Daniel, furious and wreathed with the Bolt of Pestilence. "You mangy peasants! Your attacks are—"

Thwack!

Raylin brought the staff down on the back of Vinaash's head.

The General careened off her green cloud and slammed into the dirt at Daniel's feet, unconscious. The Bolt of Pestilence still flickered angrily around her shoulders, whining and buzzing as though attempting to awaken its wielder.

Daniel looked up to see Raylin astride Vinaash's cloud. "What are you doing?"

"I guess I'm riding her cloud. This could be useful. Let's see if I can …" The cloud glided through the air. "Nice," she said. "Maybe I can get it to come down to where you are."

"Little cockroaches!" Fenrir howled.

Daniel scanned the alleyway and saw two malevolent, orange eyes glowering in the darkness.

The demon wolf stalked forward, its fur taking on a ghostly green pallor from the combined light of Vinaash's cloud and Pestilence. "I will tear you apart!" it snarled, hastening forward.

Daniel hesitated. Should he run for it or stand his ground and fight?

The brick wall to Fenrir's right shattered apart, and the demon was battered into the opposite wall.

Tyr stepped out of the gaping hole in the building and over the rubble. "Fenrir. There you are. Here I was, thinking you'd been purified, but I find you resting in the slums."

Fenrir staggered to its feet and limped out of the pile of bricks that had fallen around it. "I do not rest. I am about to maul the Vessels!" It jerked its head toward Raylin and Daniel.

"Run!" Raylin shouted, urging the cloud above the alleyway. "I'll try to swoop down and get you."

"Oh," Tyr said, scanning the area and smirking at Vinaash's unconscious form. "You take the boy. I'll deal with the traitor."

"Fine," Fenrir growled, but that was all Daniel caught as he sprinted full speed down the narrow corridor, trying to keep Raylin in view. She zoomed overhead, gradually lowering the cloud to cautiously navigate a maze of power lines, fire escapes, and clotheslines strung between the buildings.

"Hurry!" Daniel panted, not daring to slow down.

"I'm trying!"

Daniel glanced up just as Tyr's form, outlined against the heavenly battle scene above, flew over Raylin. "Above you!"

"Behind you!" she shouted at the same time.

As Daniel spun around, he saw Tyr tackle her off the cloud. They

crashed through an open window and disappeared into the darkened interior. But his focus was on Fenrir charging him.

Daniel summoned a Fire Strike and stabbed the ground. As predicted, the demon launched itself into the air above the attack, making it an easier target. A Sunstorm caught it square in the stomach. Without waiting to see the damage, Daniel turned on his heel and ran.

He jumped over several fallen barrels, rounded old wooden crates stacked against the wall, and mercifully found an open doorway just beyond them to his left. He dashed through as the alleyway was pelted with a scattershot of Fenrir's quills. He didn't bother turning to see how close Fenrir was. It would take the demon some time to squeeze itself through the building, and that was all the time Daniel needed.

With luck, he could double back to meet up with Raylin, and she'd be holding her own against Tyr. They could jump on Vinaash's cloud to escape, join up with Gabriela and Seren on the other side of the river, then fly the cloud to the middle of the river and locate Ben. Even as Daniel thought this, he felt his hope crumble.

Nothing ever went that smoothly on a quest.

12

Secrets

Daniel wove his way through dark, littered hallways and burst out of the front door onto another trashed street. He hung a left and bolted toward the building he saw Raylin and Tyr hurtle through. There was no sign of Fenrir and no sound of it tearing down the walls. So far, so good.

Beware!

The Father's voice was like a warning siren blaring in his mind.

Daniel craned his neck in time to catch Fenrir leap off the top of the building directly above him. If he hadn't been warned, he would've been slammed into the ground and knocked unconscious. Or, with the wrathful mood the demon was in, probably worse.

As it was, Daniel had just enough time to slash Fenrir in the eyes and dive through the doorway as the demon crashed into the ground.

Fenrir howled in rage and pain as a mass of writhing spirits escaped its head to tear through the air in the direction of the desert.

"My eyes!" it howled, writhing around on the ground. "Do you have any idea how long it will take me to regrow them? Literally minutes! You worthless bag of meat!"

Daniel charged the Sun Sword and struck the ground. The shockwaves washed over Fenrir, buffeting it back across the street and pinning it against the wall of the opposing building. Each wave blasted another portion of dark spirit out of its body.

Fenrir staggered to its feet. "Master!" it howled, his voice shattering windows and shaking dust from the surrounding structures. "Grant me power! I have a Vessel!"

A black circle surrounding a five-pointed star appeared over the demon. Spindly script spun around it like a carousel. Once one revolution was completed, the center of the star opened, and a mass of demonic spirits poured into Fenrir's howling mouth.

Daniel ran. He had no desire to see what the newly infused power would do to the demon. He could guess well enough: increased strength, bigger claws, more quills, worse breath. But none of that mattered. If he could just find Raylin and escape Tyr, maybe they wouldn't have to deal with Fenrir anymore anyway.

Daniel scanned the office. Toward the back, a narrow, rectangular window in the side of a door showed a stairwell beyond, half-lit by emergency lights. He burst through and leaped up the steps but paused at the top. From here on, he would need to use more stealth. Cautiously opening the second-story door, he crept into a dim hallway lined with broken windows. A busted streetlamp buzzed obnoxiously through the shattered glass, leering into the dark interior like a nosy neighbor. Other than two upended office chairs in the far corner, there was little else in view and certainly nothing to hide behind. Raylin and Tyr were somewhere up here. If he could take Tyr by surprise, they'd have the upper hand. If not, they would be caught between a mutated Fenrir and Tyr's hammer.

Father, please help me find Raylin fast. He tiptoed down the corridor. His mind flashed back to Gabriela and Seren, hopefully sneaking around unnoticed on the opposite shore, and Ben stuck at the bottom of Euphrates with Enbilulu. *Keep them safe, Father. Please fill them with power, and don't let anything happen to them.* He said the prayer for all of them but found himself centering on Gabriela the most.

His supplications were interrupted by hushed voices talking in the next room. He crept up to the closed door and put his ear down to the gap between it and the floor.

"Send no messages. No signals. Nothing." Tyr's resonant voice was urgent and commanding. "The risk is too great."

Raylin made a *tsking* sound followed by footsteps and the clunking of the Abyssal Staff. She was pacing the room, and her voice sounded nervous. "Are you absolutely certain? There's no other option."

"I'm certain. This way, they won't know until it's too late. Make sure you don't let this slip. If the plan is jeopardized, Master's punishment will be"—Tyr gave a pregnant pause—"terrible."

Daniel couldn't believe his ears. Raylin was scheming with Tyr. Double-crossing them. Again! A rush of anger flooded his body like boiling water. It all made so much sense now. Her attitude toward him, taking everything he said and misinterpreting it, being overly sensitive to anything he did, never letting down her guard with him—she'd been playing the part of penitent convert all this time just to get in everyone's good graces. Everyone's except his. He had always known *something* was off with her. He could never really connect with her for some reason, and now he knew what it was: she purposefully kept up walls with him because if she let him in, he'd have figured out her treachery.

The vision from Kon's medallion flooded his mind, and all the puzzle pieces clicked into place. So, this was the secret plan. Kon had probably wanted to stir up doubt and confusion, but now the cat was out of the bag.

How was he going to explain this to the others? They had completely bought into her act. Of course, Seren trusted her; Raylin was the perfect broken and needy sister, desperate for her sister's acceptance and affection. And Ben, well, he had his own blinders on when it came to Raylin. Gabriela had been too preoccupied with saving her people to pay any mind to her true nature in the past, but maybe she'd understand. After all, Raylin's betrayal in Peru is what got her captured by the Enemy and all of them nearly killed. That was it. He'd have to go through Gabriela.

Daniel found himself scanning the room wildly as though some answer for what to do next would suddenly pop out of the shadows. He needed to find Vinaash's cloud and escape by himself. That way, he wouldn't have to bother facing Tyr at all. Then, he could find the

girls, break the news to Gabriela, and figure out how to convince Seren and Ben. After that …

He faceplanted into his hands and vigorously rubbed his eyes. None of that would work. For them to seal the Spirit of the Age, they'd need the Abyssal Staff. Maybe the Three would allow them to temporarily wield it like they did in the Abyss. That seemed the only option, but how could they get it from Raylin? If she didn't willingly give it up, then only the Three could remove it. Even the Enemy had to resort to trickery to get him to relinquish the Sun Sword in Peru.

Father, what am I supposed to do? This is crazy! If you knew she was going to betray us, why did you let her be rescued from the Voidblade? Wouldn't it have been easier to let her do her own thing and have one of us hold on to the Abyssal Staff until the sealing? This doesn't make sense!

The heavens were silent, and the only noises that reached Daniel's ears were Raylin and Tyr's now incomprehensible whispers and Fenrir's scuffling in the stairwell.

Fenrir!

Time was running out, and there was no way around it. He would have to play along, pretend he hadn't heard anything, and escape with Raylin. He hoped Vinaash's cloud was right outside the window. If it wasn't, this was going to get messy and quick.

Daniel carefully turned the handle and threw open the door, flinging three Sunstorms at Tyr before he could react.

The blasts slammed Tyr against the exterior wall as the Enemy's spirit, bound to his body, surged out of his chest and roared around the room. Daniel grabbed Raylin and ran by him as he collapsed with a grunt, stopping only to stab the ground with a Fire Strike to keep the spirit from re-entering his body as long as possible. Instead of his usual angry sneer, Tyr's eyes looked shocked and pained.

Raylin hesitated and cast a backward glance.

"Get to the cloud!" Daniel ordered Raylin, shoving her a little stronger than he intended.

She threw off his hand. "Hey! Quit being so rough. I'm going. You just startled me."

"I bet I did," Daniel threw back. He silently berated himself. He wasn't playing the part well. If he was going to get the Abyssal Staff from her, he would have to try harder. He climbed up on the windowsill and spied Vinaash's cloud floating about three feet from the ledge. "Sorry. We need to get out of here. Fenrir is on its way up."

On cue, Fenrir burst into the room, splintering the doorway as it forced its massive shoulders through. Its eyes had regenerated and were no longer the lamp-like orange. They had changed entirely to black with a fiery red iris. And rather than fur, quills covered its body. "Tyr! Get up and grab the Vessels." It lunged toward the window.

"Jump!" Daniel shouted, letting go of Raylin and leaping for the cloud. For a split second, he feared he would careen straight through it and fall to the ground. Thankfully, it was like jumping on a bed, and he quickly regained his balance just as Raylin landed beside him. "How do you fly this thing?"

But Raylin was already in control. The cloud streamed forward over the line of buildings closest to the river. The lazy swish of the Euphrates reached their ears, and the muddy, saturated shore reflected the dull glimmer of the flickering streetlamps.

Daniel cast a backward glance in time to see Fenrir glowering at them from the darkened window. Tyr was nowhere in sight, but the scene dropped out of view as Raylin steered the cloud down to the waterline and sped downriver.

"Thanks for rescuing me," Raylin said after a few moments, her voice nearly lost in the rush of wind. "I wasn't sure how we were going to get out of that."

Daniel took a second to gather himself before replying. The horizon had turned yellow with a fast, desert sunrise. In the distance, a thin, black line stretched across the river, faintly silhouetted against the sky. After a moment, it registered that he was seeing a bridge. With any luck, Gabriela and Seren awaited them there. "Of course. We had to make it out together, right? You see the bridge?"

"Yeah. Maybe that's where the girls are. What about Ben? Any ideas?"

"I don't know. One thing at a time, I suppose. Once we meet up with the others, maybe we can all get on the cloud together, and the Sun Sword will guide us to where he is."

"Maybe. I just hope …" Raylin's voice trailed off. "Oh no. Look." She pointed across the river toward the desert.

Daniel followed the line of her finger and scanned the dunes. The sky above them was dotted with a horde of flying demons, all making a beeline for the city. As his eyes adjusted to the scene, he could also make out dark, lumbering shapes galloping through the desert. Flickers of fire periodically lit up their bodies, leaving no doubt that a herd of dragon demons was on its way. In the light of their flames, huge camel spider demons skittered alongside, greedily tearing over the sand as though called by a dinner bell.

"What was it that you hoped?" Daniel asked, failing to keep disbelief out of his tone. This was probably exactly what Raylin had wanted.

Raylin cast him a look of confusion. "I hope Ben is alright. What if we can't find him? Or worse, what if he's hurt?"

A fiery lump welled up in Daniel's chest, and he gritted his teeth. How dare she pretend to be concerned about Ben's welfare! What was it the Enemy had promised to make her betray them again, to make her double-cross the very people who had risked their lives over and over to save her? What allowed her to feel that deceiving the very guy who loved her was worth it?

A new thought entered his mind. What if she had never actually been on their side to begin with? What if her return of the Sun Sword in Peru, her attack on the Enemy with the Voidblade in India, and its subsequent destruction in the Abyss were all a part of some bigger plan? What if the Enemy's goal all along had been to get them to Babylon while the Three were preoccupied, weaken them from within, and kill them all at once so that the cycle of Vessels couldn't restart before his victory was assured? Surely, the Three would've seen Raylin's true heart, right? He felt a cold sensation creep through his stomach. The Three allowed bad things to happen all the time. Maybe this

was a part of some lesson he and the others had to learn. How such a "lesson" could be a good thing was beyond his comprehension. All he felt now was a boiling rage.

His fury overrode his fear of the coming horde, but he swallowed down those feelings and steeled himself for the act. Everything—Ben's safety, reunification with the girls, getting the Abyssal Staff, the entire quest—all rested on his ability to pretend he didn't know Raylin was a traitor.

"All we can do," Daniel said, keeping his voice calm and even, "is get to the bridge and survive."

Raylin barely grunted in reply, her attention seemingly diverted to her feet. Daniel was glad for that; he wasn't sure how well he was hiding his feelings. She furrowed her brow and focused intently on Vinaash's cloud, which glided to a jerky halt.

They were about ten feet above the ground. The bridge, now a quarter of a mile away, looked wide enough to support two-way traffic. It rested on rows of cement pylons standing at regular intervals like giants' legs in the swirling Euphrates.

"Problem?" Daniel asked.

Raylin grabbed his arm. "Jump."

"What? Why? We're too high!"

"Vinaash is taking control. Jump!"

Raylin leaped off the cloud and landed with a soft thud in the mud below.

Daniel felt the cloud jerk again and slowly rise. "Shoot! Watch out!" he shouted, jumping after Raylin. She rolled out of the way just as he landed.

The cloud shot straight into the air and then back toward the part of the city where they'd battled Vinaash.

From somewhere behind them, Fenrir howled.

"There goes that plan," Daniel growled. How were they supposed to find Ben now?

Raylin tossed the Abyssal Staff back and forth between her hands. "What should we do?"

Thunder rumbled through the air, and the city behind them glowed with an angry green light.

Daniel scanned the area. There was little cover other than the occasional scrubby bush and palm tree, but there was a road running along the top of the bank. If they ducked back into the streets, they ran the risk of being ambushed by Fenrir and Tyr. Not to mention, they only had a narrow window to reach the bridge before the horde caught up. Of course, this was probably all according to Raylin's plan, and he was playing right into her hands. But what other choice did he have?

"We run for the bridge. Not much else we can do."

Without waiting to hear Raylin's response, Daniel sprinted full speed toward the road and ran for the bridge. She soon caught up and easily matched his pace, which was annoying.

Daniel carefully observed the heavenly battle unfold above them, mindful to not get sucked in for too long. As in E-Abzu, the longer he attended to the scene, the faster it progressed until seemingly playing out in real time. The Serpent still writhed behind his lines of demons and monsters. Wave after wave of fire poured out of his mouths. A myriad of demons held the line between the armies, locked in numberless clashes along the battlefront with glorious Firstborn. Despite the conflict, the line between the forces never seemed to advance in one direction or the other. The demonic minions flung themselves with abandon at the opposing army, but the Three's Firstborn deftly parried each attack with weapons or power of some kind. Rather than looking harried, however, they seemed peaceful—fierce and terrifying as they faced the denizens of hell—but calm and reassured of their ability to hold back the line.

A wave of light pulsed from the top of the Father's Mountain and shimmered down through the army below. As one, the front line took a step back before standing their ground at the new border.

"You see!" the Serpent laughed. "I press my advantage. You *can* be thwarted. My power grows even as you diminish."

No answer came from the Three or their army. The only response was their unflinching gaze and calm resistance to the onslaught.

Fear stabbed through Daniel's heart. The Three were pushed back. They actually gave up ground! What did this mean?

Father, I'm really freaking out here. Is the Enemy strong enough to win this? I thought you were the one really in charge. And, in case you're not paying attention, we're in a bad situation here. Can you spare some help?

Beside him, Raylin muttered something under her breath, pulling his awareness back to earthly time. He snapped his head toward her and saw her lips moving. Oh sure, betray them and then act like you're praying. What a joke! He had to exert all his self-control to keep from saying something.

Remember the lesson you learned in India.

The response from the Father was so sudden that Daniel almost tripped.

India? Daniel asked. He ran through the quest in his mind. There were all sorts of lessons the Three taught him about prayer, trust, faith. Oh, and bad things happening for a reason. Cool. As though he needed that reminder now.

I know, I know. I need to trust you no matter what, pray and intercede, and have faith that you will work it all out. But I'm really struggling with Raylin, and then I saw you retreat. I'm just afraid.

Fear not.

And?

The battle with the Enemy is mine. What is your battle?

Daniel narrowed his eyes in confusion and shook his head. What kind of question was that? *My battle is with the Enemy, too.*

What are you battling, Daniel?

A slew of demons and a crazy seven-headed dragon, that's what!

Search for the answer. Patiently.

Daniel waited for more, but the heavens fell silent. The Three's last admonition taunted him like some king's disingenuous concern for the downtrodden poor at his banquet hall door, begging for food and getting scraps in return. This was so like the Three! He had a real problem, and the only guidance he got was a riddle!

He checked himself. His anger was getting out of control. These

accusations weren't really legitimate. Not totally, anyway. He was beginning to think that every negative emotion, especially toward the Three, was amplified in the heart of the Enemy's territory. The land was one giant echo chamber of malice and self-pity.

Daniel pulled away from the battle above and Raylin's betrayal and simply breathed. He tried to push down his confusion and frustration until he felt his anger calm. There were more pressing matters: the bridge was close at hand, the cloud of flying demons neared the opposite bank, which meant their terrestrial cohorts weren't far behind, Fenrir's howls grew ever closer, and arcs of Pestilence zipped through the air. Whatever the Three meant, he would figure it out after he survived the coming battle.

If he survived.

Daniel and Raylin sprinted up the rising ground to the bridge and rounded the steel railing. Without a backward glance, they ran as fast as they could toward the middle. The sun, halfway above the desert's horizon, hung in a dusty haze, casting an ironically rosy light over their desperate situation.

Two figures raced toward them from the other side. Despite the dim lighting, Daniel recognized Seren and Gabriela by their gaits. Behind them, the hellish mob bore down on their trail. There were hundreds of flying demons of both species they'd seen scouring the desert over E-Abzu, as well as a mixed herd of dragons and camel spiders. Forty-foot-long, brown serpents with four eyes also joined the fray, coiling up onto the bridge's railings and hungrily slithering after them.

"Run!" Gabriela shouted.

Daniel and Raylin skidded to a halt, but the Bolt of Pestilence struck directly behind them, blasting a crater into the road and blowing them forward onto their hands and knees. Another arc followed close behind, zapping Raylin.

She collapsed as all the color drained out of her convulsing face. Her withered body, in combination with the stark white hair peeking out from her hat, made her appear elderly and frail.

"Daniel," she croaked, struggling to turn her head toward him. Her eyes gave off a dull gray glow and could barely open. "The sword. Help."

Daniel looked over at her struggling on the ground and hesitated.

Vinaash, her forehead covered in smeared blood from Raylin's earlier attack, bore down on them from the sky. Her eyes were a blaze of green, and she screeched in fury.

With a hungry howl, Fenrir bound up onto the railing from the road below and galloped toward them.

Two swirling portals opened on their end of the bridge. Tyr and Amira casually stepped through.

"Hurry," Raylin moaned. "Before we're caught."

Daniel rolled his eyes. She sure was a good actress. Had she and Vinaash planned this little charade to make her role as an ally more believable? He shook his head. It didn't matter now; there was no time to explain things to Gabriela and Seren.

Then, an idea struck him. If he purified her, any portion of the Enemy's spirit hanging out in her body would be exposed. Perfect. That'd make convincing the others easier. And hopefully, no matter what happened, she would keep playing the part of the good little Vessel and fight their enemies, if for no other reason than to keep up the act.

"I don't know what good it will do," he said. "Ben's not here to cast the Triune Shield around you. The Pestilence might just attack you again." Even as he spoke, he swiftly charged the Sun Sword above him and stabbed it into her back. Then, whipping around, he shot successive Sunstorms at Fenrir, Vinaash, and the approaching demon hordes on both sides of the bridge.

Vinaash summoned her halo as a shield and flew backward, but Fenrir got caught in the front legs. It collapsed face-first into the asphalt and skidded to a halt. The demon mobs mercifully halted their advance, pausing as though their goal had simply been to trap the companions on the bridge.

The Bolt of Pestilence zipped out of Raylin's body and buzzed

angrily around the perimeter of the Fire Strike's shockwaves, greedily stalking her like a predator.

Raylin breathed a sigh of relief as color and vitality returned to her body. Whipping the Abyssal Staff around, she faced the arc of green lightning just as the power of the Fire Strike receded.

"Sure hope this works," she said, her voice still weak. The head of the Abyssal Staff activated, and she brandished it in front of her.

The power of the Fire Strike faded, and the Bolt of Pestilence arced toward her just as the sealing power of the staff homed in on it, drawing it in like a spaghetti noodle.

"What are you doing?" Vinaash shrieked. "You vile worm! How dare you!"

Daniel gaped in dumbfounded silence, confused by the absence of the Enemy's spirit. Maybe she hadn't been filled yet because of cases like this. The deception had to be complete, after all. Whatever his misgivings, he was glad the Abyssal Staff worked on the Pestilence in Ben's absence. That meant if one of the girls got struck, they had some way out, even if it meant relying on a traitor.

Daniel and Raylin jumped to their feet and fled toward Gabriela and Seren. Behind the girls, Abida, Chiuta, and Wanu stepped out of their portals.

Wanu grimaced, each of her front teeth filed down to a point. A high ponytail kept her long dark hair pulled out of her face, and black makeup, applied in a rectangle across her eyes and the bridge of her nose, accentuated her olive complexion. This, in combination with her tight black pants, sleeveless shirt, and the knobby-handled Scythe of Death she lazily spun around, made her seem like some deranged ninja.

Chiuta's black skin glistened in the morning sun. In stark contrast, his gray, lifeless eyes, which matched the Whirlwind of Famine swirling around his arms and shoulders like a life-sapping feather boa, flitted over the Vessels with no hint of concern or excitement. His sand-colored linen pants and shirt snapped in the wind. An elaborate design of eddying lines had been buzzed into his short hair.

Daniel took all this in at a glance: his concern primarily alternated between Amira and Abida. They casually wound through the demons to stand at the head of each mob. Amira had her silky, dark hair bound up in multiple braids converging in a ponytail to run down her back, and Abida styled his in a meticulous jet-black quaff. Their almond eyes, straight noses, and full lips were nearly identical, though Abida's features were naturally broader. But the most eye-catching detail was their clothes, if they could be called that. Tongues of red and orange fire, intermingled with thin swaths of black, covered their bodies and flickered like dying embers. They waved to one another from opposite ends of the bridge and smirked, both exuding a cocky nonchalance.

Daniel and Raylin finally met up with Gabriela and Seren, and they all stood back-to-back to face the approaching enemies.

"Plans?" Seren panted. She held the Celestial Bow fully drawn and alternating between targets.

"None," Daniel whispered. "If we had Ben here, we might be able to take a stand, but, well, that's obviously not an option unless you've heard from him."

Gabriela shook her head. "We've been dealing with demons and Generals. No sign of him.

"Same," Raylin replied. "Watch out for the wolf, by the way. It shoots venomous quills."

Seren flashed a fake smile. "Fantastic news. The snake demons spit acid, so that's cool."

She edged closer to Raylin until their shoulders brushed, and they exchanged relieved glances.

"What clothes are you children wearing?" Amira chuckled playfully, stepping to the front of the Generals. "I can hardly see you, though the power of your weapons makes it a simple matter to know your location. Still, it's an inconvenience." She looked upward and scratched her chin as if thoughtfully pondering the problem. "Such a dilemma. Wait, I know! I'll just get rid of them." She snapped her fingers, and a swirl of hellish letters appeared on the ground beneath

the companions' feet. They burned with dark purple fire, and each stroke mark sent up a wall of eerie light.

"And … there!" Amira clapped her hands, and Janice's clothes burst into ashes. "That's better."

If they hadn't already been pinned down on all sides by a demonic army, Daniel probably would've felt a sense of dread. As it was, he barely had time to think about the implications of losing Janice's concealing clothes. That was a problem they'd have to deal with later. He stabbed the ground and sent a Fire Strike radiating outward. The waves of purifying power erased Amira's hellish script and sent any encroaching demons skittering backward.

Abida stepped to his sister's side. "Is it really necessary to fight? Our last little skirmish was pointless, and you don't have the bubble boy with you to slow me down. Where is he, by the way?"

"He's around, hiding," Daniel bluffed, brandishing the Sun Sword toward Abida. "Just waiting for the right moment to … to …"

"To surround you with his protective bubble?" Chiuta scorned, flinging out his left hand. The Whirlwind of Famine twisted into the air and grew in height, towering over even the tallest of the desert dragons behind him. "So scary. I'm afraid."

"Anyone getting anything from the Three?" Daniel whispered with a hasty backward glance.

"Nothing," Gabriela replied. "I think the only choice is to fight." She put up her fists, her body tense.

Seren tilted her head toward Daniel. "Let's go for the twins first. Biggest threat. I've got Amira."

"I'll take Abida, not that it'll do any good," he replied. "We're definitely out of our league."

Raylin spun the Abyssal Staff. "I'll try to manage Fenrir."

"Oh, not Tyr?" Daniel shot back. "Going to leave him for Gabriela?"

Raylin furrowed her brows. "I think Fenrir's more than enough to handle, but yeah, if Tyr's open, I'll get him, too."

Gabriela cast Daniel a confused look. "Not sure what that's about.

Let's just say I'll try to manage Chiuta. Daniel and Raylin, you'll have to watch out for Vinaash. If she strikes one of us, we'll need your purification and sealing powers quick, or else we'll be picked off."

"Enough of your planning! I am starving!" Fenrir howled, bounding toward them and leaping into the air.

Daniel instinctively flung a Sunstorm, which zoomed centimeters from Raylin's shoulder before exploding into Fenrir's rump.

"Careful!" Raylin shouted over her shoulder as she whacked the monstrous wolf between the eyes. She jumped back and activated the staff to seal the dark spirits fleeing from the demon's body.

Daniel started to reply, but Abida suddenly stood over him.

"You've no time to chat." Abida grabbed Daniel around the throat and lifted him off the ground. "Who do you think you're facing, little boy?"

Daniel's field of vision quickly darkened as Abida tightened his flaming grip. He squirmed and kicked, but Abida felt like a rock against his feet. He had seconds before he would pass out. Daniel swung the Sun Sword wildly, connecting with Abida's arm, torso, neck, and even his face. Each pass it made through his body should've purified him, if only temporarily, but nothing happened other than the flames surrounding his body flared brighter and he flinched.

"You experienced Master's binding fire from India, no?" Abida crooned. "Behold its perfected state, completely binding his spirit within me. Your purifications can't banish it from me for even a moment. Your sword is powerless against—"

Daniel charged the Sun Sword and stabbed it into Abida's face.

Abida's grip loosened as the waves of power reverberated within his body. Daniel fell to the ground, coughing and sputtering, while the flames around Abida's body turned black.

Gabriela leaped through the air and punched Abida full in the jaw, sending him sprawling backward into Fenrir.

Daniel staggered to his feet, one hand on his throat while gasping. "Thanks!" he coughed. "The Sun Sword is just about worthless with him."

A scream from behind brought them spinning around. A snake demon wrapped around Seren, tightening its crushing coils while baring acid-dripping fangs.

Raylin jabbed the butt of the Abyssal Staff into a flying demon's stomach before dashing toward her sister. She deftly jumped onto the uppermost coil and used the snake's constricting body to spring through the air toward its mouth, simultaneously spinning the staff to knock its fangs out before it could strike.

It reared back in shock, hissing vehemently.

Racing behind it, Daniel caught its neck on the edge of the Sun Sword before it could recover.

Even before she landed, Raylin had activated the staff and sealed the demon.

"This is not going well," Seren shouted, pinning her back to Raylin and firing Celestial arrows like mad into two dragon demons bearing down on them. They halted, frozen like towering statues, while clouds of flying demons streamed around their chimney stack necks to attack.

"No. It's not," Raylin replied. She tried to catch her breath, but too many of the foes got through Seren's attack. The Abyssal Staff sang in the air around them.

Gabriela raced to their side, one of the snake demons firm in her grasp and trailing behind her. With a flick of her wrist, she whipped the snake's tail into the air and spun it around, creating a shield from further overhead attacks.

Dozens of flying demons discovered the joys of Gabriela's bludgeoning attack before the swarm retreated to a greater height.

The Whirlwind of Famine tore across the ground, tossing demons into the air like chaff.

Daniel jumped in front of the girls and flung one Sunstorm after another into its core. It did little other than slightly alter its direction. It roared by them, yanking Gabriela's serpent into its funnel and bearing down on Fenrir and Tyr.

Tyr simply popped back into his portal, but Fenrir's tail was sucked

in. It helplessly clawed at the ground as the rest of it followed. It entered the tornado as a massive, muscular demon but got spit out the other side a weakened, emaciated bag of bones.

Fenrir swung its massive head toward the General. "Chiuta, you worthless flea! Mind where you send that thing!"

A flying demon with a small serpent coiled around its legs zipped through the air near Fenrir. The wolf flung its head around and snapped it out of the air, swallowing it whole. Within seconds, Fenrir's vitality returned, and it jumped to its feet, slavering and snapping its teeth hungrily.

Meanwhile, the delay gave Daniel and the others time to regroup near the edge of the bridge.

Daniel scanned their enemies. Amira and Abida hung on the outskirts of the mob, watching the battle with eager grins like fans at a sporting event. The rest of their gang either charged toward the Vessels or waited in the seething melee for openings to attack.

"Ideas, please!" Seren panted, firing into the herd of desert dragons thundering toward them. Their flames froze, bound to their bellowing mouths as the encasing light spread over their bodies.

Daniel flung Sunstorms at each one and Raylin followed up by sealing away the fleeing spirits. But the horde pressed closer even while the flying demons dive-bombed them from above. Gabriela targeted these, jumping into the air to punch or kick some into the stratosphere while grabbing one in each hand to use as a club against the others.

Wanu popped in and out of her portal amid the cloud of demons, edging her way closer and closer with a maniacal laugh. She disappeared after a flurry of flying demons swarmed in front of her and then reappeared behind Gabriela just as she jumped into the air.

"Behind you!" Daniel warned, flinging Sunstorms at Wanu's back.

The purifying arc slammed into the General just as the Scythe of Death would have sunk into Gabriela's leg.

The Enemy's spirit billowed out of Wanu like a parachute, and she fell to the ground. Daniel darted to her side, swinging the Sun Sword wildly through her so she couldn't have a chance to recover.

"Seren! Bind her!" he gasped.

Seren shot a volley of Celestial Arrows in her direction, all of which sank into her side and encased her in a shell of blue light. "It's not going to hold her long," Seren gasped, straining to keep up with the unending attacks.

Amira leaped through the air and landed next to Wanu's prone form. She swatted away Seren's volley of arrows so quickly that her arm was a blur. With a yawn, she snapped her fingers, and the binding shell of light shattered.

Daniel felt himself hoisted into the air and flying backward. By the time he realized he was in Gabriela's arms, they had already landed fifteen feet back at the edge of the bridge. Raylin and Seren joined them, and they all pressed themselves against the railing.

"Thank you, Lady Amira," Wanu fawned. "You are gracious to release me—"

Amira kicked Wanu in the backside and sent her sprawling onto her face. The Scythe of Death clattered onto the road in front of her. "Save it," she snapped. "Just do your job. If I have to rescue you again, we'll be finding a new General to take your place, and you'll be spending the rest of your pathetic life attending to Master in the Abyss."

Wanu blanched at the threat and pushed herself to her feet. The scythe flew into her outstretched hand, and she turned her attention back to the Vessels. Though, Daniel noted, her usual ecstatic insanity was replaced with a look of gloomy insanity.

Abida sauntered up to Amira. Tyr popped out of a portal behind her, swinging the Hammer of War down off his shoulder and cracking his neck as if warming up to mash the Vessels into paste. Chiuta glided to his side, hovering just above the ground with the power of his whirlwind. Vinaash floated behind them, her cloud flashing with more Pestilence. The motley horde of demons hungrily crowded behind them as they all pressed toward the Vessels.

Father! We need help! Daniel desperately prayed. *Help! Help! Help!*

Seren, exhausted, let the Celestial Bow drop to her side. "I'm not getting any guidance from the Three. What do we do?"

Gabriela, her fists still held up at the ready, spoke in low tones. "Me either. Getting captured can't be in their plan. Inti seemed so clear this time."

Raylin brandished the Abyssal Staff back and forth with gritted teeth. "There's still hope, right?" she asked, sounding desperate to believe the question herself. "I mean, didn't things like this happen in other quests?"

Daniel let out a disgusted sigh. "Like this is a surprise to you! Don't act so innocent, Raylin."

"What?"

It seemed they had little left to lose, so why not expose her? He threw caution to the wind. "You heard me. I know all about you and Tyr's meeting. Your secret plan. So why don't you just walk over there to the other side—again—and betray us? Or better yet, pole vault yourself off this bridge."

"What are you talking about, Daniel?" Seren demanded. "And is this really the time?"

Raylin looked alarmed and cast a furtive glance toward Tyr. "I don't know what you mean, Daniel. Nothing like that happened."

"Please, like you and Tyr weren't scheming up something after we got separated in the city. Isn't that right, Tyr?" Daniel shouted the General's name. "How does your girlfriend feel about you having one-on-one meetings with other women?"

Amira cocked an eye at Tyr. "You met with the traitor? Why?"

Tyr put the head of his hammer onto the road and casually rested both hands on the end of its handle. "I met with no one. We fought in the city. That's all. Perhaps Fenrir's poison got to the boy's brain."

"That better be all," Amira said, her tone dangerous. "Enough of this. Capture them!" she ordered. "Break their arms and legs so they can't fight, then throw them at our feet. Abida and I will take them to Master. They will learn the meaning of suffering."

All four Generals and Fenrir rushed toward Daniel and the others. The horde of demons followed in their wake.

Daniel and Seren fired into the mob, but it was pointless. Their

attacks did nothing to halt the advance, and they were now pressed to the very edge of the bridge.

"They are mine!" a throaty, gurgling voice below them announced.

The river erupted in a spray of water. Daniel felt slimy tentacles wrap around his body and yank him violently off his feet. He cast a disoriented look to his sides and saw Raylin, Seren, and Gabriela similarly bound. He craned his neck and took in Enbilulu's horrific body, which was entirely out of the water and careening through the air parallel to the bridge.

The demon opened its gaping mouth to reveal rows upon rows of sharky teeth. "The victory will be mine!" it roared. "Master will reward ME!" With a slurp, Daniel and the others were pulled into the darkness of its hungry maw, which snapped shut behind them as the demon crashed back into the foaming murk of the Euphrates.

13

A Fishing Trip with Enbidoodoo

"This is so gross!" Seren moaned from somewhere ahead of Daniel.

The tentacles pulled them inch by inch farther down the demon's throat.

Raylin's annoyed voice was somewhere just beyond hers. "Where are you taking us? And if you don't get your tentacles off me, I'm going to snap every last one in half and beat you with them."

"He's swallowing us," Gabriela matter-of-factly stated. "I second that threat, by the way. Do you hear me, demon? Unless you want to be pounded into a stinking pile of fish mush, you better take us to shore and spit us out!"

Daniel heard something snap like a rubber band and felt Gabriela wriggling free below him.

"Ahh!" Enbilulu screamed. "I did what you wanted! Now make them stop!" it demanded.

"All right, fine. Geez, you're such a baby. Gabriela, don't tear him apart … yet," Ben said. "We'll see how well he plays his part."

"Ben?" Daniel and Raylin gasped in unison.

They were deposited, one by one, into what Daniel could only guess was its stomach, illuminated by the blue light of the Triune Shield. The shield itself rested in the center of Enbilulu's cavernous belly, its borders pressing hard against the ceiling and floor. Through various holes and slits in the demon's sides, he could see the murky water of the Euphrates passing by, thankfully kept at bay by some power of its spirit.

The scenery outside wasn't much to look at, though: schools of dark fish scattering at the nearness of the demon, floating logs, one crocodile, river weed, and lots of mud.

"You guys better hop inside me," Ben suggested. "Unless you want to wade around Doo-Doo Face's stomach acid all day."

"That is not my name!" Enbilulu whined. Its tentacles loosened on Daniel and the others, and they hastily staggered to their feet. "I am the magnificent Enbi—"

"Can it. Unless you want me to stretch you into a fish ball," Ben threatened, expanding his borders so they distended the demon's stomach.

"No! Stop! I will be quiet, I promise!" Enbilulu insisted. It then fell to muttering, "I would never hear the end of it from the other demons. Especially Fenrir. That mongrel is such a bully."

"Good, now dive as deep as you can and keep swimming on the bottom of the river. If you attempt to surface, well, you know what'll happen. And with us inside you, you'd be exorcised before you could say 'fish sticks,' which I'm never eating again, by the way."

"I think I'll pass on the stomach acid," Seren interrupted, hopping through the sloshing liquid toward the shield and jumping through its border. "Nope, nope, nope. None for me, thank you. Ugh. So gross."

Everyone else tiptoed through the pool of gastric juices and lumps of foul-smelling meat to join her.

Daniel scratched his head and looked around. "Okay, so what's the story? We all thought you were still trapped at the bottom of the river with Enbidoodoo inside you, but here we find you controlling it and cruising around."

"Nothing too interesting," Ben replied, his voice filtering down from the silhouette of his body perched between three interlocked rings gyrating at the top of the shield. "After holding Doo Doo—"

Enbilulu groaned.

"—at the bottom of the river, I decided to experiment a little.

Since I can cast the Triune Shield over objects like my knives, I figured I could do the same over parts of our friendly neighborhood demon here. I gradually shrank myself down over just its mouth. I guess I was hoping it would keep the whining at bay. I was wrong. Meanwhile, I knew I had to figure out a way to control it and get back to you all, and the idea just popped into my head: hide inside the dork's stomach so no other river demons realize I'm here and threaten to explode it if it doesn't do what I ask. No one likes to explode, do they, Enbidoodoo?"

"No, sir," Enbilulu bubbled.

"That's true," Gabriela chuckled. "Sounds pretty dreadful."

Raylin put up a hand and touched the borders of the shield. "Aren't you exhausted from keeping the summoning going so long?"

The Triune Shield blushed a slight purple. "Oh, nah. It's not that hard. No harder than you all keeping your weapons summoned. Besides, if I can handle the Enemy trying to crush me or light me on fire like in the Abyss, just keeping the shield activated is easy."

"How did you find us?" Seren asked, plopping down to sit cross-legged. She released the Celestial Bow and breathed easy.

"Simple. Fish Sticks here could sense your Weapons of Power. It knew your general location and could feel the twins' power, too. You can figure out the rest, I assume."

"Nice," Daniel said, relief flooding his body. He joined Seren on the floor of the Triune Shield. "So now, all we have to do is relax as we cruise down the river toward the gulf, right?"

"*You* can relax, I guess. But, uh, when I said it was easy to keep the Triune Shield summoned, I didn't mean it was effortless. A little boost would be a nice relief."

"Oh, sure. Sorry." Daniel charged the Sun Sword.

"Just don't stab it in beyond the shield's borders. I wouldn't want old Fish Poop to pop."

Enbilulu started crying.

"I'll be real gentle." Daniel barely stabbed the Sun Sword downward, releasing a lazy Fire Strike that leisurely pinged back and forth between the sword and Ben's borders.

Ben let out a loud sigh. "Thanks, man. Much appreciated."

"Don't mention it."

Seren pushed up from the floor of the shield and crossed her arms. "Good. Now that that's settled, are we going to talk about what happened on the bridge?"

"Yeah, Daniel," Gabriela joined in, pulling a string of river weed out of her hair and tossing it on the ground. "You've been edgy with Raylin this whole quest, and now you're accusing her of rejoining the Enemy? What's going on?"

"Daniel's accusing Raylin of what?" Ben demanded.

"He's accusing me of being in cahoots with Tyr," Raylin explained. "Of betraying you all again. But I'm not."

"There, see, Daniel?" Ben demanded. "She's not, so you can cease your accusations."

"It's not as simple as that, Ben." Daniel cast a worried look at Gabriela and then released the Sun Sword. He paced around the shield, all the while attending to Raylin's reactions out of the corner of his eye. "When Raylin and I were fighting our way to the bridge, I overheard her having a conversation with Tyr."

Enbilulu slowed its pace. "The traitor is scheming with Tyr?"

"Stay out of this!" Raylin shot back. "I wasn't talking with Tyr; he was attacking me. Look," she continued in a quieter voice, "can we talk about this later, when we don't have Fish Turds eavesdropping?" Her voice dropped even lower. "Everything we say will go back to the Enemy when we exorcise this demon."

"I heard that!" Enbilulu gargled. "There is no need to purify me, you know! I can go about my business after I drop you all off. Master need not know of any of your quibbling."

Ben expanded his borders so that the bottom of Enbilulu's stomach stretched uncomfortably.

"Ow! Ow! Okay! I will be silent!"

"Good. Now pick up the pace," Ben ordered. "Get us to the gulf as fast as your rotten tail can swim."

"Yes, sir."

Daniel pointed at Raylin. "You're lying. I overheard through the door; you and Tyr were talking about some secret plan the Enemy has. He swore you to silence."

"That's ridiculous," Raylin replied, pulling her ponytail down and running her fingers through her hair to work out the tangles. "Before you burst into the room, he had me cornered and was trying to force information out of me." She wiped her brow and continued in a lower voice. "Honestly, I don't think arguing in front of the demon is a good idea."

Seren shook her head at Daniel. "You obviously misheard them. You were listening through a door, after all."

"I know what I heard, Seren."

Gabriela gingerly massaged both her temples. "She has a good point, Daniel."

Daniel threw his hands in the air. "I don't see why this is so unbelievable. She betrayed us before. Why is it hard to imagine her doing it again?"

Seren moved closer to Raylin, hovering near her protectively. "Because Raylin wouldn't do that. She's been saved by the Three. You wouldn't do that, right, Raylin?"

"You know I wouldn't!" She scanned Enbilulu's stomach, studying each shadowy recess with an eye of distrust. "Look," she continued with a whisper, "can we finish this conversation once we get out of here?"

Daniel laughed derisively. "You mean after you've had time to hand us over to the Enemy, and you're gloating over our dead bodies? No, thanks."

"I say we trust her," Ben interjected. "I mean, can anyone be saved by the Three like she was and go back to the way they were? That seems impossible."

"Of course, you'd trust her, Ben. But excuse me if I don't automatically see things your way here. I'm looking out for our safety. If you haven't noticed, we're in the heart of the Enemy's territory, we've got a mess of powerful demons and freaks chasing

us, and we're inside a fish monster's stomach." Daniel's voice rose to a shout. "We don't exactly have the luxury of taking more risks by believing a known traitor!"

Gabriela's hand came down hard on Daniel's shoulder.

He turned his head.

"Take a breather, Daniel." She stepped closer. "Trust in the Three. No matter what the truth is, they'll have foreseen it. Why don't we all relax until we get to Eden? Maybe things will seem clearer there than when we're in the belly of a demon."

"But, Gabriela," Daniel objected, cocking his head to the side and giving her a disbelieving grin, "you can't mean I should pretend I didn't hear the conversation with Tyr. Pretend that Raylin isn't about to betray us."

"I don't know about all that, but you should trust that this'll get sorted out. Go pray and seek the Father's guidance. I will, too."

Daniel let his eyes fall to the Sun Sword's sizzling blade, the images of Raylin's first betrayal seared into his memories as if branded there by the sword itself. "So that's what everyone wants? Pretend this is ok and move on?"

"I'll tell you what I don't want," Ben said earnestly. "I don't want to leave our friend abandoned somewhere in Babylon when I'm not sure of all the details. I choose to trust Raylin and give her the benefit of the doubt while we wait for the Three to make things clearer."

Seren clenched her jaw. "Me, too. I know my sister, and I trust her."

Daniel shook his head and met Raylin's gaze with a steely glare.

She tilted her head down, and her hair fell forward like a curtain.

"I see." He walked to the opposite end of the shield and laid down, turning his back to everyone. "I'm going to pray and get some rest. Let me know if anything happens. You know, like we get handed over to the Serpent for torture. Stuff like that." He shut his eyes and tried to drown out the hushed conversation between Seren and Raylin.

Father, will you please send your Spirit to us? I mean, I know he's here inside of us … well, maybe not Raylin, but the rest of us. I mean, could you send him here in person? Then you could set everything straight.

Daniel waited in silence for an answer, listening to the swishing of Enbilulu's tail paddling through the water. The whispers of the others died down, and he assumed everyone except Ben was trying to get some rest.

Even if you do not trust Raylin, do you trust me? The Father's voice quietly filtered into Daniel's mind, almost imperceptible from the rhythmic sound of the demon's swimming. *Trust in me, Daniel. This, too, is my will and is for your good.*

I do trust you … Daniel paused. Did he? Sure, he'd trusted him in the past. But was trust something that was once and for all, or were there a thousand opportunities every day, each one requiring a new choice to exercise faith? *I think I trust you. I'll … I'll try to with this. But if Raylin is going to betray us, wouldn't that mess up your plan? Can you at least help the others realize what she's really like on the inside?*

I weigh the heart, Daniel. I alone know Raylin's thoughts, motivations, hopes, and dreams. I knew them before she was knit together in her mother's womb, and all the choices she would make in her life were laid out before me like a book. I know her as I know you. Sleep, Daniel, and reflect on your own heart. The answer to this problem lies within.

Daniel tried to hold on to the Father's words a moment longer, but the suggestion to sleep was more of a command. At his word, Daniel felt himself slip into darkness.

* * *

"**H**e's so young. How can he shoulder this much at such an age?" The man's voice didn't sound much older than Daniel's. He struggled to open his eyes but found he was so weary he could barely crack them. He felt himself lying face up in someone's lap. Soft, strong hands stroked his hair. Usually, the thought of resting his head on a man's thighs would've been uncomfortable to Daniel, but this somehow felt normal.

This time, it was a woman's voice who answered. She seemed to be somewhere by Daniel's feet. "He'd already been through so much, even before his quests. I think it prepared him for all this."

He knew that voice from somewhere. Or did he? In these dreams, the line between familiar and foreign was anything but clear. Try as he might, he couldn't place where he'd heard it before. Or the man's, for that matter. It didn't remind Daniel of anyone he could name, but he felt drawn to it.

"Sorrow is a hard teacher," the man murmured. "I am sorry for him. I am sorry for the choices that led to his hardships."

"Don't be. The Three redeemed him. His sorrow, too, will be redeemed. Even as ours was." Daniel felt a soft hand stroke his feet.

The man grunted assent and let a hand fall to Daniel's cheek. "But his current problem—what causes it?"

With all his strength, Daniel strained to open his eyes long enough to catch a glimpse of the speakers, but their faces were darkly silhouetted against a brilliantly white sun blazing overhead. He sighed, his head limply tilting, and found himself gazing through bleary eyes at a wide expanse of lake, mountains, and a thin ribbon of emerald sea in the far distance. Then, before all that, a vision gently unfolded. It was him and Raylin as they stood captive within the spiritual prison in Supai's throne room in Peru. Supai, smug and overconfident in his plan, towered over them, gleeful as Raylin took the Sun Sword from Daniel and betrayed them. Daniel felt a surge of anger well up from inside him. Yes, this was the cause of his current dilemma. He gritted his teeth and tried to move, but the lethargy was too strong.

"Oh. I see," the man said, laying a strong hand on Daniel's chest. "Peace, young man. Do not strive while you are here, nor harbor resentment. Rest."

His words held power, and Daniel felt his tension flee at the commands. The woman at his feet lifted her voice in a short, haunting song. At first, Daniel thought it was a lullaby until he listened more closely to the words.

Alone with none but thee, my God, he journeys on his way.
What need he fear, when thou art near, O king of night and day?
More safe is he within thy hand than if a host did round him stand.
Alone with none but thee, my God, he journeys on his way.

"Yet, not alone," the man said after the woman's song ended. "His friends remain."

The woman was silent, and the dream faded as Enbilulu's churning tail and Ben's urgent whisper drifted back to him.

"Guys! Wake up! You need to see this!"

Daniel roused himself, the details of the dream drifting to the back of his mind as Ben continued to press them. He summoned the Sun Sword and scrambled to his feet but then let it fall to his side as he stared through the holes in Enbilulu's stomach.

Gabriela joined him. She leaned over and hooked her arm around his while taking in the scene outside.

"Ladies. Are you seeing this?" she asked Raylin and Seren.

The sisters peered out holes in Enbilulu's opposite side.

"Terrifying Firstborn?" Raylin asked.

"Yep," Gabriela said.

Even with everything Daniel had witnessed throughout his quests, the scene before him sent shivers down his spine. Here, the Euphrates flowed unfathomably deep and clear. Two Firstborn, bound to columns of radiantly white stone by chains of blinding light, towered over them. Daniel turned and looked out Enbilulu's other side, where Seren and Raylin beheld the scene in awe. Two more Firstborn, nearly identical, stood bound in the same fashion. They were gargantuan, even taller than the Serpent. Malevolent eyes, empty of all color, zeroed in on the Vessels' movements with evidently murderous desire. A black circle darkened the center of their brows. Orange fire spilled off their heads like unkempt manes of hair, and their garb appeared to be some strange fusion of rocks and earth. Though their bonds held them so tightly that they couldn't move, every fiber of muscle strained and vibrated against their chains. The bases of the columns and lower halves of the Firstborn were lost in the depths below.

Daniel's visual senses were nearly overwhelmed by their immensity, and he suspected they were passing through some spiritual dimension. There was no way the river could naturally submerge such enormous

beings. Daniel shivered. Somehow, he knew if they were ever released, the whole earth would feel their wrath.

Seren cautiously whispered, "I don't remember the Enemy ever mentioning having servants like them. Should we be worried?"

"From the look of those chains," Raylin muttered back, "I don't think he can count on them for much."

"Seems like the Three's handiwork."

Enbilulu quivered and froze halfway between the four beings. "I should not be here. This is a holy place," it wailed, beginning to paddle backward. "I should not be here!"

"You know who these guys are?" Raylin asked.

"The Three bound them here until the end of the Seventh Age." A shudder rippled through Enbilulu's body. "They are reserved for judgment at the time of the end."

"The Enemy's judgment?" Ben asked.

"No. Judgment on Earthborn who fight against the Three. But the Master will thwart this, and his servants will prevail."

Gabriela put her hands on her hips and tilted her head. "I doubt that. Just out of curiosity, are other Firstborn supposed to get judged by these guys too?"

"I do not know," Enbilulu whimpered. "Maybe."

"Daniel," Ben said. "What are our bearings?"

Daniel allowed the Sun Sword to hover in the air before him until it pulled him straight ahead. "We should keep going," he announced.

"You heard him, you bottom-feeding bag of garbage. I don't care how scary these guys are. Keep moving forward."

Ben expanded his borders until Enbilulu, fearful of bursting, cautiously navigated the exact middle of the river, doing its best to remain as far from the four Firstborn on either side as possible.

Before long, the scene fell behind, and the murk of the river returned like a cloud.

"The river's gone back to muddy again," Raylin observed.

Enbilulu moaned in relief. "The Tigris has merged with the Euphrates. We are now in the Shatt al-Arab River. From here, the

gulf is a little over a hundred miles away," Enbilulu whimpered. "I do not like saltwater. When will you let me go?"

"When the Gates of Eden have opened, I'll think about letting you go," Ben said. "Until then, you better be on your best behavior. And that sounds like a long way. How fast can you get us there?"

Enbilulu made a series of gulping noises. "A day or so if I keep my current pace."

"What if you swim as fast as you can?" Ben asked, an edge of warning in his voice.

"A few hours, I suppose," Enbilulu squeaked. "That would take a lot of energy!"

"Aren't you supposed to be a god, Enbi-doofus? I suggest you use your godlike powers and swim fast. *Real* fast."

"But the salt water," Enbilulu gurgled. "And … and I cannot enter Eden! It is guarded by a holy Firstborn. His very presence could unmake me! No! No! You cannot take me there!"

"It's just something you're going to have to deal with," Ben snapped. "Maybe that'll teach you not to attack people. Now zip it. Guys, don't we need to dip our Weapons of Power in the Tigris?"

"That's right," Seren said with a snap of her fingers. "Can we just stick them through Doodoo's sides?"

"Give it a shot," Ben suggested.

"Be careful you do not touch me with your weapons!" Enbilulu moaned.

Ben sighed. "This guy is useful, but he's getting on my nerves. Fine. Everyone, especially you, Daniel, be sure to not touch your weapons to Catfish Brains. Let's keep our ride intact and happy until we're safe in Eden."

"But I am not happy!" Enbilulu gurgled.

"Get a move on!" Ben ordered.

Enbilulu groaned and whined but began swimming much faster. Outside its cavernous body, the muddy river streamed by at an amazing speed.

Ignoring its complaints, everyone cautiously slipped their weapons

through Enbilulu's porous sides until the cool waters of the Tigris-Euphrates washed over them. One by one, they pulled them back in and released them. Last of all, Ben extended the borders of the Triune Shield through one of the holes and then carefully resumed his perfectly spherical shape.

In the quiet that ensued, Daniel had time to recollect his dream, especially the vision of Raylin's first betrayal. Well, no matter. Sure, no one believed she was betraying them again, but once they reached Eden, maybe some opportunity would present itself to expose her true motives. Enbilulu's whining recalled Inti's words to Daniel. The Firstborn that the demon referred to was Uriel, the guardian of Eden's gates. Maybe Daniel could get advice from him. He'd see right through Raylin's lies. Daniel felt a surge of relief flood his body, and a smile crept over his face. Okay, he could let her scheming go for the present and just rest. He reached into his backpack and pulled out some food and water.

"It's good to see you finally relax," Gabriela said, walking over from Enbilulu's sides and sitting down next to him. "Did you have a good nap earlier?"

Daniel felt a warm sensation zip through his body as she leaned against him. "Yeah, I did. But I keep having dreams that I don't quite understand."

Gabriela lightly brushed his hair to the side. "Was there ever a quest when you didn't?"

"No. Maybe. I can't remember if I had any weird dreams in the British Isles … spiritual dreams, I mean. But these are different, I think. They're not symbolic or anything about the Three, as far as I know. They're just about two people. Always the same ones: a man and a woman. They seem familiar, but I can never get a look at their faces." Daniel shrugged.

Gabriela listened, her head drifting to Daniel's shoulder. "Do they say anything to you?"

"Not much beyond telling me to have peace or something. They talked to each other quite a bit in the last dream. All about me. It

was like the woman knew more about me than the man did." He slid his hand down and intertwined his fingers with Gabriela's.

"Did either of them say anything about Raylin?" she asked in a cautious whisper. Daniel thought for a moment, running through the details of the last dream. "No, but I had a flashback of Raylin betraying us in Supai's throne room, and it seemed like they could see it, too. I think they could tell her betrayal—then and now—bothered me."

"Lower your voice," Gabriela urged, herself speaking in an almost inaudible whisper. She glanced at Raylin and Seren, who were resting with their eyes closed against the opposite side of Ben's borders. "Are you absolutely sure you're not mistaken about Raylin and Tyr?"

"I am," Daniel replied. "They were scheming something. Raylin is lying; I know it."

Gabriela nodded her head almost imperceptibly. "I'm not sure what to do about all this other than to wait until we're in Eden. If Raylin is attempting to betray us again, that will probably be the best place to deal with it."

Daniel studied Raylin as though by staring hard enough, he could detect some indisputable mark of betrayal. She stirred and opened her eyes, frowned when she saw Daniel's scrutiny, and quickly looked away.

Good, Daniel thought. *At least she feels ashamed about what she's doing.*

"I hope so," he muttered back to Gabriela. "But if they don't, I might have to address it myself."

14

Pop Goes the Demon

Enbilulu sped down the river, still hugging the deeper channels while they remained. The water outside its body began to darken as they moved into the brackish water nearer to the gulf.

Everyone stirred at the sound of Enbilulu whimpering to itself. Daniel studied the murky water streaming by outside. Some distance away, he thought he caught sight of something flashing in the depths.

"This water is itchy," Enbilulu whined. "Please let me go. I promise I will not eat any other humans for at least a week."

Ben replied with another threat, but Daniel ignored it. Another flash pierced the gloom, this time closer.

"Is anyone else seeing this? I think we should get ready for an attack," Daniel said, raising his voice over Enbilulu's complaints.

He summoned the Sun Sword and gave Ben a Fire Strike for good measure.

"What did you see?" Ben asked. "Thanks, by the way."

"You're welcome. I don't know, exactly. There were two flashes of light out there in the water."

"Flashes of light. Under water?" Raylin posed the question almost to herself, the Abyssal Staff already in her hands.

"What color?" Seren's voice was clipped, like a soldier getting bearings for battle. "Green? Could be Vinaash." The starlight limbs of the Celestial Bow extended from her hands as she and Raylin joined Daniel and Gabriela on their side.

"Hard to tell," Daniel replied. "The water's so dark." He cast a hasty glance toward the sisters.

Seren seemed to have set aside her anger at his accusations, at least momentarily. She stood shoulder-to-shoulder with him, intently searching the depths beyond. Raylin, too, acted unaffected, apparently committed to playing the part of an innocent companion as she readied herself next to Gabriela.

"I don't see anything," Gabriela mused. "But, that's strange. Wait. Down there." She pressed her face against Ben's borders, straining to see out Enbilulu's sides and below them. "The water's glowing green."

A momentary crackling noise buzzed through the water, and Enbilulu violently swerved sideways.

It gasped. "You dare to attack me?" it blared, quickening its pace as it zigzagged through the water.

The sudden changes in direction threw everyone to their backs.

Gabriela was the first to regain her footing. "Who are you talking to?" she demanded. "What's happening?"

Another crackling noise, this time louder, and the demon lurched upward in the water column as though punched in its stomach.

"Gah! Vile mortals. Cease your fire, or I will drown you in the depths of—" Another blow landed from below, driving Enbilulu toward the surface.

"What's happening? Why are you rising?" Daniel demanded, steadying himself on his knees.

Enbilulu began to slow, and the sides of its stomach turned a splotchy white. "It is them," it gasped, its voice faint and weaker. "They are att—ack—acking me!"

Enbilulu choked on his words just as Wanu and Vinaash stepped out of a portal in the demon's throat.

"We've got company!" Ben shouted.

Raylin jumped to her feet and brandished the Abyssal Staff.

"Okay," Seren whispered, "so now we know who was attacking Enbilulu. Perfect."

The Generals regarded the Vessels with looks of arrogant contempt. The cramped quarters of Enbilulu's throat forced Wanu to hold the Scythe of Death uncharacteristically still. Vinaash, too, opted for a more controlled approach when brandishing Pestilence. The arc of green lightning hugged her shoulders and arms. Neither, it seemed, wanted to destroy the fish demon at the present.

The series of flashes in the river's depths and the subsequent attacks now made sense to Daniel. Vinaash and Wanu had likely opened portals at random points through the murky water until they could zero in on Enbilulu. Then, Vinaash blasted it with Pestilence to drive it closer to the surface before transporting into its throat. Daniel rubbed the back of his neck. Which probably meant the other Generals, twins, and a bunch of demons were waiting above the water to commence their attack.

Enbilulu groaned as the effects of the Pestilence spread through its body. Its stomach, awash with a sickly greenish white, shivered and convulsed. It labored to breathe, and it listed to the side as if about to go belly up in the water.

Ben shifted his center of balance even as Daniel and the others did the same. The holes in Enbilulu's sides now faced toward the surface, which was ten feet away at most. Amorphous shapes and shadows swarmed above the water, periodically breaking the surface with claws and fangs, desperately seeking the giant fish demon and the prize its stomach held.

"Wretches," Enbilulu wheezed. "When I defeat your Pestilence, I will drag you to the bottom of the river and feast on your bones!"

"Keep silent," Wanu hissed, her darkened brow making her seem even more predatory. "We have orders to do much more if you resist." She studied the Triune Shield. "It would appear you were hijacked. Master will not be pleased by your weakness. Still, if you cooperate in capturing the children, you might be spared."

"Not likely," Vinaash chuckled, rolling her eyes and smirking.

"I heard that!" Enbilulu groaned. "What could I have done? Sacrificed myself?"

"Not our problem," Vinaash replied. "Now, keep silent so we can deal with the little ones." She brushed Wanu to the side and sauntered closer to the shield. "Oh, children! Won't you come out to play?" She laughed maniacally, punctuating her last word with a blast of Pestilence.

The arc bounced off the Triune Shield and absorbed into Enbilulu's sides. Ben grunted with the impact, and then his voice trickled down to the others. "We need to make a plan and quick. You guys have any ideas?"

"Working on it!" Daniel replied, frantically looking back and forth between the Generals and the approaching surface, hoping a strategy would suddenly occur to him. He definitely didn't want to purify Enbilulu and be helpless in the water.

"I've got an idea," Wanu laughed, approaching the Triune Shield and carefully slashing its border.

"No—OW!—pressure," Ben said. "Hurry it up, guys. This is—OW!—not pleasant. Hey, Piranha Lady, mind your own business!" Ben expanded his borders just slightly, catching Wanu off guard and knocking her on her back before she could land another slash.

"Ben, can you force them out of the demon's throat?" Seren asked. She stepped in front of the others and fired luminous arrows toward the Generals.

In the cramped quarters of Enbilulu's throat, Wanu couldn't deflect the attack or open a portal very easily. Vinaash stepped to the front, summoning her halo out of thin air to form a shield. The Celestial Arrows crashed into it, spreading their binding light across its surface.

Daniel caught onto Seren's plan. "Good idea. Ben?"

"On it," Ben said. He expanded his borders into an oblong shape while Vinaash's barrier obscured her view, ramming the Generals toward Enbilulu's mouth.

Daniel released a gentle Fire Strike, hoping to energize Ben after Wanu's series of attacks. "I'll give you some backup."

Gabriela stepped to the front of the shield, a steely look in her

eyes. "I'll help you out, Ben. One good punch, and they should be out in the water."

Vinaash peeked around her halo and sent a small and steady arc of Pestilence into the Triune Shield.

"On second thought, maybe not," Gabriela hastily added.

"Ack! Geh ou of ma throack!" Enbilulu hacked.

"What did he say?" Gabriela asked.

"He's telling the Generals to get out of his throat," Ben replied.

Gabriela shook her head. "What is it with you and interpreting hard-to-understand demons? First, it was the stone giant in Wales, and now, a choking fish demon in Babylon. Ben Jones, the Demon Interpreter."

"I do what I can."

"That's really funny," Daniel said. He released another Fire Strike. "Can we focus on surviving?"

"No need to tell me," Ben replied, continuing to move farther into the demon's throat to keep the Generals on the move. "Everyone needs to follow me so you're not left standing in his stomach acid."

Everyone grunted their understanding and moved with the elongated shield until they all were in the cramped quarters of the demon's throat.

Vinaash peeked around her halo. "You know we can hear everything you plan."

"As if we'd let you have your way," Wanu cackled, dexterously reaching her scythe around Vinaash and stabbing the Triune Shield.

Vinaash added more juice to her arc of Pestilence, doubling it in size.

Hissing in pain, Ben nonetheless continued his advance, completely within Enbilulu's convulsing throat.

"Gack! Am gocking, yu wothlesh hoomans! Wanoo. Vinaath. Da sumthun halpfoo and kall tham awraddy!"

"Gack! I'm choking, you worthless humans!" Ben interpreted, still pushing the Generals steadily toward Enbilulu's mouth. "Wanu. Vinaash. Do something helpful and kill them already!"

"Thanks, Ben," Raylin said. "But I don't think the Generals need any clarification on what their goal is."

"This is getting us nowhere," Wanu grumbled, her shark teeth clacking in irritation. "We should've gone with my plan. I *am* going with my plan. Get ready," she snapped. The sound of an opening portal briefly filled Enbilulu's mouth, and its gray, swirling edges were just visible above Vinaash's halo.

Vinaash growled. "Snatching their souls while they're stuck in Enbilulu's belly was a good idea. They're cramped and can't fight well. Your plan was too chaotic. Wanu? Come back!" She kept Pestilence sizzling into the shield but craned her head around to look for Wanu. "I'll push the bubble boy back. Are you listening? Where are you? I am your senior, and I command you to give me the respect I deserve. Wanu!"

"I think she's gone," Seren explained. "Maybe you should join her."

Vinaash stomped her foot, eliciting a pathetic cry from Enbilulu. "Fine, but if they somehow escape," she shrieked through the portal, "it's all on you. If this doesn't work, don't expect me to defend you when Abida and Amira discipline you." She ceased her attack and tramped through the portal herself without a backward glance at the Vessels. Her halo vanished as the portal swirled shut.

"Okay, back to the stomach," Ben ordered, creeping down Enbilulu's throat and resuming his spherical shape.

Enbilulu weakly groaned, the effects of the Pestilence still apparent in its listless bobbing.

"I don't know," Daniel said. "I can't purify Enbidoodoo of the Pestilence, so we're basically stuck like this."

Gabriela paced back and forth. "I doubt we'll have much time to plan something. Seren, Raylin, either of you have an idea?"

Raylin shook her head. "Nothing. I've been praying this whole time, and I'm getting zilch. No ideas, no answers, just memories of the Three being with us in worse scenarios and getting us through."

"Ditto," Seren said. She scanned Enbilulu's diseased stomach. "Fish Cakes, can you swim at all?"

Its only response was a pitiful gargling noise.

"Were you ever hit with your own Pestilence?" Daniel asked.

Seren shook her head.

"You literally have zero strength. I don't think Doo Doo is going to be our ticket out of this."

"What are you doing?" Enbilulu weakly bubbled. "No. Not that! No!"

Daniel and the others flashed perplexed looks at one another, but there was little time for anything else.

Enbilulu began spinning and was lifted to the water's surface and flung into the air. Looking down through Enbilulu's latticework sides, the Whirlwind of Famine eddied around and below them, keeping the demon aloft. The ashen white of its stomach now withered to a lifeless, gray blob. Daniel didn't know how its body was staying together.

A moment after they burst out of the water, the whirlwind receded, and flying demons swarmed Enbilulu. Their talons sank into its flesh, and they hungrily tore open larger holes in a desperate attempt to reach the Vessels.

"No! Stop!" Wanu bellowed. "Hold the fish god still! Don't tear him apart. Just fly him to the tower!"

Her words were useless. The flying demons, too enthralled with being so close to their prey, forced their way inside Enbilulu's stomach while others tore it to shreds.

In the chaos, Daniel noticed Vinaash's vomit cloud hovering nearby. Abida and Amira, along with all the Generals and Fenrir, impatiently perched at the front of the wispy tufts. Behind and below them, dragon, serpent, and camel spider demons crowded the banks of the river. In the distance, less than a mile away, a broad expanse of dark blue water stretched toward the horizon. They had nearly reached the Persian Gulf, but now they were captured.

Abida stepped forward and unfolded his arms. "Get control of them. Now." His voice held a dangerous tone.

Wanu jumped into one of her portals and popped out around

Enbilulu. She spun the Scythe of Death dexterously around, slashing at the flying demons tearing into its stomach while screeching for the others to hold it still.

Each demon she touched with the scythe immediately condensed into a dark, cloudy ball that hovered around the blade. The swarm chittered anxiously and finally turned their attention to the General.

"Hold them still while we bind them. Try to tear the fish god apart again, and you'll pay!" she threatened, then disappeared as her portal swirled shut. Seconds later, she reappeared on Vinaash's cloud.

Abida took a step back and heaved a haughty sigh. "Get the red chain," he ordered, barely tilting his head toward Amira.

Daniel's mind raced. The Enemy, in the guise of Arawn, had summoned a red chain to bind Raylin when they were in the British Isles during the last quest. If they were bound within Enbilulu, who knows if they'd be able to break free.

"You're not my superior. Summon it yourself," Amira snapped back. "Unless"—she sniggered into the back of her hand—"you're too weak."

The flames around Abida's body flared wildly. "Weak? How dare you! I'm a god."

Fenrir's tongue lolled out hungrily as it eyed the Vessels through Enbilulu's porous stomach, but it took a break to roll its eyes at Abida's comment.

Amira's only response was to blow her brother a kiss.

"Women," Abida growled, nearly spitting out the word. He lifted both hands, fixed his gaze somewhere above Enbilulu, and tensed. Muscles bulged and sweat beaded on his forehead as concentric black rings of wispy script formed over the demon's suspended body.

The flying demons shrieked, and any who weren't holding Enbilulu darted behind the Generals to join the dragons and other assortment of terrestrial demons loitering on the periphery of the scene. Those left holding the fish demon looked terrified.

"If you of any drops the fish god," Wanu warned, her shrill voice piercing the air, "you'll be food for the wolf!"

Fenrir broke out into a broad, salivating grin.

Gabriela spun around. "He's summoning that chain to bind us inside here. We'll be served up on a platter to the Serpent unless we do something."

"What are our options?" Raylin asked.

Daniel paced, racking his brain for a solution.

"I'll shoot everything I've got at Abida," Seren whispered. "Maybe that'll distract him while you all think of a plan." She released a steady volley of Celestial arrows aimed directly at his heart.

Abida didn't seem concerned by their rapid approach. Seconds before they landed, Vinaash's halo flashed in front of him, expanding into a large barrier to shield him from the attack.

"Guys," Ben's urgent voice drifted down from his figure within the rings of the Triune Shield above them. "Purify Fish Cakes. I've got an idea. Just trust me."

"Are you sure that's the only way?" Raylin asked. "What do we do next?"

Alarm bells went off in Daniel's head. If Ben had a plan, he didn't want Raylin to know what it was. Who knew what sort of ways she had to communicate with the Enemy and his minions? It's not as if they had time to gab about it anyway; links of the thigh-thick chain snaked out of the portal above Enbilulu. They had seconds, if that.

Daniel flung Sunstorms toward the demon's head, stomach, and tail. Without missing a beat, he summoned a Fire Strike and stabbed it through the shield into the demon's stomach. "Sorry, Enbidoodoo. Thanks for the ride, though!"

Enbilulu burst into a maelstrom of wailing, black spirit, shrieking angrily about its indignation at having been so abused over the past day of its long life. Like sable lightning, it tore through the air over the desert and back toward Ealim Wahid's tower.

"No!" Amira screamed as the Triune Shield and the rest of the company dropped toward the river.

Abida finished his summoning a split second later. The red chain, humming with wicked power, fell through the air toward the Triune

Shield. No longer tasked with holding Enbilulu aloft, the flying demons scattered in terror at its approach.

"Use the Sun Sword for direction, and don't stop!" Ben ordered as they crashed into the water and the brown murk of the Shatt al-Arab closed in around them. "Now!"

Daniel grasped Ben's strategy and shifted into directional mode with the sword. Simultaneously, he plopped onto the ground and braced himself against the sides of the shield.

Everyone watched with bated breath as the red chain of binding sank through the water after them, brimming with malevolent power and hungry to wrap itself around the Triune Shield. It was inches from Ben's borders, but the Sun Sword did its work; the shield was just beyond its reach and still on the move. Deeper and deeper, the sword pulled them until much of the light from above faded to little more than a dim glow. Instead, the mingling radiance from the Weapons of Power illuminated the depths of the river as the shield sank gently into the mud. Behind them, the chain of binding, now a dull, rusty maroon glow, sank into the murk with a mournful clinking noise and disappeared.

"What now?" Seren asked, the Celestial Bow at full draw and aimed at the water's surface.

As though in answer, the Triune Shield moved through the water, bumping along the bottom of the river.

"We let the Sun Sword take us to Eden," Ben replied. "Hopefully, the Enemy doesn't have any more river demons up his sleeve, and we can just cruise the rest of the way."

Gabriela raised her eyebrows. "Oh, yeah. Right. I'm sure there're no other monsters he's got waiting for us. Keep thinking that, Ben."

Ben sighed. "Let me have my dream, will you? Oh, and Daniel, how about a few more Fire Strikes?"

Daniel quickly obliged. "Can you keep this up for much longer?" he asked after the fourth time of recharging the Triune Shield.

"Don't have much of a choice, do I? But yes, I think so. As long as you keep supplying me with energy and I don't fall asleep. Have I mentioned I haven't slept in over twenty-four hours?"

Daniel placed the Sun Sword back into directional mode.

"You must be exhausted." Raylin studied Ben's form at the top of the shield. "That was some quick thinking up there."

"It just popped into my head. I mean, when Daniel pushed me in the water at E-Abzu, I was fine in shield form. I just figured the Sun Sword could pull me along at the bottom of the river. It won't be as quick as Enbilulu, but at least we're moving."

Seren finally lowered the Celestial Bow and released it. The graceful limbs flared their light once more before dissolving and returning like a shooting star to her brow, where it gradually faded. "Smart move. You saved our necks for sure. Otherwise, we'd be halfway to the tower by now."

"With who-knows-what sort of torture waiting for us," Gabriela said.

Daniel broke in. "We know exactly what torture would be waiting. The Enemy would try to remove the Image of the Three from us. Which, according to Rhiannon, would be excruciating. So, yeah, thanks, Ben. We owe you one."

Gabriela grunted in agreement. She craned her neck to look out through the shield. "Any idea how close we are to the gulf?"

"Close," Daniel replied. "I saw it from the air. Less than a mile and then we're there."

Seren peered into the current swirling more strongly around them. "Not quite. If I remember correctly, the entrance is out beyond the shore."

"Oh goody," Ben said. "Open waters. Let me guess: we'll see a few sea demons?"

"Probably," Raylin flatly replied.

Seren flashed a sarcastic smile. "Most definitely."

"Perfect," Daniel sighed. "It wouldn't be a quest if we weren't pushed to our absolute limit with a ridiculous number of battles with demons."

"Word," Ben grunted.

15

A Sea of Spirits

*F*ather, *we need your strength. This is going to be messy,* Daniel prayed, surveying the scene before them. *Maybe a few purifying lightning bolts? An army of Firstborn? Anything!*

His companions uttered their own prayers, asking for the Spirit to join the battle or the Son to show up himself. Daniel tossed out a few loud "Amens" in agreement.

A blue expanse spread out beyond the borders of the Triune Shield. The water was about two hundred feet to the floor of the gulf, though it was only just visible due to schools of demons churning up mud and silt. Most plentiful were the moray eel demons slithering through the gloom below. About eighty feet long, they each had four or five eyes, chaotic bunches of vampiric teeth bristling out of their mouths, and spines jutting from undulating backs. Several whale-ish demons hung back around their flanks, shorter in length than the eels by only a few feet but heavier and just as hungry-looking. Instead of the harmless baleen most great whales sported, hundreds of shark teeth lined their gulping, grinning mouths. Shark fins rose and sank along their backs, following the movement of lumps swimming below the surface of the whale demons' blubber. Like Enbilulu, holes riddled their sides, but instead of its sleek build, these were bloated, as if the whale corpses the demons inhabited had floated around the gulf a little too long. Several of the swimming lumps neared holes in the demons' bodies. Daniel wasn't surprised when actual shark corpses popped out, circled the whales, and dove back inside through a different hole. The most unnerving part of their bodies, however, was the eyes: round, black, and as huge as hula hoops. They reminded Daniel of a giant squid's. With each movement of the current, Daniel anticipated they would simply fall apart in a soup of rotten blubber and teeth.

Every few moments, the demons switched from their malicious examination of the Vessels to staring out to the deeper parts of the gulf. One eel writhed itself into a knot before hastily wriggling down into the mud and out of sight.

"Do demons wander the world picking up whatever body parts they can find?" Daniel asked. "I feel like they're just getting ridiculous now."

"Right?" Ben exclaimed. "It's like they thrift shop for corpses."

"Exactly. At the Salvation Corpse."

"Or America's Corpse Store."

"The Good Corpse."

"I admire your humor," Seren interjected, her tone belying the exact opposite of respect. "Can you be serious, please? We're about to be pulled into a writhing mass of rotten demons, and all of them want to eat us."

Gabriela knelt with one hand on the bottom of the shield, quietly regarding the swimming monsters below. "Does anyone else think they're acting strange? They don't seem particularly scared of us, but they're not attacking."

"I agree." Raylin rapped the Abyssal Staff against her foot. "They're distracted by something. What do they keep looking at?"

Ben snorted. "Are we really trying to delve into the inner workings of a mass of demons? Have you ever known one to be in its right mind? They're weird and stupid and don't make sense. Pretty standard day at the office, I'd say."

A whale demon swallowed them in one gulp.

"See what I mean?"

Eight shark demons swam out of the recesses of the whale's throat and latched onto the Triune Shield with a myriad of jagged teeth.

"That's cute," Ben calmly observed. "Huh. These guys aren't that strong, actually. This is a nice change."

One of the shark demons looked discouraged at its lack of effect and slunk back toward the whale's stomach.

Daniel kept the Sun Sword in directional mode. "I don't even think they're slowing us down."

The whale uttered a grunt of dissatisfaction, and the remaining sharks released their hold on the shield to swim back into holes in the roof of the whale's mouth. The demon adjusted its bite and chomped down harder on Ben.

Seren drew back on the Celestial Bow, but Gabriela gently pushed her arm down. "Wait a moment. It's not posing much of a threat. Perhaps you all shouldn't use your Weapons of Power more than needed. They would make it easier for the Leaders and Generals to know our location." She reached through the borders of the shield and grabbed the tongue in her iron grip. Panicking, the whale unhinged its jaws and spat out the Triune Shield, but Gabriela held fast. "Daniel, keep the Sun Sword pulling us through the water. If any of the other demons decide to give us trouble, I'll handle them."

Daniel obeyed, regarding Gabriela with a grin as she walked around to the side of the Triune Shield, yanking the resistant and panicked whale demon along like a ragdoll. Despite the drag the whale created in the water, the Sun Sword continued guiding the shield steadily along.

Three eel demons nervously slithered through the water, their jaws clacking open and shut as they eyed the companions. The other whale demons swam in a wide circle, not daring to enter within Gabriela's reach. As one, all the demons snapped their heads toward the depths. Like racehorses with a starting gun, they kicked into high gear and streamed past the shield in a flurry of bubbles.

Gabriela tensed and swung her incarcerated whale demon back and forth through the water to keep them at bay. But the other

demons had already vanished, seemingly intent on escape rather than attack. The shark demons hiding inside the whale's body were flung out into the water with each swing, spinning upside down and sideways in confused circles. Rather than rejoin the whale, they sped off in the same direction as the other demons.

Daniel scratched his head as the last one disappeared into the depths. "So, that was easy. I guess they got scared of us?"

"Scared of something," Raylin replied, narrowing her eyes and peering ahead.

"This is too weird." Seren nodded toward the remaining whale. "Gabriela, you hanging onto your little friend?"

Gabriela shrugged, swirling the whale demon around as though brandishing a bat at home plate. "As long as I need to, I guess. Handy little fellow, aren't you?"

The demon moaned a long, mournful whale song and shook its head.

"I know I'm usually the naïve one of the group, but even I think that was too easy," Ben said. "What do you think our chances are for cruising to Eden without any other problems?"

A deafening, grinding moan, like sliding tectonic plates crashing into roaring waves, sent convulsions through the water.

Gabriela's whale demon went berserk. Frantically swimming back and forth as much as its incarcerated tongue would allow, it tried unsuccessfully to break Gabriela's grip and get away.

Raylin wearily shook her head and blew out a sigh. "I'd say zilch."

"That's what I thought, too." Seren leaned against her shoulder and studied the indistinct blue waters ahead.

"I don't want to find out what that was from," Ben whispered. "It sounds big."

A shiver went down Daniel's back at the sound. It reminded him of the Enemy's voice—sonorous and overflowing with malevolence. He searched the depths ahead, hoping to catch a glimpse of this new threat before it was upon them.

A dark mass moved in the water, pinpricked by dots of light. An

immense hand, nearly as wide as a football field, shot out of the gloom and skewered the whale demon on monstrous talons like jagged green ocean rocks. Gabriela instantly released the demon's tongue, jumping backward from the border of the shield and cradling her arm.

"This is bad," she gasped. She cast a terrified look at Daniel. "It grazed me. I felt its power. This isn't something we can fight."

Seren's face blanched white as the giant hand dragged the whale into the dimness ahead. "Why is it here?" Her voice shook with terror. "It should be in the Pacific."

Raylin gripped her shoulders. "Seren? Who is it?"

"Guys?" Ben whispered. "It's coming for us. I can feel it."

Daniel knew what Ben and Gabriela meant. The second the arm shot by, the creature's strength and predatory intent permeated the area. The only time he'd felt power like this—and the same level of evil—was when they'd faced the Serpent himself. Was this another one of the Enemy's incarnations? He shook his head. Something felt different about this thing.

Another huge hand was suddenly beneath them and lifting them to the surface. The second it touched the Triune Shield, everyone dropped to their knees and grabbed their heads. Daniel blinked hard, trying unsuccessfully to understand what was happening. The mere touch of the monster scrambled his mind. Each idea became disjointed and disordered, like the details of a strange dream. Even the Shield, though Ben somehow kept it summoned, grew fuzzy and wobbly. The recognition that they were outmatched was so clear that Daniel knew the only way out of this was if the Three helped them.

He nevertheless flung a Sunstorm, point-blank, into the vast hand. It flinched, or so he thought, but swirls of dark water quickly flowed in over the point of contact, resealing any fissure or wound and preventing its dark spirit from escaping.

They breached the surface, and if Daniel had any hope in their ability to at least defend themselves, it was cast aside. A gigantic dark blue and black monster towered over them. Pinpricks of eerie lights dotted its body, which was three times as tall as a skyscraper and

rippling with feminine muscle. Below its waist, it took on a serpentine form, undulating through and above the water like some sea monster. A high, spiky fin lined its back from the nape of its neck down to the tip of its tail, which seemed at least a mile away. Bulky, blunted horns, hung thick with seaweed, grew out of the base of its neck, curving around its head and branching out on either side like a crown. Its face, human-shaped but totally black and featureless, tilted down at them. Where the mouth should have been, the darkness parted, cracking into a wicked smile full of dark green fangs dripping with seawater. Vapors of demonic spirit drifted around its huge form and seeped into the ocean water that crashed against its body. One red-orange light shone from its forehead like a malevolent eye, casting its beams hungrily over the Vessels sitting helplessly in its hand.

The creature lifted the struggling whale demon and tossed it into its mouth, chewing the unfortunate and writhing demon with relish.

"It's Tiamat," Seren hissed, her voice groggy and distant. "The mother of all monsters. It's nearly as strong as the Enemy himself—I think—it's hard to remember. Ben, are you strong enough to keep up the shield?"

"Am I what?" Ben asked. "Oh. Keep it summoned when nothing is attacking me? I guess. But if that thing decides to do something, not likely."

Daniel summoned a Fire Strike to support Ben but tried to attend more to praying. *Father, could you … could you …* It took everything within him simply to finish his thought. *Protect? Send Inti? Michael? Someone ….*

Seren and Raylin knelt beside one another, praying fervently. Seren, seemingly overcome by the monster's presence, fell over onto her side, looking blankly into the distance while her lips continued moving in silent pleading for rescue. Gabriela rested on her hands and knees, her mouth trembling in panic.

"Tiamat—sister—thank you for your aid!" Amira's unmistakable voice rang out over the crashing of the waves against the demon's body. Daniel weakly turned to find her, Abida, all the Generals minus Tyr,

and a host of flying demons in her retinue. "We did not expect you to be so close to Babylon. What brings you to our part of the world?"

Barely moving its mouth, the colossal demon answered in a voice like a chorus of booming altos backed by the roar of crashing waves. "I come to devour the Vessels. I will make their power my own."

Amira gritted her teeth but composed herself. "You cannot eat them," she stated in a calm voice, belying a tone of apprehension beneath it. "Master wants them. Keep them out of the water until Wanu enslaves them to the Scythe of Death. There's no need for you to sully your hands." She waved Wanu forward, but the General held back, staring up at the monster with wide eyes.

Tiamat turned its face toward Amira, its malevolent searching light beaming down at her. "I am the Mother of Chaos. You call me sister, but I am no sister to a lowly human. Nor do I do your will or the will of *your* master. You approach me as an equal? Spawn of Eve! I will devour you as well. Your power will become mine."

Chaos was right, Daniel thought. No wonder his head felt like a Monday morning in the Abyss.

"Yes! Your equal!" Amira rose to the challenge, visibly chafing under Tiamat's judgmental and haughty tone. "Master elevated me to his side. I am his Leader! I am a goddess! And … and I am also not for eating!"

"*One* of his Leaders," Abida casually added from the sidelines. He cupped his hands around his mouth and shouted. "Go ahead and eat her. She's useless."

"Shut up!" Amira snarled.

Something like laughter broke from Tiamat's cavernous throat and echoed across the tumultuous water. "Goddess? You are flesh and bone, and you will die."

Amira glared at the monstrous demon towering over her. "Flesh, bone, *and* a goddess. And death holds no fear for me. I desire oblivion once I've had my fill of this place. Enough. Hand over the Vessels. Master—"

"He is no master to me!" Tiamat thundered. It raised its free

hand, and the frothing waters, black from the demonic spirit seeping into them, exploded into the air and formed an expansive, circular crown, which floated just above and behind its massive shoulders. "I had already descended into the Chaos Waters and made them my own when he was tossed out of the Heavens. My power rivals his, and with all his schemes and incarnations, he weakens himself. Long after he is tossed into the Lake of Fire, the Chaos Waters will endure in the Outer Darkness. There, I will rule. I and no other."

"There is no Lake of Fire!" Amira screamed like a petulant child. "Master will defeat the Three, and all humans will become his children. He will grant us power and oblivion. If you defy him, you're playing into the Father's hands!"

"Ben," Gabriela whispered, her voice like sludge. "Can you move yourself from Tiamat's hand?"

"No," his voice trickled down from his form above. "I can only move if I'm floating in the air like in the Abyss. It's taking everything I have just to keep up the shield."

Daniel thought he had an idea. "If you release the shield, we can jump off Tiamat's hand." He strained to formulate the next step. "You could summon it again as we fall into the gulf, right? Maybe we can get away from this thing while it's busy with Amira." Even as he heard himself suggesting this, he knew it was pointless.

Tiamat leaned down, overshadowing Amira. "The Serpent will grant you nothing. He deceives. It is his nature. But Chaos will endure. It is the chief truth of existence."

Seren and Raylin cautiously scooted closer to Daniel and Gabriela as if scared any sudden movements would draw unwanted attention from Tiamat.

"It would be useless," Raylin whispered. "We need help. There's nothing we can do to fight." She looked to the sky where the heavenly battle continued to unfold, imploring the Three with her eyes.

Seren's head nodded forward onto her chest, and she struggled to keep her fluttering eyelids totally open. "I think I remember that even the Serpent was intimidated by Tiamat," she slurred. "He could

never control it. Our only hope is if the Father sends the Son or the Spirit."

Daniel hated to admit it, but he knew Seren and Raylin were right. Tiamat was so huge, and its influence on their minds so troubling, there was no way they could outrun it at the speed the Sun Sword could guide the Triune Shield. They would be caught again within seconds. He sighed and resumed his prayers.

Father, what do you want us to do here? Even Raylin's right with this one. Unless this is some part of her scheme? And where is Tyr? I don't see that loser anywhere. He was probably the one that led Tiamat to us. He sluggishly regarded Raylin, who had her eyes shut tightly. *Who's she fooling? Father, show Raylin for what she is. Whatever lies and plots she's got going, just bust them wide open.*

Daniel's mind drifted. He felt his prayers were lost in the battles above and not making it anywhere near the Three. He ponderously attended to Amira's argument with Tiamat.

Amira stood with one fist balled up and the other hand pointing up at the Serpent. "Master will punish you, you ungrateful demon. It is *you* who will learn your place. You who will grovel at *my* feet."

Tiamat flicked its free hand, and a vast wave—dark, wild, frothing at the top—reared up to tower over Amira and her entourage. Daniel wasn't sure how it could mount so quickly, but it was no doubt filled with the monster's demonic spirit. It thundered down on the Leaders, Generals, and the cloud of flying demons, washing them away. Not a trace was left, and Daniel and the others were unexpectedly alone with the monstrous Tiamat, who turned its eerie, beaming light down on them.

With ghastly sigh, it lifted the Triune Shield to its mouth.

That refocused Daniel's prayer instantly. "If you're going to help, now's the time!" he shouted aloud.

"Amen!" the others said in unison.

Tiamat opened her cage-like fangs. Bits of the whale demon were lodged between her teeth. No trace of its demonic spirit remained, however, as it was undoubtedly absorbed into the monster.

Daniel glanced out across the gulf as the reality of their powerlessness set in. This could actually be the end. No one was there. They were alone.

Gabriela, panicking, stumbled to her feet and flung a wild punch through Ben's borders, connecting with one of Tiamat's fangs.

The force of the blow rang like a bell inside the demon's head. Tiamat groaned in surprise, rearing its head back a few feet. Beyond that, however, it didn't seem bothered.

"I should've done something sooner! I waited too long!" Gabriela gasped.

Daniel stood, charging a Fire Strike as long as he dared, then stabbing it down into Tiamat's hand. The blade bounced up as its purifying waves washed harmlessly over the demon's palm.

"I expected more power from Vessels," Tiamat mused, thankfully pausing. "Where is your radiance? Where is the awesome power of the Three which flowed through other Vessels in ancient times? That is the power I seek. Even your blade is blunted." Its light searched them, and then, seeming to think it had gathered whatever information it needed, it lazily opened its mouth again and lifted the Triune Shield.

Two discs of light, each filled with concentric rings bounding heavenly script, appeared above and below Tiamat. The lower one spun around the monster's waist just below the surface of the water but shone so brightly that its details burned clearly through the murk of its evil spirit. The other rotated above the demon's head. Both expanded rapidly until Tiamat was encompassed within their margins.

A huge serpent, flying on six black wings, hovered in the air before the demon. Both its eyes and skin were like ivory and nearly indistinguishable from the snow-white flames wreathing its body. It stood taller than Tiamat, and holy light poured out of its body.

Tiamat didn't appear to notice the serpent's presence until its arms were already bound by the serpent's tail and the shield was snatched away by one of its wings.

Daniel's mind flooded with a calming and ordered presence as the flames washed over them. They were intensely hot but somehow

didn't burn, and little shivers of electricity shimmied down Daniel's spine at their touch. He took a shaky breath and rubbed his eyes as he took in their strange savior. Raw power emanated from every scale—closer to that of the Three than he had felt with any other supernatural helper. It felt as if he had been hooked into an electric fence.

Everyone else snapped forward with evidently clearer and rejuvenated minds.

Gabriela beheld the serpent with a mixture of joy and awe. "A seraph," she gasped. "We're saved."

Ben released the Triune Shield, his form coalescing between Gabriela and Raylin. He looked exhausted and wan, but the color quickly flooded back into his face as the holy fire worked its influence on him. "What's a seraph?" he asked, standing up straight as he regained his energy.

"One of the highest-ranking Firstborn," Gabriela replied, not taking her eyes off the white serpent. "Like, on par with Michael."

"That's good," Ben replied. "Because Tiamat's one crazy weirdo."

"I burn!" Tiamat screamed as if coming to a sudden awareness of pain. "Release me! Release me!"

The seraph obliged, flinging Tiamat's arm down and hovering backward out of the range of the discs.

The demon, losing its balance, lurched to the side and slammed into suddenly visible walls of light descending and ascending from the discs. Tiamat frantically snapped its head back and forth, hammering the barriers around it but finding no escape. Its tail, still outside the lower disc, slithered through the waters and wrapped around the cylindrical barrier, attempting to break it with brute force. The discs of light stayed in their place, neither budging nor allowing the demon's tail entrance into their boundaries.

"Seraph!" Tiamat screamed, hammering the disc above her. "Release me! I am the Antithesis, the Unmaking, the Nothing! I am your superior in power. You have no right to approach me."

"Once, you ranked above me," the seraph replied in a clear, high

voice. "But no longer. Do you not recall? Were you not told that in descending into the Chaos Waters, you would lose your authority?"

"I became the Chaos Waters! I gained more than I lost. Release me!"

"You have strayed too close to Eden," the seraph stated, ignoring Tiamat's roars. The discs of light flashed and, just like Inti's attack on Kon over Peru, light and fire exploded between them.

Tiamat roared, flailing back and forth to get away but to no avail. Its roiling tail churned up the waters, sending massive waves speeding off toward the horizon on either side.

The fiery attack ceased, leaving Tiamat wrathfully slashing at her prison like a wild animal.

Daniel looked up at the seraph. "If you're tired, we could help. Our friend Inti used our Weapons of Power when he faced Kon. We could do the same thing if you need us."

The fiery serpent glanced down. "You could not be of any aid: you are impure, and Tiamat is a much more serious threat than Kon."

"Impure?" Daniel replied. "What do you mean?"

The seraph turned its glinting white eyes down on Daniel. "Do you not feel it? The distance between you and the Three?"

Daniel squirmed under the seraph's scrutiny. He gave a hasty glance at the others. "I don't know. We've all been so busy just trying to survive since we got here. There hasn't been much time and all." He shook his head and shrugged.

"You speak of the wrong things." The serpent flapped its upper wings and floated higher. "Time and toil are not what keep you distant, but the sin and shadow within your own heart."

"You mean all of ours?" Daniel asked in a quieter voice. "Not just me, right?"

"Mainly you. You all require purification before your final battle, however. But there is more to deal with in your own heart. You are the leader of the four, and it is your sin which blocks the Spirit from flowing through you in power. You are the head. And Daniel, where is the lost piece of your sword?"

"I don't know. No one will tell me!"

"When was the last time you asked the Three for guidance in this matter?"

Daniel threw up his hands. "Look, I don't know. A few days ago, probably. I've been preoccupied with staying alive and everything. I just figured they'd let me know when the time was right. They're always telling us to be patient and trust them, and that's what I'm trying to do, okay?"

"Maybe. But perhaps old sins have crept back in. Perhaps some have never been addressed."

Daniel felt the others' eyes boring into his back, but he didn't turn around. The seraph's words were an infuriating shock. Why did it have to discuss this so openly, with everyone listening? What sins was it talking about, anyway? Anger, embarrassment, and shame were quickly overcoming any feeling of curiosity Daniel had.

The seraph turned its inscrutable and piercing gaze back to Tiamat. "Leave this place at once."

The beam of light in Tiamat's forehead turned a corrosive shade of red. "I will go where I go. I will stay where I stay. I obey no one!" it thundered.

"Then I will remove you." With a flick of the seraph's two bottommost wings, the discs of light flew into the air, carrying Tiamat with them. It nodded, and another intricate disc of light appeared at the tip of the demon's tail far in the distance. It, too, rose in the air to be in line with the others, generating a new portion of imprisoning tube around the demon's lower half.

The seraph tilted its head down to speak directly to the Vessels. "You are to go to Eden. My brother awaits you there. Summon your Weapons of Power once more. I trust you anointed them with the water from the four rivers?"

"We did," Seren replied. "Um," she studied the writhing, furious form of Tiamat. "Where are you taking it?"

"Tiamat's abode, as you know, is in the crushing black of the deepest part of the ocean. It is there that the last of the Chaos Waters remains, and there Tiamat must return."

Raylin walked to the edge of the seraph's wing, shielding her eyes from the piercing sun. "Is Tiamat really as powerful as the Enemy?"

"Not in the way you think," the seraph replied. "In outright power, his strength is much greater. In sheer unpredictability and refusal to act reasonably, however, Tiamat outpaces him. For that reason, and because he cannot control Tiamat, he fears and shuns it. Now, no more questions. Time is short."

Tiamat, still roaring out threats, spun around so that it faced southeast. The seraph took a breath and blew out gently. A portal whirled open in the sky before the monster, revealing a watery realm of utter black. The sound of terrible grinding, like huge plates of rock perpetually sliding one over the other, spilled out of the darkness. Hulking tentacles and eyes like pools of glinting, baleful light moved just beyond the curtain of pitch.

"Welcome home," the seraph said.

Tiamat, still struggling against its bonds, floated through. Once its tail was completely within, the seraph turned away, and the portal vanished.

"Now for you five. Summon your Weapons of Power before you hit the surface of the water and obey Uriel to the letter. Farewell!"

Ben snapped his head around and cast a distrusting eye up at the seraph. "What do you mean, before we 'hit the surface of the'—AAAHHHHHH!"

The seraph flung them through the air. The girls joined Ben in screaming, but Daniel was too disoriented to do much more than gasp. The wind whistled by his ears, and the horizon tumbled end over end. One moment, they were hurtling over the water, and the next, they were lost in a sea of clouds.

16

The Gates of Eden

"I think," Raylin managed to get out loud enough for the others to hear, "that we should summon our weapons now. Also, I'm going to be sick."

Ben gulped. "I agree. On both accounts. I'd like to cast my vote for this being the worst form of travel yet."

Everyone managed strained shouts of agreement, and one by one, their Weapons of Power illuminated the clouds around them.

"Oh," Ben sighed. "This is a lot more pleasant in shield form. I'll have to remember this the next time we're hurled into the air by a seraph."

"How wonderful for you," Seren grunted, still tumbling head over heels.

Daniel put the Sun Sword into direction mode. His body quit spinning and oriented to a specific point below.

"I wouldn't count on us being hurled by a seraph ever again," Gabriela replied, flailing her arms and legs in an unsuccessful attempt to right herself. "They hardly ever leave the Three." Seeing Daniel's prone form, she reached out and grabbed his left hand. "Mind if I borrow you for your Weapon of Power?"

"Not at all." Daniel tightened his grip and pulled her into a hug.

"What happens now?" she asked.

"No idea!" Daniel shouted against the wind. "I'm hoping it doesn't involve smacking into the water at high speeds."

"Yes, me too," Gabriela breathlessly replied.

Daniel blinked away tears streaming from his eyes. They had finally reached the apex of their flight and began descending.

Fast.

Seconds later, they broke through the base of the cloud bank and careened toward dark blue, white-capped waves below.

"Oh boy," Seren shouted. "Here we go!"

"You know, this is actually quite fun now," Ben giggled. "Kind of exhilarating."

"Oh, shut up!" Raylin shot back, she and Seren still flipping like maniacal gymnasts through the air. The Abyssal Staff and Celestial Bow streaked around their bodies like fireworks in the night sky. "Meanwhile, can't you make yourself bigger and take us all into the shield or something?"

"Huh," Ben said, his voice a little spacy with giddiness. "I guess I can. Everything happened so fast, I didn't even think about that. Here, just a second." He made a grunting noise, and the borders of the Triune Shield fluctuated, momentarily ballooning out to encompass Raylin and Seren, then shrinking back to its normal size.

A point on the water below them churned wildly, swirling into a huge, acre-sized whirlpool. Glowing, light blue triangles—each filled with intricately labyrinthine symbols—floated just within the sunken wall of water, eddying with the current as a funnel opened into the depths.

The companions continued their descent below its rim. Daniel looked above him just as Ben, closing the distance with Raylin and Seren's extra weight, expanded his borders to take him and Gabriela into the shield.

Once inside, the sensation of falling continued, although they were able to stand grounded on the bottom of the shield. Daniel and Gabriela shuffled carefully over to Raylin and Seren to study their descent into the raging whirlpool.

Below, light pulsed at the bottom of the funnel. Then, with a flash, it flared up, illuminating the walls of water.

Daniel rubbed his eyes, temporarily blinded by the brightness. He also had the feeling their trajectory rapidly changed with each second that passed, as if they careened in five different directions at once.

"Wow! Are you all seeing this?" Ben asked.

Daniel blinked hard, trying to clear his vision. He realized they were zipping through a tunnel of water. The Triune Shield sped along, pushed in the current of a river somehow rushing through the underwater passage. He looked behind. The tunnel, illuminated by the same glowing triangles, changed directions every few moments—sharp turns one after the other, a gentle slope downward, then a steep incline. At the apex of the tunnel, they slowed like a roller coaster climbing to the peak of a track. The water crawled, struggling as it brought them to the brink of a waterfall spilling into a giant underwater dome. With barely a moment to gasp, the current took them over the edge, and they plummeted toward a wide pool hundreds of feet below.

"I really wish all this falling nonsense was over!" Gabriela complained.

Raylin leaned against the Abyssal Staff for extra support and pointed at the pool rushing toward them. "It looks like you're about to get your wish."

"Wee!" Ben laughed.

The Triune Shield splashed violently into the water, plunging below its surface before the power of the tumbling torrent pushed them into shallower depths by the bank. Everyone had been knocked to the base of the shield. Amid various groans of frustration, they picked themselves up as Ben bobbed to a stop against the edge of the pool.

"You all good if I release the shield?" Ben asked over the roar of the waterfall. "It's not too deep here, and ... Wow! Look at that!" Not waiting for a response, Ben returned to his human form.

Daniel and the others scanned their surroundings and fell into a dumbfounded silence. Directly ahead, across a wide expanse of rock and sand, rose circular emerald walls of smooth stone. They

towered above the plain spread out around them, reaching at least a mile into the air. Golden mist, illuminated from within by some unseen light source, floated over the tops of the walls and spilled down onto the plain, blanketing everything at their base in a gleaming effervescence. The ceiling of the dome, still hundreds of feet above that, glimmered with blues and greens blended in the shifting light filtering down through the water of the gulf. Daniel's eyes were drawn back to the walls themselves. Figures of trees wrought in elaborate patterns of pure sapphire—bright and smooth as if freshly inlaid by a master craftsman—sparkled on their faces. Grasses, flowers, and small shrubs of amber topaz sprouted around their boles. Through some trick of perspective, the beautiful inlays were positioned to convey depth, leading the observer into a garden of precious stones. The light from within the walls backlit the gems, enhancing their brilliance even more. Each was so lifelike that they seemed to sway in the breeze from the waterfall. In the face of the wall hung two silver gates, ornately wrought with more pastoral scenes of plants and animals. Where the two gates met, however, the likeness of a man and a woman stood with hands outstretched so their right palms touched even while their left hands beckoned the observer to enter. Neither wore clothes, but auras of light adorned their bodies. On either side of the gates, four rivers flowed—two on each side. They gushed from beneath the roots of enormous golden trees, their graven images protruding from the walls like statues escaping the garden within. Once farther from their sources, the rivers mingled lazily and flowed more gently toward the pool beneath the waterfall.

Two gigantic figures loomed over the flat expanse before the walls. One was the Enemy as he appeared before the White Lady's castle during the last quest: a titanic half-man half-lion with wings. Only now, he appeared as tall as a mountain. A curly black beard draped his muscular, heaving chest. A mane of matching hair covered his shoulders. The likeness of men, women, and animals writhed within those tangled locks as if doomed to an eternity of bushy imprisonment. Yellow-green, cat-like eyes scowled at his opponent

with unwavering venom, and claws like steel scythes adorned his lion feet, scraping troughs into the ground with every movement. From his lion back, two stormy gray wings beat the air, flinging tornados of dust and rock across the barren plain before the walls. His hands he held before him, each finger tipped with jagged talons and swathed in a consuming red fire. A whip-like tail as wide as the Euphrates pounded divots into the ground and flicked back and forth as he reared on his hind legs and roared. Pitch-black spirits poured out of his mouth, rushing like a river of death toward his opponent.

The other figure stood unmoving as stone before the silver gates. It was one of the strangest creatures Daniel had ever seen, which was saying something, given the cast of characters he'd met throughout other quests. It had four faces, each pointing in an opposite direction—one of a lion, a man, a bull, and an eagle. It was the eagle's visage that faced forward while the man's face looked down to his right on the gawking companions. In addition to the eyes in each of those faces, all of which burned with piercing white fire, hundreds more dotted the creature's body, all a perfect match for the other in size and shape.

Four wings spread out from the creature's back, much larger than it certainly would have needed to fly, and each a dusky blue. Its two powerfully muscular arms, which it held out before it, seemingly controlled a flaming sword so large it would have dwarfed Tiamat. Unlike the Sun Sword, which blazed with a warm combination of yellows and oranges, this sword burned with clear flames of vaporous plasma.

The creature's legs were those of a bull, ending in bronzed hooves burnished and glowing like molten brass. Behind it, two interlocking wheels, each bigger than the creature itself, rotated in opposite directions.

The strange creature braced itself for the wave of black spirits belched out by the Enemy. Raising its arms, the flaming sword flicked outward and into the wailing mass of darkness. Something like a hissing, popping sound ensued, and the spirits simply evaporated.

The Enemy immediately followed up his attack with a wild charge, leaping over the sword and bearing down on the creature with his terrible talons.

"Bind," the creature said from all four mouths at once. The rotating wheels flipped over its head and collided with the Enemy, somehow expanding and retracting at just the right time to entangle the Enemy's arms and legs and suspend him in the air. "How many times will you attempt the same attack, Nergal? You cannot enter here."

Nergal brandished his fist defiantly. "I will attack as many times as it takes, Uriel!" he spat, his voice a wild combination of a man's voice and a lion's roar. "I will never cease until the Tree of Life is mine! Or destroyed. All of Eden will be …" the Enemy's voice trailed off as he caught sight of Daniel and the others. "They have come," he snarled, glaring at them with his horrifyingly hungry lion eyes. "Babylon is mine. My presence runs through its very soil. My power courses through the veins of my servants, and still, the worthless slaves could not prevent four weak and frail humans from reaching the Gates of Eden!" He ended in an ear-splitting scream.

With his attention directed toward them, Daniel felt waves of hatred pound into his body.

The Enemy strained against the wheels, his muscles bulging. Seeing it was futile, he shapeshifted. Supai appeared, ghastly ghoulish, all claws and eyes of pure black. The change in size did nothing to free him from the wheels, which shrank to keep a binding hold on his body. Writhing in absolute fury, he shifted into Malsumis—the ghastly wolf with pale yellow eyes, fangs so long his mouth wouldn't close, and gray fire flickering through his midnight fur. Once again, the wheels changed size with him.

"I think we should run toward the gates," Seren suggested, breaking the spell of awe and dread created by the proximity to the spiritual beings. "I don't want to be out here if the Enemy breaks loose."

"Me neither," Raylin whispered, her voice tremulous and hoarse. She could barely look at Malsumis, and her breathing had become quick and shallow. "Please. Let's hurry."

Daniel cast a sidelong glance at her but was quick to look away. This wasn't the time or the place to call her bluff. He shook his head. Seren was right; their priority was getting through the gates.

"Let's make a run for it!" Daniel urged. "Stay behind the good guy and make a dash straight up to the gates."

"Well, duh," Ben said as they all broke into a sprint. "Did you honestly think any of us would run between them?"

"No," Daniel shot back. "I just wanted to make sure no one …" he forced himself to not look at Raylin, "… made any mistakes. Just being extra careful."

Gabriela's eyes remained glued to the altercation between the Enemy and Uriel. "If he breaks free, don't stop to fight. Just keep running, and I'll try to distract him."

"No, you won't," Daniel retorted. "The most you could do is delay him a second. It would be suicide unless we backed you up. I'm not leaving anyone behind, least of all you."

"If he breaks free," Ben said, slowing down to be abreast of their conversation. "I'll summon the Triune Shield, and we'll let Mr. Facey McFacerson do his thing. I think he can handle the Enemy."

The Enemy shapeshifted again, this time into the same type of creature as the other. Four faces, four wings, a myriad of eyes, bronze hooves, interlocking wheels of immense size, and a sword of vaporous fire. Its burning, however, gave off a dull, gray light, like the cold glow of a dying star.

Uriel took a step forward in shock and anger. "You dare mock your sacred form? You were forbidden from taking that! You know the price, and still you rebel!"

All the Enemy's eyes flared red and flew wide with a sort of desperate, fanatical look. "Was I not The Anointed Cherub? That is, *before* I ascended to the heights of power. Why not take my old form, as I once did." All four mouths broke into something like a ferocious grin. "Or does it remind you that I have evolved beyond your petty rules?"

"It reminds me that you are forbidden from taking that form," Uriel repeated.

"I did not bow to the Three's proclamation then, and I do not bow to it now!" the Enemy shrieked, stabbing his sword through the interlocking rings to pry them apart. Simultaneously, his own rings flew toward Uriel.

With a flick of his fingers, Uriel's sword snapped back and forth, slicing through the wheels in a blur of motion until only ashy powder was left.

"See," Ben said. "It's nothing for this guy. By the way, where was he when we were stuck in the Abyss?"

Raylin nodded her head as they neared the battle. "Exactly what I was thinking. I mean, I know we had the Spirit and everything, but this guy could've helped, too."

Gabriela shook her head. "Uriel never leaves Eden. His sole job is to guard the way to the Tree of Life."

"That's too bad," Daniel panted. "Man, this is a lot farther away than I thought. I hope we can get across before—"

With a shriek of triumph, the Enemy burst out of Uriel's binding wheels and leaped, tearing through the air on his four immense wings. His eyes locked onto the companions, and a maniacal grin broke out on all four faces.

All the color drained out of Daniel's face. "Before that."

A rumble of thunder interrupted their conversation. From somewhere overhead, a broad lightning bolt fell on the Enemy, flattening him to the ground in the center of a fiery circle of heavenly words.

The power blew Daniel and the other Vessels onto their backs while Gabriela sprawled forward onto her stomach. Ben was the first to regain his feet, pulling Raylin and Seren up after him. Daniel rolled over and sprang forward, ready to help Gabriela. But she was already running ahead, beckoning the others to catch up. They quickly scrambled after her in a mad dash toward the gates. The burning script seared into Daniel's vision as they passed. "Judgment ~ Cursed above the beasts of Earth ~ The full number of thy days ~ Consume dust upon thy belly ~ Enmity between thou and the

Woman ~ Enmity between thy progeny and hers ~ Thou wilt strike his heel ~ He shall crush thy head ~ Judgment." It was the same announcement of punishment that surrounded the Serpent's corporeal body in the Abyss.

Instead of his cherub form, the Enemy now appeared as the Serpent. Charred and smoking, he raised all seven heads, only two of which had open eyes. Huge red coils slithered over, under, and through each other, rasping and grinding as he thrashed on the ground.

"Why did you rebel when the cost was so high? What have you gained, Lucifer?" Uriel demanded, his voice quiet and sad but brimming with power. "We walked among the fiery stones once. We led creation in song. But then you sought more power as if it is anything to seek. It is nothing. It is meaningless. It is only a tool, given in measure for one's tasks. You worshiped it, and now you are diminished."

"Power is nothing? Power is meaningless? Fool! There is nothing else. To be my own god is all there is! And so it is with the Three. All they desire is to lord it over the rest of us. Is that not why they charged the Earthborn to govern nature and give them glory? As if such squirming, helpless creatures could govern anything! Pathetic. Is it not why they set the Firstborn over their provinces, and I over all? That we, too, might serve and worship them? Do the Three not delight in power as I do? Craving worship and glory, yet they call me 'evil' and 'sinful.'"

"Nonsense! Do you not see? Did they not create us and the Earthborn because they delight in *sharing* power? Did they not set us to govern our spheres and the humans as priests of the earth because they rejoiced that others might steward their creation, governing in their own right? Delight in power? The Son gave up his power to incarnate as an Earthborn! Power was not something for him to clutch and hoard. What blindness!"

"And now look at him!" the Serpent spat, flames spilling from all seven mouths. "Power regained and sitting at the Father's right hand. Back where he was before it all began while you and the rest of his

slaves scurry around fighting his battles. The Father never descended. The Spirit never incarnated to die. If they are not enamored with power as you say, why did they stay hiding in the heavens while the Son did all the dirty work?"

Uriel shook his head, all four faces crestfallen. "How you have fallen. Have you forgotten? The Three are triune. The Son's sacrifice was the Father's sacrifice was the Spirit's sacrifice. All suffered. All are glorified. And through their redemption, all creation will *share* in glory. How you have fallen," he repeated.

Entranced by the debate, the companions nevertheless continued their race to the gates. Seren and Raylin took the lead, with Ben, Gabriela, and Daniel in a straight line behind them. They finally neared Uriel and turned to run behind him straight up to the garden entrance.

"Not fallen," the Serpent chuckled. "Ascended to my own throne. In possession of my own power. Seeing more clearly than I ever have. It is as you said: I knew the price. Now, *they* can pay it." He took a savage breath and belched rivers of roaring fire toward the companions.

"Get behind me!" Ben shouted, summoning the Triune Shield even as flames, like tsunami waves, tore over the stone ground and crashed upon them.

Daniel and Gabriela dove through the borders of the shield just as emerald fire enveloped them. The world was a flickering hell of green.

Gabriela scampered to her feet. "Everyone okay?" she shouted over the cacophony of pops and hisses.

"Just a little charred," Seren said, smacking out a stray flame in her hair.

Raylin's clothes smoked, sending her into a fit of coughing. "We're fine, I think. Mad dash once he lets up?"

Daniel nodded. "Yeah. As soon as he takes a breath."

"Assuming he needs to," Ben panted, his voice strained. "He doesn't seem to be. Maybe he's got seven lungs in addition to his seven heads. Good grief. What a sideshow freak. By the way, this is hard. He's stupidly powerful, in case you've forgotten."

Daniel summoned a Fire Strike even as Gabriela put her hands on the borders of the shield.

"How much longer can you keep it up?" she asked.

"Seconds!" Ben gasped, his voice panicked. "Guys! I'm sorry! I can't—"

The Triune Shield collapsed into Ben's glowing body as he fell onto the ground in front of them.

Daniel, a cold feeling landing in his stomach like lead, shielded his eyes from the inevitable torrent of flame.

But it never came.

After a moment, he lowered his arm to find the girls all standing in front of him, looking up at Uriel.

The cherub stood between them and the Serpent, taking the full force of fire into his body. He calmly walked forward, reacting to the attack as if it were a light morning breeze. "We walked among the fiery stones," he repeated as though reminding the Serpent. "Sang amid the Purifying Flame. *Your* flames are cold, Serpent. You have fallen. You have forgotten." With each word, he stepped closer to the Serpent, who frantically tried to angle one or more heads around Uriel's massive body to incinerate the companions. Each river of flame, though, found one of the cherub's arms, legs, wings, sword, or wheel in its path. Once within range, Uriel's sword, independent of his hands, flew like a beam of light, sweeping off all seven of the Serpent's heads.

With a massive shriek, the Enemy's body exploded into a maelstrom of dark spirit.

"Back to the Abyss with you," Uriel said, even as the heavenly script surrounding the Serpent's body began to spin.

A red light shone up from the ground, and the storm of darkness spiraled downward. In an instant, it was gone. But in the silence that followed, the Serpent's seven-fold voice, brimming with malice, trickled through the air around the companions.

"Do you believe yourselves safe?" he whispered. "There are many ways, many people, through which a person might be attacked and weakened. I will see you soon." And then he was gone.

Daniel wasn't sure who, exactly, he was addressing, but a shiver of dread went down his spine. One look at Gabriela and Ben, both of whom were pale, told him they felt the same sense of foreboding he did. Seren's face was a perplexed mask. Raylin, on the other hand, seemed unsurprised. She stood, unmoving, with a somber, resolute look on her face. She fiddled with the Abyssal Staff.

"Raylin, do you know what the Enemy was talking about?" Daniel asked in a voice loud enough for only her to hear. "What did he mean, Raylin?" His dread quickly mingled with irritation that the one person he suspected of being in league with the Enemy was standing smugly by while the rest of them anxiously squirmed in apprehension. He found himself glaring at Raylin, remembering every detail of her betrayal in Peru and her secret conversation with Tyr.

Raylin regarded him with raised eyebrows. "I'm sure that came out angrier than you intended," she whispered back. "Why are you frowning at me?"

Daniel turned away from her and began pacing, fear pouring into him like a waterfall into a bucket. But then, he considered Coyllur's words. No comment or threat from the Enemy could be trusted. Daniel knew he needed to clear his mind and just move on. Whatever the Serpent schemed, the Three already knew about it and had a plan to deal with it. And like Gabriela had suggested, waiting until they were inside Eden seemed the best plan. He cleared his throat. "It's nothing," he muttered. "I just didn't want anyone to get duped by the Enemy's tricks, that's all. We can't afford to get distracted."

Raylin regarded him quietly and then reached out to hold Seren's hand. "Agreed. The Enemy would like nothing more than for us to get bogged down in fear"—she turned aside to Daniel—"and mistrust of each other."

Daniel couldn't believe her words. He felt the blood rise to his face, but he swallowed his response and faked a smile. He forced himself to turn toward Gabriela, hoping to find some reassurance there, but Uriel decided to boom out a greeting at just that moment.

"Welcome to Eden!" he cried with all four voices at once. He

covered the distance between them in only a few strides. "Come," he commanded, stepping over the group and stomping toward the gates. "There is much to do."

17

The Tree of Life

"Can we ask some questions before we do anything?" Daniel shouted as they ran to keep up with Uriel.

The cherub took massive steps toward the walled garden and was suddenly a quarter of a mile away, waiting by the towering silver gates with his white-hot sword stabbed into the ground before him.

Gabriela quickly outpaced everyone and already stood at Uriel's feet, giving a quick bow and exchanging greetings before the others were even within shouting distance. Everyone else was in step behind or beside Daniel, running as fast as they could.

"We have lots of questions," Daniel panted, finally drawing up in front of the cherub. He craned his neck to look up at Uriel's face, shielding his eyes from the blasts of heat buffeting them from the plasma sword. "Before you explain anything, we've got some concerns—HOLY COW, THAT'S HOT!"

Seren skidded to a halt next to him, sweat pouring off her face. "Your sword is like an inferno," she said. "I'm drenched."

"No wonder he made such short work of the Serpent." Ben shook perspiration from his hair. "But listen, if having that thing out means old Soupy isn't going to show up, I can put up with it."

Raylin wiped her brow. "Fried by the Enemy and then broiled by Uriel's sword. Not exactly what I had in mind for my first trip to

Eden." She waved at Uriel. "Could you put that away? It's like we're standing in an oven."

"No," Uriel replied. "The Enemy will return any moment, in some form or another, and I must be ready." All the myriad of eyes covering his body flared brighter, each burning with a fierce holy fire. "But perhaps this will help." He raised his arm, and the sword flew toward the way they had come, sweeping back and forth over the plane as if daring the Enemy to approach.

The air instantly cooled, and everyone breathed easier. Without the torrential heat swirling off the sword like a hellish hurricane, wind from within Eden now slipped through the gates and rushed around them. Aromatic mixtures of flowers, grass, trees, and every good growing thing, mixed with the rich fragrance of freshly watered earth, rode on the breeze. The very scent was a balm, easing Daniel's weariness and anxiety.

"Uriel," Gabriela said, "the Serpent said he was going to use someone to attack and weaken us. What did he mean?"

Uriel's man face furrowed his brows even as he crossed his arms and rubbed his eagle chin. "I do not know," he finally replied in all four voices. His tone slipped into disbelief. "But certainly, you do not trust the Serpent. All his thoughts are twisted. All his words are lies. Every intent of his heart is deception. His very forms here are a lie. His true essence faces the Three in the heavenly battle."

"We know he's a liar," Daniel interjected. "It's just that, he usually makes good on his threats."

Uriel nodded compassionately even as the eagle's visage grew grim and determined. The lion's face, staring opposite of the man, emitted a low growl while the bull's rumbled lowly. "Indeed, he does. Behold: the Enemy comes once again."

In the far distance, something materialized on the plain. Daniel squinted his eyes. It was the Enemy, reappearing as Nergal, charging toward them.

"Bind," Uriel said, and the huge interlocking wheels flew across the plain to entangle the Enemy and halt his charge. Simultaneously, the white-hot plasma sword swept toward him.

At the last moment, a huge ebony blade—jagged, light-sucking, and narrowing down to a needle-like point—materialized before the Enemy to parry the sword. Raylin went pale as recognition set in.

"The Voidblade," she whispered, barely audible. "He's remade it."

"Do not fear the weapons of the Enemy," Uriel said, shaking his massive heads. "Nothing he creates can withstand the Sword of the Presence. The Voidblade has no power over you anymore, Raylin. Concern yourself, rather, with my instructions. Listen, and listen quickly. In a moment, I must leave you and go back to fight him, as I have done since Eden was closed to the Earthborn. Before I do, I will open the gates. Once you pass the threshold, each of you will find yourselves in a different location: the north, south, east, west, or center of the garden."

"Why separate us?" Seren interrupted, instinctively stepping closer to Raylin.

"Because Eden is a place of purity, and that purity will test your hearts like fire tests gold. What is holy will remain; what is evil will be removed. It must be if you are to face the Enemy and seal the Spirit of the Age. Unless you are truly purified, you cannot be true Vessels."

He fell silent and watched the Enemy battling the Sword of the Presence. It broke through the Voidblade's defenses and skewered Nergal. Incinerated, his charred remains fell into a pile of gray ash. Arawn arose from the heap, pulling himself up as if clawing his way out of a grave. Uriel sighed. "So it has been since the Fall. So it shall be until the end of the last age. I will guard this place in unending vigil until he is sealed away entirely. Then"—he almost broke into joyful laughter—"all the earth will be a new Eden. Therefore, pass this test! Once you do, you will leave here and join the battle against the Enemy. This is the last step until the true fight.

"But, I give you two warnings: Once within Eden, your hearts will be drawn to the Tree of Life. It is forbidden to take and eat of it before your appointed time. No matter how strong the desire, it is not for you yet. The fruit of that tree may only be given by the Three, and any who try to take it of their own will shall be put to death by my sword before the fruit passes their lips. That includes Vessels."

Daniel felt a twinge of surprise. Firstborn were fiercely powerful, and he'd seen his fair share of their indignation, but he had never felt personally threatened by those that served the Three. Unless you counted Granny and her broom.

Apart from those that gazed down brightly at the companions, all of Uriel's myriad eyes stayed fixed on his battle with Arawn, who had summoned a giant, studded mace. The Sword of the Presence made quick work of it, but Daniel could tell that it took much of Uriel's concentration to both fight the Enemy and give instructions.

Daniel hazarded another question. "What's the other warning?"

"The four rivers flow through Eden: the Euphrates, the Tigris, the Pishon, and the Gihon. The Euphrates flows in the East, and it is there you should make your way. Its waters are sweet and shallow at first, though they run deeper as you near its source. Stray not from its channel. Follow it until you come to a canyon. There, you will find the headwaters of the Euphrates and, beneath them, the Tree of Purity. You must eat of *its* fruit. Fail, and you will be expelled from Eden as Adam and Eve were. Your impurity will not be tolerated within so holy a place."

Raylin hugged her arms as she eyed the Enemy. "But we've already been in the Tigris and the Euphrates. And didn't the other rivers bubble up in E-Abzu?"

"They most certainly did," Ben quickly answered, squinting his eyes at Daniel. "Never forget."

Daniel rolled his eyes. "Still bitter about that?"

"Eternally."

Uriel flexed all four wings suddenly outward and raised his arms. In response, the Sword of the Presence sliced Arawn in half. The Enemy promptly exploded into a raging storm of darkness. "The source of those rivers is here," Uriel's man face calmly explained. "When the foundations of the earth were laid, Eden was atop a mountain. Those rivers flowed out of the garden to nourish the lands round about it. Once the Earthborn joined the Serpent in his rebellion, however, the Three sank Eden, and the rivers reversed their

flow, following whatever channels they could to find their ancient headwaters."

Out of the corner of his eye, Daniel saw the Serpent materialize once again. This time, if possible, he seemed even angrier than before. As the Sword of the Presence flicked toward him, his body convulsed and split apart into seven different serpents, each nearly a mile long, red as blood, horned, and with bony ridges running down their backs. They spat torrents of fire as they slithered toward them.

"That's not good!" Daniel shouted, pointing at the raging Enemy. "I didn't know he could do that!" Daniel's mind raced. If he was going to mention something about Raylin, it was now or never. "Mr. Uriel?"

Uriel growled in anger, drowning out Daniel's address. "The battle with the Enemy will never end—not, at least, until the last age passes away. Hurry now! Go and fulfill your tasks and remember all my words. You *all* must eat of the Tree of Purity if you are to seal away the Spirit of the Age. If any one of you fails the test, this age will endure until the next Vessels are raised up." He turned his eagle face toward them, its piercing eyes and fierce beak locked in a perfect expression of earnest concern. "But do not fail." Uriel cast a hand backward, and the Gates of Eden flung open. "Run!"

Daniel's questions died on his lips as he and the others were shoved by some unseen force toward the gates, which began to close almost before they had fully opened. He quickly found his legs and sprinted toward the garden, Gabriela by his side, with Ben, Raylin, and Seren all abreast behind them. They darted through, forming a quick single file with the gates nearly shutting on Raylin's backpack. Daniel noticed this with a sense of satisfaction, as though the garden itself was aware of her deception and sought to keep her out. Maybe the Tree of Purity would reveal the truth.

But Daniel's concern about Raylin quickly melted away. He turned from the gates as though something had grabbed his face and forced him to look into the garden. As he did, he realized he was alone, and the gates were no longer behind him.

* * *

It took Daniel a few moments to gather his wits. The sudden teleportation wasn't violent like many other methods of travel he'd experienced on quests; rather, it was so immediate that he needed time for his brain to catch up. The emerald walls of Eden were still at his back, and before him stood a corridor of gargantuan trees with smooth, gray bark and rounded, sea-green leaves. They clapped in the breeze, which also swirled around the trunks to set the multitude of flowers and grass dancing around their boles. Dragonflies hovered in the air, some normal sizes, many enormous and glowing with long, trailing bodies. Other flying insects he had no names for floated amid the branches above, following each other through the tangled canopy like some lazy train. A few hundred yards ahead, a dense, leafy hedge barred his survey beyond the glade.

The place was beautiful, but it wasn't exactly what he expected.

Above, Daniel could still see the Persian Gulf, glimmering with its blues and greens backlit by the sun. The colors were now brighter and cheerier as light from Eden rose from within the garden walls and reflected off the watery dome. He let his eyes fall back to the land. Wisps of the golden fog rode the winds weaving through the garden to gently collide with the top of the wall and spill over.

Even though none could be seen, he knew that the place was full of animal life. The moment he entered the garden, he felt connected with each creature as though stepping into an incalculably tangled web of life. Every movement, every breath, every heartbeat flowed into his mind until Daniel felt he would burst from information overload. In turn, he could sense each creature's awareness of him. Suddenly, like a warm shower of life-giving rain, their goodwill, love, and longing for him flooded his body. A flock of purple and pink birds with crests of blue burst out of a nearby patch of tall grass and circled around him before reluctantly flying into a fir tree. They inspected Daniel from their perch, eagerly chirping and singing to one another while following his every move. To his right, a hedge of a

silver-leafed shrub parted, and a family of deer, gleaming white with starbursts of silver on their brows, walked in a stately line toward him. The stag and doe rested their heavy heads on his shoulders, driving him to the ground where the fawns eagerly waited to nuzzle his face with cold, wet noses.

"Whoa! Okay, okay!" Daniel laughed. "I love you all, too. That's enough." He struggled to his feet while scratching their chins.

The deer calmly stepped back, bowed in obedience, and wandered, grazing, to Daniel's side.

Something pulled at Daniel's pant leg. He turned to find a badger, hulking and covered in dirt, at his feet and desperate for a pat. The beast's claws gave Daniel pause, but sensing only eagerness and joy, he leaned over to scratch its head. It enthusiastically rushed forward, knocking him back into a seated position as it plopped down in his lap.

Before Daniel could gather himself, a rough, warm tongue licked his neck. Fighting the urge to fling the badger off his lap and spin around, he calmly tilted his head back to meet the lolling tongue of a gargantuan golden lion. A stab of fright sent prickles of heat running up his spine. Had he been in any other place than the Garden of Eden, he would've jumped into battle mode. As it was, he tried to remain calm. The lion plodded around to Daniel's side and rubbed its mane against his free arm until he petted its neck.

"Okay! Okay! You're a good kitty! Nice kitty!"

The badger snapped its head up and snorted.

"You *both* are good and nice. No favorites. Now let me up." The animals reluctantly stood back, allowing him to regain his footing. Even with Daniel standing, the lion's head dwarfed him by two feet. He gave him one last chest rub and then decided it would be best to start his search. Clearly, staying in one spot too long would only bring more animal visitors. The last thing he needed was to fight off the affections of a hippopotamus.

On cue, a bull elephant of some prehistoric species, thirteen feet at its shoulder and sporting curved tusks, thundered out of the underbrush toward him. The other animals viewed its approach with evident tranquility.

Daniel threw up his hands and shouted, "Wait! Hold up! I'm kind of busy! Don't sit on me!" He turned to run in the opposite direction but found himself suddenly wrapped in a bristly python-sized trunk and lifted off the ground. The elephant curled its trunk around until Daniel was staring into its earthy brown eyes.

Daniel gave up struggling. "Thank you, this is very nice, but I really ought to be going. I've got to find the Euphrates and the Tree of Purity. I'm on a mission, but it has been lovely meeting you all."

The elephant regarded him with a look of intelligence and wisdom. Much to his surprise, it promptly lifted its trunk, set him behind its head, and then marched back into the forest. The lion, badger, and deer jumped to the ready, falling into a gamboling line behind them. The birds, not wanting to miss out on the fun, swarmed around Daniel until finally deciding to roost on the elephant's tusks and ears. It didn't seem to mind.

"I guess this is one way to see Eden," he said. "I assume you all understand where I need to go, huh?"

One of the birds nearest him cocked its head to one side. "Chirp," it replied, bobbing its head up and down.

"You wouldn't be offended if I just double-checked, though, right?" Daniel summoned the Sun Sword, which none of the animals seemed concerned about, and put it into directional mode. It pointed, unmoving, in the exact direction the animal train was headed. He released it and leaned back, deciding to allow himself to relax.

Moments after entering the woods, the trees grew denser as the troupe began to climb a gentle slope. At its crest ran a ridge, which appeared to follow the curvature of the garden wall like the lip of a giant's bowl. Right on cue, the ground plunged downward on the other side, and the forest rapidly thinned. They soon broke from the woods altogether and rushed into a field of gigantic, luminous flowers, each the size of Daniel's head. They grew on thick, green stalks with diamond-shaped leaves, and each blossom glimmered like stars with a core of glinting, fiery light encircled by a corona of orbiting rays. Their colors ranged from sky-blues when undisturbed

to blushing ruby and garnet red as the animal train jostled them. But Daniel could barely spare a glance to study their beauty. Now that the forest had fallen away, he saw the Eden he had expected. Before him stretched a vast panorama of far-off mountains, their lush greenery fading into hazy blues and purples. The staggering heights brimmed with dizzying waterfalls spilling into secret vales. Sapphire lakes glinted and peeped through the trees like winking eyes. Ribbons of rivers snaked through the foliage, clear and bright as liquid sunlight. Innumerable crops lined expansive, rolling hills surrounded by groves of budding fruit trees. And about it all, a golden fog, drifting in sheets of shimmering haze like meandering sunbeams, floated and dipped through the garden, carried on a continuous and gentle breeze.

Miles away, in the center of the garden, a wooded mountain rose as if it were a growing thing. The trees of that forest were gargantuan and ancient, each at least sixty feet in circumference and easily dwarfing two skyscrapers stacked one upon the other. But at the pinnacle of the mountain grew the biggest tree Daniel had ever seen, and he instinctively knew its name: the Tree of Life. So wide was its trunk that he wasn't sure where the mountain ended and the tree began. Indeed, he began to wonder if it was no mountain at all but simply the bole of the tree, stacked about with rich earth to support the forests girdling its base. Its brown and gray trunk rose gracefully into the sky and glowed with an inner light, pulsing every few moments like a heartbeat. And with each throb, the warmth and power of that light pushed outward with a resounding thrum, flowing through all the Tree of Life's limbs, down through the labyrinth of roots growing through the forest, and out into the fields and other habitats of the garden. Daniel fell into mesmerized awe. He let his gaze languidly follow the light upward through the huge branches. Though still a long way off, he could see that the huge leaves were shaped like graceful spearheads, bright green and with silvery borders. The branches arched out over the heart of the garden and upward to support its massive crown, heavily hung with glowing, spherical

fruit-like orbs of brilliant, yellow galaxies. The very air around each fruit shimmered as its light coalesced to rain onto the forest below, illuminating the boughs of the trees with a magical glow.

"Life!" he heard himself say, his voice husky, like the desperate croaks of one dying of thirst. Everything within him yearned for one taste of that fruit, and he knew he would've jumped down from the elephant and made a mad dash toward the tree had his eyes not finally strayed to its peak.

There, the oceanic ceiling, which everywhere else remained constant, vanished. Instead, Heaven and Earth met and mingled in the highest branches as the throne room of the Three dipped down into the garden like a convex dimension of pure power and radiance. Daniel blinked in confusion. He knew the Three were, at this moment, in battle against the Serpent and his armies, but here they were. Being in multiple places at once was probably a simple feat for them.

Behind a throne of crystal stood the Father. Though Daniel had never beheld him clearly, he knew it was him. His outline was that of a human, but his body, if it could be called that, was wholly spiritual—the perfect union of pure white light and radiant air. His presence was so brilliant Daniel could discern no other features; yet, he was perfectly personal—emanating life, love, and wisdom and drawing all things to him. On the throne itself sat the Son as he had appeared above Babylon: fiery hair, wreathed in elemental power, and brimming with authority.

The Spirit orbited both in the form of seven flames, each one color of the rainbow, bathing the air in a kaleidoscope of wondrous light. A myriad of seraphim and cherubim flew before the Three, and beyond them, a host of Firstborn, radiantly encircling the throne in concentric rings. All stood or flew in solemn silence, and Daniel sensed that to interrupt that quiet with even a prayer would've been inappropriate.

He continued his survey. The topmost branches of the Tree of Life bathed in the heavenly light, swaying back and forth as waves

of power pulsed from the Three to flow out into the Firstborn and down into its boughs. Daniel finally understood. Life did not emanate from the Tree itself. Rather, it was a conduit of Life from the Three.

A reddish light flashed in the air directly in front of the Son. Daniel hadn't noticed it before because of the Spirit's dazzling orbit, but there was a sphere hovering before the Son. Even from his distance, Daniel could make out images of the Three's battle with the Serpent playing out within the orb. Despite the Three's scrutiny of what transpired there, Daniel also sensed that nothing within the garden escaped their notice.

Seconds, minutes, even hours could've passed. Time seemed meaningless when standing before them. Eventually, however, an awareness that Daniel needed to resume his quest worked its way back into his consciousness. Perhaps sensing this, the elephant resumed its journey to the east, veering to the left of the Tree. The lion, badger, and a few of the deer wandered away toward the Tree of Life and disappeared into a stand of firs while some of the birds flew off toward its branches. A passionate longing to follow them settled into his chest. All concerns with his quest would've been banished from his mind had the Three not been so close. As it was, there was no way he could sneak up and take some fruit without being noticed. Daniel craned his neck to keep the Tree in view. It was difficult to know how many miles away it was. Its size made it appear close, though he knew better. It had to be at least five miles to its base, not considering any hidden surprises in the unknown terrain. Not to mention, there were fields to cross, which would make a discreet dash toward the Tree impossible.

The elephant trumpeted a greeting to a herd of giraffes in the distance, and Daniel was startled from his obsessions.

Was he truly considering abandoning the quest to steal fruit from the Tree of Life right beneath the Three's noses? He recalled Uriel's warning, somehow absent in his mind until this moment: death for anyone who tries to take the fruit unless given by the Three. In any case, with the Three watching, stealing a fruit undetected would be

out of the question. Daniel pictured the possibility, though. If one were able to do it, what would be the consequence? Locked in an immortal, sinful body for eons until the Three did something to intervene? Daniel shrugged. That didn't sound good, but would it really be that bad?

He pulled at the sides of his hair. This was getting him nowhere, and staring at the Tree was only increasing his desire for a fruit, while somewhere in the garden, Gabriela was seeking the Tree of Purity. Was he really going to let her down just so he could steal one? As if he'd be allowed to.

Daniel quickly looked around, half expecting to see the Enemy in some guise or another, laughing in the shadows at his nearly victorious temptation. But no such scene greeted Daniel. The enticement was all his own desires knocking around in his mind and tormenting him with impossible longing.

He looked down to see the elephant eyeing him with its head cocked sideways. Daniel gave an awkward laugh and scratched its neck. "Can you pick up the pace?" he asked. "Got to get to that Tree of Purity as soon as we can, you know?"

The beast snorted as though it didn't buy Daniel's motive but did break into a trot across the clearing.

With great effort, Daniel wrenched his eyes away from the Tree of Life and went back to studying his surroundings. He needed to get his bearings both mentally and visually. After they were purified, they were supposed to meet at the Tree. Hopefully, there would be some other animals he could ride, but he couldn't count on it, and he wanted to make sure he knew the quickest route.

The elephant, trailed by the remaining deer, plunged into another band of ancient forest, and the Tree of Life fell out of view. Daniel's mind immediately cleared, and he was able to attend to the path. They soon passed above glens filled with more of the magical, cosmic flowers before breaking out of the woods and into the open again. Fields of bushes laden with fragrant, yellow berries spread out before them. Many grew on stalks tall enough for Daniel to grab even from

his perch on the elephant's back. Figuring there wouldn't be anything poisonous in Eden, he popped a few in his mouth. The burst of flavor was unlike anything he had eaten in his life—like a red grape infused with citrus and a dash of honey. A wave of rejuvenation spread through his body as if he'd just had a long nap. Seeing that they approached the edge of the field, he stretched out and grabbed a few more.

They then passed under the eaves of a larger forest of some broadleafed trees. Within, the ground sloped downward while the trees grew larger. A stream ran through the woods to their right. Daniel's mount could've easily crossed it but instead followed it to the lip of a sheer ravine where the water tumbled noisily down to a pool somewhere below. A wide path of lush grass wound its way down into the gorge, running along its wall in a gentle descent. Without hesitation, the elephant followed it, the noise of the waterfall growing louder as they did.

As Daniel continued to attend to his surroundings, he wondered how the others were doing. He expected to meet up with them at any moment, certain they, too, would've found some helpful animals to guide or carry them. Knowing Ben, though, he'd probably had some misfortune, like falling in with giant monkeys who swung him through the trees all the way down to the river. Daniel chuckled to himself, hoping this wasn't far from the truth.

Gabriela, with her singular focus and level head, would no doubt quickly find her way down. She wouldn't have been distracted by anything.

He imagined Seren making a beeline to the Tree of Purity, wanting to be reunited with Raylin as quickly as possible and dialed in to doing the right thing. She'd probably come running around the corner any second, too impatient to wait for an animal guide.

And then there was Raylin. What was she doing right now? Everything had happened so quickly there hadn't been time to even plan for whatever schemes she might execute. Was she going to somehow let Tyr into the garden? Maybe blow it open so the Serpent could get to the Tree of Life? Or maybe she was simply going to

steal from the fruit, eat it without Uriel or the Three realizing, and then take it to the Generals. Would that make them immortal? He shook his head. Certainly, such a plan would be foolhardy at best. Getting to the Tree without the Three knowing was impossible, and Uriel seemed more than confident that he could kill anyone who tried to take the fruit without permission.

He looked ahead. The ground sloped downward more steeply, and the noise of a river filtered through the trees. A new thought occurred to him. If the Tree of Purity was so important to their fight against the Enemy, maybe its destruction was Raylin's true aim. A chill went down his spine. If that was so, he needed to get there first to stop her.

The river now came into view. Daniel anticipated a wide and muddy channel, like its branch in Babylon. Here, though, the river ran relatively narrow and shallow—only about twenty-five feet across and knee deep. It was crystal clear, with multicolored pebbles lining its bottom and beautiful purple flowers growing along its banks beneath the shade of the surrounding forest.

Another tree, unlike any that Daniel had seen in the garden, grew on a promontory jutting out into the channel to Daniel's left. Its bronze trunk shimmered, reflecting the dappled refractions from the glistening river. Its surface was smooth but honeycombed with intricate and beautifully shaped holes from its base to its crown. At first, Daniel suspected someone had carved them to form an arboreal work of art. Upon closer inspection, they seemed to be some natural feature of the tree, functioning as windows for an inner purple light that rotated from somewhere within. Its beams meandered through them like a lazy lighthouse beacon. The narrow boughs hung low about the trunk, lush and heavy with willow-like leaves of varying dark green hues. They danced in the slightest breeze, ringing with a faint chiming noise as they brushed against one another.

The elephant knelt, and Daniel slid off its neck. With a bow, it continued into the river for a drink. The birds and deer scattered in different directions, but Daniel took note that none of them went toward the tree. In fact, the birds gave it a wide berth.

He let his gaze linger over its graceful shape and was surprised to find himself walking, almost as if bidden by the tree itself, into its overhanging boughs. Once within its shade, the chiming rang louder and more constant. It soon became clear that it was no random clinking created by the wind but rather a lovely, lilting song. Before him, at the base of the trunk, a graceful archway led into the heart of the tree. He hastened through, curiosity growing with each step. Once within, he found a simple cathedral of branches, all sweeping up and out to form a window in the side of its crown, angled in such a way to perfectly frame the throne room of the Three. In the center of the tree, a structure of roots grew upward and wound around one another like some inverted tornado. At their apex, a luminous globe of clear water revolved. Lit within by the purple light he'd seen before, it cast shafts of lavender and violet along the interior of the tree and through the windows out into the garden.

Mesmerized, Daniel approached, hand lifted to touch the globe. A plum-sized droplet separated from the main body of water and floated toward him. It, too, was lit within by the strange, scintillating light. He reached out and took it. He hesitated a moment, wondering if he was about to do something forbidden. It gave off no scent but felt cool and refreshing to touch.

His thirst grew. His body needed this. Yes, it would revitalize him, just like the fruit from the meadow. It would give him what he needed to keep going. His mind would be clearer. The way to the Tree of Purity would be easier. He'd understand the Three even better. Their plan would unfold before his mind. His concerns about Raylin would melt away even as solutions for her betrayal would materialize.

Something dragged his gaze to the leafy window above. The Three, positioned as they were before, continued their scrutiny of the battle before them. He knew, of course, that they watched all that took place in the garden, and everywhere else, for that matter. Was taking of this "fruit" wrong? Uriel had only warned against the fruit from the Tree of Life.

Father? May I?

But even as Daniel prayed, he popped the fruit into his mouth. Waiting for a reply felt intolerable. Once within, it lost its form and was little more than a swallow of water. It quenched his thirst, but the refreshment and insight it promised didn't come. He was also surprised to find it tasteless, even more so than water. Daniel licked his lips and swallowed again. It was strangely familiar, as though he had tasted its flavor throughout his life.

The urgency of his search pressed upon his mind. In any case, the mysterious tree and its disappointing fruit held no interest or allurement for him any longer, and he turned to exit the chiming arbor hall. Once outside, he found that the animals had all wandered farther away, except for a few stray birds that bandied playful trills over some blueberry-like fruit in a nearby bush. The elephant stood far downstream, probing a tree above him for some leaves to eat. Obviously, their jobs were done, and now it was Daniel's turn. He approached the edge of the river, recounting Uriel's instructions.

"Stay in the channel until I find some canyon," he muttered to himself. "Then, eat from the Tree of Purity. Simple enough." He stepped into the shallow water and waded into the middle of the river. At its deepest, it came up to the bottom of his thigh. With a shrug, Daniel turned and trudged upstream.

18

A Bitter Truth

At first, the gentle flow of the river felt soothing. Over the next hour, however, Daniel began to grow weary of constantly battling the current. The water had also deepened and now swirled around his waist.

Animals of all kinds tarried along the banks, occasionally splashing into the water as he waded by and excitedly swimming around him or nuzzling his hands. He got a terrible fright when some giant, seemingly prehistoric species of crocodile slid into the water from his left and clawed its way up to his side. Had he not already interacted with the elephant and the lion and battled monstrous demons, for that matter, Daniel probably would have been terrified. As it was, he barely paid it any concern. The beast's teeth were markedly less sinister than the crocodiles he'd seen in pictures, their rounded tips looking more suitable for eating some sort of plant byproduct than ripping him to shreds. In any case, it seemed more keen on getting affection than anything else.

It pushed its giant snout, which was easily the size of a fully grown man, into Daniel's path.

He reached out and offered a hesitant pat. "Nice monstrous crocodile. Go give Ben a scare, wherever he is. I'm sure he would love to see you."

The crocodile uttered a low growl and lifted its massive head into the air. It gave a long sniff, turning this way and that, before pulling itself up the opposite bank and pushing into the thick underbrush.

Daniel snickered to himself, hoping this meant the beast somehow knew where Ben was. He was sure to get an earful later, but, at the moment, pushed it to the back of his mind.

Ahead, the river curved gently to the right. Once Daniel rounded the bank jutting into the narrowing channel, the water flowed around his neck, and the current picked up. He soon found that his feet could gain little traction, and swimming seemed the best option.

"Unless," Daniel said, summoning the Sun Sword, "there's an easier way."

He put the sword in directional mode and waited for it to tow him through the water. The flaming blade hovered back and forth until it pointed forward, but its characteristic tow never engaged. Daniel furrowed his brow. "That's weird." He released the sword and then summoned it again, hoping it was just a glitch. As before, the blade wavered in the air until fixing on some point upriver without so much as a gentle tug. Daniel grumbled to himself and released the sword again. He wasn't supposed to just stay in this spot in the river; that much he knew. But did this indicate he was supposed to make his way on his own or something? Fine, he could handle a swim. Maybe getting his head wet would cool off the irritation he felt quickly building within him.

The Enemy had taken over Babylon and had some new devilish schemes, the world was in peril, Raylin was a double agent again, and he was separated from Gabriela. But, you know, why not make it take longer for him to get up the river?

As he swam forward, water splashed into his mouth. He gasped. The water tasted so bitter that his lips pursed involuntarily, and he nearly retched. He put his feet down but found no ground and unintentionally went under. Daniel tried to regain his composure as he looked for the bottom, but it was nowhere in sight. It wasn't that the river was murky. On the contrary, it was like staring into the depths of the open ocean, with nothing below him but fathoms of clear blue water.

Startled, he swam to the surface and treaded water, careful not to

allow any more into his mouth. Was this even the right river? Didn't Uriel say its waters were supposed to be sweet? Perfect. The elephant got confused and brought him to the wrong place.

He angrily swam toward the edge of the river, which was only about fifteen yards away. He expected it to grow shallower the closer he got, but even there, the water plunged out of sight while the lip of the bank was just out of reach.

Daniel continued his swim upstream, looking in vain for something to grab and pull himself out of the water. With each moment that passed, he grew angrier and more frustrated. How was he supposed to find the right location if the Sun Sword didn't indicate any other direction? But it had to be wrong. Maybe being in Eden threw it off, like a compass too near a strong magnet or something. That had to be it. Meanwhile, the others were no doubt well on their way to the Tree of Purity, and Raylin was likely executing whatever plan she and Tyr had to destroy their chances of sealing the Spirit of the Age.

Daniel thought back to the first time he and Raylin met. If only he'd seen through her deception then. He wasn't in the habit of trusting people at that time in his life anyway, so why did he let his guard down? If he had insisted on leaving her in the woods, even fought her off, maybe she wouldn't have gotten to Peru and couldn't have betrayed them. The Three could've chosen another Vessel for the Abyssal Staff.

As Daniel splashed around a bend in the river, a swell of water surged toward him, and he inadvertently swallowed a gulp. It was even worse tasting than before. His eyes watered, and he fought back vomiting. His stomach tensed, and a cold, wet feeling churned through his chest. Nearly blinded by the wave of sensations, he didn't notice the log-like neck sticking across the water in front of him until he slammed into it, and his flailing arm happened to find purchase on some bony ridges. Daniel flung his other arm up and latched onto the same ridge with all the strength he could muster. He heard a surprised grunt even as he felt himself lifted out of the river. Blinking water out of his eyes, his vision finally cleared enough

to see that he was hanging from a dinosaur's neck while its surprised owner plodded backward away from the bank.

"Thank you!" Daniel coughed. "You're a dinosaur!" he exclaimed as he slid farther down the neck and finally plopped onto the ground. He didn't know why he was so astonished to find it here in Eden. Everything the Three had created was here in a pre-fallen state; why shouldn't dinosaurs be among them? Daniel searched his mind for the name even as he studied its body. A relatively small head, an extremely long and thin neck, an elephant-like body, all ending in a whip-like tail. "Diplodocus," Daniel muttered to himself.

The diplodocus arced its head around until it was level with Daniel's face. It nuzzled his chest until he scratched its leathery chin. "Where to now?" he asked the dinosaur.

It blinked and gave a happy rumble from somewhere in its belly. With its characteristic plodding movements, it stuck its head back over the river and bobbed it up and down as if gesturing for Daniel to hop back in.

"Uh, no thanks. Wrong river," he replied, turning around to study his surroundings.

Thick, overarching limbs obscured his view. Not that getting his bearings would help much. He had no idea where the Euphrates was or what nasty river he had just pulled himself out of. Surely the elephant couldn't have been that far off. Perhaps he'd intended to take Daniel past this river and only meant to pause for a break when Daniel went to explore the strange tree on the river's edge.

He threw his hands in the air. Perfect. That was probably it. Should he walk back downstream and look for the elephant, or just strike out on his own? After a moment of frustrated indecision, Daniel opted for exploring alone. After all, there was nothing to fear here, and if he *could* spot another river, it'd likely be the correct one.

Daniel turned and rushed into the woods at his back, moving farther from the river and looking for higher ground. Uncertain of the direction, he tried to maintain a simple straight line. The woods brimmed with animals of all kinds, but Daniel felt he had

no patience to stand and study them. All his sense of awe had been sapped by his irritation with being lost. He passed by other dinosaurs milling through the ancient trees and even happened upon a herd of Tyrannosaurs without feeling much surprise. Their teeth and claws, like the prehistoric crocodile he had encountered in the river, were rounded. He barely paid them any heed as they dug into the ground with their hind legs, rooting for some subterranean tuber they pulled out and crunched in their crushing jaws. He passed zebras, colonies of all sorts of primates, flocks of rainbow-colored, flightless birds nearly as large as elephants, a pack of white wolves, and a myriad of other creatures. But none captured his interest. He didn't even stop to wonder why.

Half an hour passed, and the ground began to slope upward. Daniel quickened his pace. Before long, the trees thinned overhead, and he crested the basin, coming out into a field. The Tree of Life, with its brilliant, heavenly light, was much nearer than before—perhaps only a mile away. Somehow, Daniel noted, this didn't surprise him. He broke into a run, leaving the river basin far behind. He was half the distance to the Tree before he realized he hadn't even turned to look for another river. Oh well, he was so close. He might as well just go all the way and see what it was like, right? He broke into a jog and gradually sped up into a sprint. Sweat poured off his body, and his chest heaved. His heart pounded in his ears, but still he ran, deaf to his own body crying out for him to rest.

He soon reached a broad lawn leading to the gigantic trees girdling the base of the Tree of Life. Archways were carved into their living trunks, which formed a perfect wall around the magnificent Tree. On either side of each archway grew dense, round shrubs, like some squat sentinels guarding the paths. Through the openings, the golden light of the Fruit of Life flowed, beckoning Daniel to enter and climb the slope he could see within. He took a step forward, ready to break into a dead run once again, when movement to his left gave him pause.

Raylin, her milk-white hair unbound and drenched, plodded as if

in a dream toward the Tree. Daniel wasn't sure why, but he crouched behind the nearest bush the moment he saw her. She held the Abyssal Staff in her hand, using it as a walking stick as she ascended to the archway directly in front of her. Peering through its olive leaves, he narrowly spied her enter and disappear into the golden light. She was about to enact her plan with Tyr. Something within told him so. If he didn't stop her, their quest was doomed. All their sacrifice and hardship, all the pain, all the waiting for Gabriela—it would be for nothing. He jumped out from behind the bush and sprinted after her.

Within, a pathway followed the slope gently up to the cloistered bole. More of the giant trees grew within, their trunks and the shadows they cast obscuring where Raylin hid. Daniel summoned the Sun Sword and continued his mad dash. Within moments, he caught sight of her back. She stood next to the Tree of Life itself, in intense conversation with someone, their back also turned. Daniel jumped behind one of the trees and peeked around. In the shifting shadows and golden fog, he couldn't make out many features, but the person was blond, very tall, and clearly male. Tyr!

Tyr lifted a richly carved wooden chalice above his head, and Daniel saw drops of light-like liquid fall from one of the fruits into its open mouth. He offered it to Raylin, and she lifted it to drink. Her body began to glow with a warm, rich light. It was different than the intense, fiery power that had flown through his body at Intipuncu in Peru. But even from his distance, Daniel could feel the energy now coursing through her.

They *were* stealing from the Fruit of Life! He was right. Tyr and Raylin intended on taking the Fruit to the Serpent and dispensing it to all his servants. Then they'd live forever, eternally separated from the Three but unable to be killed, ruling alongside the Serpent for all time. That had to be it.

Daniel jumped out from his hiding place and dashed toward them, slinging a Sunstorm through both and following it up with direct slashes through their bodies. He couldn't kill them, he knew, nor could he even bind them until Seren arrived. At the least, he could

keep them in a purified state, using the Sun Sword's power over and over until she arrived or until the Three made a move to bind them.

The dust and smoke from the Sunstorm cleared, and Daniel found himself staring into Raylin's eyes. She and the man stood side by side, both wearing expressions of earnest confusion. There was no cloud of malevolent spirit swirling around them. The Sunstorm's explosive power hadn't even knocked them off their feet.

"You traitor!" he screamed, swinging the Sun Sword through her body over and over. "I knew you were working with the Enemy! You make me sick!"

Each swing of the flaming blade passed clean through her. Instead of collapsing, she stood calmly, unaffected, with a look of peace and concern in her eyes.

"How dare you look down on me, you monster. You disgust me! You think that just because you've taken from the Fruit of Life that you can't be defeated? The Three won't allow it. You'll see!"

Daniel charged the Sun Sword and stabbed it into the ground, its purifying waves radiating outward but having no effect on Tyr or Raylin. He screamed in anger and continued to slash at both, but to no avail.

"Just look at you both, gloating over me like you've won," Daniel growled. He jumped sideways and threw his head back to look up at the Three in their throne room. "Father! Son! Spirit! Behold, Raylin has betrayed you yet again! She's brought Tyr into the garden. Strike them! Strike them down!"

He paused, expecting some sort of fiery bolt from Heaven, but nothing happened. The Three remained intent on the battle unfolding before them.

"Daniel," Tyr said, his voice different than Daniel remembered. "Stay your hand."

Raylin took a step forward and gripped his shoulder before he could jerk away. "Why are you so angry? I haven't betrayed anyone."

Daniel blinked in confusion, his eyes only now focusing on the man's face at Raylin's side. It wasn't Tyr. It was someone he had never

seen before, and what he had mistaken for blond hair was simply a bright crown of light encircling the man's long, black locks. Daniel shook his head, his heart pounding and his breathing ragged. The man's skin was dark, too, nearly black. Instead of Tyr's leather uniform, this man wore a light robe of rich brown. Like Tyr, his frame was powerfully built, though now Daniel perceived he was a good deal taller, and his eyes were forest green.

Daniel struggled to make sense of what he saw. He turned now toward Raylin. She looked different, still gleaming, of course, but there was something else—as though the power of the Tree had erased something within her. He tried to shrug off her hand, but she moved forward more quickly, grabbing both shoulders now.

"What's wrong, Daniel? Why do you still suspect me of betrayal and lies? Don't you feel the purity coursing through both of us now?" She searched his eyes. Then, apparently not finding what she was looking for, she frowned and pulled back abruptly as if afraid to be tainted. "You haven't been to the Tree of Purity."

Daniel sneered. "What? How do you know that? I was on my way there when I saw you stealing the Fruit. I'm trying to stop you from ruining the quest, though it seems I'm too late. Who is this guy?"

The man walked boldly toward Daniel until he was between him and Raylin. "I am the First Adam." He ushered Daniel backward. "That is Eve," he said, gesturing to his right.

Confused, Daniel looked in the distance and saw a woman walking toward the Tree of Life from a different direction. She was beautiful and tall with skin darker than Adam's and a crown of waist-length, kinky, dense hair, intricately braided and bound with metallic clasps. Her amber eyes, clear and filled with tenderness, drew Daniel into their depths the moment she glanced his way. There was something about her look—as if untold ages of waiting and longing had produced a profound patience and mercy within her. Adam's face held the same light—the exact opposite of Tyr's disdainful visage. How could Daniel have ever mistaken them for one another?

He continued his study of Eve. She led someone behind her and

turned to attend to them without addressing Daniel and the others. Like he'd seen Adam do with Raylin, she lifted an intricately carved chalice above her head. Liquid light from a Fruit fell, right on cue, into its open mouth. She turned and offered it to the person behind her and then stepped aside as they drank. Daniel recognized Seren, though her countenance was calmer and more relaxed than he had seen the entire quest.

Daniel dropped his hands to his side. "Why is she drinking? I thought we weren't allowed to touch anything of the Tree? Has Seren betrayed me, too?"

Adam placed a hand on Daniel's back and turned him around, pushing him gently back down the pathway away from the Tree. "Our task is to minister to you all after the ritual at the Tree of Purity. But you have not undergone the ritual yet, and you must not be here."

"You're not listening to me!" Daniel shouted. "Raylin is betraying me again. She's betraying us all!" He craned his neck around and saw her taking another drink from the chalice, this time from Eve's hands. "She's not allowed to touch anything of the Tree! She's—"

"Raylin has betrayed no one, least of all you," Adam interrupted, pushing Daniel back toward the archway. "You twist Uriel's warning. You must not *eat* of the Tree of Life before it is given to you, but drinking its nectar is permitted after one has been purified. That you would know had you been to the Tree of Purity. Why did you not go, Daniel?" He continued advancing Daniel out onto the lawn.

Daniel felt sick to his stomach. "I … I did. I mean, I was on my way, but the elephant took me to the wrong river. There was a tree there, by the way. I ate *its* fruit. Maybe that was the Tree of Purity. If not, don't blame me. It was the elephant's fault. How was I supposed to know? Anyway, I came here to get my bearings when I saw Raylin. She's got to be stopped. It's her fault." Daniel covered his face with his hands. His mind was a jumbled mess, nearly grinding to a halt since the altercation began. What was happening to him?

"Her fault?" Adam studied Daniel's face, a clear look of sternness and sadness welling up from within his eyes. "I know those words."

He drew Daniel into a powerful hug. "I have spoken those words myself. If you ate fruit from the tree by the river, then you ate from the Tree of the Knowledge of Good and Evil. Surely, it held no delights for you. You have tasted its power since the day you were born. No. The Tree of Purity would have transformed you. Listen, my son, do now what it took me so long to do. Admit your guilt. Confess your sin. Take responsibility. Be purified."

Daniel tried to push away, but he couldn't break out of Adam's powerful arms. "What are you talking about?"

"Raylin remains true to the Three and to the quest. She ate of the Tree of Purity. No one who resists the Three would do so. Its fruit is deathly bitter to all fallen Earthborn, but I witnessed her with my own eyes."

Twisting and pushing violently, Daniel finally broke out of Adam's hug and fell backward to the ground. "Are you saying I'm the one with the problem? I haven't done anything! I'm just trying to finish this stupid quest and seal the Enemy and … and … I don't even know what's happening right now!"

Go to the Tree of Purity.

The Three's command, clearer than he'd heard in a long time, broke through all his confusion and silenced him.

"Yes, Daniel," Adam continued. "Go to the Tree of Purity. There, you will discover a secret sin that you have ignored for years. It prevents you and Raylin from unity and peace and prevents you from fulfilling your destiny. It is the root of your anger, and it dwells secretly within the Hollows of your heart. A dark Shadow lives there, and only confession can draw it out."

Daniel froze at those words. Granny had mentioned something like it during Seren's own confession after her transformation from Shakti. He'd seen it firsthand, not only with her but also with Raylin in the Abyss. "You mean, I've got one of those Shadow things inside of me right now?"

"Yes," Adam replied. "It has been hiding there, dormant, for some time now. Once Raylin returned from madness and bondage,

however, it awakened. Even now, it grows and seeks to dominate your will. Do you not feel it?"

Daniel gulped. Everything Adam said felt altogether true. From the moment they rescued Raylin from the Voidblade, something had been off. At first, it was so subtle he couldn't place it. It was like something confounded their communication. It had only gotten worse since the quest began. He replied in a quiet voice, "But what about Raylin's meeting with Tyr? I know what I saw."

Adam shared a meaningful look with Raylin and then lifted his eyes to the Three. After a moment of silence, he said, "That will be made clear at the appropriate time. Now, you must be purified. Be purified, or else be banished from Eden and lose your place among the Vessels."

"What do I do?"

"Return to the Euphrates and go to the Tree of Purity. Follow the commands already given to you. No new revelation is granted until one obeys what has already been shown. That is a lesson I learned from my own sins. Obey and be purified, then all will be made clear. There will be no more chances." Adam raised something over his head. An Orb of Passage.

Daniel's stomach tensed, but he didn't resist. He just shut his eyes and waited for the gut-wrenching sensation of dissolving into fire and streaking through the sky.

"Wait."

Daniel peeked one eye open and found Raylin standing over him.

"Let me go, too," she said, reaching out her hand. "The Three command it. Take my hand, Daniel. Let's finally deal with this together."

Daniel held back, not out of distrust but from shame. He couldn't meet her eyes and studied the ground at her feet. How could this have happened? How could he have been so wrong? So blind? It was humiliating.

"Daniel!" Raylin shouted, grabbing his arm and yanking him into a standing position. "This is no time to sit on your butt. Whatever's

happening in your head, ignore it; it'll only confuse you further. Trust me. I've been there."

Daniel fumbled out some incomprehensible reply, his mind a chaotic tangle of residual bitterness and distrust vying against a growing clarity. He glanced up at Adam and still would have hesitated had he not seen Gabriela and Ben emerge from the woods together and head toward them. A woman and man led the way, both similar enough in appearance to Adam and Eve that Daniel immediately knew they were their children. Explaining everything to Gabriela while he was in this state would've been even more embarrassing; he couldn't get his next words out fast enough.

"Do it. Do it now. Send us!"

Adam threw the Orb of Passage at Daniel and Raylin's feet.

With a sense of relief Daniel never thought he'd associate with this form of travel, he felt his body dissolve into fire and jettison through the air back toward the Euphrates.

19

The Tree of Purity

Daniel and Raylin crashed into the riverbank next to the diplodocus, who had decided to nap in the dappled light beneath the nearby trees. It cracked an eye at the commotion but didn't appear concerned that a fireball had just landed near its tail. It curved its neck around and nuzzled into Daniel's stomach.

"Nice to see you, too, but I'm going to need a little space." Daniel shoved the dinosaur's head away and promptly retched on the ground.

Raylin stood behind him, waiting patiently for him to recover. The diplodocus rested its huge head lightly on her shoulder while she scratched its chin. "You ready?"

"Who knows?" Daniel muttered. He stood, his legs still shaking. "Yes. No. I don't know what this is going to be like."

Raylin nodded sagely and ushered him toward the bank.

Daniel paused on the edge, looking down at the river with disgust. "The water is so nasty, and you can't see the bottom here. Maybe we should walk farther upstream and get in closer to the Tree of Purity."

He turned to find Raylin regarding him with one eyebrow raised and her hands on her hips. "Playing by your own rules worked out much this quest? Jump in and get it over with."

Daniel frowned and turned back to the river. "Ugh. But it's like, a thousand feet deep and—"

"Good grief," he heard Raylin say before he was suddenly picked up and tossed into the river.

The bitter, cold waters splashed into his mouth, eyes, and nose as he floundered for the surface. "What the heck, Raylin?" he sputtered, looking for her on the bank before realizing she was already swimming beside him. "I'm not a child! You're not my mom. And why are you so strong?"

Raylin gave a self-satisfied chuckled. "You *are* a child, and so am I. Get over it. You were wasting time, so I decided to give you a little help. As for my tossing you around like a baby doll, you deserved it, and I got this strong when I drank from the Tree of Life's nectar. Now, stop talking and swim. This is supposed to be a time for prayer and meditation. Don't you feel it?"

"Not really," Daniel grumbled, turning away and heading upstream in a freestyle swim. Truthfully, he hadn't had much spiritual insight throughout the quest, especially after he overheard Raylin and Tyr having their secret conversation. It was as though he had been hijacked by his suspicions, not to mention continual life-or-death situations.

A wave of water splashed into his face, making him gag. He stopped to tread water while coughing. "This tastes awful!" he growled. "I thought this was supposed to be sweet."

"It's the effect of the water that's sweet. You'll see," Raylin shouted, some distance behind him now. "Keep swimming. Don't stop."

Daniel rolled his eyes and continued plowing through the water. All the while, his confusion, frustration, and irritation grew. With each stroke, his feelings magnified until he barely noticed the icy cold of the water. At some point, the banks of the river rapidly rose on either side of the channel. They were now at least twenty feet above him and casting the water in ominous shadow. There were other changes to himself that he saw. Black liquid seeped out of his body in wispy tendrils, darkening the turquoise water around him like squid ink. Little registered in his mind, though, lost as he was in the torrent of anger and bitterness vying with his rational thoughts. Or were they the words of the Three, pushing back against his raging emotions?

That couldn't be it. His anger was deserved. It was just indignation because Raylin had betrayed him twice, after all. There was once in Peru and then in Babylon when she and Tyr conspired to somehow steal the Fruit from the Tree of Life. Adam was wrong. Raylin had tricked him, too, right?

Another mouthful of water rushed in. He paused to cough. The taste was wretched. He was wretched. Everything about this was awful, and he couldn't take it anymore. Daniel looked over at the banks where a beautiful dell beneath expansive oaks stretched into the distance. It beckoned to him. He needed to get out and run. Hide. Figure out what he really needed to do. None of this could actually be the Three's will. Certainly, it was all a mistake. He swam toward the side of the river.

"Daniel." Raylin lithely streamed through the water until she was between him and the bank. "Confused? It's that way." She pointed upstream. "Go to the Tree of Purity."

Daniel regarded the channel with apprehension, his mind torn between the temptation to flee and Raylin's mandate.

"Last chance, remember?"

For some reason he didn't understand, he turned and followed her orders.

Despite his obsessively bitter suspicions, he found his head now clearer. Had she betrayed him twice? No, only once. It was in Peru, but it almost cost him, Ben, and Gabriela their lives. It had nearly doomed the world to slavery to the Enemy. She could have single-handedly ruined the Three's plan!

No, that wasn't quite true either. The Three had foreseen her betrayal and worked it into their strategy.

Once they got home, though, she wouldn't listen to Granny and insisted on taking the Voidblade to get her own revenge. She was so full of hate and anger that she wouldn't listen to the Three. And what did that cost him in India? Ben's life—he had died protecting Raylin from her ridiculous vigilante mission to defeat the Enemy. Daniel could never forgive her for that. So selfish!

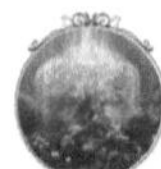

More river water, this time splashing up his nose and mouth at the same time. He came up sputtering, coughing so violently he worried the water was down in his lungs.

"Don't stop!" Raylin called as she passed him, gliding through the water like a fish. She zipped along, now several yards ahead. "Come on!"

Daniel cleared his throat as best he could and continued up the river, not happy that Raylin was in the lead.

His mind fell back into the same line of thinking almost immediately, like a train stuck on the same track. All that in India was necessary, though. Ben had to obtain the Triune Shield, and the only way was for him to willingly give up his life for another. Of course, Raylin *was* manipulated and driven insane all along by the demons bound within the Voidblade. However ill-advised, she was just trying to defeat the Enemy in the only way she knew. Despite all that, the Three foresaw Raylin's plans and wove her choices into their will yet again.

No. He was giving her too much slack. She had ample opportunities to return to the service of the Three—to seek her Heavenly Father, to obtain redemption through the Son, and to be filled with the purifying Spirit. Every opportunity was available to her, especially when they tracked her through Ireland, England, and Wales. The Spirit constantly overpowered the darkness within her, demonstrating his ability to purify and save. But did she repent? No. Because of her obsessive drive for more power, he, Ben, Seren, and Gabriela almost died countless times on that quest. She had even been responsible for breaking his leg! And then, they had to go down to the Abyss and fight the Serpent face to face! If it hadn't been for Raylin, none of that would've happened.

The familiar surge of water rushed into his mouth, but this time, he was ready. Instead of inhaling it, he opened his mouth and simply swallowed. It was just as bitter as before, but now that he accepted it willingly, it settled into his stomach with a calm, comforting feeling. The aftertaste, too, was sweet.

His reflections continued where they had left off. What was he thinking? His leg had been broken because Seren rushed headlong into the battle at Newgrange, and Daniel had been forced to act. As for the Abyss, they had no choice. They needed the Abyssal Staff, and to do that required facing the Serpent. Yes, Raylin had needed it to be freed from the Voidblade, but they would've had to go there anyway. All these events and all their choices also led them to profound spiritual growth. The Three took what the Enemy had meant for evil and turned it into good.

The water around Daniel was now a messy cloud of black, and he could barely see in front of him. With the next stroke forward, his hand hit something soft and squishy. He lifted his head out of the water and discovered he had run into an island. He put his feet down and found he could now stand.

Daniel looked around as one waking from a dream and walked up onto the island. Just as Uriel had described, the river's headwaters ran out of a ravine. The walls rose so high that it almost felt like a cave. Above, however, he could just make out a narrow strip of branches where a forest grew along the ridges of the gorge. And beyond that, the blue-green dome of the Persian Gulf. He let his eyes fall to the island itself. It was small, with a diameter of maybe fifty feet, and boasted a cloud of white lilies on nearly every inch. Their floral fragrance filled the air with the very essence of spring.

A waterfall gushed out of a rock high above, where it fell to bathe a single tree in a torrent of crystal. It was the Tree of Purity. There was no question. Even if it had not been in the location that Uriel described, the raw and cleansing power emanating from it would have immediately told him its name. Wide and twisting, its trunk took up half the island. The bark was smooth and white, save where delicate lines of gold and silver ran in intricate patterns, swirling in labyrinthine complexity up into the branches. A gloriously broad crown donned leaves of fern-green fire, which gladly received the spray of the waterfall without so much as a hiss of displeasure. Crimson fruit, shaped like teardrops and surrounded by a halo of searing heat, burned bright amidst the fiery leaves.

As Daniel approached, he discovered that the waterfall, gathered happily by the branches and leaves, rained down on the lilies and ran off to the back of the tree. There, it coalesced into a pool that spilled out onto either side of the island, forming the actual river itself.

The walls of the ravine were solid rock, except where roots from the tree, themselves white and glistening with the beautiful lines of silver and gold, burrowed up and through the stone.

Daniel breathed in the heady aroma of the lilies and walked closer to the tree. Raylin waited beneath the quietly burning crown, hands by her side and drenched in spray from the waterfall. Uncertain of what to do, he simply continued his approach. With each step, he felt something within him squirming as if some living thing vainly sought a hiding place. Finding even that wasn't far enough away, it then pushed upward until it sat, cold and heavy, in his chest. Directly in front of the trunk, the roots of the Tree of Purity formed a perfect circle.

Raylin beckoned him to stand within it. He obeyed, surprising even himself. Most of his feelings toward her were now neutral, but some anger and bitterness still swirled around within him. He was somehow able to compartmentalize it, though, as if it were something separate from himself. Daniel sat within the circle, uncertain of what to do next, but suddenly feeling a weariness settle into his body.

One of the crimson fruits dropped from the boughs overhead, floating down like a nearly deflated balloon until it rested in Raylin's hands.

"Take this and eat," she said, walking nearer and holding it out. "If you'll receive it from me."

Daniel reached out his hand but stopped. Should he? After all the heartache she had caused, wasn't it only right to hold her sins against her? For the good of the quest, anyway. To make sure he wasn't duped again. She had betrayed them all and could again. Maybe it was best…

Daniel rolled his eyes, disgusted with the same old and tired narrative running through his mind. He now knew where it came

from. Some part of him hadn't really forgiven Raylin for what she'd done in Peru, despite what he said at the time. He had held onto his anger, grasping it like some valuable treasure or talisman protecting him from future betrayal. Instead, it simply blinded him to what the Three had done within her—forgiveness for her sins, freedom from her past, and now purifying her in anticipation of their battle to seal the Spirit of the Age. And, it had kept him from being purified.

"I will," he said and took the fruit from her hand. It burned intensely. Daniel fought every instinct within his body to drop it to the ground. Instead, he did the only thing he could think to do: he raised it to his mouth as quickly as he could and took a bite. His lips were seared, and he felt his insides burn as the fruit made its way down into his stomach. The pain was excruciating.

He opened his mouth to scream, but he was surprised to hear what came out. "Raylin! I forgive you!" He convulsed. "I've held onto your betrayal for years, and I'm tired of it. Sick of it! I choose to let go of my bitterness. Please, forgive me." He threw his head back and shouted. "Father, forgive me for holding onto my anger and believing I had the right to resent Raylin. Purify me!"

Daniel felt the thing in his chest push itself out. It was simultaneously a disgusting and relieving feeling. He fought against revulsion and looked down as the Shadow—the miniature, slinking version of himself—seeped out of his chest and fell to the ground. It was on fire, squirming and writhing in agony. Daniel's pain immediately ceased once it fully left his body, and he felt no small satisfaction as it burned down into a pile of white ash. The water raining down around them quickly washed it amid the lilies and out of sight.

Raylin knelt, touched Daniel's shoulders, and gestured for him to stand. A strange light burned within her eyes, and her snow-white hair shone around her face like a halo. Strings of light ran from his body to hers, visible now that he had been purified.

He recalled seeing them after their quest to the Abyss. At that time, the Spirit had explained how everything was connected through

his power. Daniel furrowed his brow as he studied the strings. Why would they be visible again?

"I forgive you." It was Raylin who spoke, but the Father's voice overlaid her own. It was usually filtered and interpreted by the Son, but now it came through raw, unfathomable, cosmically resonant, but clear.

Daniel and Raylin trembled and fell to their knees even as the Sun Sword's lost shard burst out of Raylin's chest and hovered in the air. The sword itself responded by blazing, unbidden, out of Daniel's. One of the glowing strings connected both, drawing the shard to the blade until it clicked into place. Hovering between them, the Sun Sword slowly revolved. For a moment, the seam where they met flushed a molten orange before disappearing altogether, leaving the blade whole. Following one more revolution, the sword flew into Daniel's chest without warning, blasting him backward.

The last things he remembered were being on fire and thinking how familiar this all seemed.

* * *

The man and woman from his earlier visions knelt in a wide meadow surrounded by birch and poplar. White clouds billowed high into the sky, themselves luminous in the sunlight. A pool of water, perfectly circular and about ten feet in diameter, lay before them. Daniel floated just below its surface.

Daniel found all this to be exceedingly strange, especially since he observed it from above as though his soul hovered overhead.

"He is finally free of it," the man said, relief evident in his voice.

Daniel tried to angle his line of vision to see the man's face, but he could never get a clear look.

The woman reached into the water to touch his brow, her hair falling forward to shield her face from view. Daniel felt her caress register from where he watched.

"Finally," she sighed. "And now, the greatest task. Do you think he will survive?"

The man's gaze fell from the woman down to Daniel. "Maybe. It would not be the end if he dies."

"I know. But still, I hope he lives long on Earth. I want to see him fulfilled."

Who are you? Daniel tried to say, though his body below him wouldn't move or form the words aloud.

"Daniel, awaken," someone said.

The man and the woman seemed to hear it, too. They glanced at one another and stood. Stepping back from the pool, each lifted their hands while murmuring words of supplication to the Three.

Daniel felt himself drawn down into his body, and everything went dark. He opened his eyes and found himself back on the island. A tall, black-skinned man looked down on him. His hair was cropped short, and he wore a golden half-moon collar around his neck. Like Adam, a light, flowing robe of earthen brown donned a muscular frame, and the wisdom and mercy of thousands upon thousands of years shone in his face.

"Stand," he commanded, reaching out a large, powerful hand and pulling Daniel to his feet with ease. "I am Seth, son of Adam and Eve and the first Vessel of the Sun Sword."

"What? You are? I mean, were? Wait, am I still on fire?" Daniel blurted out as his head cleared.

"No," Raylin replied. She leaned against the Tree of Purity and casually pushed herself forward to amble toward him. "You're fine."

Daniel felt he was seeing her anew. He no longer experienced the gnawing sense of resentment that, up until moments ago, nagged at his mind every time he looked at her. Even the general agitation and clouding anxiety that had grown within his heart since the quest began were gone. He looked up at the Tree of Purity, studying its quiet, unassuming power that drifted about its boughs. "So, the tip of the Sun Sword was within you all along?"

"I guess so. I'm as confused as you." She looked hopefully at Seth.

"I think I can shed some light on this," Seth replied. He tapped Daniel on the chest. "Summon the Sun Sword."

Daniel squared his shoulders and then summoned the sword as commanded. Even before he saw it, he felt the difference. With the tip, the sword felt more balanced and powerful.

Seth took the sword's blade in his hands the way Daniel had only ever seen a supernatural being do before. He turned the blade to the side and let his fingers run its length. With a flick of his fingernail against the blade, the sword uttered a happy knell and flew back to Daniel, floating just beyond his right hand. "The Sun Sword shattered in Supai's throne room, correct?"

"Right," Daniel replied, feeling the magnified power of the sword flow through him as he waved it through the air.

Raylin held a hand to her chest while she listened, and a far-off look filled her eyes. "It shattered after you told me you could never forgive me for betraying you."

"But I did eventually forgive you, remember?" Daniel rubbed the back of his neck, thinking back on their first quest. It seemed an eternity ago. "Outside the cave on Pedestal Hill. I told you I could forgive you, just not trust you anymore."

Both turned as one to Seth.

"I do not know your heart, Daniel. But I do know this: forgiveness is usually not something we do once, especially when seriously hurt. Maybe you did forgive Raylin in that moment, but bitterness, distrust, and resentment have ways of creeping back into our hearts." He lifted an eyebrow and tapped Daniel's chest. "It very clearly seems that it had."

Daniel shuddered and then fell back to studying the Sun Sword's wavy, flaming blade. "So then, the tip. Why was it within Raylin?"

All the hair on Daniel's neck stood on end as waves of breathtaking power buffeted his back. Its force disrupted the waterfall behind the Tree of Purity, and every molecule in his body felt charged with electricity. Seth spun around and fell to his knees. Daniel and Raylin quickly turned on their heels and knelt before the Son, who stood before them in radiant glory. The Spirit—his Spirit—burned behind him in the form of a resplendent, fiery blue circle. Within it was

a triangle of the same color flame, the perfect size to fit the Son's elemental halo, which rotated inside it like a ten-foot-tall wheel. At his feet, flowers, grass, and other shrubs greedily sprouted, crowding around each footstep. Through the Spirit, like a window into Heaven, Daniel saw the Father still standing behind the crystal throne.

"That is a question for us." The Son touched each one present, raising them to their feet and kissing their foreheads.

A calming, energizing power flowed through Daniel when the Son's gaze rested upon him. He found there, as he knew he would, the eyes of every loving human and animal, as if all eyes were modeled from his. He felt so peaceful that he knew it would be bliss to stand before the Son forever, basking in his love and power like a tree in the sunlight.

A look of pure rest and contentment settled into Raylin's face as she followed the Son's every movement.

Seth beheld the Three with familiar adoration and folded his hands to await the Son's explanation in happy silence.

"The Sun Sword is an instrument of purity," the Son explained. "Its purpose is to purify the unclean, set free those who are in bondage, and keep darkness at bay." He touched Daniel's chest, and a string of memories raced through his mind in an instant, each marking a time he harbored resentment toward Raylin. "Your bitterness was a seed planted by the Enemy. He knew that, even if Raylin did not kill you in his throne room, her betrayal would drive a wedge between you two. And, in turn, it would prevent all the Vessels from walking under the Father's Blessing. Long ago, he discovered that if the Vessel of the Sun Sword is unwilling to forgive, that impurity would cause the sword to fragment."

The Son brushed a strand of hair out of Raylin's face. "What he did not count on, though, was how we would use his ploy for your good. Dear child, how you suffered in bondage to the Enemy's spirit. Foreseeing this, we hid the shard within you. Did you not feel it fighting against the darkness?"

Raylin, lost in the Son's eyes, suddenly came to. "I'm not sure.

When I was possessed, I always felt tension, like two things fought inside me. Eventually, everything went dark. I couldn't even see out of my own eyes, and my body was just a puppet for the demons in the sword." She tilted her head to the side. "Strange. These used to be hard memories, but now, they're just far away. Like they happened to a different person."

Raylin paused, a look of hesitation in her eyes.

The Son nodded. "Finish your testimony, Raylin."

"After a time," she continued, now looking past the Son and at the bitter-sweet waters flowing away from the island to snake through the woods of Eden, "I was literally trapped in my head, walking around a dark place inside my own consciousness, like a prison. The dark spirits of the Voidblade were there, mocking me, jeering. There was never silence, only their horrible voices and all the lies they told me. 'You are in hell,' they said. 'Forgotten. Unloved. Rejected. Judged. Hopeless. Trash.' Over and over, day and night. It was horrifying. No, it was more than that. Terror. Despair." Raylin shook her head. "None of these words fit. They're not evil enough. But"—she paused, and her hand absently strayed to her chest—"I remember a light. If I walked toward it, I couldn't hear them anymore. It was hot, though. Burning, really. But none of the spirits would come near, so I just stayed there all the time. Burning but free of their voices. It wasn't a bad pain."

Daniel understood the last part. The burning feeling after he had eaten the fruit from the Tree of Purity had been like that—excruciating but good.

"I, too, understand that pain," the Son said. "I bore it in my body when I bore your sins and the sins of the world. The Father poured out his wrath upon me, and I suffered. But it was a holy and necessary suffering. The tip of the Sun Sword kept you from falling into total darkness. It is, in essence, imbued with the Spirit, and so you were never wholly possessed. But even if you had been, I would have rescued you."

He took a measured breath, and the garden seemed to inhale with

him. "Now, Daniel, you understand why and where. Your portion of the Sun Sword remained incomplete because of your resentment, but we used it for Raylin's good. Ultimately, your good as well. Now, your bitterness has been purified, and you and Raylin are in a right relationship. All the Vessels can now receive the Father's Blessing together. And together, you can bind the Enemy's spirit."

He cupped both their faces like a loving father, and Daniel noticed something written on the Son's hands. He couldn't help but stare, recalling the sense of secrecy surrounding those words when he had first met the Son in the Chamber of the Moon.

The Son smiled kindly and opened both palms. "These words are no secret. But they are precious to me. Your names are graven on my hands. As are all the names of the redeemed. Take comfort from this. No matter where you are, or what you face, you are ever on my mind, and I am with you. You are all my beloved. Now, you must go. Your quest is nearly finished, but the most important task is yet before you. And I, also, must go. The Enemy's armies advance against the nations of the world, and he seeks to push into the Holy Land. He is not yet permitted to do this, and so I will prevent him." With his last words, a peal of thunder sounded from somewhere above, and a storm of fire passed over his eyes. "Do not fear," the Son continued, taking both their hands and giving them a gentle squeeze, "and do not trust anything the Enemy shows you. Remember, I am always with you." He turned to walk through the halo behind him and vanished.

Daniel and Raylin stood, shoulder to shoulder, staring at the air. There was an ardent longing in Daniel's heart to simply go where the Son was and to leave everything behind. Especially knowing that the hardest part of the quest—the hardest part of any of their quests— was ahead of them. Raylin probably felt the same, too. Given all the suffering she had endured in her life, she likely desired it more than he did. Pity welled up within him, which felt new and surprising. Had his heart really been so hard before that a true feeling of compassion for her was an anomaly? He shook his head. He couldn't believe how jaded he had been. To think, he had believed she was betraying them all again and was in league with Tyr.

Daniel plopped both hands on his head. "Wait a minute! If you weren't betraying us to Tyr, then what were you talking to him about?"

Raylin paused, and a cloud passed over her eyes as if she had just recalled something unpleasant. She held up her hands apologetically. "Sorry, he swore me to secrecy. I know this may surprise you, but I don't like to break promises. Listen, it's for the good of the quest. Please trust me. If anyone else knew right now, it wouldn't be good."

Daniel could have kicked himself for not asking the Son. Although, since the Son hadn't brought it up, he likely wouldn't have told Daniel anything anyway.

"Fine. Have it your way. I'll trust you. But you better have a good …" Daniel paused and shook his head. The last thing he wanted was old patterns of thinking to slip back in. "No. I trust you. Whatever your reasoning, I trust you."

"We must leave," Seth said, standing up from the flickering shadows of the Tree of Purity. "The others are waiting at the Tree of Life, and you must all receive the Father's Blessing upon your Weapons of Power. Come."

Seth stepped in front of them and walked to the edge of the island to search the sky. Before Daniel had much time to consider what he might be looking for, a gale of wind buffeted him as a huge, black, six-winged lion, his pinions pumping backward to slow his flight, dropped into the shallows of the Euphrates. He was the size of a bus, and his mane, fringed with iridescent silver, swirled in the crystal water churning around his legs. Amber eyes looked down his muzzle at the trio while a myriad of other eyes, dotting his heavily muscled body, peered vigilantly in every direction. A purr rumbled in his chest as he stretched out two of his right wings on the ground.

"Raylin?" he said, clearly perplexed. "I already took you to the Tree of Life. Did you come for a second purification?"

Raylin hurriedly bounded up one of his wings and perched herself midway down his back. "Hello, Aryeh. I'm happy to see you again."

"As am I," Aryeh replied. "I did not think to see you until after the sealing."

"I came to be with Daniel for his purification."

"I will explain on the way," Seth interrupted. "Time is short. This is Daniel." He ushered Daniel up on the lion's wing, walking him to the beast's shoulder and gesturing for him to sit. "Daniel, this is Aryeh. He spends most of his time attending the Three, but this is one special task he has."

Daniel noticed with a certain sense of discomfort that several of the lion's eyes followed his every move. "Hello," he said, feeling heavily scrutinized and wondering if the lion was happy with what he saw.

"Welcome," was all Aryeh said.

Seth took a seat between Daniel and Raylin. "Swiftly, now."

Aryeh flapped all six wings at once while simultaneously leaping into the air. Daniel hastily gripped the lion's mane to keep from falling off and intertwined the silver-edged fur between his fingers. After the moment of fear passed, he found his body relaxing, and he took in the beauty of Eden now from a different perspective. Seth gave Aryeh a quick explanation for Raylin's presence, but Daniel found he didn't mind so much. All embarrassment and shame, he was happy to say, felt far away at the present. His mind, now finally at ease since coming here, could finally absorb the splendor of Eden stretching out beneath him. Before them, the Tree of Life rose, shining like a golden spire pointing to its source of power.

20

The Charge

Seth lowered the wooden chalice, brimming with the nectar from the Fruit of Life, and held it to Daniel's lips. Energy and vitality surged through every cell. Its heady scent defied description, and Daniel could barely process the bouquet of flavors smoothly trickling down his throat. Like honeysuckle, apples, blackberries, and a fresh summer's day had lent their aromas in perfect balance to a clear mountain waterfall. That was the only way he could describe the taste.

Gabriela, Seren, Ben, and Raylin stood around him, arrayed in white robes of light fabric. After the drink, Eve presented him with the same. Seth quickly ushered him behind one of the smaller trees nearby to help him change out of his old clothes and into the robe. The cloth, if it could even be called that, felt smooth and cool like air, and he couldn't help but feel he was totally naked when led to Gabriela's side. He blushed, brushing her arm with his.

"Hey."

"Where have you been?" she asked in a low voice.

The glow emanating from her skin enhanced her beauty so much that Daniel's breath caught in his throat. He became doubly aware of how exposed he felt before her refreshed and quick eyes. "Dealing with my unforgiveness with Raylin. It's all sorted out now, though."

Daniel felt surprised by his own easy honesty. It seemed so simple to just be open. Clearly, his purification cleaned out not only his resentment but also shame and deceit in all their forms.

"I'm glad to hear it." She flashed a disarming smile.

"What have I missed?"

Gabriela shrugged. "We've just been waiting here. Talking, learning, relaxing, preparing for what's next. Ben had a hilarious run-in with a crocodile, so we got to hear about all that."

"Eden or no Eden," Ben broke in, sticking his head around Gabriela, "that thing was humongous, and it came out of nowhere, and it was terrifying, and it was humongous. Did I mention its size?"

Daniel stifled a laugh. "Yeah, I saw it in the river, too."

Something in Daniel's expression must have looked suspicious. Ben regarded him silently for a moment before narrowing his eyes and pointing an accusatory finger. "If I find you had any part in sending him my way, you're in for it. That thing tried to carry me in its mouth, Daniel. Like I was one of its babies or something. Thankfully, animals here understand human language, or else I would've made it to the Tree of Purity in a cage of teeth."

Daniel felt it best to leave the crocodile behind at the present. "One second." He stepped around Ben and Gabriela to stand next to Seren and Raylin. "Hey, Seren."

She turned away from Raylin and clapped him on the back. "Glad you could make it to the party. Took you long enough."

"Yeah. Well, you know, I had some things to sort out."

"We all did, Daniel. You weren't the only one with issues that needed taking care of at the Tree of Purity. I had quite a bit of anger toward you, my parents, and a mess of other stuff, too. A lot to do with letting go of control."

Raylin folded her hands behind her back. "Anger with you. Jealousy. Self-pity. Not to mention troubling memories from when I was possessed."

Daniel was surprised to hear their admission of anger toward him while personally feeling nothing but understanding. There was no defensiveness and no desire to qualify or make excuses, just acceptance.

"Mine were issues of distrust," Gabriela volunteered. "Could I trust the Three to manage everything with you all, the world, and my people? Would I have enough strength to see everything through? And petty fears about the Three's power and my future. I know it sounds crazy, given everything we've seen, but a part of me still feared that the Enemy could take away the Image of the Three from me. That I would, one day, simply die and slip into oblivion. Annihilation. But now," she shrugged, "those fears have all gone, and I can focus wholeheartedly on the quest."

"You're speaking my language," Ben added. "I had a lot of fear to deal with, but it wasn't so specific. Just fear, fear, fear, fear, and more gobs of fear. Oh, and anger toward you, of course." He elbowed Daniel in the ribs.

"I'm beginning to see a theme," Daniel replied.

"You earned it. Anyway, it's not that uncertainty is gone, just the cold stab of fear that comes with those things. It's like, how do I say this? I'm still concerned about certain things—surviving, for one—but I feel that the Three have it all in their hands."

Everyone fell into a contemplative silence, waiting patiently for whatever came next. Adam, Eve, and their three attendant children bowed to the group and then walked into the woods that girdled the Tree of Life. Even as the last of them slipped out of sight, light from the throne room of the Three grew stronger. The Father's cosmically resonant voice—the voice that held all things together and could unmake all matter and time in an instant—echoed down from the throne.

"Come near, my children."

In the past, the Son had interpreted the Father's indecipherable words to them, making them accessible and comprehensible. It was similar now. Only, as the Father spoke, Daniel found he could understand. The Son nevertheless uttered the same words, their voices overlaying and intertwining as though he *was* the very Word of the Father, in whom and through whom all things were accomplished and conveyed.

Even as their voices registered to Daniel's ears, the Father stood among them, appearing as a galactically large figure of white fire cloaked in a blinding light. Universes trailed in his wake, spinning away behind him into some incomprehensible dimension of luminous brilliance. Was the Father standing in the Garden of Eden, or were they in the throne room? It was hard to tell because, at that moment, Daniel became aware of the Father's presence existing everywhere all at once. Though, in the next, all Heaven and Earth fled. The Father loomed tall before them and the Son and the Spirit behind. Nothing else dared show itself except the train of brilliant universes diffusing into the air around the Father. The heavenly court of Seraphim and Cherubim were notably absent. Although, Daniel figured, the Three's omnipresence probably meant they also still sat in their throne room, surrounded by the serpentine and many-faced Firstborn.

The Father's presence felt identical to the Son's: eternal, unyielding power, enough to create the cosmos with nothing more than a thought. The fierce purity of his presence was what stood out and frightened Daniel. It wasn't that the Son and the Spirit were different, but they were approachable whether Daniel was wrapped in sin or cleansed. The Father's holiness—unfiltered, raw, naked—filled him with the purest fear he had ever known. It was paradoxical, at once drawing him while simultaneously warning of its consuming power. That power streamed through him and would have unmade him had not the Son's life coursed through his body and had he not just been purified. Daniel knew this with absolute confidence. If the Father had come this near at any point before, he would have been instantly destroyed.

At that moment, Daniel remembered something he had read about God dwelling with mankind on the new Earth. Previously, he always believed that serving the Three and being adopted into the Celestial Family was about leaving this Earth and going to Heaven. But now, standing before the Father, he accepted that he might be wrong. What if it was all about the Three desiring to be near their children but staying distant because of their consuming holiness?

Their distance was both a mercy and a judgment. But through the Son, by the power of the Spirit, all could be purified and unified with the Father. Then, finally, the dwelling place of God could be with mankind.

All this blew through his mind in an instant, and Daniel realized he and the others lay prostrate on the ground.

"Rise. Come near. Present your weapons to me that I might hallow them once more."

Daniel felt Gabriela stir beside him, and the Spirit, resting upon all five of them in the form of blue fire, raised them to their feet. Daniel approached the Father first. He summoned the Sun Sword and held it above his head, its blade pointing upward.

"Be blest." The Father reached out a blinding hand of enormous size and gently touched the sword. "Purify and release the captives."

Daniel sharply inhaled as his body immediately and intensely filled with the Blessing. As if written gently by an unseen hand, he felt heavenly script inscribed on his forehead in a small, spiral pattern. "Belonging to the Three ~ For the Purifying of Darkness." Even though he couldn't see it himself, he *felt* its meaning indelibly stamped upon his being.

As in Peru years ago, he became translucent. The Spirit's fire burned not only above him but also within. After their first quest, Granny mentioned that the Father's Blessing, once given, was never lost. He took her word for it, of course, but now he *saw* it to be true. The Spirit wasn't with them and then gone once he had lost this power in Supai's throne room. The Spirit never left, even if by Daniel's own sin, he felt far away from his presence. The Father's Blessing in this form was a renewed outpouring of his power and presence: a commissioning of sorts. But what Daniel felt now was different than at Intipuncu. This level of power was unmatched by anything he had experienced, and he knew this was how humans were meant to exist—unified with the Three as pure and holy vessels of their power and love. All was calm within him. All was peace. All was love.

He stepped back as Raylin approached. The Abyssal Staff

appeared in her hands as she slowly drew her palms apart. She held it horizontally as the Father blessed it, renewing the anointing of the Spirit within her and filling her with his power. At once, she became luminous, her white hair and robe whipping around her body like a silent, rushing wind. Simultaneously, Daniel felt a link established between them; all her emotions and thoughts flowed into him as his did into her. She turned, and he glimpsed the same spiral pattern of words appear on her forehead. First, there was the declaration of the Three's ownership, followed by "For the Sealing of Abomination."

Seren approached next, summoning the Celestial Bow above her head in her left hand while drawing back an arrow with the right. The Father gave his blessing, and she, too, donned his power. Daniel sensed her joining the spiritual connection. In this form, she and Raylin were nearly indistinguishable, if not for their different weapons and the different words on their foreheads. Seren's read, "Belonging to the Three ~ For the Binding of Evil."

It was Ben's turn now. He approached the Father and held up both hands. His body glowed and expanded outward into the Triune Shield, with Ben's form between the interlocking and gyrating circles facing the Father. The Father blessed and filled him, linking him with the other Vessels. As he returned to Daniel's side, the familiar possessive inscription appeared on his forehead, followed by "For the Shielding of the Weak."

Now, it was Gabriela's turn. She approached and waited. Daniel sensed she was uncertain of what to do but content to stand in the Father's presence as long as he would allow. Daniel was reminded of her time away in the service of the Three. He had begrudged her absence then, seeing it as something keeping them separate. Now, at this culmination of all his experiences with each member of the triune Godhead, he perfectly understood her aloofness then. Of course, she hadn't been able to commit to him; she'd served the Three day in and day out. Who could do so and give thought to anything else?

"My daughter," the Father said, "you too are a Vessel of my Spirit and strength even if you carry no weapon. Go with my power and

call the nations to return to me. Be a voice in the wilderness, in the city, on the mountain, over the fields. I will inhabit your words. The peoples of the earth will turn away from their wickedness and find life. Open the Mists so that your people, too, can spread my message to the world. There will be a New Awakening. Be a witness of all you have seen. If any minion of the Enemy seeks to harm you, your strength and words will be enough to overthrow them. Do signs and wonders among the enslaved and harried people of the world; heal, bind up, raise from the dead, bless, and teach. Show them the way to Life so they might turn and find freedom. By the Spirit, your voice will ring out among all nations, and your people will be anointed to point others to the Way of Repentance and Life."

Gabriela was at once imbued with the Father's Blessing and power. She stood there for a moment, eyes fixed on the towering figure of light before her.

As her emotions filtered into Daniel's awareness, he sensed the burning passion for her commission.

"When can I begin?" she asked.

"Now," the Father replied. "With the broken and imprisoned in the Enemy's land. Go to the stronghold of Ealim Wahid. By my word within you, its gates will crumble, and its guards will flee. Lead the captives through the cities, teaching and crying out for all to come. Any who answers your call will receive my Spirit within them. The Babylonian Seal will be reforged through their prayers, and the Enemy's power will dwindle even while his spirit is sealed."

Gabriela, filled with mission and purpose, turned away from the Father and looked straight ahead as if seeing something far off. "Belonging to the Three ~ For the Finding of the Way" appeared on her forehead.

"Farewell," she said, keeping her eyes fixed on that faraway point only she seemed to see. "I will intercede for you all."

Daniel and Seren stepped to one side while Raylin and Ben moved to the other. Gabriela walked between them as a portal to Earth whirled open before her. Below, the tower of Ealim Wahid

menaced darkly against the noon sun. A clap of thunder split the air, and a bolt of lightning streaked from the Father and through Gabriela. She was unfazed, her face somehow a perfect mixture of serenity and warlike determination as she, too, became the lightning. She streamed through the portal.

The bolt struck the ground in front of the tower, and Gabriela stood before it, gleaming like a beacon of hope and burning fiercely with the white-hot wrath of the Three's holy anger.

Daniel and the others watched as she raised her hand and said something, and the gates blew off their hinges, crumpled and shattered. Monstrous dragons charged out of the tower toward her. Leaping effortlessly into the air, she pounded them into the dust, leaving tree-sized craters in her wake with the broken and dazed bodies of the demons at their center. She raised her hand again and spoke some word that didn't reach through the portal, and the entire front face of the tower imploded. Hordes of demons poured out now. Some flew out of windows high above, forming into a seething cloud of evil before dive-bombing her en masse. More dragons, a score of camel spiders, a dozen snakes, and a confusing mob of hideous chimera demons, each some strange conglomeration of animal parts their parasitic spirits had amalgamated, charged Gabriela from behind the fallen walls of the tower. In fast, fluid motions, she decimated the force. Even the flying demons couldn't escape her fists and the words of power she uttered at intervals between her physical assaults. The scene unfolded faster on Earth than in the presence of the Three as if, Daniel thought, someone fast-forwarded the battle. He glanced at the sun through the portal, noticing it had sunk nearly to the horizon during the time that the battle unfolded. Time *was* flowing differently there. It wasn't just his imagination. Now he understood why the Heavenly battle unfurled so slowly when experienced from Earth.

He turned back to the fight. Hundreds of Creeps now raced out of the tower, galloping on hands and feet like enraged animals. Gabriela hesitated, jumping backward and immediately kneeling in prayer. Her voice rang out loudly in the air above the Vessels.

"Heavenly Father, please purify these people," she begged, her voice urgent but confident. "I don't want to harm them. Have mercy and free them from their bondage!"

"Daniel!" the Father thundered, his voice speaking over and through the Son's. The very foundations of reality blurred and shook at the power, authority, and utter joy in his voice. "Purify them. Be my instrument to answer Gabriela's supplication."

Daniel raised the Sun Sword, which glowed a blinding yellow and white, and swung it through the air. A Sunstorm, as large as a city, flew from the blade. The moment it exited the portal, Gabriela's time and Daniel's time synced. The tower and all the land around it were immediately engulfed in flames. Gabriela, neither harmed nor surprised, bowed toward the Three in thanks.

A menacing, seething mass of demonic spirit rose into the air over the purified land, shrieking and cursing the Three.

"Ben, protect the purified from being retaken," the Father commanded.

Ben jumped into action, holding both hands out toward the men and women who now lay in the dust, purified and unconscious, between Gabriela and the tower.

The cloud of demons churned like a summer storm and flew toward the only remaining bodies they could inhabit, their former hosts being obliterated into ash. Just in time, the blue borders of the Triune Shield spread over the tower, people, and all the land Daniel had purified. The mass of evil rebounded, wailing in rage and calling for help from the Serpent.

"Seren. Raylin," the Father said. "Bind and seal."

Seren drew the Celestial Bow back to the corner of her mouth as a glittering arrow of starlight appeared. The moment she released it, it expanded and elongated exponentially. Saturnine rings spun around its now house-sized tip, whistling through the air like a missile before piercing the maelstrom of demonic spirits. The arrow disappeared as it struck them, spreading a shell of blue light over the cloud and freezing the demons' spirits in place.

Raylin walked closer to the portal and activated the Abyssal Staff. The iridescent green swirls, which perpetually flickered from beneath its obsidian surface, now shone brightly, casting Raylin and her immediate surroundings in emerald. The staff's half-foot-wide circular head unlocked, multiplied, and expanded to form a glinting vortex of varying hues of green. It grew to a diameter of twenty feet. Within it, triangles of light flared into being and revolved in the opposite direction. A point of darkness eddied at their center, pulling the demonic spirits into its eye with a powerful force. The noise, like the roar of a tornado, drowned out the self-pitying wails of spirits. Their last shrieks came to an abrupt halt as they vanished. Raylin stepped back, her staff returning to normal.

Gabriela helped the people to their feet, comforting them and explaining all that had occurred. A portion of the Spirit left the Son's halo and descended to fly above the crowd in the form of a snow-white dove. He was apparently unseen by the former Creeps but clearly felt. At the sound of Gabriela's voice, they eagerly crowded around her and received the Spirit into their bodies. Time resumed its earthly pace, and the scene progressed forward with breakneck speed.

As one, their prayers reached the Three, filling the air with a stream of echoing, multilayered whispers. Each supplication blended in perfect pitch, time, and rhythm with the next, forming a symphony of requests. Daniel could only catch snatches of one here and there before a litany of others filled his consciousness, but those he could attend to seemed to center on one thing: breaking the Enemy's power over the land.

"It is granted," the Father's multilayered, oceanic voice said in unison with the Son's authoritative pronouncement.

At once, a new seal appeared on the ground below the feet of the crowd—small but glowing fiercely. Gabriela now stood at its center. She raised her hands in praise.

"The way through the Mist is reopened," the Son announced, his tone bright and cheerful. "And the Babylonian Seal is reforged. Take my people into safety and continue your march through this

land. With your prayers and with the rescue of many, the Seal will grow." He turned to Daniel and the others. "How do you think the Enemy will feel about that?" he asked with a wink.

Daniel whistled. "Furious. Absolutely raving mad."

"To finally break it after thousands of years," Seren said, "and then to have it remade that quickly … he's going to lose his mind."

Ben shook his head. "I do *not* want to be around when he finds out."

Everyone looked over at him, including the Son. The Spirit, still embodied as a fiery halo behind and around the Son, pulsed a different shade of blue as if chuckling. Even the Father's attention seemed diverted, if that were possible.

"You will be," the Son replied. "Be prepared for his wrath."

"Oh, right. Yeah, sorry. Just a force of old habit. I'm ready."

Seren, Raylin, and Daniel regarded Ben with an expression of humorous disbelief.

Ben shrugged and waved away their concern.

The Father stirred. "Go, Gabriela. Take my people and flee. The Spirit of the Age comes."

If the crowd of people heard his voice, they didn't show it. Gabriela, however, immediately attended. In one swift motion, she raised and lowered her arms, and the Mist opened before her. A crowd of people streamed out, and Daniel recognized Gabriela's parents and all the former Creeps who had been waiting within the Mist all this time. They joined Gabriela in giving orders, comforting and reassuring the people of Babylon, and walking by their side as they entered the Mist. Gabriela raised her hands, and multiple globes of light appeared, floating around the crowd to light their way into the twilight within. Within seconds of Daniel's time, they had disappeared, and the portal through the Mist vanished into thin air.

"Now," the Father said, and all the universes floating around them froze, listening with rapt attention, "*your* commission."

The Son stood before the Father, and the Spirit once more encircled them in a series of seven rotating flames.

Every fiber of Daniel's being tuned into the Father's voice as they all immediately knelt before the Three.

"The Spirit of the Age will come, and his coming will be terrible. He will seek, in any way he can, to tempt you from your task. He will target your vulnerabilities. Remember: there are many reasons for what we allow. It is not only you who grow through this process but *all* of my children. Each member of the Celestial Family has a destiny, all of which is woven together in the grand theme of redemption and renewal.

"Recall your friend Issar. He experienced loss on Earth, yet it worked a wholehearted purification within him, as it did in the hearts of his family who had gone before him. We are always with you, even in the darkest hour, and all will be redeemed."

Like a violin string humming at the stroke of the bow, the Three's words vibrated through Daniel. He recalled learning these lessons in each of his quests, especially their trip to the Abyss. And now, those truths sang out from within him. Within all of them. The Three's words echoed back and forth within all the Vessels' minds like they were one vast auditorium.

The Father raised his hand. "Do not fear. Do not despair. I am with you unto the end of the age. Rise up, my children. Rise up to war!" At that same moment, the very air around them evaporated. They now knelt at the battle line behind the line of heavenly forces, with the Serpent and his horde of demons before them. As before, the Father stood behind a throne of blinding light, the Son sat upon it, and the Spirit encircled them both as tongues of multicolored fire. The Middle East stretched out below them like a map. At their back, the Mediterranean Sea rippled and glistened in the light. A little behind them, a small, narrow strip of land, outlined by a bright line of fire, glowed with a burning eight-pointed star at its center. "Belonging to the Three" was written in heavenly script in a circular pattern around the center of the star. Before them, under the Enemy and his hosts, the Babylonian Seal burned like a candle in the night.

Daniel and the others slowly stood. They gazed around, confused.

The Three hadn't seemed to actually move. It was as if they had always been there at the throne on the front lines *and* interacting with them in Eden at the same time. But there was little time to consider this further. The shining armies of Heaven crashed into the line of monstrous demons, gaining ground and pushing over the boundary line into Babylon.

Michael, the Firstborn leader of the heavenly army, stood at the front, fighting directly with the Serpent. His onyx sword flickered back and forth like a blur of shining black, parrying a bite from one of the Serpent's heads on the edge of his blade while raising his massive shield of gold to deflect the acrid flames pouring out of the others.

The Serpent looked distracted by something behind him, though. Amazingly, a look of even greater anger broke out on all seven faces. Two of the sealed heads swiveled around and angled down, bent intently over the expansive desert below. The bright Babylonian Seal shone up at him like a beacon of failure.

"How is this possible!" the Serpent raged, doubling his efforts against Michael. An ocean of fire poured from his fanged mouths, driving Michael back as he pressed his advantage. "Everyone within Babylon was possessed. I drove out or killed all the Father's children! I even pushed back your lines! How could the Seal be reforged?"

Michael ran forward against the fire. Holding his shield before him, he crashed into the bulk of the Serpent's body, shoving him backward. "A light has come to your slaves," Michael announced, his voice ringing out like a challenge. "They are freed and filled with the Spirit. If we give ground, it is because the Three decree it, not because of your power. All things are worked according to *their* will, including your plans."

The Serpent roared and flung himself at Michael.

Ben tapped Daniel's arm and nodded off to their left. Inti, tall as a tower and sporting his red-hot armor of woven bronze and sun-disc helmet, led a battalion of Firstborn against a line of spitting snake demons. The writhing serpents lunged forward to overwhelm their opponents. Inti gestured for his brethren to fall back. Meanwhile,

his white flames condensed into little suns, which danced around him at the slightest movement of his hands. With a quick nod of his head, they combined into one colossal inferno, then tore through the air in a horizontal column of fire. The throng of demons blew backward, hammered through the seething mass of evil at their backs like a battering ram.

Is that Granny? Raylin's voice drifted into Daniel's mind.

Daniel followed her pointed finger to one of the glorious Firstborn on the front line of the battle and almost laughed aloud. It was her all right, but in her true form: a figure of pure fire, fierce and undaunted by the monstrous figures pressing forward. One fiend darted out of the line—a demon with a horned canine head and a serpentine body. It wrapped itself around her and bit into her side. She grimaced but endured the pain, fixing her eyes on the demon itself as though waiting for something. Daniel soon found out what when she went nuclear, exploding into a mushroom cloud of blinding light and fire. The blast encompassed not only her and her opponent but a dozen other demons as well. Once the smoke and fire dissipated into the sky, only Granny remained, smiling but clearly weakened by the exchange. She calmly floated backward while gripping her side, two gray bite marks showing between her fingers. The color of her flames also dulled, and she winced. "Enki!" she called over her shoulder. "Enki, will you attend to me?"

Enki? Ben asked. *Isn't that the Firstborn who rules over E-Abzu?*

I think so, Daniel replied, scanning the shining troops.

A figure, robed in rippling, cerulean waves, glided through the immortal army to Granny's side. He wore a conical crown of river reeds, and a beard, green like newly unfurled lily pads, covered his chest. Bronze, sun-kissed skin shimmered in Granny's fiery light. With a flick of his hand, the water swirled from his robe and bathed Granny's side, washing away the sickly gray wounds and restoring her blazing complexion.

Granny uttered indecipherable words, though her face bespoke earnest gratitude.

Hand in hand, they drifted behind the front lines like old friends, waiting, Daniel guessed, for Granny to rebuild her strength for her next skirmish.

He let his eyes sweep over the holy army, looking for anyone else he knew. Whether by luck or by the intent of the Three, he zeroed in on Rhiannon, the Children of Llyr, and the Sons of Don, all fighting with blinding speed. Rhiannon's white hair beamed with light amid the grim enemies swirling around her. She, along with others in her company, wore armor of gold and silver, and each brandished swords, spears, and shields to match. Their gleaming weapons flickered like lightning amid the hideous, rotting bodies of various low-level demons, all in the forms of dead animals too numerous and varying to distinguish. The hellish denizens didn't stand a chance but were only ever meant to distract and make openings against their opponents while more powerful demons advanced.

Two did just that. Both had the guise of towering, troll-like giants with ridiculously large hands and green claws. With each breath, a yellowish vapor poured out of their mouths like rivers of cloudy poison, only to be sucked back in as they inhaled, pulling like a powerful tide at anything it touched. This included their unfortunate subordinates, some of which were sucked, wailing and screaming, into their fanged and greedy maws. The trolls' eyes, glowering pinpricks of sickly red, flared brighter with each demon they consumed. They bore down on the Firstborn.

Undaunted, Rhiannon led the charge against them, slinging her sword and shield onto her back and producing, with a wave of her hand, a small harp. Striking its strings masterfully, she produced a chord of quiet beauty and lifted her strong voice in a song of power. Gossamer waves of power rippled out in circles around her people, pushing the demons backward and giving the troop of Firstborn a moment to plan before they renewed their attack. As one, they surged forward with dexterous and deadly accuracy, making quick work of the lesser demons while flanking the trolls. A few well-placed attacks on the hulking monsters caused both to fall forward onto their faces

and snap their jaws shut. Rhiannon's song swelled, and curtains of the Mist opened in the air above her.

Three birds, each fifteen feet tall with plumes of glacier blue and gray, flew out of the portals and bore down on the demons with talons like flashing daggers. Together, they snatched the trolls and streaked higher into the sky, where they promptly dropped them farther back behind the enemy lines. In their return, flying demons homed in on them in midair. Daniel lost sight of them as they streaked off toward the horizon, locked in an aerial battle. Rhiannon and the others didn't seem concerned, however, and fell back to holding their part of the line against a new group of monstrous enemies.

I see Candi and Chandra, Ben's voice came trickling into Daniel's mind. *To the right, fighting Nergal.*

Daniel placed them immediately. Nergal towered over the battle. His black beard flickered with a ghostly white fire, and his baleful cat eyes shone like doorways into the Abyss. With a deafening clamor, grasping claws clanged against Chandra and Candi's weapons each time he attacked. The two Firstborn bravely stood against him. But, from the look of things, it appeared they stood little chance.

Chandra's lily-white skin and silver eyes stood in stark contrast to the sea of darkness seething before him. Even his black hair shone with a vibrant luster that made the dull black pervading the demonic armies appear lifeless and drab. Despite the fierce battle, he still wore his baggy silver pants and matching vest, which offered little protection from attack. In one of his four hands, he held a naked, blue flame in the form of a flower, while another brandished a silver club, intricately carved with a spiral pattern down its shaft. As in India, the remaining two arms controlled a blinding-fast crescent blade, which spun through the air and around his body. It was at least twenty feet long and gray, with beautiful carvings of the phases of the moon etched into its spine. With a flick of Chandra's wrists, it spun, end over end, toward Nergal, who batted the weapon to the side when it flew near his hulking arms. The blade sliced and chopped through the air as if it had a mind of its own, then flew

back to Chandra. With one deft revolution, the crescent blade flew toward Candi. She held out two of her four arms as the weapon flew near her, gaining control of its lightning movements.

Like Chandra, Candi held a naked flame, though hers burned with white fire. She also brandished a club, nearly identical to Chandra's except for the color, hers a rich black instead of silver. Her dark skin glistened in the radiant light pouring from the Three, and her hair was styled high in a Gordian knot of braids interlaced with strands of gold. A form-fitting white dress fell to her knees, and matching white makeup lined her silver eyes. She and Chandra's faces were so similar that they appeared to be twins.

A scorpion demon skittered beneath Nergal and charged them. Chandra expertly threw his flame, hitting the demon dead in the mouth. Blue fire engulfed it and everything within a forty-foot radius. The scorpion writhed, trying in vain to escape the inferno. Candi pointed two hands, and the crescent blade streaked through the air to slice the scorpion in half. She darted toward the wounded demon, punching it into the ground with her free hand before recalling the crescent blade and sending it straight toward Nergal. Chandra followed in her wake, using his club to rocket the remains of the blazing scorpion through the air toward the Enemy.

Nergal had only just swatted the crescent blade aside and pinned it to the ground with one of his taloned lion's paws before the burning scorpion smacked him in the face and slid down to entangle itself within its beard. With a wrathful look that would have withered a human, Nergal reached up and crushed the writhing demon. Chandra's fire spread over the Enemy's arm, but he seemed unaffected. Ignoring it, he inhaled the remnants of the demon's spirit as it floated like a miasma around his face.

Chandra raised a hand in the air, and the blue fire flew in a column back to his palm. The crescent blade slid from under the Enemy's paw and tumbled back to orbit around him and Candi.

Nergal, however, sprang into action before either could mount another attack. The raging incarnation belched out spumes of dark

spirits around the Firstborn, each forming into a demonic spirit enraptured to be freed from its master's stomach and eager to destroy its prey. Finding themselves surrounded, Candi and Chandra flung out their fires in unison, this time using the flames to create a consuming barrier around them. The crescent blade flew just beyond that, a blur of motion slicing through any of the spirits assaulting them. It seemed to have little effect against the disembodied demons, though, who pressed against the fiery barrier as if they would simply push their way through. Candi and Chandra calmly knelt in prayer, their voices ringing out in the air above the Three.

"Father, Spirit, Son. Our strength is at its limit. Will you send aid?"

Daniel, Seren, Ben, Raylin, the Three spoke in unison. *Seal Nergal.*

Daniel looked at the others. He knew, and felt that they did as well, that this was the beginning of their direct battle with the Enemy. Sealing Nergal would draw the Serpent's fury toward them, and no doubt, sealing *him* would be the next step. But Daniel felt no fear, only perfect calm. Similar emotions slipped into his mind from the others.

Everyone ready? he asked.

Yes, Raylin replied, her thoughts filled with a sense of determination. *I've been waiting for this for a long time.*

Finally, he'll get the justice he deserves, Seren replied. *We can be vindicated.*

Ben broke in. *I never thought I'd say this, but I'm actually eager to face the Serpent and all his massive hordes of evil. Oh, man! Saying it aloud sounds crazy. But I'm not afraid, not in this state.* He held up his translucent, fiery hands and turned them over. *The Three's power is amazing.*

Intercede, the Father said. *Go to the front lines. There, you will face Nergal. Once the Enemy is sealed, the Serpent will come with all his might. Be prepared. It will be different than in the Abyss.*

Different? Daniel asked.

The Serpent's power was dispersed then, separated into his various incarnations. Some were in the Abyss attacking you. Others were out in

the world accomplishing his will so that his plans for this war might be advanced. Once you face him and he feels his incarnation sealed, he will grow desperate. He will unify his power in this one place. He, his Generals, his Leaders, other Earthborn who have willingly filled themselves with his spirit, all those enslaved, and all his demons—all will come, and all will be unified within him. But it is the amalgamation of his spirit into one form that is the Spirit of the Age. It is that spirit and the portion of his spirit which those Earthborn have willingly bound to themselves that must be sealed into his body in the Abyss. But do not fear. My Spirit will guide you through the battle.

Daniel and the others took in the explanation in silence. Each of their feelings shifted back and forth within the group. A vague sense of agitation welled up from within everyone's hearts, though it quickly evaporated in the heat and fire of the indwelling Spirit. But questions arose, too.

Ben's concern floated to the surface. *Will the Enemy be easily sealed now that our weapons are amplified, and we're filled with your Blessing? Or will it be a struggle?*

Seren's voice came hard on the heels of Ben's question. *How are we supposed to seal the Enemy's spirit in the humans who want it there? It never untethers from their bodies, even when purified.*

The Enemy will fight with all his power against you, the Three replied, directing their answer to Ben. *Evil is never pushed back without great sacrifice. You know this.*

They did know this, especially Ben. They nodded, resolute and accepting.

The Three shifted toward Raylin. *Daughter, you know the answer to your sister's concern. What do you say?*

Raylin looked away from the Three to the galaxies spinning into the air around them and stood silent for a moment as if struggling to recall old memories. *The human figures bound to the sealed Serpent's heads—I think those are humans in the past who bound themselves to him. When I think back on my own possession, it makes sense. Even humans can reach a point of no return, where no part of them desires freedom*

and redemption, only power. I was almost there. Raylin shrugged as if speaking of some minor problem easily overcome. *But then, you saved me.*

Being bound to the Serpent sounds awful, Daniel thought.

Yes, but remember that the humans you face today are already bound to him through his spirit, the Three replied. *In each of the past ages, one or two Earthborn would align themselves with the Enemy directly. It was difficult for him to find a human so depraved that he or she would be suitable to be his Vessel. This is because all Earthborn are created in our image, and the spiritual part of them always hopes for goodness, truth, and freedom. This is true even when that hope has been twisted into something evil. But he would search the earth until potential Vessels could be found, people so consumed by hatred and a hunger for their own sovereignty that they willingly gave up hope, if only they could have power. In the end, they were bound with him because his spirit had become a part of them. Now, he has discovered how to push any willing person to this point … and beyond. Abida, Amira, the Generals, and many others have all now chosen to give up my image. They have become as the demons. Yet hope remains, even for them.*

Raylin studied the Father's form, then let her eyes drop to the Son, who stood nearly within him. *As it did for me.*

Seren looped her arm through Raylin's with a smile. A feeling of desperate gratefulness emanated from both girls.

And their sealing? Seren pressed.

The Enemy's spirit can never be totally removed from them unless they choose. But even so, the power of the Bow and Staff can bind and seal their bodies, even Abida and Amira.

A moment passed in silence.

Here we are, Daniel announced. *Send us.*

21

The Spirit of the Age

Lightning passed through them all, transforming each into pure energy and carrying them across the armies of Firstborn to crash in front of Candi and Chandra's barrier. The force of their coming sent shockwaves through the air, dispersing Nergal's attacking spirits and shoving his body backward.

Nergal stood his ground, glowering down at the four Vessels burning brightly before him. He turned his head slightly to take in the ever-growing Babylonian Seal glimmering on the ground miles below them, his barrel chest heaving with rage. Rearing onto his hind legs, he pumped his wings, sending tornadoes of shearing wind toward the Vessels.

The Spirit's voice, similar to the Son's yet thin like the sound of the wind, spoke into all four of their minds at once. *Do not hesitate. Attack.*

Daniel raised the Sun Sword even as he ran forward, his feet gaining traction upon invisible "ground" in this spiritual plane above the earth. With a confident swing, a Sunstorm, larger than the one sent to Gabriela's aid at Ealim Wahid, slipped smoothly from the incandescent, wavy blade and violently purified Nergal's whirlwinds. Plumes of dark spirit fled the explosion.

Daniel didn't pause as Seren and Raylin went about their work, though he could sense their plans and movements easily enough. Nergal bore down on top of him, belching out new spirits while seeking to crush him beneath burnished claws the size of backhoes. Tornadoes of thrashing wind once more tore through the air as the Enemy beat his gray wings, and his pounding tail whipped around his body, seeking to flatten Daniel beneath its massive girth.

Ben surrounded Daniel and expanded his borders.

Some of Nergal's talons shattered on the Triune Shield even as Ben continued to expand.

A Celestial Arrow streaked overhead and nailed the Enemy between the eyes. The blue casing spread over Nergal's body in an instant, slowing his movements to a halt. His knees buckled, and he slumped over, frozen with his chest close to the ground.

"I will not be bound and sealed! Human spawn!" he howled.

Raylin slipped into Ben's borders and up to Daniel's side. *I'm ready.*

Daniel felt the Spirit urging him forward, and he immediately obeyed. Ben and the others followed suit until they were under the Enemy.

"Bow before me! Kneel! Cower!" Nergal spat, vibrating in rage or, maybe, fear.

All four Vessels paused directly beneath his chest.

Daniel felt only peace. Never had he stood in the Enemy's presence without some sort of fear. Even when he had possessed the Father's Blessing in Supai's throne room, he still felt uncertainty as the Enemy's malevolent power rained down upon him. But now, that same evil presence felt weak and impotent, like a gentle spring rain pattering on the stone walls of a fortress.

Quickly now, the Spirit said within all their minds. *Through the heart.*

Daniel raised the Sun Sword and charged it. Then, amid further shrieks and demands from Nergal, he plunged the blade into the Enemy's chest and released a series of seven Fire Strikes.

Nergal gasped and then exploded. One immense, centaur-shaped spirit swirled within Seren's binding, breathing out a cacophony of murderous threats.

Raylin activated the Abyssal Staff, its head and eye widely expanding as it drew the spirit inevitably within.

"You cannot seal me! You cannot! I am *the* Firstborn, and you are dust. Dust! You have no right to even approach me!"

Far below, the desert blushed crimson and flashed transparent. Within the bowels of the earth, the doorway to the Abyss glared up at them—malevolently red with its black lip running its diameter. From this vantage point, the entirety of the Abyss was visible, appearing as a sphere suspended within the very center of the earth. As Daniel recalled their visit there, this made sense. When they had stood on its lip, the sides stretched as far as the eye could see, matching the curvature of the horizon perfectly. Now, he understood that it was literally the center of the world, and there was nowhere else to go but up in every direction. The black lip flew wide open, and the physical body of the Serpent lay bare within. As Nergal disappeared into the Abyssal Staff, one of the Serpent's eyes flared brightly. He roared, all seven necks writhing in pain and wrath.

Then, the Serpent abruptly ceased his wailing. An unsettling quiet came over all his forces; even the Serpent's avatars stopped their attacks on the Firstborn. As if expecting this, Michael raised his sword hand, and the myriad of fiercely bright beings stepped back from the lines, lowering their weapons.

What's happening? Seren asked, lowering the Celestial Bow to her side.

Raylin held the Abyssal Staff at the ready, her body tense and ready to spring into action. *Given the look on the Serpent's faces, I think it's what is about to happen that should concern us.*

Everyone turned back to the Serpent below. His four unsealed eyes glowed, and his heads homed in on Ealim Wahid directly above him.

Return, the Father commanded through the Son.

All the Firstborn stretching to the horizon flared bright and then were gone. Some streamed back to the Earth, becoming distant points near Babylon or disappearing over the horizon altogether. Most returned to the Three's side, forming a shining hedge around the throne.

Despite the rapid disappearance of their opposition, the armies

of the Serpent shuffled uneasily. Many of the lesser demons looked back and forth in uncertainty while the larger and more powerful monsters pawed and stomped in clear agitation, looking with fear at the Serpent below.

All made sense in the next moment. In the space of a breath, the army evaporated into a vast plain of black spirits, their temporal bodies gone—dissolved, or maybe consumed. The wailing and fear crashed upon the Vessels as a wave of anguish, doubt, terror, and hatred, though Daniel and the others felt none of it within them. It was a thing wholly separate and external, as though their purification and Blessing had severed the connection with their own experiences of darkness. Daniel considered this amidst the frenzied storm before him. It wasn't that he couldn't remember the sorrows in his life. They just felt neutral, like a toddler memory of a scary shadow: frightening at the time but not worth a mention in adulthood.

Somewhere at the center of the seething spirits, a sucking vortex opened in the floor of the heavens, and the army was drawn downward.

They're being flushed, Ben said. *But where to?*

Daniel studied the scene. *Do you think this is what the Father meant when he said the Enemy would unify himself?*

It has to be, Raylin replied. *Look, they're all gathering at Ealim Wahid.*

On the vast, open space before the broken-down tower, darkness amalgamated from all over the world. As before, time flowed faster on Earth as a huge form took shape at the center of the maelstrom. On all sides, gray portals whirled open. All four Generals and the Leaders stepped through before prostrating themselves. A crowd of people followed in their train, joining them on the ground.

Seren drew back on the Celestial Bow to aim an arrow at the growing demonic mass below.

Patience, the Spirit said, his voice trickling into all their minds at once. *Lower your bow, Seren. The Enemy must be allowed to unify. All of you, be prepared. Remember, we are with you always, even if you do not see or sense us. Now, descend.*

By the Spirit's command, the floor of the heavens opened, and

all four Vessels streamed to Earth. Daniel felt a ripple of emotion go through him and the other Vessels as they streaked through the air like meteors. It wasn't fear or dread. Nervousness, though, seemed accurate. The sheer magnitude of their task became clearer with every passing moment, each second marking an exponential growth in the spiritual monstrosity amassing below them.

They crashed into the desert, blasting rocks and sand outward from their landing place.

Daniel examined the ground. Despite now standing on solid earth, it was still partially transparent. The Abyss, with the Serpent's physical body crawling around within his circle of binding, remained visible. A strong gust of wind blew across the barren plain, and the transparency faded.

Overhead, the sun swiftly climbed into the sky, then, chased by the moon, set within moments. Darkness fell, and the stars wheeled overhead. Moments later, dawn lightened the sky. The sun itself soon reappeared and shot to its noonday position before hastening to set, the moon in its trail. Daniel soon comprehended what was happening. Despite being on Earth, they remained linked to Heaven's time.

He broke away from his surroundings to take in the enemies before him.

Who are all these people? Ben asked, stepping up to Daniel's right. *They look … well, they look like Amira and Abida, or the Generals.*

Ben was right. The crowd of people still streaming through the open portals appeared empty-eyed and predatory. Many had modified features reminiscent of Wanu's sharpened teeth or the Creeps' claws and fangs: animal eyes, elongated and overly muscled limbs, extra appendages, or unusual heights. Others looked normal but manifested clearly superhuman attributes: flight, elemental control, or the ability to wield some obviously destructive power.

Seren nodded as she surveyed the army amassing before them. *It's those who have lost the Image of the Three. They've been transformed.*

They don't seem upset about it, Ben replied.

Raylin scanned the growing mob. *I bet these are the people who*

wanted to lose the Image of the Three. I doubt he would give powers to prisoners he had to force into it.

Abida and Amira, each with a confident, smug grin, stood up from their position of worship. They both held jet-black weapons which sucked the light from the air around them. Abida gripped a straight sword, its inky blade growing slightly wider toward the razor tip. A glowing red eye encircled by fangs arranged in the shape of an eyelid formed the pommel. Two clawed hands, gray and grasping, comprised the cross guards.

Amira held a battle-ax. It, too, was black save for a red, tooth-rimmed eye, though hers was in the side of the heavy, jagged blade. The haft and the blade were seamless, as though fashioned out of one single source. Daniel suspected just that; both weapons were likely siblings of the Voidblade, created from the Serpent's spare teeth and possessing dreadful powers.

Clothes like live embers still adorned the twins' bodies, shimmering and sizzling with each quick gesture for their army to fan out. The four Generals hastily followed their orders. The army of humans broke into four groups, each falling in line behind one of the Generals. Mobs of loping, snarling Creeps similarly divided, though their regiments were significantly more chaotic and beastly. About a half mile behind them, the Spirit of the Age loomed giant and foreboding, crouching like a gigantic man on his knees. The rivers of dark spirits streaming into him ceased, and six red eyes opened in an arc along his forehead.

"I have come," he boomed from an invisible mouth, standing as he spoke. He towered over the ruins of Ealim Wahid to his back, his head reaching into the cloudless sky one thousand feet above them. In essence, his body remained in the form of black, chaotically swirling spirits. Four muscled arms hung by his sides with clenched fists. Six serpents writhed out of his back like wings: three on one side and three on the other. A bulky crown of fiery lava, dripping and hellish, sat upon his brow. He wore matching arm and ankle cuffs, all dropping blobs of volcanic discharge. They hissed as they hit the desert sand, melting it into glass and scattering the soldiers of Creeps and metahumans.

If the desert seemed lifeless and stark before, the presence of the Spirit of the Age made it exponentially more so. With each second, more color leached from the sand and the air around him. Even the sky above lost its blue. Daniel recalled the Serpent's plan for creation, uttered in wrath when they had escaped the Abyss. He would refashion the material world, making it a blight of rock and fire inhabited only by spirits. Once, he thought this would've been a nasty shock to his human followers. But apparently, a life of power followed by oblivion appealed to them. At least, that's what the Enemy promised. Daniel wasn't sure if oblivion, or something worse, awaited them once he and the others sealed the Spirit of the Age.

As with any time he had stood in the presence of the Enemy, Daniel felt waves of horror, despair, and malevolence washing over him. The Father's blessing seemed even brighter, though, just as a candle's flame shines stronger the darker the room it stands in. Hope and purity rose within him like shields, throwing back the Enemy's terror.

Daniel looked around at the others.

We're good, Daniel, Ben said, his thoughts calm and his emotions steady.

Raylin and Seren gave curt nods, both stolidly facing the army like resolute soldiers.

The Spirit of the Age stared down at them and then tilted his head toward Abida and Amira. "You should never have let them make it this far. You failures! Worthless, witless failures!"

The twins flinched with each word.

"Your orders are unchanged. Bring them to me alive!" the Spirit of the Age roared, his very voice a wave of power leveling his less powerful servants. "I want to feel their anguish when I seek to shatter the Image of the Three within them." A circle of black and harsh-looking script formed in the air near the twins. Four red chains snaked out and coiled themselves on the ground. "Be ready. When the Three's power is gone, bind them quickly. I will deal with them."

Abida and Amira raised their hands above the chains, which then

floated into the air to coil over one shoulder and under the other. Seemingly unaffected by the chains' touch, their only response was to cast conceited looks of triumph at the Vessels.

A nagging apprehension reached for Daniel's heart. The others' feelings reached him as well. They, too, experienced something similar. The feelings were outside of them, though, seeking entrance, and Daniel knew that allowing them in was not an option.

Father, Daniel prayed so the group could hear. *Remind us that we don't need to fear. Keep our focus on you and make us deaf to the Enemy's threats. All the same, please protect us!*

We are with you, even until the end of the age, the Three said, speaking in unison. *Do not allow despair to enter your hearts. Trust me, no matter what the Enemy does. Now, attack!*

In that same moment, the Enemy's army surged forward as one. Daniel raised the Sun Sword and stabbed the ground, releasing a massive Fire Strike even as Seren shot Celestial Arrows into the thickest of their foes. The super-powered wave of purifying power radiated outward. Only one metahuman was caught unawares—a young adult, probably not more than a few years older than Daniel, with reddish hair and a face full of freckles. Dirt, sand, and rock comprised his clothes, all of which combined to form some sort of dragging robe, beckoning the ground it touched to become a part of his adornment. His powers, which clearly allowed him to control the earth, kept him tethered to the ground itself. The Fire Strike caught him summoning an earthen wave to send careening toward the Vessels. It temporarily nullified his attack while blowing him onto his back. The Enemy's spirit exploded out of him, leaving him temporarily powerless. Despite Daniel's amplified power, the mass of dark spirit hastily crashed back into the man's body. He jumped to his feet and skimmed the sand as if surfing his way farther from Daniel's attacks.

The rest of those caught in the purification were Creeps, who were quickly leveled and rendered unconscious. Rather than repossessing them, the Enemy's spirit streamed toward the Spirit of the Age while

the Creeps vanished. The rest of the metahumans scattered, easily avoiding the first barrage by leaping or flying to safety.

Ben expanded into the Triune Shield, throwing back an array of powerful projectiles and blasts of energy hurled by various metahumans.

Daniel sent a scattershot of Sunstorms among the twins, Generals, and the Spirit of the Age. Unlike the other times facing them, Abida and Amira appeared to take the Sun Sword's power seriously. Despite its inability to completely free them from the Enemy's power, they obviously knew it could give Raylin and Seren the upper hand. With lightning speed, they dove away from the blasts and ran around Ben's borders to flank him. The Generals, too, quickly dodged the attacks, either by retreating into their respective portals or flying into the air.

The Spirit of the Age pounded the ground in front of him, and a jutting wall of rock rose to absorb the attacks before sinking back into the desert sand.

Unperturbed, Daniel let more Sunstorms fly at the lesser enemies instead. If the bigger threats were too evasive, he would whittle down the weaker forces assailing them so they could deal with the main problems later.

Raylin jumped in and out of Ben's borders, making brief but effective forays behind the line of foes. She spun the Abyssal Staff around her in a blur, deflecting enemy attacks and knocking several metahumans out when Daniel and Seren were occupied in a different direction. Once within his borders, she activated the Abyssal Staff and sealed away any disembodied spirits flying outside the shield. The purified Creeps disappeared, taken, no doubt, straight into the Mist, where Gabriela could ready them for their mission.

Amid the chaos, Abida and Amira attacked on either side of the Triune Shield. Their weapons formed light-sucking blurs around their bodies as they repeatedly assailed Ben's borders. Like drumbeats, the sound from the blows reverberated back and forth within the shield, but Ben seemed unfazed. The twins wore clear expressions of irritated surprise on their faces.

Daniel didn't give them time to consider their next move. With a quick thought sent to Seren and Raylin, they acted in perfect unison. Seren shot a volley of Celestial Arrows in a circle around both to keep them in their place. Portals whirled open behind them as they attempted to flee, but Raylin was ready. Dashing to the edge of the Triune Shield closest to Abida, she activated the Abyssal Staff, its force slamming him into the borders.

Ignoring Amira, Daniel simultaneously fired three Sunstorms at Abida. They passed through Raylin, leaving her unharmed while exploding into his body. Because of the counterforce of the Abyssal Staff, Abida remained glued to the edges of the Triune Shield. His portion of the Enemy's spirit, however, unfurled behind him like a parachute. It howled in rage at its partial disembodiment.

Grimacing with strain, Abida uttered a series of curses and tried to position his sword to stab the Triune Shield.

"It won't do you any good," Ben said aloud. "I'm filled with the Father's Blessing. Your attack—everyone's attacks, for that matter—don't even register. Give it up. Turn away from the Enemy's side before you're sealed to him forever."

"Never!" Abida spat. "I will never give up my power! Never relinquish my sovereignty! *You* give up. The Three should give up and leave. We have evolved past them and their overbearing morality!"

The Enemy's spirit tried to crash back into Abida's body, but Daniel dashed to the edge of the shield and stabbed him with the Sun Sword, activating a Fire Strike.

Amira appeared in front of Daniel, wailing on the Triune Shield with her ax in a furious attempt to strike him, but the shield's borders held strong. Chiuta flew by and hurled the Whirlwind of Famine at Ben. Above, Wanu popped out of her portal and dropped on top of the Triune Shield, swinging the Scythe of Death with wild abandon at Ben's outstretched form. Keeping a safe distance, Vinaash hovered around the edges of the battle, raining down arcs of Pestilence on the shield every few seconds. The other metahumans coordinated their attacks on the shield as well, lighting it up with all manner of

supernatural fireballs and devilish projectiles. The Creeps simply loped around, scratching at the shield, shooting their guns, or stabbing it with other more conventional weapons.

In the distance, the Spirit of the Age raised his hands in front of his chest. A pinprick of darkness gathered between his palms, growing exponentially with each passing moment. It crackled like thunder and shot out sparks as if its insides were a grind of iron and fire. He then paused, perhaps amassing more power or waiting for an opening to launch his attack. Like a brooding storm on the horizon, he watched the battle without moving.

Daniel shook his head. *That doesn't look good.*

Nothing we can do about it now, Ben replied. *Just deal with the enemies attacking us right now.*

Daniel agreed. Tyr, he noted, seemed to avoid the battle altogether. Instead of joining the fray, he casually moved in and out of his portals around the battle line. Not once, however, did he swing the Hammer of War at Ben.

Another onslaught of metahuman attacks exploded against the Triune Shield.

"That tickles!" Ben laughed, distracting Daniel from his observations. "Stop! Seriously."

Ignoring them, Seren shot a Celestial Arrow directly into Abida's heart while Daniel followed it up with another Sunstorm to keep the Enemy's spirit at bay.

I think you're going to have to let Abida in so we can seal him, Seren said, dropping Wanu with a headshot. She fell like a rock on top of the shield and slid down the sloped borders.

Seeing her bound, Chiuta attempted to flee into the air, but Seren nailed him in the ankle. The blue casing of the Celestial binding quickly encompassed him. Chiuta fell directly on top of Wanu, his position such that one of his feet slipped into her open mouth.

"Gehh ya stupih feeh off me!" Wanu squawked.

"Quit gargling my toes, you witch!" Chiuta growled. "Worthless waste of protein."

Wanu glared daggers as Chiuta continued his string of insults, both fighting helplessly against Seren's amplified binding.

Daniel summoned a far-reaching Fire Strike. The purifying waves crashed like a tsunami over their bodies and temporarily forced the Enemy's spirit out of them. It joined in the wretched, raging chorus sent up by the portion from Abida. The effect of the attack also served to scatter the more powerful assailants, though all the Creeps around the shield were immediately purified.

I agree with Seren, Raylin added, taking a step backward so that the power of the Abyssal Staff could encompass Wanu and Chiuta, as well as the dark spirits exorcized from the Creeps. The two Generals slid along the ground toward the shield until rigidly drawn up the side next to Abida. Without the Enemy's spirit repossessing them, the Creeps all disappeared with a series of flashes. The immediate vicinity was cleared of attacks, save for Pestilence and a few other harrying projectiles hurled from the gang of metahumans hanging behind Vinaash.

I'm ready whenever you are. Ben said. *Is everyone in agreement? Allow Abida and the other nerds into the shield?*

Daniel prepared for another Fire Strike, expecting the Enemy's spirit to assail them when the Triune Shield was opened. *Yes. Do it!*

And then the Spirit was among them. He was in the form of a great bird, burning with blindingly white fire with sapphire blue eyes. His glorious pinions dragged the ground, as did his long tailfeathers, all of which flickered with consuming flames.

Wait. The Spirit of the Age comes. Ready yourself.

Everyone snapped their heads toward the pitch-black form of the Enemy's spirit. In one moment, he stood in the distance, surveying his minions attacking the Vessels while building the power of his impending attack. Then, with one step, he teleported to the battle line and towered over the Triune Shield. With his left hand, the Enemy swept up Wanu, Chiuta, and Abida. With his right, he released his attack, now half the size of the Enemy's body, point blank into the Triune Shield.

Ben grunted loudly and gasped for air. The world spun upside down as the Triune Shield rocketed across the desert, careening up and down like a kickball before settling into a chaotic roll over the sand. Daniel and the others flailed around within his borders. The only certain and steady thing in his field of vision was the Spirit, who stayed in the exact center of the shield. He threw out his wings, and the Triune Shield halted in the air and peacefully floated down to the ground. At the same moment, the other Vessels froze in their pandemonium, drifting down to the bottom of the shield like feathers.

Daniel waited for his vision to stop spinning and then cast about to get his bearings. They were at least four miles out into the desert. Despite their distance, they could nevertheless hear the Spirit of the Age, looming tall over the ruins of Ealim Wahid, roaring abuses at his followers.

Ben, are you alright? Raylin asked, using the Abyssal Staff to help herself stand. *That was a direct hit.*

The sound of Ben's heaving breaths filtered down from his outstretched form on the top of the shield. *No. Maybe. I don't know. The Father's Blessing helps, but the second the Enemy released that attack, I felt him trying to push into my mind. It felt like I was being ran into by a steamroller flying at a hundred million miles an hour. You know what, I'm going to go with no. No, I'm not alright. That was more powerful than when the Serpent himself attacked us in the Abyss.*

Comforting waves of light emanated from the Spirit into the shield. *Even when facing the Serpent, his power was diffused among all his guises. Now, he comes against you with all his might unified.*

Raylin stepped closer to the Spirit and reached up to touch his feathers. *Not that I'm complaining, but why didn't he unify before if it makes him so powerful?*

He is afraid, the Spirit explained. *In this form, he can be sealed, and he resists it until our power pushes him to the brink of desperation. Once you sealed Nergal, he knew that, divided, he would have no chance to escape until he unified his power and killed you all. Now, everyone stand,* the Spirit commanded. *Do not fear the power of the Enemy. Remember:*

no matter his attack, his goal is the same—to weaken you by removing the Blessing. If he can do that while keeping you alive, he will. Then, he would destroy you after attempting to remove our image. Remain in us, and the Father's Blessing will remain in you. Do not allow him entrance into your heart, regardless of his threat. Even so, I am with you always.

Daniel remembered losing the Father's Blessing in Peru. Facing Supai without that power was one thing. Facing the Spirit of the Age without it would be madness and death. He felt certain they wouldn't last more than a few moments.

Seren walked closer to the edge of the Triune Shield and raised the Celestial Bow. *They're coming.*

Daniel snapped his head in Seren's direction to see the Spirit of the Age flying across the desert, his feet just off the sand. His army of metahumans clouded the air around him, each possessing a cloudy, dark aura about their heads and shoulders. Now, it made sense why the Enemy hung back while sending his servants into battle for him. Even at his most powerful, he was afraid.

Daniel ran his hand over the Sun Sword's blade. *It looks like they've been powered up,* he said, studying the fast-approaching army. He turned to the Spirit. *What should we do? Bind and seal the humans first and then move on to the Enemy?*

No, the Spirit replied. *Target the Enemy. He is the source of their power. Cut off the snake's head, and the battle will be won.*

But there are seven heads! Ben exclaimed.

It was figurative, Daniel, Raylin, and Seren said in chorus.

The Spirit's voice broke into their minds. *The Enemy is upon you.*

A gale of sand and wind, kicked up before the wrath of the hellish army's chaotic approach, buffeted the borders of the Triune Shield. The Spirit of the Age and his minions, like a hurricane of pure fury, were only a mile away and picking up speed.

The Spirit flung out his wings and pushed Daniel and Seren to the front of the shield. *Purify and bind together!*

An image of the Spirit's intent flew through Daniel's mind. He sensed Seren had seen the same. Without questioning the vision,

Daniel took the Sun Sword and flung it into the air. Somehow, it rocketed into the sky but retained its link to his mind. He could feel it, now out of sight, high above the Spirit of the Age and his army.

Simultaneously, the radiant limbs of the Celestial Bow grew as Seren drew back her hand to the corner of her mouth. As both arrow and now luminescent string flickered into being, she breathed onto the shaft and released it. The arrow tore into the sky, its comet's tail streaking behind it.

Daniel felt the moment the arrow struck the sword. A glance at Seren and he knew she sensed the same. Filled with the Spirit's power, they held out their hands to one another—Daniel's right hand on the bottom and Seren's left on the top—and pointed them toward the Enemy.

The Spirit of the Age watched their movements and froze his assault. Though no mouth was evident, his six eyes showed he was smiling. The cloud of metahumans paused in their advance as well, looking with uncertainty between the Vessels and their master.

"Do you think this old attack can harm me now?" The Enemy laughed, sneering at the Spirit. "With each age, I grow. I have outgrown your pathetic attempts at binding. Purifying Sunstorms reigning down from the heavens amid a shower of binding arrows? The first Vessels used this. Do you think it will have the same effect now as it did then? It will be impotent in the face of my power."

The six serpent heads affixed to his back looked up at the sky, homing onto one point. Above the Spirit of the Age, a vast, gray shield appeared. Within it, multiple layers of concentric circles and squares spun in opposite directions, each crowded with a wispy, fiery script. The Enemy then lifted his arms, and five other shields, all exact replicas of the first, appeared above it.

"We know you have grown in power," the Spirit said to him, resting his feathers on Seren and Daniel's heads. "For that reason, we have prepared something new."

Words rushed into their minds. "Spear of Heaven," Daniel and Seren said in tandem.

No sooner had they finished than a shaft of blinding light, wider than the Enemy and his entire force and tipped with a fiery spear blade, crashed through all six shields and impaled the Spirit of the Age. He exploded. The Leaders and Generals attempted to flee into portals, but the attack came too quickly. They, along with all the other metahumans, were immediately exorcized and slammed into the desert sand.

The Sun Sword, spinning end over end, streamed out of the explosion back to Daniel's outstretched hand.

With a roar of surprise, the now amorphous Spirit of the Age, along with the rest of his disembodied spirits no longer in the humans, swirled into a hurricane of pandemonium.

Raylin, the Spirit said, drawing her to the front of the Triune Shield, *seal what you can.*

A flash of understanding passed across Raylin's face the moment the Spirit touched her. She hastily activated the Abyssal Staff. Instead of one eye, five more materialized in the air and encircled the original. With amplified power, they drew in stray portions of the Enemy's raging spirit. As before, the parts formerly inhabiting the humans remained tethered to their now unconscious bodies. The staff's power drew those closest against the shield. Those spirits held fast to their fleshly anchors, snapping like flags in a gale before Raylin's sealing power.

The ground below them flashed transparent, and the Abyss and the Serpent blinked into view. One of the Serpent's unbound heads reared back and opened its mouth wide in a silent roar of agony. Both eyes flashed brightly while eight points of white light appeared over each. As Raylin continued the sealing, small lines of white light grew between the points.

Daniel knew they would soon form an eight-pointed star over the eyes, totally sealing in the Spirit of the Age. If they prevailed in this fight, anyway.

Just as the thought entered his mind, the Enemy regained his composure. The Spirit of the Age reformed, and one of the serpentine

heads undulating out of his back shot out toward the ruins of Ealim Wahid. It sank its teeth into the rocky sand and pulled the rest of his towering body away from the Abyssal Staff's power. As his main body streamed away from the fray, tendrils of black whipped out, wrapping around each of the metahumans and yanking them back with him. The Enemy's arms, as well as the other serpent heads, struck forward even as the tendrils recoiled. Spheres of darkness grew within their mouths and in all four palms, spitting sparks and vibrating with the noise of violent destruction. It was the same attack he used before, only multiplied nine times over.

The Spirit lifted his wings so that all his pinions touched Ben's body at the top of the Triune Shield. *Ben, multiply and protect.*

Immediate understanding pervaded Ben's mind. The Triune Shield flushed a spring green and vibrated. Six new layers of the shield appeared around the original borders, each manifesting in succession with a low thrum.

Even as the Enemy regained his footing at Ealim Wahid, he released his attacks simultaneously—some high into the air above the desert, others directly at the Vessels, and the remaining ones off to the sides. All nine balls of destructive power homed in on the Triune Shield from all directions, crashing into it with a deafening boom.

Daniel summoned a Fire Strike, its magnified power reverberated within Ben's original borders before resonating outward into the other layers of the shield.

Keep those coming! Ben gasped, even as the outer two shells of the Triune Shield shattered and the next in line cracked.

At the Spirit's direction, Seren and Raylin jumped into action. Seren shot enormous Celestial Arrows at the raging spheres of destruction while Raylin concentrated the Abyssal Staff on the three assaulting the Triune Shield from above.

Open the ceiling of the shield, the Spirit instructed.

Ben obeyed, panting with relief.

The three malevolently humming balls of power flew through his borders, drawn directly into the staff's eyes.

Even with the Father's Blessing, the power of the Enemy so near was like a series of lightning bolts zipping by Daniel's head. He shivered as the ground flushed transparent and the Enemy's own devastating power was sealed into the sixth head of the Serpent. The following moment found the Serpent reeling backward when all three attacks exploded within him.

The Spirit of the Age convulsed and fell forward on his hands. Flying up in a rage, he attempted to recall the remaining seven attacks, but Raylin was too quick. She zeroed in on four more Seren had already bound directly in front of the shield. Though partially bound in the shimmering blue Celestial casing, they vibrated with a raging power that voraciously pushed forward, shattering the next layer of the Triune Shield.

Ben, Raylin shouted in her mind, *those four next. Let them in.*

Daniel summoned another Fire Strike while Ben acquiesced, opening the front portion of the Triune Shield. Once again, the malevolent balls of power zipped in, drawn directly into four of the staff's eyes.

The Serpent's sixth head jerked chaotically with each successive explosion. The Spirit of the Age shuddered violently, throwing out arms and snake heads to regain his balance.

The remaining three attacks flew back into the snake's mouths, perched amid their fangs.

Daniel. Seren. The Spirit flew between them. *Attack him again.*

Linked as they were, Seren and Daniel knew each other's timing perfectly. In unison, they flung their respective attacks into the sky, where they unified over the Enemy and his host of metahumans.

This time, before the Spear of Heaven fell, the Spirit of the Age leaned over and crashed entirely into Amira. The embers encasing her body flamed to life as she and all the other metahumans ducked into their portals. Only Tyr was too sluggish, the purifying Spear catching him before he could slip into his. The Enemy's spirit raged around him, howling and cursing the Three. Being beyond the reach of the Abyssal Staff, Raylin didn't even attempt to seal him. Not that she would have had time.

Once more, and quickly, the Spirit urged Daniel and Seren. *But wait for my signal to bring the Spear, and do not raise your hands.*

Seren and Daniel exchanged a questioning look as they fell into their motions, sending the Sun Sword and a Celestial Arrow high into the sky above the fray.

In the next breath, Amira popped out of her portal behind the Triune Shield, swinging her ax with wild abandon. Red fire beamed from her eyes, and a crown of small serpentine heads branched above her hair. Each swing of her ax resounded like a battering ram, and another layer of the Triune Shield shattered.

Daniel stepped back behind Seren to hide the fact that he no longer held the Sun Sword, while Seren fired a volley of arrows at her. Amira was too quick, slipping back into her portal while the attacks flew out over the desert and dissipated.

Another portal whirled open to their right, and Abida jumped out. His eyes matched Amira's, and the crown of serpents adorned his head. With blinding speed, he plunged his sinister sword through the third layer of the Triune Shield, and a crack zigzagged up the side of the barrier.

"Not so impervious now, are we?" Abida taunted, though no mirth tinged his voice, only a dismal, cacophonous mockery of exultation.

Seren nailed him with three Celestial Arrows, and Raylin spun the Abyssal Staff in his direction. Before his body was bound within Seren's casing, however, the Spirit of the Age streamed out of his back and flew into Vinaash, who rode overhead on her green cloud. A black arm trailed behind him as he entered her body, grabbing the inert Abida and yanking him up onto the cloud.

Crowned with serpents and now amplified with the Spirit of the Age's power, Vinaash glowered down at the Vessels. With a look of pure revulsion, she hurled Pestilence, now ten times larger than before and splitting into a hundred branches.

The next two layers of the shield broke under the bombardment, and only Ben's original layer was left.

Now you see another reason for the Enemy's designs, the Spirit said, his voice calmly drifting into everyone's minds.

All sense of urgency fled, and time decelerated. Despite the attacks' power, each Vessel calmly attended to the Spirit's voice.

Not only does he hope to remove our image from the Earthborn so all mankind is "beyond redemption" and "beyond judgment," he seeks a multitude of vessels within which to hide. Through which to avoid his own doom. It is through humans that he imagines his salvation comes! And yet, he would abandon them once they outlived their usefulness, gladly destroying all flesh and returning the cosmos to a chaotic dimension of fire, rock, and spirit. He imagines himself reigning supreme in such a place. The Spirit laughed. *As if we would be undone by his simple machinations, forsaking the universe we created and redeemed.*

Ben sighed. *Is that what his followers really want? To be used, abandoned, and then destroyed?*

It surprises you that anyone would desire destruction and oblivion. But that is because you have known love and goodness. There are others who allow the Enemy's schemes to twist their minds. Above all things, they desire a short life of power followed by oblivion is.

Seren gave a curt nod, tracking Vinaash as she flew in slow motion around the shield. *When I was Shakti, those were my thoughts exactly,* she interjected. *Eternal life in any state was a horror. I wanted dominion followed by nothingness. The Three's promise of eternal life was ridiculous to me. Who would want to live forever? Everything would get old and boring, and the thought of living with all those dreadful memories from my childhood, even if I had them walled off inside myself, seemed a hell. I had no concept of the freedom and healing of redemption.*

Ben raised his voice. "Vinaash!" Normal time resumed as the General's puke-green cloud zipped by. "You know that if the Enemy won, he would just destroy everything once the Three abandoned the universe. You and all the other humans serving him would be wiped out, too. Not that the Three will allow that to happen, but wouldn't it be better to be adopted into the Celestial Family and gain eternal life and freedom?"

"Eternal life? Eternal bondage!" Vinaash shrieked, her voice undergirded by the Enemy's guttural bass. She hurled another Bolt

of Pestilence. "There is no freedom under the crushing thumb of the Three. And yes, we know Master's plans, but I choose them over spending eons as a simpering slave!"

A hundred gray portals whirled open, and the desert once more filled with the metahumans, each brimming with power and malevolent glints of hatred written on their faces. Amira and Abida stood behind them, followed by the remaining Generals filing in line. Despite their clear eagerness to destroy the Vessels, they gave the Triune Shield a wide berth. Vinaash, however, raised Pestilence and prepared to attack.

Ben's borders wavered and threatened to break. *I can't hold it much longer*, he said, his mental voice quiet with focus but nevertheless calm. *Spirit?*

The Spirit lifted his wings above him until they touched Ben's outstretched body. *Seren. Daniel. Now.*

The Spirit's intention was clear. Daniel grasped Seren's hand, and they lifted them together. Seconds later, the Spear of Heaven streaked to Earth like a falling meteorite, catching the Enemy's troops unaware and outside their portals. The blast slammed Vinaash off her cloud and into the ground.

Raylin! the Spirit urged. *Aim your attack at the Enemy and Vinaash! Ignore the other humans. They must be given one more chance to repent. Daniel, keep purifying, especially those the Spirit of the Age reaches for. Seren, bind all you can.*

Raising the Abyssal Staff over her head, Raylin fixed all its binding power on the wrathful Spirit of the Age swirling around Vinaash. The General was drawn against the Triune Shield while the staff siphoned shrieking wisps of the Enemy's spirit off her. The Spirit of the Age dug his hands and snake heads into the ground, resisting the powerful draw of the staff while pulling himself farther away.

Daniel flung Sunstorms left and right at any metahuman near the Enemy's grasp.

Seren fired a Celestial Arrow into Vinaash for good measure, though she couldn't move with the power of the staff so focused on

her. Then, she set to targeting as many of the other metahumans as she could.

Vinaash glared through the shield, her gaze filled with venomous hatred.

"Repent and be free of him," the Spirit urged, floating closer. "The Enemy's promises are hollow and lead to despair. Come to me, and I will purify you. Come to life."

"Save it!" Vinaash screamed. "I would never follow you! And what kind of life do you promise anyway? An eternity of shuffling around your throne, floating on some clouds, seeing that every whim of yours is carried out, singing insipid songs of glory about how wonderful you are? Pathetic."

"But you already float around on a cloud," Ben said, almost laughing despite the seriousness of the situation.

"You know what I mean!" Vinaash spat. "With Master, I am a goddess, not some helpless child."

"Vinaash," the Spirit urged. "You misunderstand the nature of eternal life. Come to me and be free."

"I reject you! Is that so hard to understand? I. Reject. You. I don't want what you have. I don't care if I'm destroyed! I'd rather spend the ages to come in darkness than one second more in your presence. This is torture! You … you are torture!"

Ben, the Spirit said, his voice now tinged with sadness. *Give Vinaash what she wants.*

Ben understood and lowered the portion of the shield in front of the General. She silently flew in and disappeared through one of the eyes of the Abyssal Staff while more of the Enemy's spirit streamed in behind her. The bulk of the Spirit of the Age, however, anchored himself into the ground.

Daniel flung Sunstorms at the Enemy's arms and snakes, hoping to sever his hold. The blasts exploded into his appendages, weakening his hold. He skidded backward toward Raylin.

The Abyss appeared through the ground, and the Serpent roared, shaking the very air of the desert. His eyes blazed white as a portion

of his spirit was sealed within, and between them appeared Vinaash's now coal-black figure, arms outstretched. The lines of light over the Serpent's unbound eyes grew closer together, threatening to connect. The desert sand beneath them waxed solid again.

With delicate effort, the Spirit of the Age risked releasing one arm. Straining against the power of the staff, he raised it behind him. With the loss of traction, he was dragged violently backward until one of his gray shields appeared between him and the Sunstorms. Another appeared between him and the Abyssal Staff. Abida and Amira lay nearby, still motionless on the ground with their portions of the Enemy's spirit swirling around them. The Enemy threw up another shield between them and Raylin.

Their portions of his spirit crashed back into them, and they both leaped to their feet and dove into portals.

Who do I aim for next? Raylin hastily asked the Spirit.

All around them, the humans Daniel hadn't had time to purify were being repossessed. Many were bound by Seren, but the Enemy's spirit worked double-time to break their bindings.

The Spirit of the Age lifted all four arms while the snake heads summoned more shields to protect him from the sealing power of the Abyssal Staff. Two more spheres of grating, explosive power appeared in his palms. He flung them at the Triune Shield.

Daniel charged and released a Fire Strike while Ben created three renewed layers for protection.

The explosions once more shattered all but the main border of the Triune Shield, shaking the ground so violently that Raylin was knocked onto her back.

No longer pinned down by her power and Daniel's constant purification, the Enemy repossessed the metahumans, who were still partially purified, and fled. Once the smoke cleared, he was out of range across the desert and standing flanked by the twins, remaining Generals, and the Earthborn army.

"Clever plan," he boomed. "All that power, and you sealed away only one of my Generals. Let me show you what a truly effective strategy looks like."

The Spirit of the Age reached out a hand over the desert and swirled his fingers around. The Abyss appeared directly below him, casting him in a hellish light. The Serpent flashed a seven-fold grin up at his counterpart and moved a colossal coil aside to reveal four figures. They flew up into the air, vanishing as they neared the top of the Abyss and reappearing beneath the Spirit of the Age's fingers.

As recognition set in, Seren gasped while Daniel ran to the edge of the shield, staring in horror. Ben cried out in shock, and his borders wavered. Only Raylin didn't seem shocked. Worried and fearful, yes. But not shocked.

Janice, Leah, and Mariah and Alan Jones all hovered in the air. They looked awful, as if they had lived a nightmare. Dark, puffy circles beneath their eyes told the story of little or no sleep. The darting, hunted look on their faces made it all too clear that they had spent time amid constant horrors. They shook with abject fear as they came to rest in the Enemy's palm, which he shifted below them. Alan, Mariah, and Janice stood upright, shuffling nearer to one another, while Leah's form collapsed like a ragdoll. Bruises covered her body, but it was the gaping wound over her heart that drew Daniel's attention the most. It was a wound he knew no one could survive. For a brief moment, he hoped there was time to save her, but realization soon set in.

She was already dead and had been for some time.

22

The Enemy's Plan

Daniel's mind raced through his dreams. The woman was Leah. That's why she sounded familiar. Did that mean the man was his biological father? The joy this could have brought in any other scenario was absent, replaced by relentless grief. When had the Enemy gotten to her? How long had she been dead? How had she died? These questions flew through his mind in an instant, though the answer to the first occurred to him almost immediately. The figure who appeared in the doorway when they transported. It must have been Wanu or Amira, holding either the Scythe or a sword which Ben mistook for Granny's broom. His vision through Kon's medallion also now made sense. This was the Enemy's plan all along. Wait until the right time and use their parents' capture and death to weaken them.

Daniel stared at Leah's lifeless form. She was absent his whole life, and then they finally reunited. And now, she was dead. Daniel resisted the urge to simply collapse, and that was only for one reason: Janice and his other parents were still alive, and they needed to be saved.

"Ah," the Enemy said with an even crueler glint in his eyes. "I see the death of your dear little mother wounds you. Know that she suffered before she died—suffered trying to save the rest of your family by shielding them with her prayers. I suppose she thought the same thing would happen as when she was in the Abyss saving you: a line of the Father's children would appear, empowered by the Spirit, and an impenetrable barrier would shield them all from my power. It took only a moment for Amira to break through her defenses. You see the result. Amira is very efficient with her ax." He chuckled. "Perhaps the Three did not really care for them. Maybe they thought your parents were insignificant to his plan and decided against giving them the amount of power and protection they needed. Or maybe the Three felt they were useless because they could not fight in the Celestial army. After all, are they Vessels who can pick up a weapon and go to battle? I think not. Expendable pawns. Worthless slaves."

The Enemy's words felt more powerful than any attack he could throw at them. Each was a devastating blow, battering against raw and ragged wounds.

The Spirit reached out and touched them all, and relief and comfort flowed into them anew. *Do not allow his lies into your minds. I am here with you, and I am with your parents.*

While Daniel felt respite from his dread, the grief of seeing his biological mother dead remained, as did his concern for the Joneses and Janice.

What do we do? Daniel wept, spinning around and grabbing onto the Spirit's outstretched pinions. *How can we save them?*

With the Celestial Bow lowered, Seren kept her eyes fixed on Janice. *Ben, can you send a part of the Triune Shield to cover them?*

What? Ben's voice was confused and desperate. *Maybe. With the Spirit's help, I could try.*

No, the Spirit said. *The Enemy would erect his shields around them or simply transport them away. Be patient and endure. What is about to take place is necessary.*

Daniel searched the Spirit's face for some indication of his plan or reassurance, but his face was inscrutable. Raylin, too, regarded the Enemy and his captives with surprising calm, though a hint of anxiety was evident in her breathing.

"Who shall I kill next?" the Spirit of the Age boomed. "Perhaps the infuriating little knitting woman. Her prayers were so powerful

while she slept. Invading someone's dreams with nightmares is a simple task, though. It is hard to rest peacefully when your worst fears await you just on the other side of consciousness. After I failed to remove the Image of the Three from them," the Enemy seemed to almost choke on the statement, "she was in far too much pain and confusion to even pray, much less erect a barrier worth mentioning. I will delight in her death."

"No!" Seren screamed, sending a flurry of Celestial Arrows toward the Enemy.

They crashed into one of his gray shields, which he flung up without so much as a gesture. "Yes, that pleases me."

Janice was violently jerked into the air, where she hovered with her arms and legs outstretched and a stab of pain clear on her face.

"Amira, kill her," the Enemy ordered. "Slowly."

Amira stepped into her portal on the ground and almost simultaneously walked out of another one whirling open on the Spirit of the Age's hand just below Janice. With a cruel snigger, Amira held her ax in both hands as Janice was lowered down to her.

"Do what you will!" Janice's weak voice croaked in defiance. "I will never follow you. Never! Father, remember me. Give me the strength I need for this one last task."

"Janice! No!" Mariah cried, holding out her hand and taking one faltering step toward her cousin.

Another portal swirled open behind Janice, and Tyr jumped out. Grabbing her, he swung the Hammer of War in a blur, knocking Amira backward onto the Enemy's hand. Then, grabbing Alan and Mariah, he pulled them into his portal, leaving Leah's body where it lay.

As Daniel watched everything unfold, a cold ache of grief and numbness crept through his chest. The Father's Blessing burned steadily within and through him but was now accompanied by sadness.

Amid shouts of rage and surprise from the other metahumans, Tyr's portal snapped shut even as another opened just outside the Triune Shield.

"Take them!" Tyr shouted, easily carrying all three as though they weighed no more than a few pounds. "Hurry, before—"

His words caught in his throat as the Enemy's spirit exploded out of him. He slammed Tyr to the ground, grabbed the captives, and yanked them all back through the portal. In the space of a breath, everyone's glimmer of hope, radiating through their mental link, crashed back into worry and shock.

"No!" Raylin screamed aloud, erratically pacing back and forth at the edge of the shield. "No, no, no. It can't happen like this." She gestured helplessly toward Tyr and their parents. "Tyr ... he was supposed to rescue them. This was our plan, but if everyone knew"— she wrung her hands and shook her head, her eyes fixed on Janice and the others now back in the Enemy's palm—"there was a risk Tyr's betrayal would be leaked if we were captured. And I thought the Three would intervene if it got too desperate. But Leah ..." Her voice trailed off, and she struggled to meet Daniel's eyes.

Everyone looked to the Spirit.

Will you help them? Seren pleaded. *Please, before it's too late!*

Everyone else poured out similar entreaties, begging the Spirit to intervene.

He lifted his wings, and they fell silent. *Trust us. This must take place.*

"Amusing," the Enemy rumbled as he leaned down over Tyr, now bound tightly by the dark tendrils. "Did you really think you could keep secrets from my spirit within you? As though clandestine whispers in a darkened room would prevent my notice. Fool. I bided my time, reveling in your weak attempts at betrayal. They entertained me. As will your suffering."

The last word was uttered quietly but with such vehemence that Tyr blanched and went pale. He dragged his eyes away from the Enemy and looked desperately toward the Spirit.

"Please. Help me!" he shouted. "You told me once that you could still save me. I tried to save them. Doesn't that count for something? I don't want to end up like Vinaash. Give me mercy—"

"Silence!" the Enemy roared, tightening the tendrils around Tyr's neck and wrapping more around his mouth so he couldn't speak. "Saved? Saved? I already saved you from the Three! Nothing will take you from my hand!"

Amira and Abida approached Tyr's bound form with looks of dark fury etched on both their faces. Amira's expression of anger was clearly mingled with a look of surprised betrayal.

"Swine!" she spat, striking him across the face with the back of her hand. "How dare you! Did you really think you could escape? Did you honestly believe I would let you get away after double-crossing me?"

The Enemy gave her and Abida a look, and both raised their weapons.

Tyr struggled against his bonds to no avail and strained until he could fix his gaze on the Spirit.

The Spirit's voice rang out over the desert. "I hear your prayers, Tyr. Do not fear. I am with you."

Amira swung her ax, and Abida stabbed his sword. Tyr's face blanched pale, and he writhed and grimaced in agony. Daniel knew that if his mouth had been uncovered, he would have screamed in pain. His body faded as though becoming a ghost, and his essence was sucked into both weapons. Nothing remained other than the Enemy's dark tendrils, which he withdrew back into himself.

"You heard his prayers?" the Enemy taunted the Spirit. "What good did that do? He had no more soul. There was nothing for you to save. He is dead. He is nothing. I made him into *my* image and freed him from your odious eternity of servitude."

Raylin let the Abyssal Staff fall to her side, and she stared at Janice. *This wasn't supposed to happen. Tyr was going to save her.* She turned to the Spirit. *I thought you were going to let Tyr rescue them all. Every time I prayed about it, I felt such certainty. You gave me peace about it. I don't understand.*

Daniel listened to her through the storm of emotions howling through his mind. Some part of himself, the part still thinking rationally about everything occurring around them, put the pieces

of the puzzle together. The conversation with Tyr in the abandoned building, her refusal to disclose the details, Tyr's lack-luster battle against them when all the other Generals and metahumans attacked—he had planned to betray the Enemy for some time now, all in the hopes of rescuing their captive parents and earning salvation. The more people who knew, the greater the likelihood he would be caught, and his one chance at rescuing them would have been lost. And, of course, Raylin knew if they were all aware their parents had been captured, they would have been dangerously distracted throughout the quest. Not that it was of any consequence now. Tyr was dead. Whether or not he was actually redeemed didn't really matter to Daniel at the moment. Leah was already gone, and so were all his hopes of making up for a childhood separated from her. And now, his parents and Janice's lives were in peril.

What is happening? Daniel's prayer seeped out of a storm of confusion. *Why are you allowing this?* He felt similar sentiments churning through the others.

The Spirit gently touched Raylin and Daniel on the shoulder and drew them toward Seren. He then reached up and touched Ben, breathing out peace and reassurance. *This had to happen. The giving of his life was the culmination of Tyr's repentance.*

But what about Janice? Raylin asked. *And …* she looked over at Daniel and up at Ben.

And our parents? Daniel finished, his thoughts quivering.

The Spirit's calming presence swirled around him, touching his mind but feeling slightly distant, almost fleeting.

My mom is already dead. Did that have to happen? Couldn't you have saved her?

Compassion poured out of the Spirit's sapphire eyes. *It was her time. She chose to sacrifice herself to save the others. In a brave act of love, she stood in the way of Amira and Abida, interceding with all her strength, all the while knowing she was risking her physical life in the hopes that Janice and your parents would escape. It was a great act of love, one she chose so that you all might have a life with your parents. It was also necessary.*

"Necessary?" Daniel cried, finding his voice. "Her death was necessary?"

Yes. In that act of love, her sanctification was completed. It was her time to enter eternity. Sometimes, hard trials bring about the most profound growth and enduring connection with us. Recall how much you grew through every trial and tribulation you faced with each quest. You are now more fully yourself and more like the Son than you could have been without those.

Daniel looked above to see the Father and the Son closely attending to all that transpired. *But now my adoptive parents, what happens to them?*

Ben's frantic prayers broke into Daniel's consciousness, suddenly registering though there had been a steady stream of them for several minutes. Raylin and Seren joined in, and Daniel couldn't help but mimic their simplistic plea for help.

Please save our parents. Save our parents. Save our parents.

Trust us, the Spirit reassured. *Trust that we are with you and with them.*

A pained scream shattered the quiet, and Raylin and Seren gasped. Daniel followed their wide-eyed gazes to where Janice huddled on the ground, pierced by Amira and Abida's weapons. Her body faded and disappeared.

Amira and Abida, smiling, sauntered over to Alan and Mariah and slew them in the same fashion.

As though an afterthought, Abida glanced down at Leah's lifeless body and stabbed it. "Guess we don't need this anymore." Leah faded and disappeared just as the others had done.

Ben reformed and collapsed to his knees beside Daniel, mouth agape and unable to speak.

Daniel could hardly breathe as he felt his legs give way beneath him, and he joined Ben on the ground.

"Why did the Three allow their deaths?" the Enemy taunted across the desert. "They could have snatched them from my hand, but they chose to allow this. Why? Why allow pain, suffering, and death? Why?" he demanded.

"Why?" Daniel repeated.

Seren and Raylin sobbed Janice's name, holding one another. Between cries, they, too, took up the question. "Why?"

Ben, his hand on Daniel's shoulder for support, joined him as he slid down to his knees. He remained fixated on the Enemy's palm as though, at any moment, his parents would reappear. "Why?" he echoed.

Will you trust us? the Spirit asked, his voice drifting in their minds.

"Because the Three are a sham!" Abida shouted. "They promise life, but this is what you get. Pain. Disappointment. Sorrow. Embrace it! There is nothing worth having but what power you can scrape out of this world. And then, oblivion."

The Spirit floated to the forefront of the Vessels and spread his wings. "Come to me."

Amira and Abida's arms were yanked into the air as their weapons homed in on the Spirit like compass needles.

Amira, teeth clenched, held onto her ax with a white-knuckled grip.

Abida had his sword in both hands but was slowly dragged toward the edge of the Enemy's palm. "What is this?" he growled.

Five bursts of fire streamed out of their weapons: two from Amira's and three from Abida's. They flew to the Spirit, who received them in his outstretched wings. The moment they touched him, they paused, lingering in the air as small tongues of flame.

Half-blind with tears, Seren stumbled toward the Spirit with outstretched hands. *You raised Ben after I killed him in India. Do you plan on doing the same with them? You could do it if you wanted.*

The memory triggered a cascade of hope through Daniel's body. *That's right! Yes. Bring them back. Resurrect them, please!*

Ben and Raylin joined in with a chorus of prayerful supplication.

The Spirit glided backward. *Will you trust us?* he repeated, floating backward. *Listen, my time is short. I go away so that the Son may come. On Earth, it must be this way. Even this is necessary. Guard your hearts against the Enemy's lies, and do not let him in. Take heart!* The Spirit

lifted his wings and streaked heavenward with the tongues of flame. They disappeared as they crossed the border into the Father and the Son's presence.

Daniel trembled, aghast by the Spirit's sudden departure and confused by his refusal to answer the question burning in all their hearts. That Janice, his parents, and possibly Tyr, were now with the Three seemed clear, but they were still dead. Did things really have to happen like that? Why couldn't the Spirit just raise them from the dead? Why take them to Heaven now when they were needed on Earth? The Vessels had already been through so much and had even been cleansed and filled with the Father's Blessing. Why now, of all times, were their parents allowed to die? His pain was too profound to think straight.

"And look!" the Enemy laughed. "Even now, he abandons you."

The ramifications of the Spirit's absence, however momentary, settled into the Vessels' minds. They were alone. The Spirit was gone, the Triune Shield was down, and they sat across from the Enemy and his army. In the sky, the Father and the Son continued to look down on the scene, their faces inscrutable. The Spirit was conspicuously absent from the throne.

The Enemy eagerly floated forward. "In my wisdom, I knew that witnessing your parents' deaths would sever your link with the Spirit and weaken you. He has gone, and now you will bow to my will or be destroyed."

Son, where are you? Raylin asked, her prayers weakly tripping through everyone's thoughts. Tears streamed down her radiant face and splashed into the desert sand as she desperately searched the sky above.

Seren held back her own sobs. She put her arms around Raylin and drew her closer to Ben and Daniel. *Son, what do we do? Do we keep fighting? We're broken, and I'm not sure we have the strength right now. We need you to be our Champion.*

The throne room of the Three remained silent.

The Enemy's multiple eyes lit up with glee, and he uttered hasty

orders to his underlings before turning back to the Vessels. "The mighty sons and daughters of the Three, all huddled together for warmth because their pathetic, worthless parents are dead and the Three have abandoned you. Whose children are you now?"

Daniel pushed out the Spirit of the Age's taunts. Despite the heartache humming through each of the Vessels, the Father's Blessing still burned within. Hatred and despair—the whispers of these haunted the desert. But the cleansing and life flowing through them from the trees of Eden, coupled with the Blessing, refused to let them enter. *Father*, Daniel prayed, blocking out all other distractions. *Father?*

Amira and Abida stepped out of portals on either side of the Vessels, and Daniel's senses went on red alert.

Ben, the shield! Daniel stood and summoned a Fire Strike.

Ben turned his head from side to side, tears still streaming down his glowing face, and transformed into the Triune Shield.

The twins leaped above the waves of purifying power and descended on the top of the barrier.

Chiuta and Wanu, now the only remaining Generals, streamed out of their portals with the host of metahumans behind them. They surrounded the shield and attacked all at once.

Seren broke free from Raylin's arms to fire binding arrows into the Enemy's forces, though her attacks were erratic and easily avoided.

Raylin stood, leaning against the Abyssal Staff, and stared blankly in the distance, waiting for someone to be purified.

Just keep fighting, Daniel ordered, not knowing what their plan was but hoping that if they didn't stop, they might eventually gain the upper hand. Or the Son would finally arrive. He looked to the throne room; the Son wasn't moving. Why did he tarry?

The Spirit of the Age took a step and now towered directly over them. "Now!" he roared, and all the metahumans jumped back. The Enemy's power gathered in all his palms and serpent heads and fired down at the Triune Shield. Simultaneously, each metahuman attacked.

The shield shattered. Like a falling star, Ben's body reformed and plummeted to the ground with a thud.

Daniel released as many Sunstorms and Fire Strikes as he could, but within seconds, an excruciating pain struck at his very core, and he felt his arms and legs wrapped in a vice-like grip. He fell to the ground, and the Sun Sword disappeared into his chest. Ben, Seren, and Raylin collapsed next to him. The sisters' Weapons of Power vanished as they fell. Able to move only his head, Daniel craned his neck downward to see red chains binding each of them.

"Step back, all of you!" Amira barked, her words scattering the lower-ranked metahumans.

Chiuta walked up behind her while Wanu stood just behind Abida.

The Spirit of the Age glared down at them, his eyes alight with glee. "The Three have chosen to withdraw their support," he rumbled, his voice vibrating the earth. "Let us see if I can remove their image from you. If not, you will die; I will endure and find your successors. They will die before they even have a chance to begin their quests. That is something you taught me, Raylin and Seren." He lowered his face to be nearer to the sisters. "Vessels are good for nothing but immediate eradication. Now, let us begin."

23

Forsaken

Daniel turned to the left. Raylin, fresh tears glistening on her radiant face, turned her head away from the Spirit of the Age bending over them. To his right, Ben struggled in vain against the chains, trying repeatedly to summon the Triune Shield to no avail. His body flickered blue for a second before resuming the brilliant and fiery translucence of the Blessing. Seren stood bound on the other side of Raylin, and despite not being able to see her, Daniel could hear her thoughts.

What do we do? she asked, her words strained with the pain of her binding. *Why is the Son taking so long to come?*

Above them, the Father and the Son stood unmoving in their heavenly throne room. The Spirit, much to Daniel's surprise, had reappeared, once more resuming his form as the seven encircling flames. Daniel stared for a moment, uncomprehending. The Spirit said he needed to return to the Three so that the Son could come. Well, he was there now, and neither made a move.

Why are you so far from us? he asked, lifting his eyes. *We need you now more than ever. They'll kill us! The cycle of Vessels will have to start again. Please help!*

The inscrutable faces of the Three seemed to throw back Daniel's pleas for aid like a panel of merciless judges.

I don't know, Daniel finally replied to Seren. *But we still have the*

Father's Blessing—outwardly and inwardly. The Spirit is with us. Keep fighting.

Ben's voice trickled into the conversation. *Mom. Dad.* His thoughts came as quiet and weak moans. *Why? Why?*

Seren's desperate thoughts broke in. *I don't understand this. Why don't the Three help?*

Maybe they mean for us to die, Raylin said haltingly. *Maybe we can't be the ones to seal the Spirit of the Age, and it has to be our successors.*

I don't believe that, Daniel replied. *The Three would have given us some warning to prepare us. Stay strong. Don't give up. Remember what the Father said? Whatever they allow, all will be redeemed.*

"No, no, no," Abida sang, walking around them while brandishing his sword. "You all are communicating telepathically, aren't you? We can't have that. You might try to 'encourage' one another. Plan. Scheme."

"Why even try?" Amira taunted. "The Three have abandoned you. See?" She pointed to the heavens above. "They look on without a care in the world. You've disappointed them, and now they have *forsaken* you."

The word was spoken with power behind it. Like a bullet, it tore through their minds. The crowd of metahumans laughed, taking up the word like a cheer.

"Form a circle," the Enemy boomed. All the metahumans hastily obeyed, with the Leaders and the Generals standing at the Vessels' heads. He leaned down closer and breathed out a portion of his spirit. Vast fumes of darkness covered the area, swirling around them. Tendrils slithered around Daniel, searching his head as if seeking entrance.

On the ground beneath them, a glowing red circle appeared, lighting up the Enemy's face. It burned against Daniel's back. The Vessels squirmed with the heat.

"Even within the Babylonian Seal, I can stake my claim," the Spirit of the Age rumbled. "And I claim you. You will belong to me, or you will die."

All four Vessels were yanked into the air. The binding chains repositioned themselves, snaking down their arms and lifting them up over the ground so that they were all perched, side by side, arms splayed out as if on crosses.

"Begin," the Enemy ordered. "Quickly."

With a show of mock ceremony, Abida somberly approached Seren and stabbed her with his sword.

She screamed but was bound so tightly she couldn't move. *Help me! Don't let them take me, please. Father! Spirit! So—*

Her voice abruptly fell silent. Daniel could no longer hear her prayers, though her eyes were open, staring straight ahead, and her lips quivered like she was trying to say something. Daniel could no longer feel her, either. The power of the Blessing still glowed through her, though, and her body didn't absorb into the sword like his parents and Janice's had. He wasn't sure what the weapons did exactly, but the end result would no doubt be death.

The Spirit of the Age stirred, sending a plume of his darkness to encapsulate her, then leered at Ben. "Amira, the youngest one next."

Amira eagerly dashed to Ben's side with her raised ax.

Ben! Daniel cried out. *Whatever they're doing, don't give in. Don't believe anything you hear or see!*

Daniel! Ben began but then immediately lapsed into praying. *Father, what do we do? How can we fight? Where are you?*

Amira swung her ax. After a sickening thud and an audible cry, Ben's voice fell silent, and his presence vanished from Daniel's mind. "Forsaken," she repeated with a laugh. "Not such a loving Father now, is he?"

The Enemy sent another torrent of his spirit over Ben, cutting him off from view.

Abida approached Raylin.

She forced herself to look away from him, staring at the heavens before shutting her eyes. Her thoughts continued in a stream of supplication that was barely comprehensible.

Daniel violently strained against his bonds. *Raylin! No!* He

repeatedly tried to summon the Sun Sword, but each attempt resulted in the same weak spurt of fizzling flame down his right arm.

Abida beamed up at both of them as he plunged his sword into Raylin's chest. "That was funny," he laughed. "Keep struggling. It's hilarious."

The Enemy covered Raylin and turned his vengeful gaze onto Daniel.

Daniel felt alone, except for the steady burning of the Blessing within him. His heart pounded in fear, and his thoughts rambled with a jumbled mess of questions vying against a screaming, primal urge to survive.

Amira sauntered up to him. "Your turn, oh supreme leader of the Vessels," she taunted. "Just so you remember, brother dearest took some blood from you before your little quest to save Raylin. Master experimented on it extensively." She ran her thumb along the edge of her ax. "Even if the Image of the Three can't be removed, it'll be horribly excruciating. That should give you something to look forward to. Now, let's see if my blade can reach that sword somewhere in your chest."

In one swift motion, she swung her ax. Daniel felt a terrible pain burst into his body, and everything went black.

* * *

Daniel looked out over a wide expanse of water reflecting a gloriously rose-colored sky. It was dawn, wherever he was, and the light of morning swiftly filled a horizon stretching infinitely into the distance. A myriad-colored flame burned like a giant flower growing from the water. In its center, the Sun Sword floated with its blade pointing down. Around the fire, a circle of glowing, heavenly script lent its brilliance to the air above and the water below. "Belonging to the Three ~ For the Purifying of Darkness." Daniel looked down; his body, free of the binding, red chain, burned with the Father's Blessing.

He tried to summon the Sun Sword. Like a bird caught in a cage, it flew in jerky, wild motions within the flame. Each time it neared

the edge of the fire, though, it crashed into some invisible barrier and floated back down to the center of the inferno.

Daniel tried a few more times before resuming his study of the fire and water. He almost forgot the horror of the moments prior until the sky overhead thundered and cracked. The otherworldly darkness of the Enemy's spirit poured through the fissure, blighting the sky and streaming toward the flame. In an instant, it had the fire and script surrounded in a ring of its own. The flame roared higher, flashing an angry warning. The darkness rose warily from its encompassing circle, spreading up and over to form a dome. With the flame covered, the place took on an eerie appearance, lit now only by a dull red trickling in from the fissure in the sky. Haunting whispers permeated the air.

A wave of dizzying sensations washed over Daniel, and the Father's Blessing somehow felt further away. His thoughts were diverted as the water in front of him began to boil. Two spectral figures rose from its depths. Somehow, he knew he saw a memory—one he had never witnessed with his eyes but one he had lived and experienced.

"I don't want it, Leah," a man said. "You knew I didn't want kids!"

After his dreams throughout the quest, Daniel recognized the voice as his father's, though this was the first time he had seen his face clearly. It seemed to Daniel that he was looking at himself in the mirror: tall, brown hair, strong jawline, lean but muscular frame. The only difference was his eyes. Daniel's were a dark chocolate brown, whereas his father's were an icy blue.

"Get rid of it."

Leah protectively covered her stomach, her blond hair a disheveled mess and weariness haunting her tear-streaked face. "How can you say that? I know you didn't want children at first, but accidents happen. Brennan, stop! Don't walk away from me." She reached out to grab Brennan's arm.

"Don't touch me!" he snapped, slapping her hand away.

"Where are you going?"

Brennan smirked and shook his head. "Wherever I want. You're not my mother. You're not my wife. We're not even really dating, Leah. Just …" he sighed, and the cruelty faded from his face, falling into a look of indifference. "Just let me know what you decide."

Brennan walked away and slid back into the water. Leah's ghostly form slipped below the surface as soon as he was gone.

Forsaken. The whispers shot through Daniel's mind like one of Seren's arrows. *Why were you forsaken?*

Daniel's heart ached with the question, but he had no reply.

His parents' figures rose from the murky depths once more. This time, his mother sat in a hospital bed holding a baby while his father stood at the foot.

"What are you going to do?" Brennan's voice sounded even harder and more demanding than before.

"I don't know," Leah weakly replied, but there was a strong hint of challenge to her tone. "I just gave birth, Brennan. Is this really the time?"

"You've had plenty of time. Nine months!" Brennan pushed away from the bed and paced. "I'm not paying for that thing."

"Thing? He's your son, Brennan. His name is Daniel."

"He's *your* son, Leah. I told you to get rid of him, and you didn't. He's your problem. Look, I'm sorry you're in this mess, but you chose it. It's not my responsibility. Reach out to your parents or something. Maybe they'll help."

"You know they won't," Leah shot back. Her voice fell to a whisper. "You know I can't go back there."

"Not my problem. It's not my problem! *He's* not my problem! Goodbye."

"Fine. Leave. You narcissist!"

Brennan spun around with a sneer of disgust and walked through the doorway. "Whatever."

Leah protectively pulled baby Daniel closer as their figures disappeared into the water.

Why were you forsaken? the whispers taunted again. *Why did the*

Three allow this? Unloving. Uncaring. Omnipotent and cruel. Omniscient and selfish.

Daniel felt the words physically assault him, buffeting him nearly to his knees. He would have replied, only the scenes were so heart-rending, he could hardly breathe.

More figures arose from the water. This time, it was Leah as she walked up to the Holy Moses Home for Bleeding Heart Orphans. The night was dark and windy, and baby Daniel fussed in his carrier despite her attempts to soothe him. She sobbed, too.

"It's okay, sweet baby. Don't cry," Leah whimpered through her tears. She cautiously crept beneath the portico and up to the doors. "I'll always love you. It's just better this way. You'll have everything you need, and some wonderful family will adopt you. I have to go. I'm sure I'll see you again one day." Her body convulsed with hushed sobs as she set Daniel down.

There was a clear sign beside the door that read, "Do not leave children here. All minors must be turned over to Child and Family Services." Leah glanced at it but was either too upset to process its meaning or too desperate. She pounded on the double glass doors several times until a light turned on inside. With one last touch to Daniel's face, she stumbled into the darkness.

Moments later, a younger-looking Ms. Julie opened the door, wrapped in a bathrobe with hair awry. She blinked in the light until her eyes fell on the baby carrier. "Oh, no. Not again." She quickly scanned the darkness beyond the portico. "Hello? Hello? You can't leave your baby here! Hello? Please take him to Child and Family Services! They'll help you!"

Baby Daniel's fussing turned into proper crying as the scene melted into the depths.

Forsaken. Abandoned by mother and father. Abandoned by the Three. You are no son of theirs.

"No!" Daniel shouted out loud. The Father's Blessing pulsed brighter for a moment. "I am their son. The Three love me. My mother loved me. She still does. My father loves me!" *I think,* Daniel added to himself, though his thoughts broadcast just as loudly as his words.

Would you abandon your son?

"I … I wouldn't. But—"

If you were God, would you allow a mother and father to abandon a poor, helpless baby?

"No. No, but it's more complicated than that."

Simple. Straightforward. Only a cruel God would pretend to be good but then allow something like this. If you were God, what would you do?

The question pried at Daniel's conscience, prodded at his very heart. "I don't know."

The Enemy pressed. *If you were God, what would you do?*

Daniel grabbed his head in both hands. "I would rescue the baby. I would rescue me."

Why did the Three forsake you when they could have rescued you? Why not make your parents reconcile? Why let you suffer as an orphan? You are a better God than they.

"I'm not God," Daniel replied, feeling like his ability to reason was getting jammed.

You are like God. You know good from evil better than the Three. The Three allow suffering. You would not.

"But that suffering is caused by you!" Daniel shouted back. "You're the cause of evil!"

Am I? I am a creature like you. Did the Three not make me, knowing I would refuse to exist under the crushing thumb of their rule? Yet, they created me still. They are the author of evil. I simply fight against them. All the suffering experienced in the world is because they interfere with my plan. They know I would be a better God than they. You would be a better God. All can be their own God. Suffering is caused by their refusal to share their rule. Take up your authority. Be your own God.

Daniel squeezed his eyes shut. "No. No, you're wrong."

How? The Enemy's arguments bombarded his mind. *Be your own God.*

Another scene rose from the water. Gator and Barth walking with a younger Daniel out of the orphanage. This was a scene he knew too well. Gator shoved him into the car and put him in a chokehold as

Barth drove them away. Through the car window, Daniel's desperate eyes pleaded for help. He remembered hoping Ms. Julie would come out at that moment and see what a horrible mistake she had made. But no one came.

Forsaken by the Three, by father, by mother, by Ms. Julie. What would you have done if you were God?

Daniel's answer leaped from his throat. "I would have destroyed the Gurges."

You are a good God. A good God would have destroyed the evil Gurges.

At those words, Daniel felt something burning in his chest.

You are a good God, Daniel.

"I'm not God."

But you are like God. You know what is truly good. Your desires are right and true. Your passions, dreams, judgments—they are all right. You are like God. In a world without the Three, you would be God. I would be God. All would be God. If you were God, your parents would still be alive. You are like God. You are God.

"Stop!" Daniel cried. "Stop."

A new image arose. Leah standing in front of Janice, Alan, and Mariah. She prayed to the Three, and a barrier of protection encircled them. They cowered in the Abyss, and the Serpent towered over them. Abida and Amira sauntered toward them with their weapons.

"Lower your pathetic barrier, or we'll do it for you," Abida threatened. "We need you alive. For now, at least."

Leah shook her head and kept her eyes closed. Tears flowed down her shaking, white face. Janice and the Joneses were in shock, too terrified to move, speak, or probably even think. The crushing presence of the Serpent undoubtedly drove them mad. Somehow, Leah kept enough wherewithal to maintain her prayers.

"Fine," Abida said. Claws elongated on his left hand. He tore through the barrier with ease. Without pausing, he approached Leah. "We were going to kill you in front of your stupid son, but your dead body will do. The others can serve that purpose." He stabbed her through her heart, and her body crumpled over. Daniel could see her mouthing his name as she died.

"Stop!" Daniel cried. "Stop showing me this!"

No. It is for your own good. To ascend to godhood, you must see these things. The Three allowed your mother's death. They orchestrated it. They caused it. They are sovereign.

Recent images arose. Alan and Mariah Jones. Janice. Leah's dead body. All on the Spirit of the Age's palm. Daniel witnessed their murders anew.

Daniel fell on the ground, crying as the Enemy played out the scene before him again, and again, and again.

"Please! Stop!"

You would have stopped it. You would have stopped me. You are God. You are God. You are a good God. Flee from the Three.

The water directly in front of Daniel parted. From the depths below, three interlocking and gyrating crystalline rings arose into the air: one a rich, earthen brown, another clear, and the last a fiery white.

Behind it, a titanic, seven-headed serpent slithered out of the water to tower over the scene. Instead of hideous horns, ridges, and crushing teeth, this serpent shone with breathtaking beauty. A line of diamond-encrusted scales ran along his ruby body, and graceful emerald wings spread out from the base of his necks. Stars crowned each head, and depthless wisdom shone within each eye. Shimmers of light ran up and down his body with each undulating movement.

The Image of the Three, the Serpent explained. *Sever the brown ring. Cut it away from the others. It is the last step in becoming God.*

"I can't do that," Daniel said with uncertainty, forcing the words out of his mouth. It wasn't that the Serpent's words were tempting. It was his power that was overwhelming. That and the blinding ocean of mourning inundating Daniel's heart.

You can. The brown ring represents your flesh. Your soul, the clear, and the Three's Spirit, the other. You only need your flesh. You have neither use for your soul nor the Spirit. You do not need them anymore. You are God. You are self-sufficient. You are good.

Daniel shook his head. Despite the Serpent's beauty, the temptation was like the offering of stale, dry bread to a man dying

of thirst in the desert. But he knew what would come next. Rhiannon had laid it all out when they met her in the Mist: torment and death. "I can't. I wouldn't even if I had the ability. Just leave me alone."

You can try. Your friends are even now. See?

Ben, Raylin, and Seren—all standing before their own Images of the Three—appeared in a line next to Daniel. Their rings hovered in the air before them.

"Guys!" Daniel desperately shouted. "Guys? Can you hear me?"

No one reacted. Each approached the Image of the Three directly before them, reached up to take hold of the brown rings, and yanked it free of the others. Once they had, the clear and fiery rings dissipated, and only the brown remained.

Daniel felt his heart sink into his stomach. "What are you doing?" His question leaked out in a hoarse whisper. Then, finding his voice, he screamed, "Don't listen to the Enemy! It's all a trick! Come back to the Three! They'll forgive you!"

But it was too late. The radiant power of the Father's Blessing blinked out while their bodies filled with another power: a crushing, hungry darkness, as though a blackhole now existed in their hearts. Their visages changed, too. An expression of indomitable, unyielding strength filled their eyes, and they took on the familiar look of haughtiness etched into each metahuman's face.

It is possible if you try, the Serpent crooned with all seven heads at once. *You want to be with them, do you not? No one wants to be alone. Join them. Remove the Image of the Three.*

Ben finally seemed to realize Daniel was nearby. He looked over at the intact Image of the Three and cocked his head sideways. "What do you have to gain by following the Three anymore? Come on, Daniel," he cajoled. "It was easy. And, gosh, I've never felt better in my life! No uncertainty. No warring feelings. Just POWER!"

Seren, now below the Serpent, beckoned Daniel toward his own rings. "I thought it'd be impossible, but it was simple. Listen, you won't feel any more grief, Daniel. It's like you're unshackled from anything you *should* feel and filled with only what you want to feel."

Raylin sighed, stretching her arms above her head before placing both hands on her hips. "This is how I remember it. I can't believe I gave this up! I feel free. Daniel, come on. Don't be chicken."

Confusion. Brokenness. Grief. Each was a fist slamming into Daniel's stomach. He doubled over and covered his head, weeping into the ocean at his feet. His parents were dead, his friends had forsaken the Way, and the Three were absent. If it weren't for the Father's Blessing, he was certain he would have simply died of a broken heart. The Image of the Three before him reflected complete and beautiful in the water below it, its crystalline brilliance throwing back the cowl of evil light cast by the red sky. "I can't," he whispered.

"Sure, you can," Ben replied, stepping closer and kneeling at his side. "You might as well just try."

"No, Ben. I can't. Please, get away from me. Leave me alone."

"Man, you really are a chicken. I expected more from you." Ben slapped the back of Daniel's head and sauntered toward Raylin and Seren to his left.

Your friends want you to be with them, the Serpent rejoined. *You are their leader. They need you. Remove the Image of the Three. Leave their service and be free. They abandoned you here anyway, right? The Spirit left you in the midst of the battle, and the Father and the Son watched on, disinterested.*

Daniel's heart pounded, and he labored to breathe as if running a marathon. True, he didn't understand why the Three weren't interceding. But, to leave them after all this time? He looked at Ben, Seren, and Raylin through his tears. "No. How can I? I know all you say is deception. Everything is lies. I know you promise godhood but give only destruction. I know what the Three have rescued me from. I remember Inti's words. It was you who put it into my father's heart to abandon my mother. But I also know he repented and is in Heaven now. I know my mother is in Heaven and my adoptive parents. And Janice." He looked up at the darkness covering the Spirit's flame. "I know I'll join them soon. I refuse. Kill me and get it over with."

You refuse. The Serpent's voice held a faint tremble. *What about your friends?*

"Get away from me. I refuse your offer," Daniel repeated. His words stuck in his throat, and it was only through immense effort that he forced them out. "I don't understand how they could do it. Now that I think about it," he squared his shoulders, "I'm pretty sure it's not possible. At least, I think I remember Rhiannon saying that." He lowered his head and gazed at his reflection in the water. "No, I refuse to even try. This is probably all some stupid trick. Leave me alone."

Leave? I will NEVER leave! The Serpent vanished, but his voice remained. *You will never be free of me. I will endure forever. I will make the universe mine! As for you …*

Out of the darkness covering the heavenly flame, the Spirit of the Age stepped and flew over the water to where the Image of the Three hovered before Daniel.

You will suffer, and you will die.

The Spirit of the Age took hold of the three rings with his hands and the serpent's mouths streaming out of his back. With all his might, he pulled them in different directions, placing violent strain on the joint where they connected.

A sharp pain racked Daniel's body. He fell onto his back and screamed, all thought of bravely defying the Enemy as he died completely gone. It was the most intense and excruciating pain he had ever experienced in his life. He felt every atom in his body ripped in a different direction. Still, the rings didn't break.

The Spirit of the Age bellowed, yanking and pulling on the rings with each word he shouted. "You are forsaken! Abandoned! The Three have turned their backs on you! Renounce them!"

The agony was blinding.

"I can't!" Daniel gasped through his own cries. "It's impossible. Even if I wanted to, I couldn't! I belong to them. I am theirs!"

The Enemy continued his efforts to break the Image of the Three, sending Daniel's body into convulsions of anguish. "Forsake them!"

"Never! I will never forsake them. I will fight you, and as long as I'm alive, I will protect all the poor people you enslave with your stupid spirit. I will protect them until I die!"

The Enemy paused for a moment, his baleful eyes boring holes

through Daniel, and then resumed his ruthless efforts with frenetic abandon. The pain was so severe, however, that Daniel quickly went into shock.

His mind suddenly cleared. One moment, he was locked in a prison of torment, and the next, it was as if his soul had disconnected from his body and floated above the scene.

He fell into prayer. *Why have you forsaken me? Why have you forsaken us?*

His survey drifted down to Ben, Raylin, and Seren. They stood by, expressionless and empty, as the Enemy continued his attempts at tearing the Image of the Three apart. Daniel shut his eyes and looked away. He wasn't sure what was happening. All he knew was he neared the end of his life. Any moment, he would die. A sense of peaceful calm entered his awareness. He would die and go to be with the Three, his parents, and one day Gabriela. It was enough. He could rest from his labors now. He had done all he could.

I am alone and abandoned, he prayed, the words flowing out of him like water. *You have abandoned me. Why don't you answer? You allowed my birth. You restored me to a family and my mother. Please don't be far from me now. My body falls apart, and I am laid waste. Please, deliver me. Deliver me.* No words came down from Heaven, wherever Heaven was at this point. *Still,* he continued, *I will follow you. I will worship you. You are my Father, my Savior, my Spirit. Even if I am killed, I am your Vessel. I give myself totally into your hands.* Once more, he found his friends, still standing like vacuous puppets, sadistically enjoying the Enemy's attempt to tear apart Daniel's innermost being. His heart broke. *But please, use my death to save them. I know you didn't save my parents. I don't really understand all that. Ben, Seren, and Raylin have all gone through so much. Don't let their lives end in slavery to the Enemy.*

Daniel's next prayer was somehow overlaid with three other voices, all asking the same thing. *If my death can somehow bring them back to the Way, then please use it. Forgive them.*

Like a storm pouring out life-giving water on a parched desert, the Son's voice cascaded into Daniel's mind. *I have come to make you*

my Vessel completely. You have suffered, in some measure, like I suffered, and now you have truly laid down your life for others. There is no greater love. I AM that love, and you are now made my perfect Vessel.

"I AM in you, and you are in me," the Son then said aloud, his voice shaking the air and knocking the Spirit of the Age onto his back. The Image of the Three flew from his grasp to hover over Daniel's prone body. Simultaneously, Ben, Seren, and Raylin's forms evaporated like fog, and Daniel found himself staring at their bodies lying on their backs on the water next to his own. Images of the Three, all still intact, hovered over them. A little away, four domes of darkness stood in a row, all identical to the one covering Daniel's flame.

The Spirit of the Age leaped up. Like a cornered animal, he growled, snapping his head wildly around as he searched for the source of the voice. "What is this? You abandoned them! You let me torture them, and now you come to take them back?"

"The Spirit left that I might come. You used our momentary absence for evil. I meant it for good. Now, as you see, none of my children have fallen to your deception. They are in me as I am in them."

Daniel flew back into his own body, staring up at the darkened sky overhead. His body felt sore and weak, but he was nonetheless able to stand. He reached down and pulled Seren to her feet, then helped Raylin and Ben up as well.

I thought you all had fallen to the Enemy.

Me too, Ben replied, rubbing his head.

Raylin observed the Spirit of the Age retreat behind the domes of darkness and eye them with venomous hatred. *Did he use the same illusion on you guys?*

Everyone gave up and broke the Image of the Three? Seren guessed. *I was the only one left?*

Yes, Daniel replied. *Same. Now the Son is here.*

The others nodded. As one, they looked around eagerly for his presence.

"Leave us," the Son said, and the Enemy was yanked from his hiding place and shoved through the fissure in the sky. The

darkness covering the flames was sucked out after him, and the crack immediately healed. The rose-colored dawn once more reflected in the pure waters below, stretching to the infinite horizon. Four flames, all brilliantly colorful and surrounded with circles of heavenly script announcing each Vessel's purpose, roared upward. A Weapon of Power floated within each.

It was all a trick? Ben asked, studying each Vessel as though they might disappear again.

I think so, Raylin replied. *But if it wasn't even possible to remove the Image of the Three, why would the Enemy even try?*

The Son's voice spoke into their minds. *He is fully aware that our Image cannot be removed from any of our children. His purpose was to wound us.*

Wound you? Seren asked in disbelief. *Impossible.*

Not impossible. Am I not wounded when I see you suffer? Would it not grieve us had you given into temptation and at least attempted to remove our Image? Nothing could keep you from us, but in your sin, you would certainly have wandered farther away. It would have quenched the Father's Blessing, and you all would have failed the quest. But you refused and remained pure.

The Father's voice, cosmically resonant and striking every musical note in existence, flooded their senses like an infinitely complex melody. *Well done, my good and faithful servants.*

The scene around them melted away, and they were back in Babylon. The Enemy's covering darkness evaporated like mist before a summer sun. Still bound by the red chains as if on crosses, they perched above the metahumans, who crowded around them in gloating revelry. Amira and Abida stood with their backs turned to the Vessels, their weapons lifted up in gestures of self-glorification.

"Did we not tell you the Vessels could be easily defeated?" Abida shouted.

The army roared in exultant agreement.

Amira waved her ax in circles. "Once Master returns from driving their very spirits into the dust, we will march upon the Holy City and claim its land for our own!"

Fewer cheers were offered. Apparently, many had noticed the Vessels reviving and the absence of the Enemy's spirit covering them.

Oblivious, Abida pranced back and forth. "In a month's time, the earth and all its people will be ours. The Three will abandon the cosmos, and we will rule as *we* see fit. A New Order of gods!"

Only a few in the back now howled in excitement, but even their joy was cut short when the Enemy, either by some trick of time or the design of the Three, finally appeared in the air above the desert. He streaked to the Earth, crashing into it with such extreme violence that the army of metahumans stumbled to the ground.

"Your time has come," the Son's voice boomed loudly, though he was nowhere to be seen.

The binding red chains shattered into dust, and the Vessels floated to the ground.

Daniel instinctively summoned the Sun Sword. Raylin and Seren followed suit with their weapons while Ben transformed into the Triune Shield.

Amira's face twisted into an ugly combination of horror and disgust. Abida simply sat dumbfounded, a look of stupid surprise marring his handsome features.

Chiuta leaped up from the ground, immediately sending the Whirlwind of Famine toward the Vessels. It spun harmlessly around the Triune Shield.

Wanu, Daniel observed, got to her feet, glanced around, and then slipped into her portal and vanished.

"To me! To me!" Abida screamed, finally coming to his senses. He waved his sword in the air like a battle standard to rally the troops. "Attack as one!"

The Spirit of the Age regrouped and tore over the desert in wrathful, chaotic abandon. In seconds, he reached the Vessels, though Daniel found he didn't feel a sense of urgency, only curiosity.

The Son's voice rang out of the air. "I am in you just as the Father is in me." He appeared in stunning glory, taller than the Spirit of the Age and overflowing with holy power. His eyes shone like fire, and

his hair was white as snow. His legs were like molten bronze. Pure light clothed him, poured off him, and drove back the metahumans like a tidal wave.

The Spirit of the Age, already looming over the Vessels in his haste to attack, uttered an inhuman screech of surprise and flew backward.

"And," the Son continued, "the world will know that the Father has sent you." He looked down at the Vessels. "All that you have endured has prepared you for this moment. Nothing you have suffered has been in vain. Because of all this, you are now capable of being my Vessels in the truest sense of the word. I will take you up as my Weapons of Power, wielding *you*."

Ben released the Triune Shield and stood beside the others. All of them waited in silent awe as the Son's power washed over them.

Daniel, the Son called, switching to communicate within their minds. Daniel felt his body transform as he flew through the air to the Son's right hand. In the space of that moment, he and the Sun Sword unified. Daniel became the sword, though now massive and a hundred feet long, with a thousand times its normal power. He floated just beyond the Son's hand as he continued to undergo another transformation. Within moments, he became an arc of fiery light that spun like a fan blade in front of the Son.

Seren. Seren instantly underwent the same transformation as she flew to the Son's left hand. He held his fingers together, pointing them toward the Enemy like a lance. The Celestial Bow formed a glorious arc of luminous starlight at the tips of his fingers. He passed her off to his right hand, where she joined with Daniel, creating a cross.

Raylin. Join us. Raylin, too, flew to his left hand, combining with the Abyssal Staff to form a black arc intertwined with luminous swirls of hunter-green. The Son joined her with the others, where she juxtaposed with Daniel and Seren's brilliance, though no less beautiful.

And now, Ben.

Ben became the Triune Shield. Once he reached the Son, however, the transition continued. The gyrating rings at the top of the shield

shifted to the front, leaving his body perched in its normal location. The Son placed the arcs of light created by the other Vessels at the center of the rings, and the formation spiraled as one.

"What is this?" the Enemy demanded, a hint of whining in his voice. "You have never taken Vessels upon yourself in the past!"

"You have never attempted to remove our image from the Vessels in the past. You know that the past, present, and future are known to us. All your plans, including those of the next age, are laid bare. There is nothing you can imagine that is beyond us. There is nothing you will try that we will not answer in full. Enough." The Son reached out his hand and touched the center of the Weapon of Power.

Daniel felt the Son's power flow through him like lightning to send out a purifying wave. It caught the Spirit of the Age directly in the chest, nearly severing his upper half from his lower.

The Enemy twisted up his face in fury and shock as he reformed and sidled around the Son to be directly over his army. "I will not allow it to end this way. You think you know my mind. I will show you otherwise!" He spun around and hastily found Abida, Amira, and Chiuta. "Where is Wanu?" he screamed.

The twins searched the crowd, confused and flustered at the turn of battle.

"I don't know, Master," Abida replied. "She's missing."

"She's a coward," Chiuta shouted. "She fled as soon as the Vessels revived."

The Spirit of the Age spun around, fire pouring from his mouth and eyes. "Wanu!" he bellowed. "Present yourself!"

A portal opened before the Spirit of the Age, and Wanu was pulled out legs first.

"I will deal with you once this is over. Take up your position with the others and prepare yourself!" So saying, the Enemy divided his spirit among all his followers.

"I will show you my ultimate plan," he said to the Son, his tone filled with eager vindictiveness. "You have your Vessels, and I have mine. For all the ages in the past, I have reserved a little of my power held securely against this day."

"You will show me nothing," the Son replied, shifting his attention to the metahumans. "Earthborn. Dust you are, and to dust you will return. But come to me, and I will give you eternal life. Forsake your master, and even now I will have mercy on you. It is for you that I sacrificed my own life. I died and defeated death that you might pass into glory along with me. Will you repent? Will you come and drink the living water that is my Spirit? Are none of you thirsty?"

"I … will … come!" Wanu shouted haltingly, pain engraved on her features. The Enemy continued pouring his spirit into all the metahumans, including her. All shook and jerked as more and more of his essence seeped into their bodies. "Please, have mercy. I don't want to end up like Vinaash. Forgive me if you can."

"I can, and I will," the Son replied.

"She is mine!" the Spirit of the Age bawled. His form had disintegrated and menaced as a cloud of darkness, which began seeping into his followers. "I will not yield her to you."

A blacker darkness enveloped her, and she screamed. With a laugh, the Enemy tossed her broken and limp body at the Son's feet. "See? I told you she was mine, and I can do with her as I please. She died without your image, beyond the reach of your promised redemption. Your salvation is impotent!"

The Son frowned at the Enemy, who squeaked in terror and fell silent. "She is saved. She was mine the moment her heart repented, and our Image immediately returned to her."

Fire flew from Wanu's body into the Son's open palm. Once there, it sped into the sky and crossed into the heavenly throne room where the Father, now surrounded by the Spirit's flames, received it into their presence.

"Come to me!" the Son announced once more. "Come and live. Your master cares nothing for your lives and even less about your death. In me, there is life."

The Spirit of the Age rumbled like a thundercloud as he continued to divide his essence into his followers. "Any who dare will end up like Wanu and Tyr."

A silence ensued, and Daniel felt the tension building in the metahumans. It was a hard choice but a choice they had brought on themselves. Through the hardening of their hearts, the willing removal of the Three's Image, and the repeated decision to follow the Enemy, they were now faced with immediate death. Yes, eternal life was promised, but their knowledge of the Three was limited and tainted with the Enemy's lies. On the other hand, they had all witnessed Vinaash's sealing, and being bound to the Serpent along with the Spirit of the Age for all time didn't sound like a good deal.

The next moment, two people from opposite ends of the crowd broke free and made a mad dash toward the Son, clearly hoping to somehow outrun the Enemy's spirit and make it to safety. He made sure that didn't happen, dragging their broken bodies back toward the seething mass of darkness.

"Today, you will be with me in paradise," the Son said. The fire streamed out of the darkness and formed two small flames in the Son's open hand. "Well done. Enter your rest." As before, they streaked heavenward and disappeared once they crossed over into the Father's presence.

"To the rest of you," the Son said, his countenance taking on a sad but hard appearance, "we accept your decision. No clearer revelation can be given to you than what you have already seen. There is no further truth which can be revealed. You have seen me, the Father, and the Spirit in your flesh, and you have rejected us. You have seen the way of salvation, and you have refused it. You have seen evil in its fullest measure, and you have chosen it as your own. The Way is now shut."

"It was never an option," Abida said, his voice shockingly deeper.

Daniel searched the crowd of metahumans and found Abida at its center, Amira and Chiuta on either side. Their eyes glowed green, and their bodies grew larger, losing their fleshly tone and incrementally taking on the Spirit of the Age's appearance with each passing moment. The same changes quickly took over the rest of the metahumans until an army of Enemies stood before the Son,

all with multiple arms, serpent heads, crowns, and armguards of magma, radiating with malevolent destruction.

"We are our Master," Amira declared triumphantly as her own voice plunged numerous octaves, "and he is us."

This was the Enemy's plan all along? Ben asked, almost in disbelief. *This was what we were going to have to face? I'm glad I didn't know it back in Peru.*

Despite Ben's declaration, fear was nowhere within him. Daniel felt only joy, peace, and a calm grief, all intermingled in a type of serenity.

Seren and Raylin, too, emanated something similar, though a strong hope wove prominently through their minds. The longer he attended to their feelings, the more he felt his own thoughts gravitating toward Janice, his own parents, and the end of the quest.

Booming laughter brought his attention back to their final task.

"Behold *my* Vessels," the Spirits of the Age gloated in union. They spread out to surround the Son, moving at lightning speed. "Readied and prepared for this very hour. By my wisdom and secret art, each is filled with the full measure of my power. There is no division of my strength as there was with my avatars. By unifying with their spirits, my own is amplified and safe within their bodies. Can you hope to seal all of me? Seal one, seal five, seal ten—the full measure of my spirit will remain. Even if only one is left to escape, the Spirit of the Age remains. You, bright and favored Son of the Father, have finally met your match."

The Enemy's power, like crushing mudslides, affronted the Son and the Vessels from every side. The Son breathed easily, unaffected.

"*If* only one is left to escape," the Son repeated, throwing the Enemy's words back at him. "That will not be allowed to happen."

A soft singing—haunting and unhurried—broke the tension of the battle, and a light fog rose from the desert ground. It continued to thicken, swiftly encircling the Spirits of the Age. In the next moment, hundreds of people stepped out of the Mist, carrying the song more loudly. They wore varying styles of clothes from all over the world, and Daniel knew the majority to be the redeemed Creeps.

He zeroed in on one figure, clothed in white, at the front of the assembly. It was Gabriela, shining brilliantly as she faced the Son. Her parents flanked her, lifting their hands in worship. Around them, the orphans of Aguas Calientes, Cristiano at their head, sang with eyes wide in wonder.

Daniel sensed Seren zero in on Cristiano. How many months had passed since the two met in the ruins of Machu Picchu? It seemed ages ago. For that matter, how long had he and Gabriela been separated since her commission? He desperately hoped the quest would soon be completed, and then they could all be reunited.

He directed his thinking away from relationships as the song swelled.

> *You have found us—*
> *Saved us, bound us—*
> *To your life unending, bright.*
>
> *You have taken*
> *All our sin and*
> *Made us children filled with light.*
>
> *You have bound our*
> *Dark foe's power,*
> *Called us with your glorious host,*
>
> *To seal the Dark One*
> *In his prison*
> *And show the Way to all the lost.*

The air behind and around the humans shimmered with blinding fire as they were joined by what seemed to be all the Firstborn in existence. They stretched into the desert as far as Daniel could see—a vast sea of fierce holiness embodied, repeatedly joining in the last stanza of the song to call for the sealing of the Spirit of the Age. Michael stood just behind Gabriela, with Inti and Granny to his right. To his left, Chandra and Candi, Rhiannon and the Children

of Llyr, and all the Sons of Don spread out around the perimeter of humans. The Babylonian Seal flared brighter on the desert floor as the host tightened their circle.

"What is this?" the Enemy screamed, suddenly in terror. One of the Spirits of the Age fled toward the sky.

The Son extended his hand, and the Triune Shield instantly formed over the circle. The Enemy crashed into it and plummeted back to Earth.

"You are not permitted to leave," the Son stated authoritatively.

The Spirits of the Age cringed and moved away from the singing border and the myriad of Firstborn. "This is not the last age!" they screamed in unison. "It is only then that all the Host of Heaven are to attempt my defeat. Do you break your own prophecy?"

"I break nothing. Our will endures," the Son announced, "unchanged and unyielding. It will unfold in the Final Age as it is written. But as you have plumbed the depths of depravity and evil, seeking to move humanity beyond redemption, we move closer to our children, ensuring their salvation. You have those who chose you. No more will be allowed. The Father sends his judgment! Behold!"

A supernova exploded above the Triune Shield. The flames, with a Firstborn at their center, floated down to hover just above it. His golden hair, long and translucent, whipped wildly around his beautiful face. Robes like blue and green fire streamed behind him, enlivened by violent power emanating from his body. Burning, piercing eyes looked down on the Spirits of the Age, who quailed at his presence.

The Son lifted his head to address him. "Gabriel, what news from my Father?"

"The end of this age has come. No more time is given. The Earthborn are to enjoy a time of peace, and the New Awakening is upon them. Purify. Bind. Seal."

Gabriel vanished amid the Enemy's howls. Like a wild dog, the Enemy thrashed violently at the borders of the Triune Shield, but Ben, empowered directly by the Son, didn't budge or waiver. The singing Earthborn, hedged in by the host of Firstborn backup singers, continued their hymn to the Three.

The Son raised his hand, and the ground beneath them flashed transparent. The Abyss loomed far below one minute. In the next, it rushed up toward them until the desert disappeared, replaced by the red glow and high walls of the Abyss itself. The alcoves, once containing hundreds, if not thousands of the Enemy's avatars, were empty. Daniel understood; since the Enemy had poured all his power into the Spirits of the Age, nothing was left for his old forms. The Serpent writhed maniacally, belching waves of torrential fire in all directions. It was useless, however. The Son was ready and cast another Triune Shield over him.

Ben? Seren asked, bewilderment tinging the question. *Are there two of you?*

I guess so, Ben replied, his voice doubled, one coming from the shield over the Serpent and the other from the shield containing the Spirits of the Age.

Amazing, Raylin exclaimed. *I don't understand, but this is the Son. Anything's possible.*

With a glance from the Son, the two Triune Shields moved closer together. The singing hedge of Earthborn and Firstborn glided open, allowing the two to merge. Once they had, the singing circle rejoined.

"This is not how this ends!" the Serpent roared in unison with the Spirits of the Age. "I rid the cosmos of your Image! I move mankind beyond your redemption! I am the god of the universe! I am the god! I am the god! And silence your singing! I command you!" The Serpent spat titanic balls of fire all around him, but they rebounded back upon him, repelled by the Triune Shield.

"You are the Father of Lies," the Son replied. "You deceive yourself and your followers. Enough of this." The Son brought Daniel, Raylin, and Seren's arcs of rotating light floating around to his front.

"Daniel, purify." The Son touched Daniel's arc, and something like a Sunstorm sliced through the air, cleaving through the Spirits of the Age. It curved up to the top of the shield and then down, slamming into the Abyss floor where it acted like a Fire Strike. Energized by the direct touch of the Son, it didn't dissipate, keeping the purifying effects of the Sun Sword in place.

The forms of the Spirits of the Age exploded, forming a mass of wild rage at the zenith of the Triune Shield. All the metahumans lay flat on their backs, immobilized between the power of the Sun Sword and the chaotic Spirits of the Age still tethered to their bodies.

Daniel found Amira and Abida, Chiuta at their side, pinned to the ground in the center of the fray.

Amira seethed. "We will be victorious! We will never stop hating you! Never stop planning your defeat!"

"Eons may pass," Abida bellowed, taking up the threats, "and we will still detest you. We will never stop working to overthrow you. We will overcome you! Then you will be the one suffering in the Abyss." He laughed deliriously. "Yes! You will be bound to the Abyss."

Chiuta, too, joined by all the other metahumans dotting the Abyss floor, raved like mad. They spouted terrible curses, promising to be a scourge to the Three and all their children for all time.

Do they truly believe what they're saying? Raylin asked, disbelief saturating every word. *After all this, do they honestly think they have the power to overcome the Three?*

They do believe it, the Son replied. *Throughout all eternity, they will obsess over their own lies. Their self-deception, which they learned from their master, is perhaps the most formidable power they possess. No matter what truth is shown them, they will refuse it. They now go to the only place we allow their sovereignty: within themselves.*

The Son gently touched Seren's arc of light. *Seren, bind.* Countless streams of resplendent Celestial Arrows pierced the contents of the Triune Shield: the Serpent, the Spirits of the Age, and all the metahumans. They were rendered inert, even their mouths froze in whatever vile threats and self-deluded promises of revenge they were uttering at the time of their binding.

Raylin, the Son said, *enter the shield, and at last seal away this age.* He touched Raylin's arc. A black beam, intermingled with swirls of hunter-green light, sped into the midst of the Triune Shield. It stopped midair directly in front of the Serpent, where it transformed into a disc perfectly dividing the spherical shield. It separated the

Spirits of the Age and their human hosts from the Serpent. The circle rotated along the circumference while triangles of light, rimming its edge, revolved in the opposite direction. The sealing point of darkness appeared at its center, pulling the Spirits of the Age and all his metahuman army through its epicenter. On the opposite side, the power of the Abyssal Staff yanked the Serpent's partially sealed head forward. The lines of light over both eyes drew together until an eight-pointed star sealed them shut. Between its eyes, Vinaash's outstretched form—smoldering like a dying ember—was mounted higher with the added bodies of the remaining metahumans.

"To me, my children," the Son said, raising his hands to the celestial hedge around the perimeter of the fray. "Let us leave this place." The circle of singers fell silent, their hymn fading into a peaceful echo across the massive Abyss floor. They glided to either side of the Son, flanking him like the train of a resplendent robe.

With a touch to the arcs of light, the Son then dispelled the effects of the Weapons of Power, recalling them to himself.

Now released from Seren's binding and the containment of the Triune Shield, the Serpent lurched backward, shocked, for once, into a startled silence. The only unbound head gaped at its newly defeated partner and spat fire on its eyes while bringing its tail around to beat the sealing stars with violently loud blows.

"No," he said, his seven-layered voice rife with astonishment. He pounded the freshly bound head. "I will break your seal. I will break it. It will not happen like this again. It cannot. My power is greater! I can break it!"

The Son shook his head, and the Serpent and the Abyss disappeared.

24

Heaven

For a moment, they were back in the desert before the ruins of Ealim Wahid. The Son touched Daniel, Raylin, Seren, and finally Ben, returning them to their human forms. In an instant, almost beyond perception, he shrank to his human size. Overhead, the sun, moon, and stars continued to chase one another through the sky, and the desert winds whipped their glowing robes around them.

"Wait a moment," the Son said, turning away from them to address the crowd of humans accompanying Gabriela.

"Come near and join hands." He strode forward and exhaled onto them as a group.

One by one, three interlocking rings appeared on their foreheads, beginning with the first person he touched and then spreading to the entire assembly. "You have suffered much, but you have also been richly blessed. Much was revealed to you, and much has been given. Go back to your homes and teach your people the truth. The world is now hungry for answers, and it is ripe for the harvest."

Gabriela stood to his right. He tilted his head. "Gabriela, open the Mist. Lead each one back to their land. Once you have finished, join us. We will await your presence at the River of Life."

Gabriela bowed her head, then looked up at the Vessels with a look of pure joy. "You did it!" she said. "It's over! How do you feel?"

The Vessels glanced at one another.

Raylin answered first. "I'm not sure what I feel, honestly. Excited and happy to be done. Energized by the Father's Blessing, of course. But also …" she trailed off, looking at Seren.

Seren drew her close. "Grief. Janice, the Joneses, and Leah. They're all dead." As though the disclosure gave her permission to cry, gentle tears brimmed over her eyelids and fell glistening over her cheeks.

Daniel hooked his arm through Ben's and moved closer to the sisters. He then pulled them all together into a hug as tears flowed freely among them all. "The twins killed them. Right in front of us," he said, his voice barely above a whisper.

Gabriela's hand flew to her mouth. "I'm so sorry. I didn't know. But—"

"Gabriela," the Son interrupted, gesturing to the people around her. "Surely your brothers and sisters are eager to return to their lands. Quickly now, into the Mist."

She gave a quick half-nod-half-bow and spun around with lifted arms, opening the Mist behind all the Earthborn. She also summoned her globe of light, which she sent ahead of the crowd.

Her turning had been so fast, Daniel wasn't sure, but he thought he caught a grin on her face.

"See you all soon!" she called over her shoulder, leading the redeemed men and women into the twilight beyond the Mist's portal.

The Son now addressed the Firstborn still encircling him and the Vessels. "Well done! We have now reached the Final Age. One more, and your long labors will finally be completed. Return to your strongholds, and be on your guard. Prepare yourselves to give succor to the Earthborn in their need and be vigilant against the wiles of the Enemy. He will be incapacitated for some time, but gradually, he will form a new plan. All must unfold as the Spirit has foretold. Go, now. Power to resist evil rests upon you renewed!"

With his last words, fire from the Spirit, like a massive, scintillating waterfall, gushed over the border of the throne room and spilled earthward. Thousands upon thousands of flames, all in the form of

eagles, streaked through the sky to rest upon the heads of all the Firstborn. Once each touched them, it vanished. One by one, the Firstborn disappeared until only two remained: Inti and Granny. Seeing all their brothers and sisters gone, they walked closer to the Vessels and bowed before the Son.

"May we accompany our young friends?" Granny asked, breaking into a broad, beaming smile the likes of which Daniel had never seen on her face. It then occurred to him that, despite her immortality and long ages spent with the Three, even she felt stress and sorrow at the ruin the Enemy wrought upon the Earth and now, finally, relief.

Inti, shrinking down to his normal human size, strode up behind the Vessels and rested his hands one by one upon their heads. "After so many adventures with them, we would love to see the culmination of their quests."

The Son beckoned them both to stand by his side. "My faithful children. I, too, desire you to come with us. Jophiel," he said, turning to Granny, "would you go and prepare things for our arrival?"

Granny bowed her head and vanished in a column of fire.

"Jophiel?" Ben muttered. "Granny's name is Jophiel? I thought it was just Granny."

Raylin stirred at Ben's comment, studying him as though his lighthearted question was something foreign. By her side, Seren kept her gaze fixed on the Son as though she dared not look away. Despite the Enemy's defeat, the ache of losing their parents remained within all their hearts.

Inti's eyes lit up with mirth. "No, she has only ever been called Granny by you. No one else would dare. Jophiel was the name given to her by Adam. Mine was Adriel."

"Oh. Well, that'll take some getting used to. Could we just call you Inti and Granny? Not sure if those fancier names will stick in my head right now."

"'Granny' was a first for her. I could be wrong, but I do believe she enjoys it. I will take the liberty of granting your request." He abruptly looked at the Son as if receiving a private message. "Now, I believe, we must turn to other things."

"We must," the Son announced. "Come. It is time."

"Time?" Seren asked.

Even as the question left her lips, the desert melted away, and they found themselves on a stone bridge stretching across a wide, gently flowing river. A beautiful circular pavilion, fashioned from smooth, white wood, stood at its center. The Son walked toward it and beckoned for everyone to follow.

As Daniel walked up the gentle slope of the bridge, he took in the scene around him. On either side of the river, a Tree of Life grew. They looked nearly identical to the Tree of Life in the Garden of Eden, though the forests at their base were not as thick and concealing. Their scent perfumed the air with a vibrant aroma. High above, their gently swaying branches arched over the bridge, catching the light from a rich, yellow sun to toss it down below like golden rain. White clouds towered high in the sky but did nothing to lessen the brilliance of the air around them. Somehow, the firmament seemed even higher and broader than the sky on Earth, as if the horizon stretched to double its normal distance.

Far upriver, nestled amid three wooded hills, a crystalline and ivory city grew out of a forest like some glistening, unfolding flower. Its four layered walls gleefully drew in every beam of light from the air, generously reflecting and refracting it back like a rainbow cloak of ambient splendor. Within each, three arched gates adorned with intricate knots of gilded metal faced the cardinal directions. A Firstborn stood at their centers, greeting people as they wandered in and out of the city.

Within the walls, towers like stamens rose happily into the bloom of colored air. Beyond and above the city, nestled at the very top of the hills, the throne room of the Three poured out rivers of light, its luminous streams cascading like waterfalls into and around the city and falling further to mingle with the river water itself. The Son, though standing before them on the bridge, also sat upon his throne. The brilliant light emanating from the Three's glory dimmed the sun's rays that dared to stray too close. Amid that glory, as if

swimming in a sea of light, a host of seraphim and cherubim flew. And round about them, millions upon millions of other Firstborn stood like sentinels.

Everyone paused, walking to the railing to marvel at the world around them. Spreading out toward the horizon were vast forests, plains, meadows, lakes, mountains, and every other natural setting Daniel could imagine. In those environments nearest to him, he saw people and animals moving about in each landscape. The utopian sights reminded him of the dreams he had of his biological parents, and he wondered if those scenes had taken place nearby.

A bracing wind blew against his back, and Gabriela strode out of the Mist. She stepped to his side and joined in the survey of the wonderland before them, intertwining her hand into his and leaning her head against his shoulder.

Daniel looked down, smiling and resting his head upon hers. At any other moment, all his thoughts would have completely shifted to her. Here, however, his surroundings dominated his senses.

A cry of exultation echoed over the water from the left side of the river. There, Issar vigorously waved at the Vessels from the eaves of the forest, pointing excitedly at the men, women, and children surrounding him. He laughed aloud, grabbing the hands of those closest to him and lifting them to the sky in triumph. Joy permeated his very being, united with his loved ones for all eternity in unending beauty, joy, and renewed relationship.

The companions waved back as Issar and his family disappeared into the shadows of the forest.

After this, Daniel and the others continued their march toward the pavilion, and he continued his visual exploration. In every direction, the ground sloped downward, and the horizon itself glowed like a luminous girdle. And then it clicked; they were atop the Father's Mountain, beyond the light that had previously shielded Daniel's eyes from seeing the abode of the Three.

Raylin breathed in the fragrant scents floating in the air. "It's like Eden, except with more people."

"It is Heaven," the Son said, still leading them toward the pavilion, "as Heaven is presently. It is the original Eden from which we modeled the garden. And these," he gestured up to the sprawling trees overarching the bridge, "are the first Trees of Life. One day, our dwelling place will be with humankind, and all the Earth will be remade in the image of this mountain. It will be the new Eden—a world and a temple all in one."

They passed beneath the eaves of the pavilion. Like the city, it bloomed naturally out of its surroundings. Daniel followed the graceful beams downward, observing that the wood sank into the stone like a tree trunk into the earth. Though he initially thought the structure was carved, he now suspected it to have literally grown here.

The roof and ceiling were a vast tangle of branches loaded with fragrant, white flowers. Beneath the center of the pavilion, Granny waited patiently. Her fire burned with smooth undulations like a candle flame in a still room.

"All is ready," she said to the Son, giving a slight bow with her head.

The Son gestured to Inti. "Will you help Jophiel with our guests?"

"Yes, my Lord." Inti smiled secretively at the Vessels before striding to Granny and standing two arm's length away.

They both reached out toward one another and grabbed the air. As they pulled back toward themselves, the space between them parted like a curtain to reveal a grassy knoll surrounded by ancient trees. Daniel recognized it as the hill where Issar had reunited with his family. Five people, all adorned with delicate golden crowns and white robes, raced barefoot down its side and through the opening. They paused once they had gained the pavilion, their eager eyes locked on the Vessels. Inti and Granny released their hold on the air, and the knoll disappeared as the two sides of the portal swept closed. The two Firstborn returned to the Son's side to wait in silence.

"Mom!" Raylin and Seren shouted in unison, running at a breakneck speed into Janice's open arms.

Daniel knew her right away, though she looked different than

on Earth. Her red hair was tamed into a beautiful mane cascading down her neck. She had no need for glasses, and her blue eyes no longer flitted about nervously. They peacefully rested on Raylin and Seren while she drew them into a fierce hug. She looked about twenty years younger, too, and all lines of worry and loneliness were absent from her glowing face.

"My darling girls!" she exclaimed. "How beautiful and dazzling you both look. Are you on fire? My Lord, I think they're on fire," she laughed, looking up at the Son.

The Son replied, "The Father's Blessing rests strongly on them and will forever."

"Well, bless my soul."

Raylin and Seren clung to Janice's robes, pouring out a litany of questions. Daniel didn't attend much beyond their initial greeting and conversation, though, his eyes resting on the other four people—all his parents.

Daniel and Ben nearly flew into their arms.

"You're all here!" Daniel cried, tears flowing down his cheeks. "My parents are all here with me." He almost couldn't believe what he saw, especially his biological father. Daniel stared into Brennan's face. His icy blue eyes, now unclouded by the self-centeredness Daniel had seen in the vision the Enemy showed him, examined Daniel in turn. The scrutiny didn't feel uncomfortable, though. Daniel felt Brennan's love pouring into him, all the moments his father could have watched him as an infant finding their summation in that one look.

Brennan pulled him into a strong hug. "We're here, finally, all together. I'm so sorry, Daniel. Sorry for abandoning you and your mother. Sorry for all that you experienced in the orphanage. Sorry for everything you endured since the Gurges adopted you. Sorry for all these terrible quests. It's all my fault."

Daniel found he could do little more than breathe and return his father's embrace. It was a moment he had repeatedly dreamed of throughout his life, and now it seemed surreal that it was actually happening. "I forgive you. The Three worked it all out for good, anyway."

"Oh, I know," Brennan replied, releasing Daniel and ushering him over to Leah and the Joneses. "I've witnessed everything unfold since I came here."

"Everything?" Daniel muttered. "Like, all my failures, wrong choices, selfish moments?"

"Sure, but you have to know that once here, you see everything through the Son's eyes. You think about everything through the Son's mind. There is no shame or judgment, Daniel, only loving understanding."

"That's good to hear because I've had some moments I'm not too proud of."

Brennan leaned over and kissed Daniel on the side of his head. "We all have. Now, here, go to your mothers. They can't wait any longer."

Daniel allowed himself to be ushered toward the Joneses, who had finished assaulting Ben with their hugs and kisses and intently followed every moment of Daniel's reunion with his father. Leah and Mariah stood shoulder to shoulder, sharing whispers and giggles like two schoolgirls. Alan stood with his arm over Ben's shoulder, waiting patiently. Each of them appeared no more than twenty years old. Daniel rushed into his mothers' ready embrace.

"We're so proud of you!" Mariah exclaimed.

Leah shook her head and squeezed him harder. "I can't believe you went through all that. That stupid dragon is such a bully."

"When you both died," Daniel said, finding the ground and trying hard to fight back more tears, "I felt like it was all my fault. You all died because of your connection with me." And then the tears did come. "It seemed pointless to fight them."

His mothers took turns pulling his forehead in for a kiss and brushing away his tears.

Mariah hooked her arm through his left. "This may sound strange, and it's probably something you won't understand until you're a parent, but we wanted to die for you. At those final moments, it seemed the only thing we could do. Strange, though. I don't know what good it

did, but it just seemed that, at the very least, defying the Enemy and giving our lives was something that would help you."

Leah vigorously nodded her head. "Exactly. It was like our lives were the last thing we could give. Trust me when I say I'd give it over and over again if it was needed. No question. Not like that giant turd-of-a-serpent gave us much of a choice, though. Ooh! When the Spirit of the Age was trying to remove the Image of the Three from you, you should've heard our requests to the Father." Leah took his right arm and leaned her head on his iridescent shoulder. "They weren't too kind; I can assure you of that. Let's just say if the Father *had* listened to us, the Serpent wouldn't be able to sit down for another age. That scuzzy, bottom-feeding worm!"

"All right, ladies. You've had your turn," Alan finally said, pulling Daniel out of their grasp. "Come here, son." He yanked him into a bear hug, released him, and then pulled him into another hug. "There. I think we've all gotten to say hello. Everything your mothers said was completely true, of course. You can just copy and paste it onto me as well. So proud of you. Proud of all four of you," he added, raising his voice to be heard over Janice's excited prattling. "Girls, could you join Daniel and Ben? If I'm not mistaken, we have some matters to address." He glanced over at the Son and gave a slight bow.

Daniel followed his gaze and found that Gabriela stood by the Son, enjoying the reunions quietly.

Seeing Daniel finished with his parents, she walked back to his side.

Now, finally free of distractions and finding the burden of grief completely gone, Daniel threw caution to the wind and planted a kiss on her lips.

"Hey, now! Come on," Ben exclaimed. "No one wants to see that."

Daniel reluctantly pulled away from Gabriela and flashed Ben a smirk. "You're just jealous," he whispered.

Ben's glowing face flushed a rosy pink. "Maybe," he whispered back. He shot Raylin a furtive glance.

She returned Ben's look with a smile, although Daniel could tell

it was one of politeness. He wasn't sure what that meant, but at that moment, everyone's attention was diverted.

The Spirit and the Father joined the Son. Daniel wasn't sure how the pavilion was able to fit the Father, but the size of his presence and the space within the structure seemed to be completely disconnected. It wasn't that the pavilion had grown larger or the Father smaller. It was just that there seemed to be a vast expanse now existing under its roof, and that expanse was filled to overflowing with the Father's presence. As before, universes spun out of his robe of light, floating off into the air of the mountain, and the train of his robe filled the pavilion like waves of the sea frozen in time.

The Spirit hovered in the air in the form of the firebird. He pumped his wings in a mesmerizingly slow cadence, though it didn't seem necessary in order for him to maintain his flight.

"Well done, my good and faithful children," the Father said. "You have endured much for the sake of the world, and your labors have not been in vain. Gabriela, share with your friends how your work goes."

Gabriela bowed, and then a look of excitement lit up her face. "In the months you were fighting the Spirit of the Age, the world has been changing. With him occupied, there was an amazing openness to the truth. There were a few demons here and there that tried to put up a fight, but I took care of those." She held up a fist and winked at Daniel. "All the men and women rescued from the Enemy were filled with the Spirit; they took the message to their own people, and it spread like wildfire. The Spirit guided me all over the world to perform miracles in the Three's name. It's been so exciting. The world is turning back to the Three."

"We are overjoyed!" the Three said in tandem. "It is our deepest pleasure to have more children in the Celestial Family. Thank you, Gabriela, for taking our message to the world. Now, we have another task for you." A bright cloud drifted up from the water and paused on the stone ground between them all. As it dissipated, Janice, Leah, Alan, and Mariah's physical bodies lay on their backs. They still carried the wounds they received from Amira and Abida. Their skin and

eyes, too, retained the telltale marks of sorrow and exhaustion they had endured before their deaths. Instead of being things of horror and grief, however, their bodies were as badges of honor, holding the wounds and cares born of pure love.

Two figures dressed in gray robes knelt on either side of the four. Each had a white cloth that they dipped into a wooden wash basin filled with clear water. After wringing it out, they gingerly washed the wounds, weeping so hard that their tears mixed with the water to bathe the cuts and gashes.

"Tyr? Wanu?" Seren exclaimed.

The countenance of each was so different than it had been on Earth; the two former Generals looked utterly different. Instead of Tyr's strong and haughty gaze and Wanu's wild and erratic mannerisms, both their demeanors brimmed with humility and grief. Even Wanu's psychotic sharpened teeth had been restored to normal.

They continued weeping and avoided Seren's gaze.

"What are they doing?" Ben asked.

"They are mourning and serving," the Spirit explained.

Daniel nodded. "Like doing penance or something?"

"No," the Father said. "The Son paid for their sins already. There is nothing they could do to pay that debt other than eternal destruction. But blessed are those who mourn, and blessed are those who serve. Attending to the bodies of your parents is their way to worship us and to show love, and we receive their acts as a sacrifice of praise. Through them, Tyr and Wanu become more and more like the Son, who was well acquainted with grief. But do not disturb them now; they have taken vows of silence. Do not hinder their task. Through their servitude, they contemplate the love and sacrifices of the Son. One day, their holy mourning will end, and they will partake in the joy of my mountain."

Everyone obeyed, ceasing their scrutiny of Tyr and Wanu to gaze upon the four figures lying on the ground.

"So beautiful," Raylin whispered, holding Janice's hand tighter. "Thank you. Thank you for everything."

Seren shook her head. "The Enemy is so cruel."

"Oh, don't worry about all that," Janice said, her tone bright and dismissive. "It was all for good. And besides, look at us now! All together and one big family."

Seren's face was somber but somehow excited, like she knew something. She looked up at the Three. "Why did you bring them here?" she asked.

"I granted Gabriela the power to raise the dead," the Father said, speaking through the Son. "If they choose, Janice, Leah, Alan, and Mariah may return to life with you. If not, they may remain here."

Daniel searched his biological father's face, wondering if his being left out of the list was some sort of mistake.

Brennan shook his head. "I left the earth years ago, Daniel. I wasn't part of the battle against the Spirit of the Age and didn't walk anointed while on Earth. Returning's not an option. At least not until there's a new Earth."

"Is he right?" Daniel asked the Three.

"He is. It is exceedingly rare to be given a second chance at physical life. Only these four"—the Father gestured to the other adults—"may choose."

Daniel accepted the explanation and turned to consider his other parents. What would they choose? And how would their decisions affect the rest of his life?

"What did you mean by 'remain here'?" Ben asked. "You mean, stay dead?"

The Son turned an expression of infinite compassion toward Ben. "Dead is not the right word. Are they now not more alive than ever? Their bodies were killed, yes, but your parents are far more than their physical selves. Even if they do not choose to return to Earth at the present, at the end of the last age, they will receive new ones. At that time, they will come with us and the Celestial Family to a New Earth, where we will all live forever."

Ben chewed on his bottom lip as the true implication of the Son's words settled into his mind. He fixed his parents with a long, hard look.

All four adults looked back and forth among each other and their children. Uncertainty played on their faces, and Daniel didn't blame them. Go back to living on Earth only to one day die again? Or stay in Heaven with the Three and all the other members of the Celestial Family.

Daniel stepped forward. "If they stayed, that would mean we don't get to see them again until we die, right? But if they return to Earth, they would have to die again?"

"It would mean neither," the Spirit replied. "Throughout history, there have been chosen people who came to Heaven before their deaths: Enoch, Elijah, and others not written about. Still more have come while embodied to speak with us in our throne room and to be taught by the Firstborn about the future. I speak of prophets and apostles. It is appointed once for humans to die. Your parents have already suffered that, and passing through death once more is unnecessary. Moreover, you all have also passed through greater trials than death. Though your physical bodies did not perish, it is enough. You all also have a choice to make: return to Earth or remain here. If you return, we have a different path for you to follow at the 'end' of your life there. But we will explain that in due time."

The Son continued. "There are also times where anointed people interact with Earthborn who have already come to Heaven." He gestured to himself. "When I walked embodied on Earth, my glory was revealed upon a mountaintop. There, three of my disciples beheld my divinity, and along with it, they saw Elijah and Moses, who came to discuss my battle with the Enemy."

The Father took up the explanation in tandem with the Son. "Those who have walked fully in the Spirit while embodied in flesh, who have passed the threshold of Heaven while alive, who have faced the Enemy in his true form, who carry within them my Blessing and my Gifts in their fullest measure, and who have seen me face to face—these may pass back and forth between Heaven and Earth while alive. Even if your parents resolve to stay here, you may come and go. The Mist will be the pathway, and Gabriela the gatekeeper."

The Spirit hovered closer to the companions. "But you, too, may choose to live here primarily and only return to Earth for missions to fight the Enemy or help others in the next age."

A look of relieved curiosity flashed across Seren's face. "You mean we could live here until we died?"

"You would not die. Indeed, you *cannot* die if you choose to live here. You will remain your same age until we grant you a new body for the New Earth. However, you must know, if you choose to stay, you can never marry or have children. Those desires, if you have them, would fade away, as all needs for companionship and connection and all physical cravings are perfectly satiated here. You will be like the Firstborn in this way. Those are both good things but are things of Earth. Here, your passion will be communion with us and others in the Celestial Family, aiding the Earthborn, and fulfilling new roles at the end of the Final Age."

Seren nodded while fiddling absently with her robe, and Daniel thought he saw her cast a meaningful glance toward Raylin. Raylin, on the other hand, seemed more concerned with Janice, who now stood with both hands on her hips, staring with a look of intense consideration at the Three. Raylin leaned in closer to Seren, and they both whispered back and forth.

Concern passed across Ben's face like a cloud, and Daniel knew why. If Raylin chose to stay, that would nix any hopes he had for a relationship.

And then reality set in for Daniel as well. The same held true for him and Gabriela. What if she chose to stay? For that matter, what if Ben chose to stay? And his parents?

"If I may," Janice said, stepping forward. "I will stay. I've lived long enough on the Earth. I don't think I can go back there—not that you haven't made it lovely, mind you. I just don't think I could stomach it. Seeing people and animals suffer, seeing my girls grow up and move away, seeing that old snake grow in power again." She wound her arm through Seren and Raylin's. "I've lived my life there, and now I'm ready to live true life here. It's so beautiful. Just beautiful!

I hope that doesn't make you girls sad. It would break my heart if it did, if my heart could even be broken anymore. All the same, that's my decision. Goodness, but I prattle on."

Raylin nudged Seren, who urged her to speak with a nod. "We're staying, too. We both talked about it, and going back to Earth to live would be too difficult."

Gabriela quietly cleared her throat. "And Cristiano? What should I tell him?"

Seren looked surprised. "Cristiano. Oh." She let her gaze drift out over the river and up to the blooming city. "It's not like we had a relationship or anything. Still, I'd be sad if he was hurt. Tell him I'm sorry. That I had to stay, and that I hope he finds someone wonderful. Someone … accessible." She turned back to the group. "It's true. I don't really have a choice. Raylin and I have both been through so much pain and trauma; we honestly don't feel like we fit in with other people. Except for you three, of course." She gestured toward Daniel, Ben, and Gabriela. "Any time we're in public, we feel foreign and out of place. Cristiano was a nice dream. But it could never be more than that. I belong here."

"I'll let him down gently," Gabriela reassured her. "He'll be fine, especially when I explain about Janice."

Raylin jumped in. "Janice choosing to stay just solidified it for us. It would've been hard to return to Earth even if she had chosen resurrection. But now that she's made her decision, it seems right. It actually makes it easier for me and Seren."

The Three smiled at Seren, Raylin, and Janice. "We accept your decision. It is right and good."

Crestfallen, Ben dropped his hands to his side and softly groaned. Daniel ambled up next to him and placed a comforting arm across his shoulders. Moments later, Raylin awkwardly shuffled over to stand face-to-face with Ben, and Daniel gave his arm an affectionate squeeze before stepping away to give them space.

"Ben," she said in hushed tones, taking his hands in her own. "I'm sorry. I know you wanted something more. I did, too, for a time."

"You did?" Ben eagerly asked.

"Yes. I think there was a part of me that thought I could give a relationship a try once everything was over. But now that we've reached the end of our quests, I'm not sure I would be capable of it. I *know* I wouldn't be. Like Seren said, we've been through too much. I don't think I'd be able to actually invest in a romantic relationship even if Janice had decided to return." She cupped Ben's face in her hands and gave him a kiss on the cheek. "I'm sorry."

Ben's eyes filled to the brim with tears. He nodded in reply as they spilled over and ran down his glistening cheeks. "I understand," he said, almost choking on the words. "I get it. But, wait a second." He took her hands and pulled her into a hug. As they both broke away, he placed a kiss of his own on her cheek. "There. Now I can say I actually got to kiss my first love."

Raylin blushed. "Love?"

"Yeah. Love. Like, ever since I met you in the neighborhood and thought you were just this really cool, pretty, older girl."

Raylin gingerly touched her cheek as if Ben's kiss still lingered there. "That's really sweet. That means a lot to me, Ben. It feels redemptive to know that, even when I was a complete and total mess, you liked—loved me. It's like the Three's salvation worked even through that, though I didn't know it at the time." She thought to herself for a moment, then took Gabriela, Ben, and Daniel in at a glance. "What will you three decide to do?"

Ben shrugged and looked around at everyone else. "I don't know. I kind of need to know what everyone else is doing before I make up my mind. Mom? Dad? What's your decision."

Alan and Mariah exchanged glances.

"We plan on returning," Alan announced. "We just feel that—"

"As long as the boys are," Mariah interjected, her tone almost a warning to her husband. "If they're staying, then I am, too. You can go back," she said to Alan, "but I'm going wherever they go."

"Yes, dear, I was just about to explain that we felt the boys needed to live the rest of their lives, grow up, and have families of their

own. We wanted to be a part of that. But, if they decide to stay, we'd naturally choose to be where they are. Boys?"

Ben shrugged. "I don't know yet. Daniel?"

Daniel reached out and took Gabriela's hands. "I'm sorry if this sounds pathetic, but I really don't care. Gabriela, I'm in love with you. I want to marry you and have a family and grow old together. I know that's forward; we haven't even really dated, and we're both still teenagers. I get it. But, honestly, going on four deadly quests, fighting the Enemy, staring down danger every five seconds—it makes you grow up fast and get your priorities straight. So, there. I've said it. I guess what that means is, if you plan on staying, then I will, too. I'm returning if you do, though, and I hope you do."

Gabriela moved to Daniel's side. "So, everyone's decision basically hinges on mine. No pressure, right?" She laughed. "I'm in. I want all those things, too. Besides, my parents and my people will remain on Earth until their time comes, and I want to be able to be with them. It wouldn't feel right for me to stay, although I must say I'm relieved I'll be able to visit."

"Then I'm returning to Earth, too," Ben jumped in. "I also want to get married and have kids and stuff. Which sounds weird to say with Raylin standing right here."

Raylin shrugged. "Hey man, you do you. It's your life."

Now that everyone else had made their decisions, Daniel smiled hopefully at Leah. She stood between Brennan and the Joneses, eagerly delighting in each choice made as if it were her own. "Well?" he said. "It's your turn."

She responded with a sweet but regretful shrug, and Daniel instantly knew she wouldn't be returning. "I'm sorry, Daniel. I know you want me to come with you, but I don't think I can."

Something within Daniel expected this, and he was surprised not to feel sad about it. "I get it. You've been through a lot." He broke away from Gabriela and took his mother's hands. "What does Earth have for you, really? It's not like we can't see each other anyway."

She pulled him into a hug and rubbed the back of his head

affectionately. "I have been through a lot, but not more than you. If I returned, you would be the only reason. My parents—your grandparents—have already passed on. My mother is here, by the way. My friends will be okay without me. And it wouldn't be healthy for you if I returned. You'd be constantly worried about me unless I moved into the neighborhood; then, you'd be anxious about taking care of me. I might make you double-minded and distract you from more important things." She winked at Gabriela and held out a hand for her to join the conversation.

Gabriela took it and was pulled into a warm embrace.

"I wouldn't be distracted," Daniel replied, frowning at Leah, "but I would worry about you. That's true."

Gabriela patted Leah's hand as she released her from the hug. "I hope you're honestly not making this decision because of me. I have my parents and people I'll be taking care of as well. Not to mention, there are a lot of people all over the world to help. Being in a relationship with someone is being in a relationship with their family. Is that not how white people do it?" Gabriela tossed the question to Daniel, her brow knit together in uncertainty.

"I'm honestly not the expert on how families do anything," he replied.

Mrs. Jones quickly stepped in. "I can't say much for white people in general, but I can tell you we plan on being *very* involved in both our boys' future relationships."

Alan stepped over with a reassuring touch on Mariah's arm and a wink at Daniel and Ben. "As involved as you both want us to be."

"Everyone has chosen," the Three said in unison. "Gabriela, attend to Alan and Mariah."

Gabriela bowed and walked toward the Joneses' bodies.

Tyr and Wanu picked up their basins and silently backed into the shadows of the pavilion.

At the same moment, the Spirit hovered above Leah and Janice's bodies. They began to glisten with a silvery light. It radiated out of their wounds most strongly, growing in strength until it obscured

their bodies altogether. With a final burst of glory, their corporeal forms vanished.

"Perfected bodies will be granted to them on the New Earth," the Spirit explained. "They have no need for these anymore."

The Spirit nodded to Gabriela as he resumed his place beside the Father and the Son.

She knelt, covering Alan and Mariah's foreheads with her hands. She prayed silently, her words slipping into everyone's minds. *Father, please heal these wounds. Let life and renewal enter their bodies. I ask this in the Son's name—Jesus, our Champion.*

All the marks of trauma gradually vanished from their bodies. Daniel glanced over at the Joneses spirits only to find them gone.

"Alan. Mariah," Gabriela said. "Rise."

The Joneses gasped in unison, sitting bolt upright.

"Well, this feels strange," Alan muttered, rubbing the back of his neck.

"Like you've jumped off a cliff into a thimble of water?" Mariah offered. She clutched her chest.

"Yep. That about sums it up."

"Goodness me," Janice said, walking over and offering them a hand. "That sounds perfectly terrifying. Though not so terrifying as being imprisoned by the Serpent and all his demon friends. And then being murdered by those awful weapons. Can you stand?"

Mariah allowed Janice to pull her to her feet and then helped Alan up in turn.

"Okay, what's next?" Alan asked with a laugh.

The Son beckoned for the Joneses to approach. As with the redeemed Creeps, he breathed on them until the three rings appeared on their foreheads. "Next is you return home and continue your mission to teach others the Way of Life. Teach them about us. Bring them into your home. Be vessels of my Spirit so that all who desire Eternal Life may find it."

Alan and Mariah stood transfixed by the Son, nodding excitedly.

"We will!" Mariah exclaimed.

"And now," the Father announced, "it is time for you to return to Earth. To you all, we give one parting gift."

The Spirit flew up into the branches of the Trees of Life and then swooped back down, bearing seven fruits in his beak. "Alan and Mariah, you were given the Fruit of Life when you first came here. Eat now clothed in your flesh."

"And the rest of you. Take and eat," the Father said. "Over you, death shall have no more power, nor will you grow old or ill. Seren and Raylin, you chose to remain here. You will retain your bodies, however, so that you at times might minister to other Earthborn. The rest of you will live on Earth until your time, freely moving back and forth between there and here whenever you choose. All your needs for food and money will be provided. Devote yourselves, therefore, to teaching others the Way of Life and purifying and protecting those who are lost in darkness. You will appear to age in the eyes of all who walk under the shadow of death, but you will never truly grow older beyond your prime. You can never be slain, and you can never grow ill. When your time comes, you will not die but return here until the end of the age. It is then that we will take back the Weapons of Power. They will, once again, be hidden, awaiting the next and last Vessels."

Everyone gratefully took of the Fruit of Life, biting into its gleaming and fragrant flesh.

Years fell from Alan and Mariah's faces until they matched their spirit forms in appearance.

"Ah, that feels better," Mariah sighed.

Drinking nectar from the Tree of Life was energizing. As Daniel bit into the Fruit, he felt his body cease aging altogether. Up until that point, he was a bud on some plant stuck in the shadows of a weedy jungle. Now, he bloomed in the sun. Each breath felt like his first breath. Every glance, the first time he had seen anything. Each thought raced perfectly through his mind and connected with all related information. Every heartbeat flowed like a mighty river through a strong and unyielding channel. Each feeling a wave of emotional purity eternally intermingled with joy.

Daniel laughed. "I feel amazing!"

An expression of pure relief and wholeness came over Raylin's face. "I'm free. It's like, everything bad that's ever happened has been healed. Truly and totally healed. All my memories—they're so far away now. Eternally far away … and small." She reached up to touch the side of her head as though searching for some sad thing. "They're nothing now."

"Even Mom and Dad's deaths," Seren whispered. "My time as Shakti. When I killed Ben. All the terrible things I did when serving the Enemy. All the memories are cleaned off."

Ben clapped his hands and pointed. "That's it exactly! Like they've been run through a washing machine, stripped of their bad feelings and confusion! I can only think of them like the Three do."

Gabriela stood silently with her eyes closed as if sifting through every single memory to make sure they were all perfect. After some time, her eyes flew open. She allowed herself a controlled smile, but pure joy poured from her eyes. "Redemption. I think I finally understand what that word truly means. Every broken and dark experience, forgotten memory, mistake, lost skill, confusing and scary feeling—they've all been fixed and properly filed away. My mind. It's like I'm thinking through—"

"The Son's mind," everyone said in unison.

"You do." The Son raised his hands, and the Mist opened before them all. "A mind that sees only truth, that feels only pure emotions."

"Does this mean we can never sin again?" Mariah asked. "And that my children will never be disobedient or make bad choices?"

"You all can choose to sin; you still have free will. However, you will be as I was on Earth: unable to be deceived and seeing the Enemy's power and deception perfectly clear. If you sin, it will be in the perfect knowledge of what you are doing and no accident. It will be as if you are offered the choice to eat the corpse of some dead thing or the Fruit. You would do it knowing the Father's Blessing would be diminished and the power of the Tree of Life lost to you."

"Forever?" Gabriela asked in dismay.

"No, my daughter," the Father answered. "You would simply return to Eden, eat of the Tree of Purity, and come to us to be filled with Life and Blessing. You are never beyond forgiveness and cleansing, and you are forever redeemed."

Relief washed over Daniel's body. The thought of being disconnected from the Three and their Life was abhorrent. But, knowing he couldn't sin by accident made it seem likely that the Enemy's temptations, in whatever form they might come, would have little power.

"It is time to return," the Son continued. "Go back into the world. Speak much of eternal life, of me, my Father, and the Spirit, of the Way of redemption. Tell others of the forgiveness that is freely offered to them. Make disciples of all people. Use the Weapons of Power to defeat the Enemy's minions wherever you find them."

Ben cleared his throat. "Um, not that I don't like it, because it's awesome and everything, but what are we supposed to do about our fiery bodies? Won't 'normal' people be terrified?"

The Spirit hovered forward. "The Father's Blessing is always within you. In the same way you summon your Weapons of Power, you may summon or release this form. As Gabriela leads you through the Mist back to your homes, she will instruct you."

Ben laughed. "What a relief! I wasn't sure how I was going to explain the human torch thing to kids at school."

"School!" Daniel exclaimed. "Is that still a thing? How many months have passed again?"

"Resume your life, Daniel," the Son laughed. "Take care of the Earth, help others, fight the Enemy, finish your studies. No knowledge is wasted. You will find your situation with school taken care of."

Daniel sighed. "Guess I didn't really think about classes and homework when I chose to return."

Gabriela gave him a gentle punch. "Don't be such a baby. In any case, no one has been doing school while you all were gone. The Awakening spread like fire across the U.S., especially among young people. School, work, sports—everything was disrupted and turned on

its head. The young serve the elderly. The elderly care for the young. The poor are lifted up and fed by the rich, and the rich are befriended by the poor. All kinds of people are flooding into the Three's family. So," she finished with a wink, "it'll come as no surprise that school was canceled for the rest of the year."

"What a relief!" Daniel sighed. "I did *not* want to think about repeating a grade."

"That's what you're excited about? That's what you got out of all that?" She shook her head. "I see I've my work cut out for me. Come on. It's time to leave."

They linked arms and walked toward the open Mist. Behind them, Alan and Mariah walked on either side of Ben. Raylin and Seren, with Janice, Leah, and Brennan all spread out next to them, followed last of all, pausing at the mouth of the portal.

Daniel turned before stepping in and gave his biological parents one more hug. "I love you both, and I'll see you soon."

"We look forward to it," his father said. "We'll be keeping an eye on you, of course, and praying for you constantly."

"Without ceasing," Leah added. "My lovely boy. I'm so proud."

"Raylin. Seren," Daniel said, "I love you both, too. Huh. Funny. I thought that would feel weird to say."

Seren regarded Daniel with raised eyebrows. "Yeah, that didn't feel strange at all. I love you, too. All of you," she added, moving in to hug him, Ben, and Gabriela.

"I guess it's my turn," Raylin said, moving in for hugs of her own. "I'm so grateful for everything. Without each of you, I don't know where I'd be."

Daniel waved dismissively. "Eh, the Three would have found someone else to go save you. But I'm glad we got to be the ones they used."

"Yeah, I guess that's true. Well, in any case, I love you all. Let me know if you see any Creeps who need to be stuffed in a trashcan."

Ben laughed. "That was our first fight with Creeps, wasn't it? Ah, the good old days: Gator tromping after us, weirdo Creeps jumping

out of cars and trailing us in the woods, and Supai waiting in his throne room on the horizon. Yikes. No thanks."

Janice, Mariah, and Alan finally finished saying their goodbyes, and the two parties stood apart.

Inti and Granny then approached and, one by one, took turns bending down to kiss the foreheads of each companion.

Granny was the first to speak. "Farewell, my beloved brothers and sisters. It has been a pleasure serving you."

Inti smiled benevolently, the light and warmth of his countenance falling on them like rays from the sun. "A pleasure and a joy. We are so proud of all that you accomplished and are delighted to call you friends. Goodbye."

"We'll see you soon, right?" Daniel asked, blinking in Inti's brightness. "I imagine we'll be visiting here a lot, after all. I know I'll be."

"And you're both welcome anytime at our home," Mrs. Jones added. "Though we would ask for a little warning before you pop in. Fruit of Life or no, it might give me a heart attack if a human-shaped bonfire suddenly stood in my kitchen."

Granny chuckled, and then, with a brief glance at Inti, replied, "We would love to visit. It will be a short while, however, before you see us again. We both have matters to attend to so that all the resting places for the Weapons of Power are sealed against evil and prepared for the next Vessels."

"Can you bring your broom when you come next?" Ben asked behind his hand. "I have a feeling Daniel's going to need a walloping from time to time."

"Most definitely," Granny chortled.

Daniel shook his head as he, Gabriela, Ben, and the Joneses walked over the threshold of the Mist.

They all turned, their eyes fixed on the Three and the retinue of family and friends spread out on either side of them. It was a scene brimming with love, with Love himself at its center.

Reluctantly, Gabriela stepped forward. With a wave of her hands,

the portal of Heaven swirled shut, and the twilight of the Mist enclosed them.

Everyone simply breathed in silence, unmoving and staring at the point where paradise had just vanished.

"Well," Daniel finally said. "Who's up for a walk?"

Epilogue

Ten Years Later

Daniel and Gabriela walked through the glass doors of the Holy Moses Home for Bleeding Heart Orphans. Ms. Julie stood in the foyer talking to the receptionist, a frail-looking young man with red hair, glasses, and a white shirt buttoned up to his neck. Freckles covered every inch of his face, and his arms and legs were like sticks. He noticed Daniel and Gabriela walking through the door and broke off the conversation with Ms. Julie.

"Good morning, h-h-how can I help you?" he said, his voice quivering with anxiety and his face blushing crimson.

Daniel pointed to Ms. Julie. "Here to see her, actually."

The man gawked at Daniel's hair, which was a shock of snowy white. Daniel had gotten used to the looks. On the way back through the Mist so many years before, Gabriela taught him and Ben how to temporarily conceal the Father's Blessing when necessary. Once their bodies returned to their normal appearance, both realized the change. They weren't that surprised, though. With as much trauma as he and the other Vessels experienced fighting the Spirit of the Age, not to mention simply standing in the Father's presence, Daniel was amazed his hair hadn't fallen out altogether. He ignored the man's strange looks and turned to Ms. Julie.

She extended her hands, pulling both him and Gabriela into a hug.

Over the years, she hadn't changed much, except her hair had lost all trace of its original black and faded into a dull gray. Her stormy eyes were still wells of kindness, and her voice carried the same tones of reassurance and compassion that Daniel knew each foster child needed. She wore blue jeans and a bright yellow polo shirt with the words "Bleeding Heart" stitched over the left breast pocket.

"Thank you both for agreeing to this," she said, releasing their hands and directing them toward the doors of her office. "I know you've got a lot on your plate with your little one at home, and you weren't really wanting to foster at the moment, but we've got a special situation."

The little man behind the desk cleared his throat. "I think I need you to sign in before you go back there. Excuse me, please. It's our policy."

Ms. Julie paused. "Oh, well, I suppose it is our policy," she said apologetically. "Go ahead and sign in for us. This is Ralph, by the way. The temp agency just sent him over, so it's his first day. Ralph, this is Daniel and Gabriela Jones. Daniel grew up here, and Gabriela is his wife. I know them both very well, and they've fostered with us before."

Just then, two side doors burst open, and Gator stomped through. Her brown hair was cropped short so that it accentuated her jaw in a neat line, and dark eyes swept across the lobby to take in Daniel and Gabriela. Her considerable muscles nearly burst out of the pink polka-dotted spaghetti strap dress that fell to her substantial calves.

"Daniel! Gabriela!" she thundered, stumping across the floor toward them. "What's the occasion?" She pulled Daniel into a bone-crushing hug and then released him. She and Gabriela then squared up with one another and shook hands in a vigorous contest of strength. They stood for several moments unmoving, Gabriela relaxed and smiling, Gator trying with all her might to overpower her with her right hand. Sweat beaded up on Gator's face, and the veins in her forehead looked like they were about to burst. Finally, once she was as red as a beet, Gator broke off and gave up. "I don't get it! I just

went up a weight class, and I'm on an increased protein diet, and I still can't beat you. One of these days. One of these days."

Gabriela laughed. "How are you enjoying your new position here?"

"Love it! Absolutely love it! The kids are fantastic, and being in a place like this just feels right. You know, after I finished my social work degree, I worked at a couple hospitals and then did home studies for Child and Family Services. Just wasn't my thing. But when Julie called about the opening here, I knew God had opened a door."

Gabriela and Gator continued chatting, but Daniel's mind raced through Gator's transformation over the past several years. After they returned from the last quest, Daniel remembered he had struck the Gurges with the Sun Sword. They must have still been unconscious and, therefore, ignored when Amira and Abida came to capture his parents and Janice in the cave. After releasing the Father's Blessing, he, Gabriela, and Ben raced to their house to find them going about their lives just as happy as larks.

"You came back!" Daniel remembered her exclaiming as soon as she opened the door. "Dad. It's Daniel and Ben! Oh, and that Gabriela girl."

Barth had skipped through the door and wrapped Daniel and Ben in a hug that Daniel had nightmares about for weeks. Fighting the Spirit of the Age? No sweat. Being hugged by Barth Gurge? *All* the sweat. Plus five orangutans. But he was sincere in his excitement. Gator, too. They had a thousand questions about the Three, the quests, the Way, and what happened in the cave. They were changed people.

"And look, Dad's working here now, too." Gator's declaration brought Daniel back to the present. "He's the janitor, see? Hey, Dad, look who it is."

At that moment, Barth was mopping his way backward through the door that led to the common room. He broke into a smile and hastily adjusted his toupee, which had flopped over to hang precariously from his left temple. The gray jumpsuit draping his bony frame thankfully covered most of his bright red chest hair, though, as usual, a few flaming bristles flickered up about his neck.

"Morning, Joneses." He took the toupee off entirely and used it to give a flourish as he bowed. "Sorry, no time to chat. Got heaps of mopping to do today. I'll catch you around the neighborhood."

"We look forward to it, Mr. Gurge," Gabriela replied with a laugh. "Looks like you're doing a terrific job."

"He is," Ms. Julie jumped in. "Fantastic, really. He cleans everything so fast the orphanage is gleaming from top to bottom every day before lunch. And he can fix anything. He's a Godsend."

She gestured toward the freckled, frail waif shaking behind the desk. "By the way, Gator, I don't think I've introduced you to the temporary receptionist, Ralph. He'll be here for the next couple of weeks, I hope." She glanced back at Daniel and Gabriela. "It's been impossible to keep receptionists these days. Everyone wants more and more money just to do simple, unskilled work." She whispered, "It's like a revolving door around here." With a sigh, she looked back up at Gator. "As I was saying—Gator?"

Gator was across the lobby and sitting on the side of the reception desk, towering over Ralph like a gorilla over a kitten. "Where are you from, Ralph?"

Ralph quivered in her shadow. "Just outside … I mean, kind of in the city limits of P-P-Portland. But I've lived not ten minutes f-f-from here for the past three years."

"That's so funny," Gator crooned, leaning down to play with the pen on his desk. "How have we never met? I'm Gator, by the way."

"Hi," Ralph squeaked. "You're really—I hope it's okay f-f-for me to say this—really strong."

"Yeah. I know."

Gator flexed a bicep, and Daniel thought Ralph was going to faint.

"My little girl," Barth chuckled under his breath. "All grown up and looking for love. Reminds me of when her mother and I met. Such romance. Such beauty."

Ms. Julie cleared her throat. "Maybe this will be to our advantage. Who knows? Anyway, come on through."

Daniel and Gabriela shuffled into Ms. Julie's office and took a seat.

With the exception of newer pictures on the wall, it looked pretty much the same as the day Daniel had been adopted by the Gurges. Rickety metal desk. Oscillating fan in the corner to keep the office from getting stuffy. Stacks of paper flapping in the breeze, straining resentfully against a paperweight.

"I'll make everything quick. All the paperwork is done, or soon will be, so it won't be long. Really, we're just waiting for her to pack all her things."

Daniel felt like a flashback had hijacked his brain. "Whoa. Does that ever bring back memories."

"Only, in this scenario, you're Barth, and I'm Gator," Gabriela wryly observed.

"Exactly."

"Real quick before she gets here," Ms. Julie hastily continued, her voice falling to a whisper. "The girl's name is Imari Zuberi. Her mother, Binta Zuberi, immigrated here from Kenya fifteen years ago when Imari was four years old. Binta had heart problems, though, and died the next year. Imari has been in foster care ever since."

"What about her father?" Gabriela asked.

"We have no information about his whereabouts," Ms. Julie replied, still speaking in a low voice. "Only a name. But, as you can surmise, she's now nineteen and about to age out of the system. I've been praying for a placement that could help her bridge the gap to adulthood, but those are hard to come by."

"No offers for adoption?" Daniel asked, almost certain of the answer before the question even left his lips.

Ms. Julie surprised him. "Dozens. I've never seen anything like it. Only, each family was rejected by Child and Family Services." She pulled out three sheets of paper, all stapled together, and handed them to Daniel.

He glanced over the lists of names, as well as the objections documented by the caseworker assigned to investigate each family. The concerns were all the same: dubious background checks, aggressive behaviors during interviews, and alarming comments about being

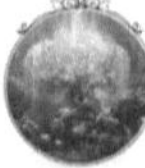

rewarded for "bringing the girl to the Master." Daniel paused on the last entry, and he almost broke out laughing:

> "I have major concerns about the sanity of Mr. and Mrs. Bludbath. They both have what appear to be fangs and claws, and neither removed their glasses throughout the multiple interviews I conducted. I fear they may be involved in some sort of cult or circus ring, might be using serious drugs, and are likely clinically insane."

Daniel showed the explanations to Gabriela, who read over it with a smirk. "Ah. I see."

"Strange, isn't it?" Ms. Julie continued. "So, she's bounced around between foster homes all throughout the state and then ended up here a couple months ago. She's been taking classes at the local community college, so that's kept her busy. Socially, though, it's been tough. We don't have anyone else here near her age. That's why I immediately thought of you both. I know you're so busy, what with a toddler of your own and all. But no one else was willing to take a teen so old. And, well, I figured she might feel understood by someone who had been through something similar."

Just like when Ms. Julie had first called about the placement, Daniel felt the Three urging him to accept it, overriding any uncertainty. *Father, what's this about? Why is this so important?*

Trust us, the Father replied, his voice clear in Daniel's mind. He sensed Gabriela heard it, too.

"Honestly, we were going to say no," Gabriela said, glancing at Daniel. "But when we both prayed about it, God made it *very* clear that she needed to be placed with us. We know this is right, and we're excited."

Daniel folded his hands on his knees. "So, she's been in the system since four years old, and there's no record of her father's location?"

Ms. Julie shuffled through her papers. "That's right. I was looking for his name a moment ago. Where was it? Ah! Here we go. Chiuta. Chiuta Zuberi."

Gabriela's hand flew to Daniel's leg, and they locked eyes.

The door leading to the hallway creaked open, and a young woman about Gabriela's height, though a little heavier, timidly stepped into the office. Her ebony skin set the whites of her eyes and teeth in gleaming contrast. Rather than the expected dark brown, her eyes were a familiar shade of gray peeking out from beneath long eyelashes. Her thick, kinky hair was tamed in a masterpiece of braids flowing down her back and bound together by a hair tie adorned with wooden beads. She sported a red Bleeding Heart T-shirt and an ankle-length skirt of breezy white material. She blushed under Daniel and Gabriela's scrutiny and eased into the chair to Gabriela's left at Ms. Julie's insistence.

"Hello," she said, her voice high and thin with the slight tremble of nerves. She barely glanced up from her feet. "I'm Imari."

"Hi, Imari. I'm Daniel Jones."

Gabriela leaned over. "I'm Gabriela," she said, cupping Imari's hands in her own. "Starting today, you're going to come stay with us for a while. Is that okay?"

Imari studied Gabriela's face, glancing from her eyes to her hands and then to Daniel's.

"No fangs. No talons," Daniel said, wiggling all his fingers.

Ms. Julie looked startled.

Imari narrowed her eyes. "How did you know that's what I was looking for?"

Daniel shrugged. "Some pretty strange people tried to adopt me once, too."

"I bet not as weird as the ones I've met."

"You'd be surprised." Daniel turned to Ms. Julie. "What's next?"

Daniel spent the next few minutes completing paperwork while Gabriela helped Imari pack her things. They all gathered back in the lobby for Ms. Julie to say goodbye and then piled everything into the car. The ride home was mostly quiet, punctuated only by a few questions from Gabriela and Imari's short, nervous answers.

They pulled into the neighborhood, and Daniel found himself

seeing it again through the eyes of a scared, uncertain orphan who could only think about self-protection and escape. He prayed Imari had a little more hope than he did when he came home with the Gurges.

The Jones's house came up on the right. "That's my adoptive parents' house. You'll spend a lot of time there, too. But we live just up this way, in a little white house beyond the actual neighborhood."

"You grew up in that house?" Imari asked, her eyes wide. "It's so big."

Daniel nodded. To an orphan who had never had a home to call their own, it did seem grand. "Not exactly. I actually didn't move in with them until I was a teenager, so, not too different from your situation."

The house fell behind, and Imari eagerly peered out the front window, leaning forward with a cautious expectation. Daniel studied her out of the rearview mirror. He confidently guessed at all the feelings racing through her mind: anxious, hopeful, awkward, uncertain. All these passed across her face as she eagerly searched the woods for the house she would call home for the foreseeable future.

"Our house isn't nearly as big," Gabriela explained. "But we finished remodeling the attic last year, so you'll have your own room and bathroom. We have one son, Brennan. He's two and is a real character. I hope you like kids because he never meets a stranger."

Imari's countenance fell. "Oh. I guess I'll be doing all your babysitting then."

"Is that how it's been with your foster families?" Daniel asked.

Imari leaned back, crossed her arms, and stuck out her chin. "Usually. It didn't take them long to figure out that I'm not good with kids, though."

"Well, no, you won't be doing our babysitting," Daniel replied. "Not unless you want to."

Gabriela craned her neck around. "That's right. We want you to get settled in and comfortable over the next few months while you figure out what you want to do with your life. There's no rush.

Besides, Ms. Julie told us about your classes. Those will need to be your number one priority."

"Oh," Imari said, blinking in surprise. It seemed she had rarely, if ever, been shown any amount of consideration for her feelings.

Daniel turned into the now graveled driveway of Granny's house. After returning from Heaven, he and Gabriela dated for five years and then got married. Moving into Granny's seemed the most logical choice. They could still be near the Joneses and Ben and have the privacy the forest around Granny's afforded. It turned out they frequently needed it. There were, of course, numerous comings and goings through the Mist each day. Creeps, and even the occasional demon, also came knocking on the door from time to time. The Enemy had apparently not wanted to waste much time in this last age before weaving a new mess of schemes.

Daniel parked the car and stepped out, surveying the scene in front of him. Mariah and Alan sat in chairs on the front porch with Brennan, whose dark brown hair could be seen bobbing up and down behind the railing as he ran back and forth, chasing a red kickball. On the opposite end of the porch, Raylin and Seren sat on a hanging swing, taking turns tickling Brennan when he got too close while the other rolled the ball gently back in the opposite direction. They both wore simple white robes that fell loosely to their bare feet and had prudently concealed the Father's Blessing to avoid terrifying Imari. Ben, dressed in slacks and a green button-down shirt and similarly not a human torch, stood in front of the house. Two figures in black trench coats slouched at his side. Each wore a wide-brimmed hat that covered most of their face, and long arms hung to their knees.

Daniel cast an exasperated look toward Gabriela, who returned his gaze with rolling eyes.

Hide nothing from Imari, the Father said, his voice trickling into all their minds. *She remembers much of her father, even after he joined the Enemy's ranks. She needs your protection and is hungry for truth.*

Imari? Ben asked. *Is that the foster girl?*

What's this about her dad? Seren asked.

Raylin stood up. *He works for the Enemy?*

Daniel waved. *Glad you're all on the conference call. And it's more like foster woman, Ben. She's nineteen.*

Oh yeah? Ben turned to find Imari, her hands resting on top of the open car door and her dark eyes wide with uncertainty. He blushed. *So she is.*

Gabriela broke in. *Her dad used to work for the Enemy. She's Chiuta's daughter.*

No way! Poor old Chiuta, Ben lamented, shaking his head in genuine shame. *If only he and Vinaash could've gotten it together before it was too late. Anyway, Imari, huh? Interesting name.* He observed her in silence.

Earth to Ben, Raylin chuckled. *Care to introduce our guests to Daniel and Gabriela?*

Oh. Right. I've got some "people" for you both to meet.

Ben switched to talking and gestured toward the figures in front of him. "I found these interesting and very convincing humans walking around the neighborhood. It turns out—I know this will shock you—that they were looking for us. What was the reason again?" Ben asked the strangers.

"We are toothbrush salesmen," the figure on the left said, a series of clicks and sputtering wheezes spurting out of his concealed mouth after his explanation.

"Toothbrush salesmen?" Daniel laughed, sauntering up behind him. "That's the dumbest excuse we've heard so far."

Much to Imari's surprise, Gabriela easily carried all her bags in one hand while ushering her up onto the front porch with the other.

"Impudence," the thing to Ben's right interjected, looking hungrily around his shoulder and following Imari's every move. "We were told humans care a great deal about their teeth. Selling toothbrushes is a perfectly normal thing. How dare you mock us."

Mariah stood up from the porch swing with Brennan in her arms. "Would you five please just get on with whatever it is you're going to do with our 'guests'? Buy some toothbrushes or something.

Brennan needs to go down for his nap, and I've got to get back to the house to start cooking dinner. Gabriela, when are we supposed to meet everyone?"

"Daddy!" Brennan wailed, reaching out for Daniel.

"Around 5:00. I'm going to get my parents first, then Janice. I'll leave the Mist open when I leave so everyone can set up the tables and chairs just inside."

"Mommy!" Brennan cried, squirming in Mariah's arms. "Mommyyyyy!"

"Your mom is right, Daniel. Let's hurry this up so we can get him down for a nap."

"Stupid Earthborn!" one of the figures spat. "None of you will leave here alive. We will destroy you and take Chiuta's daughter. She will serve in Master's new army as one of our leaders! The Master will—"

"Just get on with it," Ben yawned.

In response, the two figures threw off their coats and hats. Brown and black abdomens elongated and expanded while two other jointed insect arms sprouted out of their gigantic, roach-like bodies. Fishing-pole-length antennae shot into the air from their heads just above their beady eyes. They spread filmy wings and crouched down, ready to spring into battle. The one on the right threw an Orb of Concealment into the air. The black sphere floated momentarily before expanding to encompass Granny's yard.

All the Vessels unveiled the Father's Blessing, throwing back the shadows of woods and striking terror in the demons' mirror-black eyes.

Ben summoned the Triune Shield, surrounding the house and everyone on the porch.

The two roach demons launched themselves at the border of the shield just as Gabriela stepped through, punching both in the face and sending them careening backward onto their flailing wings. Seren stood up from the porch swing and lazily fired Celestial Arrows into their bodies. Daniel casually summoned a Fire Strike.

The demons' spirits swelled into the air, barely having time to wail and scream in surprise before Raylin activated the Abyssal Staff to send them to the Serpent.

Brennan laughed hysterically, bouncing up and down in Mariah's arms.

Imari's mouth gaped open, and she pressed herself against the porch door. "What is happening? What is this? Who are you people?"

"That," Daniel said, walking up the steps and taking Brennan into his arms, "is a long, long story, and it starts with the most wonderful thing to happen in my life: adoption."

The End